Duke of Normandy

Book 10 in the Norman Genesis Series
By
Griff Hosker

Duke of Normandy

Published by Sword Books Ltd 2018

Copyright © Griff Hosker First Edition

The author has asserted their moral right under the Copyright, Designs and Patents Act, 1988, to be identified as the author of this work.

All Rights reserved. No part of this publication may be reproduced, copied, stored in a retrieval system, or transmitted, in any form or by any means, without the prior written consent of the copyright holder, nor be otherwise circulated in any form of binding or cover other than that in which it is published and without a similar condition being imposed on the subsequent purchaser.
A CIP catalogue record for this title is available from the British Library.
Cover by Design for Writers

Contents

Duke of Normandy	1
Prologue	4
Chapter 1	7
Chapter 2	18
Chapter 3	32
Chapter 4	41
Chapter 5	52
Chapter 6	65
Chapter 7	75
Chapter 8	86
Chapter 9	96
Chapter 10	111
Chapter 11	123
Chapter 12	141
Chapter 13	150
Chapter 14	161
Chapter 15	173
Chapter 16	184
Chapter 17	195
Chapter 18	208
Chapter 19	218
Epilogue	231
Norse Calendar	233
Glossary	233
Maps and Illustrations	239
Historical note	240
Other books by Griff Hosker	245

Prologue

I was now the Lord of Rouen. It was not a title I afforded myself. It was forced upon me. My wife, Poppa, liked the title of lady. She had been the daughter of a Frankish Count and such things mattered to her. The men who had been jarls under my grandfather and were now my lords wished me to have the accolade. Partly that was because they were all lords of the places we had conquered. They enjoyed their own titles. It meant more to their wives than that of jarl. We were becoming, in some ways, more Frank than Norse. That was not surprising for most of my men, like me, had married Frank or Breton brides. Our language was changing. It was not Norse and it was not Frank. Like our people, it was evolving.

What had not changed was my warrior heart. I was still Göngu-Hrólfr Rognvaldson. I was still Rollo! I was the warrior who had been drowned and reborn. I was the warrior with Long Sword and now, after many attempts, I had fathered a son. William Longsword would follow me. He would have a land which he could rule. Until my brother had tried to murder me I had had no wish to rule. Now I saw that if I ruled then my family and people would be safer. My grandfather had shown me that. His benevolent ways on Raven Wing Island at the Haugr had proved to be too gentle and we had lost all that we had once had. It had taken both blood and death to recover it. I could not allow any to question my rule. I also had a prophecy to fulfil. My grandfather had been told by a witch that his heirs would rule the western world. We had but a toe hold on the land. Before I died I needed to make something my son could hold.

King Charles the Fat ruled the Franks but he was old and there was enough division amongst them for them not to be a threat to us. We had raided Paris and while my men and I had profited, many of the other

Vikings who took part in the raid perished for they were too greedy. We took the bribes offered by the Franks and we left. They tried to take more and were slaughtered. The coin we took built strong walls. It paid for good swords and it made us stronger. Count Odo of Paris had resented the bribes and it was rumoured he sought the crown for himself. We would exploit such divisions.

The threat which was on our doorstep was the land of Brittany. There had been a civil war and Alan, son of the Count of Ridoredh now ruled. Emperor Charles, known as the Bald, of the Holy Roman Empire, had been so desperate to find allies to fight us that he had made Alan of Vannes, King of the Bretons. It was a title to keep the Breton away from his borders. It made him look at us. We had taken the Cotentin from him and he wanted it back. Although his homeland was around Vannes in the south the Breton had begun to cast covetous glances at the lands of my lords. It had been a Breton who had suborned my brother and I bore them no love. I would have made war on them but I was dissuaded by my wife. She had been related, through her husband, to Bretons. I listened to her. It was a mistake. It was a mistake which cost me dear. It drove a wedge between us that never truly healed. She had given me a son. That would be enough.

Duke of Normandy

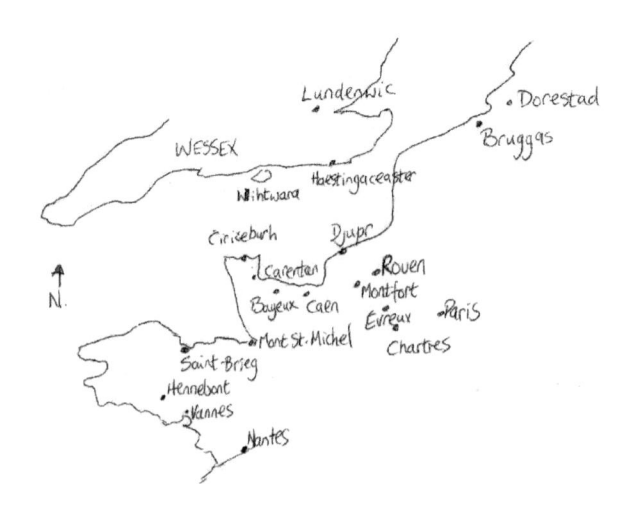

Chapter 1

Rouen

My son, William, had seen more than two summers before I went to war again. I had tried to do as my wife wished and live like a lord. I had tried to live at peace with my neighbours but it had sent out the wrong message to my enemies. They thought I was growing weak. However, the time of peace was good for the land and the mix of Norse and Frank. My people prospered. We traded. We ploughed, farmed and fished. Life should have been good. The first signs of danger came when many of the warriors who had followed Guthrum in the land of the Angles had come to our land. The time of the Danes was drawing to a close. King Alfred of Wessex was in the ascendancy. They thought to raid up the river but I had promised King Charles that I would stop Danes from raiding. My reputation and my friendship with Guthrum prevented violence but it was a warning that when Guthrum died we might have to fight Danes once more.

Then my lords who lived in what the Franks called the Cotentin were raided for slaves by the Bretons. Saxbjǫrn the Silent of Carentan had families taken. The families who were taken lived to the west of his domain. Halfi Axe Tongue was the lord whose land suffered the most losses. They lived far from others and their loss was not discovered for a month. Landbjartr was a hersir who farmed the land ten miles to the east of Carentan. He had been one of Saxbjǫrn's hearth weru. When we returned from the raid on Paris he had taken a wife and gone, along with his brothers to live in a secluded valley. It was good farmland and the sea was just a few miles to the west. It was perfect. His two brothers married and they took their families to live there. When a messenger was sent to invite them to a wedding feast in Carentan they found nothing save the heads of the three brothers and farms which had been destroyed. Despite a search, Saxbjǫrn could not find who had taken them. That had been half a year since and the lord of Carentan had put it down to a raid by Danes. King Alfred's rule drove many Danes back to the sea. Landbjartr had lived too close to the sea.

I was summoned late one afternoon when Saxbjǫrn's drekar, *'Moon Dragon'* was seen approaching my stronghold. Despite the peace I still had men walking my walls. They were the ones who did not farm. They were not bondi. They were my hired warriors. They had sworn an oath to me and the twenty of them would be the heart of my crew when I sailed to war. Harold Strong Arm had served my father as a warrior and he had once led my oath sworn. He had relinquished the role for one he thought a better leader. Such was the way of good warriors. Æbbi Bonecrusher led them and he came to inform me. After he told me he said, "She does not have a large crew, lord. She rides high in the water."

"Have the warrior hall prepared. I am guessing they will stay the night." I found myself looking forward to spending time with the Lord of Carentan. I missed the company of my warriors. A life of comfort did not suit me.

As I hurried down to the gate to greet him my wife stopped me, "We have visitors?"

"Saxbjǫrn the Silent. I have ordered the warrior hall to be prepared."

She wrinkled her nose. She did not like my lords. "This is not the way a civilised person conducts himself. He should have waited to be invited."

Before my son had been born my wife and I had got on well. A rift had begun to appear when I forbade her priest Æðelwald of Remisgat to attend the birth of our son. I had drawn a little blood. Now they were closeted together each day. She prayed, apparently, for my soul and her priest helped her. While Sprota watched William, my wife would be on her knees with her priest. My wife had a thousand ways to annoy me. Each day she found a new one.

I smiled, "Saxbjǫrn is like me. He is not civilised. He is a Viking. Have a feast prepared for this night."

She snorted. It was not attractive. "That is all we need! Drunken Vikings vomiting in the hall!"

I smiled again for I knew it annoyed her. "It is good to see that we are in agreement!"

Since Gefn, my adopted mother, had died, I had used the widow of one of my warriors to run my hall. My wife should have done it but she had not been taught the skills by her mother and she thought it beneath her. Ágáta hid her smile as my wife stormed off. As Æbbi Bonecrusher often said, 'she flounces better than any woman I have ever met!'

"Ágáta Silver Hair, see the cooks and ensure that this is a feast fit for warriors. They will want real food and not the delicate little titbits which the priests, my wife invites, seem to enjoy."

She smiled. She had raised four children. All lived in other parts of the world but she knew how to cook and she knew what filled a man. "Fear not lord, they will not let you down."

Two of my oathsworn followed me. Harold Strong Arm and Haaken the Bold were my shadows. There had been killers sent to do me harm. One had managed to get into my hall before he was killed by me. After that attempt, the hearth weru arranged for two men to watch me at all times. Some of the killers were obvious ones. I had not given them the judgement they wished in my court. Others had asked for a piece of land and I had not acquiesced. There were some, however, that I did not know. The one I had slain outside my sleeping chamber had been one that I did not recognise.

Harold said as we stepped into the sunlight, "Perhaps this will bring us some action." I flashed him a look. He shrugged, "Since Paris, lord, I have not used my sword to draw blood. I do not have many more years of war ahead of me. I am a warrior and I crave action."

"Does not your new wife give you action enough?"

Haaken laughed, "She is too young for this old goat, lord. She tires him out and that is why he wishes to go a-Viking."

Although Haaken was joking I knew that most of my men wished me to raid, or to go to war. Despite the fact that they had married Franks and had the title of lord none were yet ready to hang up their swords.

The idea of swords put something in my mind and I asked Harold Strong Arm, "Whatever happened to my father's sword?"

He looked sadly toward the north. My father had been murdered on the Tamese. His body had been brought back and buried but I had been in Norway when that happened. In the time since I had come back I had asked many questions but not that one.

"I was young when it was made but I still remember that it was engraved."

Harold nodded, "It said, '*Bagsecg made me. I come from the past and reach to the future. Enemies of the clan, fear me.*'" He closed his eyes and clutched at his amulet. "We never saw it after the battle on the drekar. I assumed it had been lost overboard but…"

"But what?"

"When we look back we have perfect vision. I fear your brother might have taken it."

"We did not find it when I slew him. He did not use my father's sword."

"Then it is lost but, in my heart, I know it was not killed. It lies somewhere waiting."

We had little time to talk for Saxbjǫrn's drekar had already turned around so that when they left they could do so quickly. We liked to use the tides and we were always prepared. We had met Saxbjǫrn the Silent, Halfi Axe Tongue and Nefgeirr Halfisson in Dyflin. The port which had once been a haven for Vikings had become a dangerous place with little honour amongst those who ran the port. They had followed my banner. All three had settled close to Carentan. Saxbjǫrn the Silent was the lord who ruled them but the three were still as I remembered them. They were close.

I clasped his arm. "It has been too long. How goes the world?"

He gestured toward my hall, "You are lucky here, Lord Göngu-Hrólfr Rognvaldson. You do not live on the edge of the Norse world."

"Trouble?" He nodded. "Harold, take the jarl's men to the warrior hall. I will be safe."

"Aye lord."

We were alone as we passed beneath my gatehouse. "The families we lost?"

"Aye."

"You have discovered their fate?"

"It was Bretons. It has happened again. Some of Halfi's people were taken and this time they were seen. One of the shepherd boys was making water and he saw the Bretons taking the women and children back to their ship. Now it makes sense. The ones who were taken both the last time and this time all lived within a few miles of the coast. The Bretons are beginning to copy us and I do not like it."

We had reached my hall and Ágáta had ale and horns waiting for us. She was discreet and she hurried away. We were alone. We would not be disturbed for my wife disliked my jarls. She found them both uncouth and, in her words, malodorous. She had had to explain to me what the word meant.

"You wish help?"

"No, lord. We are Vikings and we fight our own battles. It is just that we intend to raid the land around their Mont St. Michel and as the King of the Franks has given it to the Bretons we thought to ask for your approval."

I nodded. This showed respect. "You do not need to ask permission for the Bretons, by raiding, have declared war on you."

"We have three drekar and many men. If we can we hope to take prisoners and exchange them for the families of those who were taken."

"Good. If you wish me to make war on the Bretons then I am happy to do so. The King of the Franks cannot give away that which he does not control and the Cotentin is ours by force of arms and blood."

He looked relieved. "When we are done I will return and tell you what we have discovered."

"You have no need. It has been some time since I took *'Fafnir'* to sea. We will visit you in two months' time. I too have men who wish to raid. How long do you stay?"

He smiled, "Just overnight although I daresay that will be enough to annoy the Lady Poppa. She will be sending for boatloads of lavender from Provence."

I laughed. Everyone, it seemed, knew of Poppa's views.

The next morning I watched *'Moon Dragon'* head down the river and I had my drekar hauled from the river. It was good that Saxbjǫrn had come for it had made me realise that I was still a Viking. We might not be raiding the Franks but the Bretons were a different matter. I had not made any promise to them. I saw that weed clung to the hull of my ship. We had shipwrights on the river and they would examine her for me. "Clean the weed and replace every strake and sheet. I want *'Fafnir'* to fly."

"Aye lord." Leif the Ship hesitated, "Who will captain her?"

Olaf Two Teeth had been my captain. Even though he was lord of Djupr I had always felt comfortable with him on my steering board. He was a link to the past and my grandfather. He had suffered an illness. Some said it was a punishment from the gods. I did not. He had woken one morning to find that half his face and his left arm were useless. All else was fine and his mind was as sharp as ever. His son Siggi was a powerful lord and he helped his father. He could rule Djupr but he could not fight in a shield wall and he could not sail my drekar. I believe it was the three sisters who sent his affliction. They had often spun their webs and tied my life to that of another. This severed a thread. I was still tied to Olaf but it was not as tight. I knew as I answered Leif the Ship, that another thread was being spun even as the words came from my mouth. "You know ships. Whom would you have holding the steering board?"

He tried to evade the question, "I know how to sail a ship and not fight with one."

I laughed, "Do not worry, Leif, I know how to fight but I need someone who can put my ship where it will do the most good; next to a foe. Do not be coy with me. I can see in your eyes that you have a name. Spit it out so that I may hear it." My wife often told me that when I spoke in what I considered a reasonable way it sounded threatening and intimidating. She urged me to speak quietly as her priest did. It was nonsense of course. My men knew that my loud voice was a gift from the gods and came with the huge body I had been given.

Leif the Ship nodded, "If I was to speak truly then I would say my son, Erik Leifsson. He sails a knarr and makes the swiftest of voyages." He shrugged. "You asked me, lord. Ask others if you wish. I have a half share in my son's boat and he makes me rich. If he serves you I may be poorer."

I snorted, "Unlikely! My ships come back laden with treasure. Is he in port?"

"No, lord he has sailed to the Haugr to take goods to Finnbjǫrn."

"Then when he returns ask him to speak with me."

As we headed back inside the city I asked Snorri Snorrison if he knew Leif's son. "I have heard that, despite his age, he makes swift voyages and he has skill. He has no experience in a drekar, lord."

I nodded. I knew what he meant. A knarr did not use oars. A drekar captain had to know when to use oars and how long to make the crew row. I decided to wait until I had met the young man before I committed. "Have Harold Strong Arm warn my men that I will need them a month from now."

He cocked his head to one side, "I thought you told Saxbjǫrn that it would be two months, lord?"

Despite my loud voice those whom I trusted knew that they could question me. I smiled, "It has been two years since we went to war. I know not about the crew but I feel rusty. Besides, from what Æbbi Bonecrusher said my men are eager to leave Rouen. We will raid!"

He laughed, "They are that lord. A woman in your bed gives you comfort but only for a short time. Then you need to have the freedom of the seas. You need to hear dead comrades screeching from above. A man needs his blood to rush through his veins as he raises his sword. It is what makes him a man. I was curious only."

My wife's reaction was the opposite. I do not think that she minded the fact that I would be away. In fact, I believe that she relished it. It was my intent that she did not like. "The Bretons? You know that I am related to Alan of Vannes?"

I shrugged, "You are now my wife. As I recall there was little rush to pay your ransom when I took you. And, if memory serves, you were happy to become my bride!"

Her mask slipped a little as she snapped, "Perhaps I thought I could turn this sow's ear into a silk purse. I might have had the idea that if I made you Christian then you would become a Frank."

I turned and said, a little colder than I intended, "Then you were wrong."

"You have changed, Rollo!" She refused to use my Viking name and used the name the Franks called me. "I gave you a son and now you need me not!"

"Then give me another son!"

It was the wrong thing to say. We rarely coupled these days and she appeared to be indisposed more than when we had first met. She stood, "You are a barbarian but I am Christian! I will go to Æðelwald of Remisgat and we will pray for your soul!"

I knew that they would be closeted together for hours in the chapel she had built in my town. I missed Gefn. She had been the one who had been the bridge between Poppa and me. Since she had died I had grown apart from my wife. Left alone I went to the door which led to my fighting platform. It looked out on the river. I had chosen this land. My grandfather had chosen this land but the more I thought about it perhaps the Norns had chosen it for us. If that was the case then perhaps they had chosen Poppa. I no longer had someone with whom I could confide. My grandfather was gone, and my adopted mother had been taken. Sven Blue Cheek and Bergil Fast Blade lived far from here and now had their own families. I would try to change my ways. I needed to build bridges with my wife. Perhaps the time I spent away from her might make her warm to me.

I liked Erik Leifsson as soon as I met him. Although young, I estimated that he had seen twenty or so summers, his skin had the leathery look of a man who spends most of his time at sea. He was also unafraid of me. I liked that too.

"Your father has spoken to you?"

"Aye lord. He said you need a captain for your drekar. She is a fine ship." I nodded. "I have a ship of my own."

"I know. I do not need a captain for long periods. If you agree then you will just sail my ship when we raid. It might be for a month at a time."

"A month when I will not be earning coin."

"A month when you will earn more than when you sail your knarr."

"What will my share be, lord?"

"You have a tenth of the coins and treasure we take but you pay for your ship's boys from that."

He nodded, "That is generous."

"Trust me Erik Leifsson, you will earn it."

"And when do you need me?"

"We sail at Harpa."

I watched him considering. "I will tell you what, Lord Göngu-Hrólfr Rognvaldson, I will sail your drekar when you sail at Harpa. When the voyage is over then we should sit and talk. Perhaps you might not wish me to continue and perhaps I will go back to my knarr."

He was confident and forthright. I knew of lords who would have taken offence at his words but they suited me. I held out my arm. "I am happy at the arrangement. I leave the ship to you."

He smiled, "Do not worry, lord, I may not know of battles but I know ships. She will be ready and she will fly."

There were some things I enjoyed about being Lord of Rouen. We had good walls. We had ready access to the sea. My people were prosperous and the climate was pleasant. What I missed were the warriors who had helped me to take this enclave of land in the heart of Frankia. This had been one of the jewels in the crown of Frankia and now it was mine. But warriors like Sven, Bergil, Sámr. Ragnar, Finnbjǫrn and Olaf were no longer warriors who lived in my hall. I missed the ease with which we could speak. We had been shield brothers. They were closer than any family.

My wife was still with her priest and so I went to the town square. It was where we held a market each morning. As I reached it the farmers who had come into town to sell their produce were packing up. Snorri was my bodyguard. Each stranger was viewed with suspicion. I did not think I would come to harm but it did not pay to be careless.

"Come Snorri. I see that Dómhildr the alewife has brewed fresh ale. Let us go and taste it." When an alewife brewed fresh beer, she hung out a sheaf of wheat. We went to drink not simply because the ale would be good but because it would draw many men there and this was my way of gauging the mood of my people.

Snorri rubbed his hands. Dómhildr had taken over Brigid's mantle including some of her secret recipes. My men enjoyed good ale. I did not tax Dómhildr. Her beer brought in far more coin to my town than any other business. I taxed the other stallholders and the ships who not only used my port but the river as well. At first, the merchants and captains had complained of the cost but as the river was now much safer they realised it was an investment. It was another reason why the Franks tolerated us. We kept their river safe.

The market was where I was most popular. There had always been a market in Rouen but until I had captured it the townsfolk had suffered raids not only from Vikings and Frisians but Angles, Saxons and, increasingly, Bretons. I was hailed and offered all sorts of delicacies as I headed toward the alehouse with the upturned barrels and trestle table. Dómhildr beamed. Her husband was a tiny man which contrasted with the huge Dómhildr. They seemed happy enough together. I envied them.

"Abel, fetch some sausage for the lord." As her husband hurried away behind the curtain to the food, Dómhildr bobbed a curtsy. "You must have known that I had brewed some of your favourite ale, my lord."

"Black jet?"

She nodded, "And I think I have managed to keep to Brigid's recipe too." She pointed above her. "If there is a wind from the west then we know I have it wrong." Dómhildr was not a Christian. She believed in signs, portents and omens. "The sausage is a new recipe. I hope you enjoy it!"

"I am sure we shall. How is business?"

"I cannot make enough ale to satisfy demand, lord. I am looking for slaves to work in my brewhouse. If you could find some I would appreciate it. Saxon girls would be best. They know ale and they can be trained. Not Bretons or Franks. They do not know ale and they run. It is hard to run across water."

Her husband appeared with a wooden platter and two horns of black ale. They both looked at Snorri and me as we took a mouthful. You did not sip ale, you swallowed it! It tasted dark with a slightly bitter aftertaste. The foam stuck to my beard. A sure sign of a good ale. "It is better than Brigid's!"

"Lord, you are too kind." Just then some of the market traders who had finished clearing their stalls arrived. "Business lord. Just shout when you want more. Valka! Fetch more horns!"

We chewed on the sausages and washed them down with more ale. Snorri wiped his greasy hands on his breeks. "We have not raided the Saxons for some time, lord. It might be worth raiding there before we visit with Saxbjǫrn. He will have dealt with the Bretons himself."

"Do not be too sure, Snorri. This Alan of Vannes has shown himself to be a survivor. I will not underestimate him."

It was late in the afternoon when we returned to my hall. I had learned much in the short time I had spent amongst my people. There was no unrest. The Franks who came to trade also spoke of the peace they enjoyed but they also spoke of the threat of the Bretons.

My wife sat with William and she and Æðelwald of Remisgat were teaching him to read. I frowned. The priest had too much influence on my son. I feared he would try to turn him into a Christian. One day Æðelwald of Remisgat would upset me and then he would pay for all the trouble he had caused my family and my land. He was the one person who never saw me smile for each time I saw his face I wished to draw Long Sword and take his head.

"The market is prosperous and it is growing."

My wife sniffed, "When they bring and sell fine cloth from Bruggas then I will enjoy the market until then it is a place for ale, beans and cabbages and the people there smell! None of which will entice me there."

I sighed, "When I raid I can always make a raid on Bruggas."

It was the wrong thing to say. I knew not why I said it but my wife stood and jabbed a finger at me, "You are a barbarian! I do not want clothes stolen from some poor gentlewoman! I want to pay for them!"

I did not say that we would be taking from the merchants and traders who would have made a profit. I just shrugged and went to my chamber. There I had maps and I would study them. Perhaps we could raid the Saxons in Cent and then sail to Carentan. As Snorri had said it was some time since we had sailed and there would, inevitably, be a new crew. I found myself looking forward to the opportunity to draw my sword and spend some time with my warriors.

I sought out Padraig. Although he was a priest he was not of the same church as my wife's priest. He was a clever man and he organized the taxes and the running of my hall and town. "How long will you be away, lord?"

"Fourteen nights would mean that events have not turned out the way I might have hoped."

He hesitated, "You do not need to go, lord. Your men would happily raid for you and the result would be the same."

"Perhaps. You are right that they are well trained but I do this for me. Besides neither my town nor my family need me at the moment. William is too young to train to become a warrior and my wife…."

He looked nervous. I think it was because he was a man of God. "I do not know women, lord but it seems to me that Lady Poppa just needs someone to be gentle with her."

I was puzzled, "I have never raised my hand to her!"

He sighed, "I am the wrong man to ask, lord, but if I were you I would speak with those warriors who have been married for a long time."

I knew that he meant well but he sent me to sea in a confused state of mind.

Chapter 2

I stood with Erik Leifsson on the steering board as we sailed gently down the river toward the sea. I had made a blót and been rewarded with a gentle wind from the south and east. It would take us to the land of Cent which lay to the east of Wessex. When we returned we could use the wind to head into the open ocean and then return home. We planned to land on the south coast of Cent. We would be far enough away from the ships Alfred of Wessex used to hunt down drekar. Other Vikings had told me that the Saxons had improved their ships and seamanship. I was not worried. Alfred might have tricked poor Guthrum and made him a Christian. I was made of sterner stuff.

"How long for us to reach Cent?"

"This is a fast ship. In my knarr, it might take four or five days, even with a wind like this. This is a drekar and *'Fafnir'*, if we used the oars, could do it in two."

"There is no rush. We can take half a month for this raid. I am not due at Carentan until another moon has passed."

Erik was a clever young man, "This way you can see if I am any good and which of the crew you wish to change."

I smiled, "Perhaps but it may be that I just wish to enjoy the raid. It has been more than two years since I went to sea."

He nodded. "Is it true, lord, that once you sank to the bottom of the sea and did not drown?"

"I was pushed into the Tamese and I was under the water a long time. When I surfaced I was alone on the ocean. Ran came to my aid." I turned and holding my horse amulet, bobbed my head at the sea, "For which I am eternally grateful."

"Then you truly are a chosen one for I have never heard of any who sank to the bottom of the sea and lived."

I smiled, "Even one as tall as I?"

"Even one like you, lord." He pointed toward the mast fish. "I have used oars on my knarr but I have never had thirty-two men pulling at the same time. You know that I will need advice."

"It is not hard. For this voyage, I will command them to be run in and run out. You need to use them to change direction. You can make an even more extreme turn than you can with a steering board. You order one half to be out of the water and by putting the steering board over you can turn a drekar almost in its own length. By backing one set of oars while rowing forward with the other you can spin the drekar around."

"All of this sounds good. I thought we just used them when there was no wind."

"That often happens. We are just single crewed. If we had a double crew the men can keep rowing for half a day and more. That can prove useful."

I was pleased with all the questions he asked me for it showed he had a mind and that he wanted to be the best that he could be. Once we cleared the headland south of Djupr and left the estuary the motion of the drekar became busier. We also moved far quicker. We were out of the river and had the wind pushing us hard. It would not be on the outward voyage where my new helmsman would learn to use oars.

I left him to discover the drekar's secrets and joined my men by the mast. We had my oathsworn and another twenty men. Some, a handful, were younger warriors without mail who wanted coin to buy some. Half of the others were married men who had had enough of life at home and wanted adventure. The others were farmers who needed either coin or animals. For them, a perfect world would be one where they found animals and treasure. They would choose to take part of their share from the animals. I remembered when I had been a young warrior who needed to raid. When I was picked up and taken to Norway I had had nothing. Everything I owned had come to me after I had sunk to the bottom of the river. I knew that was the work of the Norns. This trip to the land of the Angles and Saxons had not been my idea. The seed had been planted by Dómhildr. Who knew whence the seed came? The Norns had made a prophecy to my grandfather and it had still come to fruition. My son and I were tools of the Norns.

The wind was benevolent and took us where we wanted to go. We would land where it took us. There would be people. If they were men they would die and if they were either women or children then they would become slaves. My grandfather had been one such slave and he had ended life as one of the most respected Vikings anywhere. Dragonheart had been a Saxon slave and yet he had become the most famous of warriors. Slavery was not a bad thing. A man made of it what he could.

They made space for me to sit down. I was the largest man on the drekar and everyone had to move. I took the horn of ale Harold Strong Arm offered me and leaned with my back against the mast fish. I listened to them as they bantered and joked. Without even knowing I recognised the ones who were farmers for they were more intense. I heard the bravado from those who had never yet fought and I listened to those leaving wives behind who laughed and joked about their women. All had different motives but once we went ashore then we would all have to be as one.

Siggi Svenson was one who had a farm. It was south of the river. He had been a warrior who had raided with me. He had a short mail byrnie, a well-made helmet and a good shield. When he had married he had left his life as a Viking behind. I was pleased to have him for he was a doughty warrior. He turned to me, "Where do we raid in Cent, lord?"

I pointed to the sail above us, "Where Ran sends us. There are many towns. There is Hamwic in the west, Haestingaceaster, Hastingas in the centre and Dwfr to the east. In between, there are many beaches, many small ports and inland there are many towns. It is a rich land."

"But they have burghs. They have walls to defend them."

"And we will not touch the ones with walls. We need slaves and animals. If we find a church then the gods truly favour us. If not..."

He nodded, "I have four children, lord. I have good land but I need animals. The animals from Cent will be hardier than the beasts we buy. He shook his head, "And they are expensive!"

I laughed, "Then we will try to get as many as we can then!"

Normally I would not have stood a watch but my captain was new and so I did. We were out of sight of land and it was night. There were no stars but that did not worry me. We were heading roughly north. We had to hit the coast at some point and it would not be during my watch. The two ship's boys who shared the watch with me were more excited than any crew I had ever seen. It was their first voyage and Erik was not only their captain he was also their uncle. Added to that they were watching with the Lord of Rouen. I had to find tasks for them to keep them occupied. I wondered how William, my son, would behave. Despite what his mother might say I intended to bring him to sea as soon as he was able. It would make a man of him and also help him to get to know the men with whom he would be fighting. Poppa could posture all she wanted now. It did not matter for the present. He was too young. When he became old enough then he would be mine!

During the night I felt the wind veering. It became more east southeast than southeast. I made corrections but we would need the sun to get a more accurate position. I woke Erik well before dawn. "The wind has shifted, Erik, I adjusted our course but…"

"We have all day before we see the coast of England. Thank you for standing a watch, lord. Next time I will bring my first mate with me. Lars is a good man."

"There will be a next time?"

"I think so but let us not tempt the Norns for this voyage is not even begun properly yet."

As I laid down in my furs I realised that Erik had an old and wise head upon his shoulders. I had one less matter to occupy my mind.

My sleep was filled with dreams and pictures I did not understand. My wife laughed at me as I lay pinned to the ground with a cross lying upon me. I saw Alan of Vannes leading horsemen and burning farms. I saw Danes trying to take my town. The dream disturbed me and I woke when it was still dark. I stared up at the black sky and then tried to get back to sleep. I forced myself to think of my grandfather and the days I had lived with him at the Haugr. They were happy times and I fell asleep.

They let me sleep until the fourth hour of the morning. I made water and then went to the steering board. Erik pointed to the sun. "The wind took us further west than we wished, I have corrected but it means we are moving more slowly. Should I run out the oars?"

"No, we have time. I will relieve you in the afternoon watch. My mistake means we will not reach the coast until nightfall now."

I ate and we ploughed north. The ship's boys spotted a sail at noon but it was on the horizon and it could have been anyone. A drekar had a high mast and kept a good lookout. Few other ships had such a good view. I doubted that we had been seen. When we drew closer to the coast then we would be in danger. Our newly painted shields and fresh sail would make us stand out. Perhaps I had been meant to make a mistake so that we could land at night.

Snorri joined me when I took the steering board. "Fetch the chart, Snorri. Erik is a good mariner and he has marked our last position on the map. I would estimate where we might land."

I saw from the map that our course would take us close to the old Roman fort at Haestingaceaster. The Saxons had made it into a burgh. There were, however, many beaches close by and I knew that there were farms. I had taught my oathsworn how to read maps and Snorri pointed to a small bay marked with a cross. "What is this, lord?"

I looked closely at it. At first, I could not remember. It had been some time since my grandfather had drawn the map. I closed my eyes to recall him. That often helped. When I saw him then I heard his voice and it came to me. "Bulverhythe, it is a safe haven. It has a shingle beach but it has two arms of sand and a ship can land there." I smiled, "We told Guthrum about it and the Danes used it before they began to bend the knee to Alfred. You have a good eye Snorri. We will make for there. It is close enough to both Haestingaceaster and Hastingas to allow us to raid and to have a secure boat."

"We could have brought more men. There was no shortage of volunteers."

"I know but this crew will suffice." I needed to confide in someone. "I fear that the Bretons mean us mischief. I hope that when we reach Saxbjǫrn that he has dealt with them but if not then this will mean war and that will take every warrior we have."

"We are Vikings, lord. War is something we relish."

Snorri was right but the world was changing. When my grandfather had been a young man a single crew could raid and be successful. The last raid I had been on had involved more than three hundred ships. We had unleashed the beast and now the Bretons and the Franks were organising to counter that threat. Alfred had already defeated Vikings on the island the Romans had called Britannia. We had a toehold on the river and the land around us. An alliance of the Franks and the Bretons could drive us hence.

"How many men from Rouen could we call upon if we had to go to war?"

He stared at the mast and then back at me, "That is a hard question to answer, lord. This is not like Norway. We do not have bondi. Warriors? Perhaps a hundred but many, like Siggi Svenson, live far from Rouen. The ones who are not warriors could defend walls but I would not put them in a shield wall." I was silent and I think Snorri took that to mean I was not happy with his answer. "I am sorry, lord, but you asked me."

"And you have given me a good answer. We are no longer Norse. We are a mix. The same will be true of Sven Blue Cheek, Bergil Fast Blade and all the other lords of my towns. We need a different system. I have this voyage to come up with one."

I enjoyed such mental challenges and after I had handed over the drekar to Erik, I sat and ruminated. Darkness fell and I slept a little. Harold Strong Arm woke me. "Lord, Erik says he can hear the beach. He has taken in the sail."

I nodded, "And he wishes us to use oars."

Harold's teeth showed white in the dark, "Aye, lord, he is a good sailor but he does not know a drekar yet."

I stood, "Run out the oars!"

There would be no chant. It was the middle of the night but we did not want to alarm those nearby. If we were seen then that would be the work of the Norns but if we alerted our enemies then that would be our own carelessness. I donned my mail. When we landed I would jump ashore with the ship's boys and the warriors who had yet to acquire mail. It would be enough of us to secure the beachhead. With the oars manned Erik had the sail furled and the crew pulled to drag the drekar ashore. We had the tide with us and that helped. I placed my helmet at the prow and patted the dragon prow. It never hurt. The ship's boys awaited me. Two had ropes and the rest would help to secure us. I could see the white of the surf and hear it as it shifted over the shingle. The land was just a black line. The wind took any smells of the land away from us. This was always the time when excitement and nerves coursed through my body in equal measure. I had missed this.

I pulled myself up onto the gunwale. The ship's boys barely came to my waist. I spied the shingle. It glistened. I leapt into the black water. When I landed I realised that it came up to my chest I said, "Hold! It is too deep!" I waded ashore as the oars pulled the drekar closer. I heard the splashes behind me as the boys leapt into the sea. I was already on dry land seeking something to secure us. There was neither rock nor tree.

Sven Blue Eyes was close by. He had the hammer and the metal stake. "We will need another stake. Fetch one." I strode further up the beach until I had passed the high-water mark. I began to hammer in the metal spike. To dampen the noise, I placed my cloak over the head of the spike. It did not ring but made a dull thud which I hoped would be masked by the sea. Lars brought a rope from the ship and when the spike was embedded he tied it. Sven brought the second spike and I took it thirty paces west. I repeated it. By the time we were secure, my men had formed up. Lars gave me my helmet and shield.

"Tell the captain to keep a close watch on the ship!"

I raised my Long Sword and my men formed up on me. There was no cliff here and the ground just rose to a grassy area. I guessed that Haestingaceaster lay to the north of us and if that was so then Hastingas would lie ten miles to the northeast of us. It would be dark for some hours and that would give us the opportunity to head into the inland areas and take as much as we could. When daylight came we would head up the coast to Hastingas. Although the wind was behind us I recognised that there was a church of some description ahead of us. It was partly the sound of chanting and also the smell of incense and candles. Both were clear signs of monks. I stopped and waved Harold and Haaken ahead to scout. Æbbi Bonecrusher organised my men behind me. He had my oathsworn in the front rank, then the mailed, experienced warriors and finally the untried youths at the rear. I was the only one without a spear. My long arms and Long Sword meant I had the reach of a spear anyway.

My scouts were only away a short time. Their smiles told me that we had found treasure at the first attempt. "Lord, it is a monastery. They have neither guards nor weapons but they do have animals."

"You two go around to the other side. Take the untried warriors and stop any from leaving."

I gave them a few moments to disappear and then I led the rest forward. I had twenty warriors with me and that was more than enough to deal with monks and priests. We soon heard the sound of prayers and the ringing of small bells. As we drew closer I could make out the words. They were in Latin. I sensed movement ahead, close to the gate which led to the walled enclosure. I held up my hand and my men stopped. They knew better than to make a noise. When I heard clucking, I knew that there were hens. These would be monks or servants collecting eggs. I frowned for the words I heard were Frankish. What were Franks doing in Cent?

I turned and waved Snorri and Æbbi Bonecrusher forward. I slid a finger under my chin and they nodded. They slipped down the wall and climbed over. The only sound I heard was a soft sigh as the two warriors slit the throats of the egg collectors. The gates were opened and we slipped inside. I smelled the animals. There were hens, sheep and at least one cow for I heard her lowing. She needed to be milked. We headed for the church. I waved for Siggi Svenson to go to the place they cooked. I could smell bread. He took two men with him. One was his brother. When we reached the door to the church I paused. I sheathed my sword for I would not need it. These were monks. They might flee but the door to the apse was guarded by my men.

I flung the door open. Faces turned and froze as I ducked under the door frame. I shouted, in Frankish, "Stay where you are and I promise that you will not be harmed. Offer us resistance and you will die."

I saw Snorri frown at my use of a foreign language but I knew that I had been right to do so when the Abbot shouted, also in Frank, "Save the treasure!"

I sighed for it was not only futile it would show us where the treasure lay. Two friars began to move the altar. Another two picked up incense burners and swung them at my head. I batted them out of the way and then punched one in the face. He fell backwards and did not move. I snarled at the other, "On your knees!"

When two tried to flee out of the back door they were stabbed by Harold and Haaken. When Æbbi Bonecrusher cuffed the two men who were trying to move the altar then all resistance ended.

"Harold Strong Arm take two men and escort these back to the drekar. They are Franks!"

Harold nodded and said, "You priests walk ahead of me. We are going for a paddle in the sea."

The Abbot complained, "You said we would not be harmed!"

"And I also said if you offered no resistance. Pick up your priest and be thankful that I did not draw my sword else you would have ended your lives here." While my men began to strip the church, I went out of the church to the sleeping quarters. I took Æbbi Bonecrusher with me. As I had expected the grandest quarters belonged to the Abbot and yielded a chest containing both jewels and coins. Æbbi collected all the fine linens too. "Search the other rooms and I will see you back at the drekar."

After he had gone I went to the table. Æbbi had taken the candlesticks but there were parchments. One was still sealed. I was intrigued. I might not be able to read them but Padraig could. I found a leather satchel and I jammed them inside. Siggi and his men were outside. They had a hand cart and it was laden with food. There were hams, cheeses, honey, a barrel of beer, two jugs of wine and bread.

Siggi looked happy. "With this and the animals, lord, we have raided enough and we can go home."

I shook my head, "We need slaves too but this is a good start. The gods smile on us." I was the last to leave. Normally we would have burned the church. We did it to show that our gods were superior to the

White Christ but we did not wish to alert the burgh of Hastingas. We left it. I was still intrigued by the presence of the Franks. What were they doing in Wessex?

The animals were being loaded onto the drekar when I arrived. This was where Erik excelled. He knew how to load a ship. He had rigged a block and tackle. Turning the drekar beam on facilitated the process. I handed the documents to Lars, "Keep these safe and dry."

"You wish them as kindling lord?"

I shook my head, "These are as valuable as coins! We do not burn them!" I saw a worried look flash across the face of the Abbot. I walked over to him. "Tell me, Abbot, what is a Frankish monastery doing in the land of Wessex?"

"King Offa of Mercia gave the land to the monks of Saint Denis. King Alfred has confirmed the land to us. You have made a grave error, Viking. The King of Wessex will punish you."

I laughed, "Abbot, I do not worry about Saxons. I leave the worrying to them. I am Göngu-Hrólfr Rognvaldson. Even your Frankish master, Charles, fears me."

He wagged a finger at me, "Your days are numbered Viking. Just as Guthrum now serves King Alfred so shall you serve King Charles!"

"We will see." I turned to Erik, "I will leave you six men to watch these monks." I changed to Frankish, "Abbot if you and your friars help my men to load the ship then we will not take you to be sold as slaves." In truth, I had no intention of taking them back. Priests had lost value and we did not need them.

"You give your word?"

"I give my word and I am never foresworn."

"Very well."

"Erik, they will help you."

I saw that dawn was on the horizon and I led the rest of my men north and east to seek slaves and more animals. We had no pigs yet. We halted at a small copse and examined the land which lay close by. There was a town further along the coast, Bexelei. As the sun rose I saw smoke from the houses. We could now see the fields. Animals which had been brought indoors at night were being brought out. Close to the shore was a stone tower. It was unoccupied.

I turned to Siggi, "Take the men with mail and the youths. Search the farms and capture the animals north of us. Return by noon. My oathsworn and I will go to Bexelei. It is not far and there is no wall."

"Aye lord. Come, men. We hunt for slaves." I led just twelve men. It would be enough.

We turned and headed for the river we could see which meandered down to the settlement. It was lined with trees and bushes. It would afford cover and we soon discovered that it was fordable. I slung my shield over my back and hung my helmet from my Long Sword. I had a short sword, Hrólfr's Vengeance I could use. We were just four or five hundred paces from the settlement when we were seen. A shepherdess was squatting in the river making water. She turned, saw us and screamed, "Vikings!" Her strident voice would carry to Bexelei.

I drew my short sword. "Get her. Capture as many as you can." We ran down the river bank as Haaken grabbed the girl and slung her over his shoulder. She would be a perfect slave. She looked to have seen less than fourteen summers. I could hear the alarm, as people reacted to the shout. The wise ones would just run. The foolish, or the greedy, would try to take as much as they could before we arrived. They would be the ones we would capture or kill.

My long legs meant that I reached the settlement first. As I had expected three men had decided to slow us up to allow their women and children to escape. Holding my short sword in my left hand I drew Long Sword from over my back. I saw the fear on the faces of the three Saxons as they saw the size of my sword. With their small shields and spears, they held their ground. I wore mail and I did not hesitate. I swung Long Sword in an arc. One of them made the mistake of misjudging the length of my swing. He jabbed forward with his spear. Although the spearhead hit my byrnie he was already dead as my sword tore across his neck. I instinctively parried with my short sword as the other two tried to jab at me and step back at the same time. One stumbled as he stepped out of the range of the now bloody Long Sword. I changed to overhand and brought my sword down from on high. The second Saxon thought his hands were quicker than mine. They were, almost. His spear struck my mail even as he twisted to break the mail. My Long Sword came down between his neck and his arm. I ripped his upper body into two parts. He fell screaming. The one who had fallen was bespattered with blood. He regained his feet and hurled his spear at me before running away. I batted the spear out of my way with my short sword.

I whirled around to see if any other men survived. Two more lay dead. They had small chests with them and the rest had shown common sense and run. I knew that they would head to Hastingas. They would raise the fyrd and we would soon have company. Snorri and half of my men were guarding the twelve or so captives. The rest were ransacking the huts and homes.

"Anyone wounded?"

Æbbi Bonecrusher laughed, "You fought the only ones with weapons lord. You are too fast and your legs are too long for your oathsworn!"

"Aye well, we had best hurry for they will run to Hastingas and there will be warriors there for it is a burgh."

I walked to the two dead men and wiped my swords clean on their kyrtles. Their weapons were of poor quality. I left them.

"Ready lord!"

I looked up at the sky. It was almost noon and Siggi Svenson and his men would be back at the drekar. "Get the captives and the captured animals moving. Harold, Æbbi and Siggi, stay with me. We will be the rear guard."

I picked up the two spears the Saxons had used. They might come in handy. I saw that my men had managed to get a cow and a calf as well as eight sheep and two goats. Four dead fowl hung from Haaken's spear. They would be made into a stew.

"We found coins in the chest. Farthings and halfpennies mainly but enough pennies to show that they were doing well." He shook his head. "They should have had a wall."

I pointed to the empty tower. "They have that instead. I am guessing that it should have been manned and that there is a fire at the top. They had them on the river by Rouen when we first arrived. When warning came they would have fled to Hastingas. Their lack of vigilance has cost them dear."

Æbbi Bonecrusher shook the second of the chests. It rattled showing it was far from full. "These folks are not as rich as the Franks."

Shaking my head, I said, "I told the Franks that so long as they left me in peace we would not raid. Do not worry, Æbbi Bonecrusher, the Bretons will prove a worthwhile source of coin."

Siggi looked behind us, "It seems they have lit signal fires." I looked back and saw a beacon burning on the headland to the east of Bexelei.

"We must have a four or mile start on them. We should make the ship." Then Harold pointed west. Another column of smoke rose. It looked to be coming from beyond where we had moored our ship. "Then let us see how fast the animals and the captives can move." We started to run and I shouted, "Make them move!"

Haaken roared in Saxon, "Move! I have an itch in my pants!" He leered at the women. "I am a Viking and I am ready for a woman who is too slow to move!" It was all an act of course. Haaken was like all of my men. He had honour but his threat worked and the women ran. The animals were harder to move. I saw one Saxon woman glare at Haaken and then speak to the others. They listened to her and they moved faster.

We saw the mast of the drekar at the same time that we heard the thunder of hooves behind us.

"Haaken, take the women to the drekar. Use the priests and monks as a shield before us while we load. Petr, go with him and the rest of you with me!" I had ten men with me. "Shield wall. Five men with me and the rest behind. We stop the horsemen and get back to the drekar quickly. There is little in this battle for us." That was confirmed when we saw the twenty horsemen riding the little horses the Saxons like to use. None of the Saxons had mail save for the leader who had a short byrnie and a helmet with a plume. They had round shields and none had stiraps. We knew horses. We could ride to war and a few of us could fight on horseback. That was because we used stiraps. As we waited I saw that they had raised the fyrd and a warband was some way behind the horsemen. The horsemen were there to slow us and then the fyrd would slaughter us. It was an ambitious plan. Perhaps when the men who had escaped us had reached Hastingas they had reported just thirteen men. Even now they would spy my drekar.

The thegn who led the men was not a complete fool. He halted just a hundred paces from us. If he thought we would turn our backs then he was a fool. It came to me that he was waiting for the fyrd to arrive. "On my command, we walk backwards." I banged my shield and began a chant to help us keep in step.

> ***Clan of the Horseman***
> ***Warriors strong***
> ***Clan of the Horseman***
> ***Our reach is long***
> ***Clan of the Horseman***
> ***Fight as one***
> ***Clan of the Horseman***
> ***Death will come***

As soon as the thegn saw what we were doing he dug his heels into his horse's flanks and shouted, "Charge!"

"Halt! Wedge!"

We had practised this many times and Æbbi and Siggi stepped behind me while the next three moved back a little. The last five formed a rear rank. I had two spears. As the Saxons hurtled toward us I waited until they were five paces and then hurled my spear at the thegn. He held his shield up and deflected it. Sadly for the man next to him, the spear was deflected into his face. As he pulled his hand up he slipped from the saddle.

"Brace!"

I felt Siggi's shield in my back. The Saxons showed their lack of experience. Some tried to throw their spears. Unless you had straps one of two things happened: you either fell from your horse or the throw had no power behind it. Two men fell from their horses and another four spears hit shields or glanced weakly from helmets and mail. The others like the thegn tried to stab down. To do so they had to close with us. Three spears stabbed at the thegn and his horse. My spear struck his leg and Siggi's, his horse. The horse reared and the thegn barely held on as his wounded animal galloped off away from the spears. I thrust upwards at the second Saxon as Æbbi rammed his spear into the chest of a third. My spear came up through his arm. As he pulled around the spear broke. Their attack was broken and the fyrd was coming closer. I drew my Long Sword and swung it in an arc. I caught the rump of one horse and the shield of a Saxon. They withdrew. One of the horsemen was tending to the thegn's wound. I saw that the fyrd was less than half a mile away.

"Stig, how far to the drekar?"

"Four hundred paces."

"On my command, we run for the drekar." I was counting on the fact that we could cover a hundred paces before the Saxons knew what we were doing and that Harold Strong Arm would have men with bows ready to repulse them. "Now!"

I let my men run first and I stood waiting. One of the younger riders saw his chance and he galloped toward me. I slipped my shield around my back and held my sword two handed. Some of the other riders followed him. I was not being heroic. I knew what I could do with my sword. I let the tip rest on the ground and when he was twenty paces from me pulled it back and began to swing. It was all in the timing. The sword sliced the horse's skull in two. The rider fell as the horse tumbled to the ground. The others who had been following stopped and stared in horror as the dying horse thrashed its hooves. I could not let the animal suffer and I strode up to it and in one blow took its head. The rider lay quivering on the ground. I said, "Today, you have been lucky! I give you your life!"

Sheathing my sword, I turned and began to walk back to my ship. I heard the sound of the fyrd as they ran along the road but they would not catch me. Even with my back to the horsemen, I knew that I had broken their spirit.

As I neared my men they began to chant and bang their shields.

Göngu-Hrólfr Rognvaldson
Göngu-Hrólfr Rognvaldson
Göngu-Hrólfr Rognvaldson
Göngu-Hrólfr Rognvaldson

The animals and captives were all on board. Harold had three men watching them. I saw, in the distance, more Saxons approaching. "Get aboard! Abbot, you may go to your people." He looked at me apprehensively. "Run lest I change my mind!"

I saw that he was afraid I would break my word. I had no intention of doing so. They ran. Running toward the fyrd, I knew that would slow up the advance of the fyrd and allow us to sail. The ship's boys were ready to loosen the ropes and retrieve the spikes.

I shouted, "Release the ropes!" My men hurried to clamber aboard. I went to help Lars who was struggling to pull out the metal spike. He was a little flustered, "Fear not, Lars, we have plenty of time!" I picked up the spike and he coiled the rope. Already the drekar, even without the sail, was tugging to be free of the land. Lars ran to the water. It came up to his chest. I hoisted him on my shoulders and walked to the side where he grasped a rope. The water was up to my chest by the time he had scaled the sides. I began to walk up the side. As I landed a cheer went up.

"Where to, lord?"

"Where is the wind?"

"Still east by southeast."

"Then sail west and find a beach on Wihtwara. I am hungry and keen to try the monk's ale!"

The men laughed. We had lost no one. We had achieved our objective and we had food. Life was good.

Chapter 3

We did not need to row for we sailed south and east with the wind. The women wailed and the animals complained but the children seemed just to be interested in the drekar. My men liked children. Most were fathers and they smiled at the youngsters. It was the women who were fearful for they were anticipating a hard life. The only way it would be so would be if they chose to make it hard. I noticed a woman, she was the one who had glared at Haaken. I put her age at twenty or more summers. She looked calm and she had no fear. The others, even the ones older than she looked to her.

The coast of Cent disappeared behind us as we headed toward Wihtwara. Although part of Wessex there were many places where we could land. The island was a mass of beaches and coves. Some were protected by high cliffs. As the captain of a knarr, Erik knew them all. He found one before dark. I sent four men to check the surrounding land while we tied up and lit a fire. We slaughtered one of the older sheep. With the four fowl we had killed and the shellfish we gathered on the beach it would be a good feast for all; even the slaves. We did not share the bread, ham or cheese with them and we heavily watered the beer we gave them. We were warriors and we deserved a reward.

I was desperate to examine the parchments I had taken but I needed someone to read them. Instead, we gathered all the coins together. While the coins we had from the villagers were bronze and silver, those from the abbey were silver and gold. I saw the eyes of the younger warriors light up. They were rich. The battle had yielded little in terms of weapons and mail but they could afford to pay the smiths of Rouen to make mail for them.

Æbbi asked, "Lord, you seemed disturbed to find that the Franks had an abbey in Cent. Why?"

"I like not links across the water. Alfred has had the better of Guthrum. I thought he would be King of Britannia. If he had controlled that land then he might have aided me to rule Frankia."

"Frankia, lord? That is a mighty mouthful!"

I nodded, "True Petr, but think what we have attained already. We have the Cotentin and the northern side of the River Seine. The land between, close to the coast, is ours. That is why I think the Bretons have made a mistake. Had they let us lie we might have grown indolent. Now we are roused."

My men nodded. Our shield brothers had died. A Viking was a vengeful creature and we were the best of the Vikings. Guthrum and his Danes might have been cowed but we would not be.

Siggi Svenson came over to sit by me, "Lord, I am happy with what I have from this raid. I would that I could stay on my farm."

"You do not wish to make war on the Bretons?"

He shrugged, "I do not mind but summer is coming. I have a farm. If you were raiding at Gormánuður when the crops are in and we have culled our beasts then I would say aye."

I nodded and drank some more ale. I had been thinking of this problem for some time. I saw an answer. "Siggi, you are a good warrior. What if I said I needed you for thirty days each year to be as a warrior. Would you go whence I asked?"

He nodded, "Of course, lord save…"

Æbbi Bonecrusher snorted, "Save that it has to be convenient for this farmer!"

I saw Siggi's face colour and his hand went to his seax. I held up my hand. "Peace Æbbi! Siggi, if you gave me thirty days it would be when I needed you. You have a wife. You can get thralls and you have children."

I saw him subside and his hand went from his seax to the bread. He broke a piece of the bread and used it to wipe clean the wooden platter. He glowered at Æbbi, "The way you say it, lord, it sounds reasonable and I would agree."

Arne Green Eye said, "What if a warrior wanted more than thirty days, lord?" He smiled, "I prefer being a warrior to a farmer's life." He pointed to Siggi, "I have no mail yet. I have just a small piece of land which has more weeds than grass. If I took a goat from this raid it would enrich me beyond words. I would wish to raid as often as I could until I became as rich as Siggi."

Siggi whipped his head around, "I am not rich! I have a farm which I work from sunrise to sunset."

My voice took on a commanding tone, "Peace Siggi! Take it as a compliment that Arne envies you." He nodded, "Aye Arne but if I had every warrior for thirty days, at least, then think what we could do. When we have been to Saxbjǫrn 's then I will summon my lords. This only works if all of my people adhere to the same system."

Æbbi said, quietly, "Lord, you are Lord of Rouen. Men rule because you allow it."

"And if I wish to continue to enjoy their loyalty then I must work with them. This is good. I was just using you to sound out the idea. I need to speak with others."

That night I slept well despite a deck crowded with animals and captives. I had an idea and I saw a way to make my clan stronger. The gods had been kind to us for the wind had veered to east by southeast. We could sail due south and would not need to row. Erik was in good spirits. He had sailed his first voyage and, so far, not made any mistakes. If the wind continued from the same direction then we would be home within two days. We sailed swiftly south. At noon Erik was already estimating our speed. The ship's boys were singing as they skylarked in the stays. Perhaps their merriment was the reason that they did not see the sails of the two ships until it was too late.

Lars pointed to the east as he shouted from the masthead, "Captain, two ships to the east." There was a pause. "They are Saxons!"

My captain's face showed his thoughts all too clearly, "These are the ships King Alfred uses to hunt for Vikings. We are in trouble, lord."

I shook my head, "We are in trouble when I say we are. To arms." As men grabbed their weapons I looked east. They lay between our present position and our home. They would continue to close with us and drive us over the edge of the world. I had to remain calm. I had been outwitted by this King Alfred. I should have known how clever he was. He had defeated Guthrum.

I went to Erik, "Keep calm, captain. We are faster than they are."

"But they have the wind. Eventually, they will catch up with us and then with odds of two to one they will win."

I laughed, "They need odds of greater than five to one to defeat Vikings! Just keep sailing and do not lose heart."

There was a contrast between Erik, his young crew, the first-time warriors and those of us who had seen this before. It was the inexperienced ones who developed a crick in the neck turning to see the two Saxons bearing down on us. They had hours of daylight to catch us. Although we did not stare at the Saxons my hearth weru and I were thinking of how we would escape the enemy. We had to elude them for our decks were crowded. If it came to a battle then we would have to abandon the animals and captives over the side. Panicking animals could destroy our drekar.

"I would fight them, lord."

"Throw the animals and the captives to the sea?"

Harold Strong Arm shrugged, "If we do not then we are lost."

Æbbi Bonecrusher shook his head, "You know me, Harold, I would fight any man and Saxons? As many as are foolish enough to come within range of my sword but there is little to be gained from fighting and much to be lost. We outrun and outsail them."

Snorri lowered his voice, "But our captain is young and lacks experience."

I had heard enough, "The Norns have spun. This is meant to be. I asked for a raid which would make my newer warriors and sailors stronger. Is this not what we asked for? And Snorri, has Erik done anything which Olaf Two Teeth would not have done?" He shook his head. "We sail until dark. You are right, Æbbi, we will not be fighting which means we can row. When it is dark we lower the sail, take to the oars and sail north and east, into the wind."

I saw Petr the Slow frown, "Into the wind? Toward the Saxons?"

Haaken the Bold explained, "The Saxons would have to stop, furl their sail, run out oars and then row to follow us. Is there any crew who can row as long and hard as us?"

Harold was like a dog with a bone, "What about the younger warriors?"

"They will have muscles which will burn and their hands will be redraw but we will do that which our lord wishes, we will have a crew!"

Æbbi had the final word.

I rose and went to Erik. He was worried. "The wind is helping them, lord. They are eating into the lead we have and I can go no faster."

"Suppose you mirror their course and sail with the wind?"

"Then we will head further out into the ocean and…"

"And you have never been this far west." He nodded. "I have. I know not where the edge of the world lies but it is further west than I have sailed. Keep the same distance between us. When it is dark you will have the ship's boys furl the sail and you will turn us to face them. We will row until we lose them. When they are no longer in sight then turn to sail due east. As the men tire we can use the sail again."

"We are single crewed."

"And at night we will be hidden. Once we have passed them we can change direction once the men are tired. All that this does is to give us a longer voyage home."

He nodded, "Perhaps I am not the man to captain your ship, lord. I do not have the experience."

"And the Norns know this. You do not think that this is an accident, do you? This is meant to be."

I saw him nod and clutch his amulet, "Aye, lord."

"When you have changed course have your boys fed. They will have to work all night while my men row. This is how we forge your crew into the steel that is the heart of this ship."

I wandered to the prow where my men kept watch on the animals and the captives. We had taken no boys older than seven years. Most of the captives were women and children. I spoke with them all but I addressed my words to the matriarch who sat in the centre. She was the one the others looked to and she had young children by her. I watched her eyes as I spoke.

"We have a long voyage home and your ships are chasing us. They will not catch us." I gestured to the animals. "One of the cows will need milking, the other has a calf. You can have the milk. You have young children and it will feed them and help them to sleep. My ship's boys will bring food later. They do not speak your language. If you need to speak then send for me. Ask for Göngu-Hrólfr Rognvaldson." I said the words slowly. "Keep the animals calm. I say this for your own safety. If they become restless then their hooves can hurt."

The matriarch said, "What do we do with their dung? How do we make water? Would you have us piss on the decks?"

She was not afraid of me and I heard a challenge in her voice. I smiled, "You are right, gammer, to ask such questions. The animal dung can be thrown over the side and that too is where you make water and…" I waved a hand. I remembered Bergljót and Gefn when we had sailed from Norway to Northumbria. "It helps if one holds the woman's hands while she sits on the gunwale." I tapped it so that they knew what I meant. "We will be sailing in a straight line for a while. Make water now, while you can."

I saw them taking it in. The matriarch said, "And what is our fate when we reach your home? Do your men use us as playthings?"

"You have slaves in your land. Do your men use them for pleasure?"

"No, but we are Christians and not barbarians!"

"We have priests and we have churches. My wife is a Christian. Some of you will become servants in the halls of my lords. Those with skills such as bread and cheese making or brewing ale will perform those tasks. Those without skills will be taught them. We are not barbarians. In Rouen, we live in stone houses. We took you from wattle and daub huts. Think about that!" I was about to head to the steering board when a thought struck me. "When you hear my men say," I changed to Norse, "come about," I reverted to Saxon, "then hold on for we are about to change course." The woman repeated my words. I nodded. "And I dare say you will pray to your God, the White Christ, at the same time!"

As I walked astern I saw that the Saxons had not gained on us. I examined them. They were a copy of the drekar but they were not as narrow. We could outrun them. They did not have their shields at the side but I saw that they had ports for their oars. They did not have as many ports as we did but I guessed they would have a larger crew. King Alfred had done well. However, it is one thing to have ships and quite another to have the experience which courses through the veins of a Viking.

As I passed my men I said, "Eat and rest. When it is dark we row and we row hard!" I joined Erik and I took the steering board. "Go, eat, drink, make water. I have spoken with the captives. We are now in the hands of Ran and the Norns."

"Aye, lord and thank you. Your words have calmed me. I began to feel unmanned. This is not like my knarr. There I worry about four others. Here I worry about many more."

With my hand on the steering board, I felt connected to my drekar. She was alive. Each slight touch brought a response. It was a joy to captain her. I glanced up at the sail. The crew had done well. The stays and sheets were taut and the sail billowed perfectly. Erik knew his business and he had set the sail so that we kept pace with the Saxons. Had we wished then we could have left them far behind but that would have taken us further from our home. Already we would take a day longer to reach Rouen. More if the tide was against us.

The sky was darkening behind us when Erik returned. "I am ready, lord."

"I would have us turn when there is still enough light in the sky for the Saxons to see us. I will have the men ready with their oars. Turn when ***'Fafnir'*** hides the sun from view but there is still a soft glow ahead."

"Aye lord. I will not let you down."

I joined my men. Harold Strong Arm handed me some pickled fish and the last of the bread. I ate. Haaken passed me the ale horn. When I had finished I said, "Get your oars from the mast fish but do so discreetly. Do not let the Saxons see what we do."

I stood and wiped my hands on my breeks. I lifted the first oar and held it horizontally. I walked to my chest and sat on it. I laid the oar next to the side. One by one my men did the same. All the time the sun was getting lower. While I waited I wrapped linen around my palms. I was the front oar on the steerboard side. Even if others were changed or stopped rowing I would not. Harold Strong Arm would be opposite me and we would be the last two to cease rowing. When we were all in position I put the oar so that the blade was at the port. Harold's oar rested upon my knee. I watched Erik. I could not see the sun setting. All that I could see was the darkness to the northeast and the sails of the Saxon. Erik nodded. It was time. I shouted, "Out oars!"

Erik shouted, "Come about!"

The ship's boys were already at the spar and they began hauling up the canvas almost as soon as Erik began to turn us. The motion was uncomfortable as the drekar lurched from side to side. Some of the women screamed and the animals began to complain. I pushed the oar out and, like the others, held it horizontally. Erik had never done this before. He would shout the signal to row and then it would be up to us to take us between the Saxon ships. I knew when he would shout for we suddenly became still as he completed the turn and the sail no longer propelled us.

"Oars!"

I looked at Harold and, as one, we put our oars in the water. The rest followed and then I began the chant. The chant dictated the speed. I chose the song of our old drekar. It had a regular beat. We needed a long steady row for we were single oared.

Skuld the Dark sails on shadows wings
Skuld the Dark is a ship that sings
With soft, gentle voice of a powerful witch
Her keel will glide through Frankia's ditch

With flowing hair and fiery breath
Skuld the Dark will bring forth death
Though small in size her heart is great
The Norn who decides on man's final fate
Skuld the Dark sails on shadows wings
Skuld the Dark is a sorcerous ship that sweetly sings
Skuld the Dark sails on shadows wings
Skuld the Dark is a sorcerous ship that sweetly sings
Skuld the Dark sails on shadows wings
Skuld the Dark is a sorcerous ship that sweetly sings
The witch's reach is long and her eyes can see through mist
Her teeth are sharp and grind your bones to grist
With soft, gentle voice of a powerful witch
Her keel will glide through Frankia's ditch
With flowing hair and fiery breath
Skuld the Dark will bring forth death
Though small in size her heart is great
The Norn who decides on man's final fate
Skuld the Dark sails on shadows wings
Skuld the Dark is a sorcerous ship that sweetly sings
Skuld the Dark sails on shadows wings
Skuld the Dark is a sorcerous ship that sweetly sings
The witch's reach is long and her eyes can see through mist
Her teeth are sharp and grind your bones to grist

    At first, we seemed to be barely moving. When the two Saxon ships slid down our side I knew that many of the newer men would think we had misjudged it. That was not so. The Saxons had not known what we intended. When they saw us stop and turn they would have parted so that they could block our move one way or another. I saw that the one on my side was a hundred paces from us. Even as we moved northeast I saw her as she began her turn. I watched as oars were run out. Our pace picked up as the oars bit into the sea. There was still just enough light in the west for me to see that the Saxons had managed to furl their sails and run out their oars. They were at least ten lengths behind us and they were stopped. They would be able to see us for some time but once the darkness fell all that they would have to follow us would be the white from our stern where we had made bubbles. Eventually, they would lose that too and they would have to guess our course. I was now in the rhythm. The chant helped. I had longer arms and I was stronger. If I had rowed at a pace I could manage then the others would have struggled to keep up. By the time we stopped chanting we had the rhythm and Harold and I kept a steady pace for the others to emulate.

Lars came with ale. I shook my head, "Keep an eye on the captives and animals." He nodded. "Did we lose any in the turn?"

He laughed, "Two women brought forth their supper, lord but we lost none over the side."

It had been many years since I had taken a turn at the oars. I felt muscles I had forgotten I had. I knew that the new men would be finding this even harder. I could just make out the two Saxon ships for they were silhouetted against the last glow from the sun. As soon as we lost them I would know for Erik would turn us and then, a short while later, he would lower the sail. We would not stop rowing immediately. We would put sea room between us and the Saxons. As I rowed I told myself that from now on I would double crew my drekar. With a double crew, we could have taken on the Saxons and beaten them!

Chapter 4

It took us two days to reach home. Despite the fact that we had been forced to run from two Saxons the raid had been successful. We had the wind with us for the last day and as we edged up the river, I divided the coins and animals. Some men, like Siggi, wished for animals in lieu of the coin we would get from the slaves. The first choice of the female slaves would go to Dómhildr. Her ale was popular and kept men happy. She provided barrels for our voyages. It made sense. The rest would be assessed by Ágáta. When she had been alive Gefn would have done so. I missed my adopted stepmother. Poppa found the whole issue distasteful. The captives had come to accept their fate once they saw the coast of Frankia. The fact that they had been treated well and fed helped. The matriarch, Popæg, proved to be a rock. She was calm and reassuring. The children nestled close to her when the ship rocked. I would mention her skills to Ágáta. I saw a role for her in Rouen.

We were seen when we were still downstream of Rouen and the families of the men we had taken flocked to greet us. There were also those who sought to make money. There would be slave traders and merchants eager to buy from us. They would have to wait. I was Lord of Rouen. I was the one who made those decisions. Poppa, of course, was absent. That was no surprise. Padraig was there but not my wife. I did not expect her but it would have pleased me had my son seen me arrive. Every day he was growing further from me. Each moment away from me he was falling under the influence of Æðelwald of Remisgat. As soon as I could I would take him to sea with me. One day he would come to war with me too.

I took the chest of parchments from the ship myself. I was the first ashore and was greeted by cheers. As the animals and captives were unloaded Padraig spoke with me, "I am pleased you had a safe and successful voyage, lord."

"Aye Padraig, the gods smiled on us."

"Lord you overestimate your so-called gods and underestimate yourself."

I smiled. I enjoyed these debates with Padraig. We differed in our views on the world but we agreed to differ. We both agreed that his God and the Allfather were probably the same Supreme Being. With Æðelwald of Remisgat, it was different. To my wife's priest, it was as though the differences were a chasm which could not be crossed. I knew that he influenced my wife and that was why she had drawn apart. I had thought to take another wife. Many warriors did so but Gefn had liked Poppa and I would not be disloyal to Gefn. I handed him the chest. "The abbey we raided was Frankish and there were documents. One was a sealed letter. When you have time read them for me and let me know if there is aught I need to know."

"Aye lord."

"We met King Alfred's ships. He has learned from us."

"He is a clever man."

Just then the captives were unloaded. Popæg stopped and spoke, "You kept your word and the fact that you speak with a priest bodes well. You may rise in my opinion, Lord Göngu-Hrólfr Rognvaldson." She followed the others and I saw Padraig smile.

I shrugged, "She was useful on the voyage and, to speak truly, I admire her courage and stoicism."

"No, lord, I smiled because you are the most feared Viking Warlord and yet you let a slave speak to you as though you were equals. It is remarkable."

When Siggi passed me, he was leading the cow and the calf. That and a purse of coins was all that he had taken. "Will you be coming to Carentan with me, Siggi? You are a good man in battle."

He looked at the cow and calf. "I now have a cow. The calf is a heifer too. We can produce milk. I can buy some seeds with the coin. When do you leave, lord?"

"Harpa."

"Eight days then." He looked reflective. "That should be enough time and there may be more treasure for me there." He smiled, "Unless disaster awaits me at my farm I will be with you!"

When the crew had left I walked with Padraig and my oathsworn to my hall. Padraig asked, "Why did you ask Siggi? Why not command?"

"I have decided to ask each man who lives in Rouen to give me thirty days of service. It would seem reasonable."

The priest smiled, "Forty days is too Christian for you?"

"No, but thirty is a twelfth of the year. A man can serve more but I would have a minimum. That would go for those who live within my walls."

He looked surprised, "Merchants? Swineherds? Farmers? Fishermen?"

"All. It is the price they pay to live under my protection. You have often told me how prosperous the people are under my benevolent rule. It is worth such a price, is it not?"

"To me, it seems eminently reasonable but then I would not have to serve."

I stopped, "Of course, you would and Æðelwald of Remisgat. You would not need to fight but you are both healers! You can come to war!"

He laughed, "That is a wonderful jest! For myself, I do not mind for I can minister to men's souls anywhere but Æðelwald of Remisgat likes his comfort. I pray you to let me be there when you tell him."

"I intend to convene a meeting of the town's men. When I tell them of their tax commitment I will tell them of this."

"And if folk refuse?"

I smiled, "The world is broad and there is room for all of them. It will just be beyond my borders! I intend to tell my lords that I require the same from them." We walked inside. I knew that my lords would be more than happy about the arrangement. They could ask for the same from their men. It was fair because all had the same duty, lord and labourer, poor man and priest.

My wife and her priest with William in tow met me at my hall. My men and Padraig parted. "I will read these, lord and speak to you later."

I nodded. I would rather they had stayed than Æðelwald of Remisgat. He had an oily voice, "Papers, lord? Perhaps I could read them for you."

"Why? Padraig is doing so."

Poppa frowned, "Because Padraig is a wild Celtic priest and Æðelwald here knows more of the world."

"Padraig suits me. I like his honesty." I bent down to pick up William. "You are getting bigger. What say we go to my ship? It is time you saw her."

Poppa shook her head, "I would rather he stayed here. The sun is bright and there are many common folk outside. I would not have him catch some disease."

"The sun will do him good and he will lead these people. Let them see him." She did not look happy. "And you should know that next spring William will be coming to sea with me. It is time he learned of his heritage." If I had slapped her she would not have looked more shocked. I left before she could say more.

Once I left my hall Harold and Petr fell in behind me. William giggled, "Your men are following us, father!"

"They are my oathsworn and when you are a warrior then you will have your own oathsworn." He nodded. "You want to be a warrior do you not?"

"Wear a helmet and mail? Carry a shield and a sword? Of course!"

I put him on the ground and took his right hand. "Good. We will see my ship first. We go to war on a horse or in a ship."

We walked toward the river, "Father Æðelwald says war is a bad thing and men who fight will go to hell."

"We believe that warriors who fight and die with a sword go to heaven. Which sounds better to you? To fight or to spend your life on your knees?"

He screwed up his face as he thought. "Fight!"

"Good. Soon you will have your first sword and my men will teach you how to use it. I have men who will show you how to use a bow too."

He stopped and looked at me, "I would rather you taught me!"

My heart swelled with pride, "Then it shall be me!"

Erik and the ship's boys were busy cleaning the drekar. The captives had cleaned as much of the animal waste as they could but it had not been complete. Erik was proud of his ship. William asked if he could help and he was given a mop. I knew his mother would be apoplectic with rage for his clothes would be both wet and dirty. I did not care for he was enjoying his time with the ship's boys all of whom made a great deal of fuss over my son. William was the one who was sorry when the work was finished. His threatened tears did not come for Lars took him on a tour of the drekar. I spoke with Erik.

"Now that you are safe in port have you considered if you sail with me again?"

"You would have me again? Even though I had to ask many questions?"

I laughed, "Had you not asked questions then this would have been our last voyage. I am happy with you as are the crew. You made no bad decisions and you handled our escape from the Saxons well. You cannot learn to be a drekar captain overnight. You will grow in confidence. Our next voyage will be but a few hours."

He held up his chest of coins, "If I can gain rewards like this then I will be happy."

"Sometimes we take nothing."

"It will balance out. It is good. My boys and I learned much. After we left the Saxon shore we thought we were safe and we learned we were not. Next time we will know what we have to do."

William was animated as we headed back to the hall. He chattered non-stop and I felt, for the first time, like a real father. That ended when Poppa saw him. Æðelwald made the mistake of tutting. I erupted for he ruined the moment, "You are an apology for a man! This is my son. Get out of my sight. Ask permission to be in my presence from now on!"

My two men smirked and William grinned but the look Poppa gave me was one of pure hate. Æðelwald went white. He bowed and hurried out as quickly as he could. Poppa took William away and I knew that I would pay for my outburst.

"My lord?"

I turned and saw a grinning Padraig, "I thought to speak with you but if you are in the mood for tearing off priest's heads then…"

I laughed, "Get in here! Have you read the letters?"

He nodded and laid them out. "Most are just about goods which have been ordered and there is one from the monastery at Saint Denis asking for a list of the brothers who have died. But this," he held up one with a broken seal, "is the most important one! This is a letter sent from King Charles to King Alfred and it concerns you, lord."

I was intrigued. "Then the sisters sent me there for a purpose."

Padraig sighed, "Or perhaps it was just a lucky accident."

I smiled, "The same thing. What does it say?"

"King Charles asks King Alfred for help. There are those like Count Odo of Paris who think he is too weak and the problem appears to be Vikings. He needs his ships. King Alan of the Bretons is beginning to eat into Frankish land. The Count of Anjou is also being threatened by the Bretons. King Charles suggests an alliance of the three men to defeat King Alan and then turn their attention to you."

"I am mentioned by name?"

"They call you the barbarian." He gave me a questioning look.

"Speak the truth. They are not your words and I will not be offended."

"He says he has tolerated you but you are an abomination." He put the letter down. "He says he knows he can weaken you for he has a man in Rouen who reports all that you do."

I picked up the letter. I could not read it but I wanted to look at it. "And we know who that is."

Padraig shook his head, "You cannot be certain, lord. There are many men in this town who have links to the Frankish court."

"And all profit from my town. There is only one who wishes me gone and that is Æðelwald of Remisgat."

"But you cannot prove it!"

"I am the lord of Rouen. I am a Viking, I do not need to prove it."

Padraig slapped the letter, "And when you have him hanged or murdered you confirm the view that you are a barbarian. If it is Æðelwald... "

"We both know it is."

"We both suspect it is. Then we try to trap him. When you come back from this Breton raid feed him or your wife false information."

I whipped my head around, "My wife?"

"She is under his spell lord and we cannot deny it. If you can feed them false information then you will have your proof."

I shook my head, "I need no proof."

He said, patiently, as though talking to a child, "Yet if you wish to be a legitimate leader then you must prove it to the other kings and princes."

This was the one aspect of being a leader I did not like. I could no longer be as honest and forthright as I had once been. I sighed and nodded. I would play this game of power until I was strong enough to fend off any enemy or foe. I would be my own master and make my own decisions.

I did not mind that my wife kept from me for the next eight days. That meant I did not have to look at her priest. I had banned him and he hid from me in my own hall. My wife kept him company. She left my son with me and it was a delight. He helped me prepare my ship. He helped me to speak with the extra men who would come with us. He, in fact, was desperate to join us. It was too soon to sever the ties with his mother but I knew that day would come. My wife had had a choice; me or the priest and she had chosen the priest. It was a mistake.

By the time we came to leave I was sorely tempted to take William with me but he was still too young. I did not think we would have to fight but if we did then William would be at risk. He was tearful when I left but I persuaded him to accept my departure. I knew that the priest and my wife would work on him and so I asked Padraig to watch over my son. The Celtic priest was happy to do so.

We headed downriver. Erik was much more confident about this voyage. The drekar was laden. A third of the crew were untried warriors. A third had a little mail but the rest were the best. I was not worried about them. My mind worried about William. I had become a father. Until I had returned from the land of the Saxons that was not so. I had had a son but I had not yet learned to be a father. Now I was learning. Were the sisters spinning a web? Whose thread was now linked with mine?

It took just a long day to reach Carentan. We had to be vigilant as the Bretons claimed these as their waters. They were better sailors than the Saxons but their ships were poor. We could ram any of them and confidently expect them to sink. Carentan lay inland a little although the land between the town and the sea was either boggy or flooded. Saxbjǫrn and Halfi Axe Tongue had built a wharf there and we tied up. There was just one drekar moored, '**Sun Dragon**' and she looked to be a little worse for wear. She was not Saxbjǫrn's. Leaving just the ship's boys and Erik on board we headed up the track which led to the town. It was a healthy walk. I knew not what I expected but the muted and sad faces on the walls were not it.

We were admitted. Where was Saxbjǫrn? Halfi Axe Tongue? Nefgeirr? The oathsworn warrior with the fresh wound on his arm said nothing. I would not ask the oathsworn to speak with me. That was not right. His lord would tell me his news. The hall was filled with warriors but none of the three jarls was there. I looked at the oathsworn. He bowed, "Lord, if you leave your men here I will take you to the jarl."

"Haaken, come with me. The rest make yourselves comfortable!" I gave a pointed look at Bonecrusher and he nodded. He would discover the reason for the atmosphere.

We went to the back of the hall. A curtain shielded a sleeping area. When I went in I saw Saxbjǫrn. He had his left arm in a sling. He gave me a wan smile. "As you can see, lord, it did not go well." He looked pointedly at Haaken.

"Haaken, leave us alone. I am safe." My oathsworn left.

"Tell me all!"

"We were betrayed and we were outwitted. I discovered, too late, that Beorn Straight Hair, one of my oathsworn, had been bought by the enemy. They knew we were coming. We sailed our drekar toward the Mont for it had a good anchorage. We landed after dark and felt confident that we could strike inland and hurt the enemy. Nefgeirr and half of his crew stayed there. They would take the treasures of the abbey. We headed for Avranches. It was close by and Beorn Straight Hair told us that they had no wall. He lied. He went ahead with two men to scout it out and we prepared to attack. We never saw any of them again. As dawn broke the Bretons came. They used horses and swept all around us. Halfi Axe Tongue died in the first attack. I ordered a retreat and we fought our way back to the coast. Men fell all the way back to the coast but we slaughtered many Bretons. When we reached our ships two were afire and Nefgeirr and the last of his men were defending **'Sun Dragon'**. We fought our way to their side but Nefgeirr and his oathsworn died. They saved us for we boarded the drekar and sailed away. We sailed to the land of the Bretons with over two hundred and fifty men. I brought back less than forty. Had I not left a healthy watch on my town then it would have been worse. I am sorry, lord. I have wasted your time and lost all that I held dear. Your faith in me was misplaced."

"No, you have not. You were betrayed. Beorn Straight Hair will pay. I know that we cannot repay King Alan of the Bretons yet but his time will come. Can you defend your walls?"

His face showed a gritty determination. "Aye lord. They shall not have this pretty jewel but we have lost Benni Ville and the other towns we had built."

"Good, then recover and I will put together an army which will defeat this King Alan but first I will visit with him. I will speak with him." I smiled my wolf smile, "I will leave him a Viking's words!"

"Is that not dangerous lord?"

I laughed, "Aye, for him!"

We stayed for two days. I wished to ensure that Carentan could be defended. I spoke with his men and assured them that they would have my help. They were broken men. To have lost two jarls in one night was unheard of. I sent Haaken the Bold on a mission. I sent him to the jarls who lived in the Cotentin and asked them to meet with me in Rouen in two months' time at Sólmánuður. Leif Sorenson was sent east to deliver the same message to Bergil, Sven, and Sámr. I left with my drekar, I had a message to deliver to King Alan. I had a spy in my town just as Saxbjǫrn had one in his. None knew what was in my mind for it was only as we left Carentan that I told Erik of the course he should take.

"Sail west. There is a small town with an abbey, Sant-Brieg. I would tell King Alan that I have received and understood his message. There will be war."

He nodded and picked up the chart. "That means sailing close to Sarnia and Angia. They have pirates who race out to take unsuspecting ships, lord."

"And we are not unsuspecting. If any race out to take us they will find we are no juicy morsel. Besides we will be sailing through their waters at night."

His face showed his displeasure, "Lord there are many rocks and shoals there."

"We have a man with a wax-covered lead weight in the bows. We need to have complete surprise. The Bretons have spies in Carentan but Saxbjǫrn and his ships made it easy for the Bretons. They would have been seen sailing toward Mont-Saint Michel. I intend to surprise those who live in Sant-Brieg by striking at dawn."

I walked to the prow to think. I trusted all of my men but if I told them of the spy in my town and disclosed the contents of the letter they would act. I had had time to think about Padraig's words. The priest had been right. There was little to be gained confronting Æðelwald. I knew he was gathering information through my wife. It would be easy to dry up that particular source but there might be others too. What I did not know was how he was getting information out. I had charged Padraig with the task of watching Æðelwald. I saw, in the distance, the Haugr. I had grown up there and yet it did not feel like my home. The fjord in Norway was the place I thought of as home. The threads of the Norns had stretched across oceans and lands so vast that it made my head spin to think of them. I had been complacent. The peace with the Franks had dulled my instincts and two jarls had fallen. Worse, we had lost almost two hundred men. A Viking was a warrior. A Viking raided and was vigilant. The lesson was learned. Lord Göngu-Hrólfr Rognvaldson would show his teeth. The Franks and Bretons thought I was duped. That might have been true once but no longer.

A young warrior appeared next to me. "Lord Göngu-Hrólfr Rognvaldson?"

I glanced down and when I saw his face realised that he must have been standing there for some time. It was a young warrior whom I did not know well. I knew his face. This was his first raid. I struggled for his name and then saw his hair, Egil Flame Bearer. He was so named for his red hair which looked like fire. "Yes, Egil?"

"The ship's boys tell me that we sail to Sant-Brieg."

"They do. Do you know it?"

He shook his head, "No lord but it is not far from Raven Wing Island."

"As the seagull flies but it is on the other side of the coast. Why?"

"My family lived there. When Hrolf the Horseman took the clan to the Haugr my family stayed for a while. My great grandfather was one of the warriors who followed Finni Bennison. His name was Karl the Red."

I struggled to remember him. The name was unfamiliar. I knew Finni Bennison but not the man who had followed him. I nodded, "Finni served my grandfather well."

"I know. My family made a mistake when we did not follow Hrolf the Horseman. It has taken us three generations to remedy that mistake. After my grandfather was killed by Bretons my mother and father brought us to the Seine. My father died in the raid on Paris."

"Did he sail with me?"

"No lord. He sailed with Sven Stormchaser. All in his crew perished."

I remembered Sven. He had had one of the smaller drekar. I had begun to wonder why Egil had come to speak with me. Now I began to see. "Who is left from your family?"

He said, simply, "Me. I was the one left at home to watch over my mother and grandmother. My two brothers perished with my father. My grandmother died when she heard the news and then my mother had the sickness of the worm. She grew thin and died from within. It took her months to die. I buried her two months since."

I looked at him. He wore leather mail and had a simple round, pot helmet. His shield was well made but his sword was short. "The farm?"

"I gave it to Ralf the Pig Man in return for half of the profits. I would be a warrior, lord, and the little coin I receive will feed me."

"And you have made a good start for you have joined a good crew. This is your first raid?"

"It is. Lord, you should know that although I have never raided my father and my brothers trained me well. I will be a good warrior."

"You have never killed a man?" He shook his head. "Had to fight for your life?" Again, he shook his head.

"But lord I would serve with you. My life will be that of a warrior. I would be an oathsworn!"

It was my turn to shake my head. "To be oathsworn is an honour reserved for the best of men. I am not saying that one day you will not be oathsworn but now it would be like giving you a death sentence. My oathsworn fight where the battle is hottest. Sail on a few voyages with me and learn to become a warrior."

"I will, lord, but I would have you take me each time you sail. I have nothing for me at the farm. It is full of the ghosts of the past."

Now I understood. "You would live in my warrior hall!"

He grinned and I saw that he was young. He looked to be the age I had been when my brother had tried to kill me and I had sunk to the bottom of the sea. I could almost hear the Norns spinning. My thread was connected. His great grandfather had broken the thread and the family had suffered. The Norns were giving us another opportunity. "I am happy to be as a sentry on your walls when you do not raid, lord. I wish to learn. I wish to atone for the mistake my great grandfather made and which plunged my family into this pit which has all but consumed us. I know that we were cursed." His voice became quieter, "Lord, we all know of your curse. You overcame yours. This is my chance to overcome my family's curse."

I clasped his arm, "Then, Egil Flame Bearer, you shall live in my warrior hall and I will try to help you but know this, a curse is hard to overcome. I needed the help of Ylva Aidensdotter the mightiest witch in the world."

"Aye, lord, but you are Lord Göngu-Hrólfr Rognvaldson and you are the mightiest Viking of your age. This is *wyrd*!"

The Norns were spinning. They had a prophecy to fulfil and another thread was added to their spell.

Chapter 5

Erik might not have been familiar with Angia and Sarnia but I was. There were hidden shoals, reefs and rocks but I knew where they were and what to watch for. As well as a man with a lead weight at the prow I stood there too. I shouted my commands down the drekar and Erik adjusted his steering. It was nerve-wracking but years of sailing these waters had given me the ability to almost sniff out the course. When we saw Sarnia on the steerboard I knew we were safe and I strode back to Erik. "Your course is clear now."

"Thank you, lord. You are truly a mariner."

"The Lord of Rouen must be many things to many men. I will rest. Have me woken when the coast is close." I curled up and slept. I had learned to do this years ago and I was able to sleep instantly and be awake just as quickly.

"Lord, it is time!" Æbbi Bonecrusher shook me awake. He waited as I stood and then handed me a horn of ale. "We can smell the land. Erik is a good captain. By my estimate, the town and church are not far away. We heard a bell sound."

"Are the men ready?"

"They are mailed and prepared. All have eaten." He proffered some bread.

I shook my head, "There will be fresh in the town." He helped me to don my mail. Petr the Slow offered me my helmet. I shook my head. "I should not need it nor will I take my shield. Unless they are ready for us then I doubt there will be much opposition." I walked to the mast where most of the men were gathered. "When we land the larboard crew will secure the wharf, the warehouses and the ships. The steerboard crew will come with me and take the town. I want King Alan to know who did this. We take everything. Every man will be slaughtered. Kill the priests. Drive the women, children and old from the town."

Petr said, "We do not take them as slaves?"

Æbbi Bonecrusher shook his head, "They are too close to home. They can flee or there might be a rescue attempt. Lord Göngu-Hrólfr Rognvaldson is wise. This gives the Bretons more mouths to feed and fewer men to provide for them."

"We take every coin, each animal, all their sacks of flour and even their loaves of bread. When we leave we burn all to the ground. We destroy all of their ships."

Snorri said, "That will make him attack us."

"Aye and that is what I want. I will have a battle and it will decide who rules the land between the Cotentin and Rouen and when that is done I turn my attention to the Franks."

The two kings did not realise what they had done when they roused me. I was the sleeping dog they should have let lie. Although it was dark the shadow that was the small rise upon which the town stood could be seen. We knew that the river below the town was small. I had passed the port but that had been many years earlier when I had been but a boy. As I recalled there was a wharf which ran along the river below the houses and I could not remember a wall. This raid had a good chance of success as they did not know we were at war yet. As soon as they did then they would build walls and have a town watch. When the lookout at the prow heard the sound of waves on the shore he whistled and Erik had the sail furled. Half of our men went to the oars. They pulled us gently in to the shore. The tide was with us. The half who were not rowing gathered at the prow and stern on the steerboard side.

I had my sword raised. As soon as I judged it right I would lower it. The steerboard side would stop rowing and the larboard side would make but one stroke. If I timed it aright then we would bump gently into the wharf. Five men had bows with arrows nocked in case there were any watchers. There were ships tied up and, alarmingly, one looked to be big enough to be a ship of war. I had cast the bones. We would have to deal with whatever we found awaiting us. I pulled myself up onto the gunwale and held on to the forward stay. I held my sword up. I waited until we were a ship's length away from the wharf and I dropped my sword. The oars were run in and we turned sharply. Erik compensated and when the larboard oars stopped we bumped gently into the wharf. Even while the ship's boys were tying us up I had leapt onto the wooden wharf and was racing for the path which led to the houses.

Glancing to my left I saw that Egil Flame Bearer was there close to me. It was he who slew the first Breton. There was a sentry who had been sleeping. He paid for his carelessness with his life. As he stood, startled by the noise of feet on the wharf, Egil rammed his sword into his middle. The sentry died silently. My long legs took me up the steps which led to the church, the hall and the merchants' houses three at a time. Once my men joined me I knew we would be heard as we thundered up the wooden steps. Those in the houses closest to the steps would wonder what they heard. Some brave soul would venture forth and then the alarm would be given. I wanted to be close to the church when that happened. The stairs were few in number. As I came out on the flat area by the town square the first man stepped from his house. Even as he shouted, "Vikings!" my Long Sword hacked into his chest.

My speed had taken me ahead of my men. I ran for the church as men poured out of houses. They were armed but my men were awake, mailed, and ready for war. I heard steel on steel behind me as I burst into the church. It was an abbey church albeit a small one. Two priests knelt by the altar. One threw a candle holder at me. Although I batted it away with my sword it allowed the two of them to run through the back door of the church. They had gone empty handed.

Egil and Petr followed me into the church. "Collect all that is valuable."

I ran out of the back door. One priest was helping the other onto the back of a horse. I swung my sword. The priest on foot ran at my swinging blade to buy his companion the time to flee. His dying body fell at my feet. I shouted, "Tell King Alan that Lord Göngu-Hrólfr Rognvaldson makes war on the Bretons! Fear me and fear my Long Sword!"

More priests ran from the chapter house. These were armed. They charged me. It was not glorious but it was necessary. I swept my sword left and right until a bloody pile of corpses lay before me. None were left. I ran into the chapter house and I was joined by Einar Ketilsson and four other men. "Search it and then burn this and the church."

"Aye lord. "There are mailed men in the square. They are defending the warrior hall."

"I will deal with them!"

I turned and ran toward the square. I could hear screams from women and children as they grabbed what they could and tried to flee. A woman and three children ran from their home toward the church. When they saw me, they dropped their precious goods and ran up a side alley. Life was worth more than the few items they had saved. I saw that some of my men lay dead. More Bretons had been in the town than I had expected.

There were two shield walls. Æbbi Bonecrusher and my hearth weru led one and a mailed warrior led the Bretons. Even as I watched he stepped forward and slew Bjorn Axe Hand. I heard a roar from Æbbi Bonecrusher for Bjorn had been his friend. I did not want my men to become reckless. I shouted, "Hearth weru! On me!" My voice seemed to echo in the night. My men had blood in their heads but my voice brought reason into them. They stepped back. I held Long Sword above my head in two hands. My men parted so that I could join the front rank. Bjorn's body lay between us. The Breton lord, who had an open face helmet, grinned at me. He raised his sword and hacked off Bjorn's head.

I heard Æbbi roar and I shouted, "Hold! I command!"

"Aye lord."

I began to stamp my foot. My men copied me and banged their shields. I saw some of the Bretons look at each other fearfully wondering what it meant. Their leader shouted, "It is nothing! These are barbarians and we have God on our side."

Just at that moment, flames began to lick at the roof of the wooden church and the fire crackled. I shouted. "Charge!" and I leapt at the enemy. I swung Long Sword as I ran. The Breton lord held up his shield and my sword crashed into it. He was not supported by men behind and he reeled. My sword continued along its long swinging arc and hit the next warrior in the neck. As he fell Æbbi and the rest of my hearth weru hit the Breton line. Had their leader still been in the front rank they might have held but the anger of my men coupled with the lack of leader meant that they broke. The Breton lord regained his feet and he punched at me with his shield as he slashed with his sword. I grabbed the edge of his shield and blocked his sword with my own. Had I been wearing my helmet I would have head-butted him. Instead, I brought up my knee hard between his legs. He fell as though he had been hit with a war hammer. He lay on the ground and I gripped my sword with two hands and brought it down to slice his body in two. Even as I did so I realised I had ruined a good suit of mail and destroyed a helmet. I cursed my anger. I had allowed the death of an oathsworn get to me. The rest of the Bretons were butchered. The sun began to rise behind the burning church. The screams of the women and the children had grown fainter as they fled. Now there was just the sound of men dying.

I roared, "Empty the houses. Take everything from within that is of value to the drekar. Take all the mail, even that which is damaged."

Æbbi and the rest of my men took out their anger on the dead. When the Bretons came to view the town, they would be horrified at what they saw. The terror we inspired was part of my plan. King Alan of Vannes might well be unafraid of me and my men but his people would be. When we came to make war, the battle would be half won before we began. I cleansed my sword on the Breton lord's cloak. I saw Egil Flame Bearer. He had been with my oathsworn. "Egil, here is a good sword for you. I fear I have destroyed the mail and helmet."

He grinned as he took the sword, "I thank you, lord, but," he held up a good helmet with a nasal, "I have found a helmet already and the warrior had coin but I will take the mail. I am handy with a hammer."

I smiled for the young warrior looked elated. "You are walking down the warrior road now, Egil. I hope the journey is long."

I headed down to the drekar. I could see that Erik had already lifted the decks and sacks were being loaded along with chests. We would share them in Rouen. For now, we had to ensure that the drekar was evenly loaded and that we had left nothing of value behind.

"Erik, there are still ships which need destroying."

"Lord they are good ships. It breaks my heart to sink them."

"They are the ships of our enemy and I would hurt them." I pointed to the hillside. "See how we burn the town? If the crops were not still green I would burn them too. That is what we do. If you hurt a Viking we hurt you more. We make you fear us."

He nodded, "I understand. Lars, take an axe and drive it through the keels of those ships."

My men began to filter back toward the drekar. They carried chests, bolts of cloth, hams; all that the town had contained was ours. Æbbi Bonecrusher came toward me with a loaf. He handed it to me. It was still warm. He smiled. "You said you wanted freshly baked bread. It does not come any fresher."

"Thank you, Æbbi Bonecrusher."

He shook his head, "Thank you, lord, I forgot that I followed a great leader and I almost lost my head. It will not happen again."

I nodded and bit into the warm bread. "Have our dead brought back to the drekar. We will bury them at sea. They died well."

"Aye, lord, and they are now in Valhalla!"

The fire began to spread as my men moved down the hillside. The very steps we had used began to burn.

The last of my men boarded. "Tie ropes to the wharf."

Erik gave me a strange look and then nodded, "Lars, do as our lord commands."

I shouted, "Take to the oars and hoist the sail."

I think I had bemused them all. I sat next to Sweyn Oak Arm. I began the chant.

The Clan of the Horse march to war
See their spears and hear them roar
The Clan of the Horse with bloody blades
Their roaring means you will be shades
Clan of the Horse Hrolf's best men
Clan of the Horse death comes again
Leading Vikings up the Frankish Water
They brought death they brought slaughter
Taking slaves, swords and gold
The Clan of the Horse were the most bold
Clan of the Horse Hrolf's best men
Clan of the Horse death comes again
Fear us Franks we are the best
Fighting us a fatal test
We come for land to make our own
To give young Vikings not yet grown
Clan of the Horse Hrolf's best men
Clan of the Horse death comes again
Clan of the Horse Hrolf's best men
Clan of the Horse death comes again
The Clan of the Horse march to war
See their spears and hear them roar
The Clan of the Horse with bloody blades
Their roaring means you will be shades
Clan of the Horse Hrolf's best men
Clan of the Horse death comes again
Leading Vikings up the Frankish Water
They brought death they brought slaughter
Taking slaves, swords and gold

The Clan of the Horse were the most bold
Clan of the Horse Hrolf's best men
Clan of the Horse death comes again
Fear us Franks we are the best
Fighting us a fatal test
We come for land to make our own
To give young Vikings not yet grown
Clan of the Horse Hrolf's best men
Clan of the Horse death comes again
Clan of the Horse Hrolf's best men
Clan of the Horse death comes again

We had to row hard and there was resistance but eventually, the wind, our drekar and the strength of our men prevailed. The piles which held the wharf were dragged into the river. The wood from the wharf would have to be removed and the sunken ships shifted. The port would need much work until it could be used again.

"Cease rowing! Cut the ropes! It is time to go home!"

I watched the fire burning as we headed north. I knew that Bretons would be galloping to try to save their town. It would be too late. The ancient monastery was gone. The lord, whose name I did not know was dead, along with every warrior in the town. The ones who had escaped would not boast of their escape. They would count themselves lucky that they had avoided the wrath of the Northmen. The priest who had fled would report the tale to his bishop and to the King. My message would be delivered.

With the wind behind, I sailed close to, first Sarnia, and then Angia. I was taunting the Bretons. I was letting them know that these were my waters. I could bring twenty times the ships and none could stop me. There were ships in their harbours but none ventured forth. As night fell the wind diminished. Before the sun set, we sent our dead into the waters. They had died with their swords in their hands and would be in Valhalla. Their bodies would be safe from the vengeance of the Bretons. We were in a sombre and reflective mood as we headed home.

I had much to think about. I had declared war on the Bretons. I had fought them before. We had beaten them. I had been remiss. The peace had seduced me and I had grown lax. Erik Gillesson was my master of horses. There had been a time when Stephen of Andecavis had led horsemen who could fight the Breton and Frankish horsemen. They had given us parity on the field with their horses and that had allowed our shield walls to win. Erik and his son Bagsecg still bred fine horses. They had even bred a horse big enough for me. The training of my young men as horsemen had not been as rigorous as it ought to have been. We needed horsemen again. Horsemen would have found the Breton raiders before they could take my farmers and their families. I could have stopped the war before it began.

I glanced up at the masthead. My pennant flew there. It did not stand out enough. I wanted something which told the Franks and the Bretons who came to fight them. I wanted them to fear me before they fought me. I would have a larger standard made. It would be red. The blood-red sign with a yellow horse would tell them that the Clan of the Horse was coming. Egil Flame Bearer had shown that he had courage. He had yet to prove himself as an oathsworn but he could stand with my standard. His red hair seemed to mark him for that task.

The voyage up the Seine was slower than normal and we did not reach Rouen until after dark. We had no throngs to welcome us. It did not matter. We had a war to plan. As we sailed the last few paces to the wharf I said to the crew, "You have all done well but this is only the beginning. Go home and see your families. I would have all of you sail with me." I looked at Siggi, "But if you cannot then do not worry. I will call upon you again in the spring. It is late but come the morrow I will divide the treasure we have taken. If there are those of you with long journeys then fear not, I will send your share to your homes. We fought as one and we share as one. Clan of the Horse!"

The crew roared, "Clan of the Horse!"

I waited until all had landed before I left. It was so late that all were in bed save for Dómhildr and Padraig. Padraig was finishing a goblet of wine. Dómhildr bobbed her head, "I will fetch you wine, lord, and congratulations!"

She left and I frowned, "Congratulations?"

Padraig gave me a weak smile, "Your wife, lord, is with child."

I could not get excited about it. She had been with child once since William and the babe had died stillborn. I wondered about the curse for she had been pregnant six times and only produced one live child, William. Our daughters had died. "I hope the gods are kinder to me."

He saw that something was amiss. "What is wrong lord?" I told him my news. My riders would not be back for a few more days. After I had told him he sipped from his goblet. He did not use a horn. "War with

Brittany might be expensive lord. We know of the secret alliance between Wessex, the Empire and Brittany. Are you not playing into their hands?"

"If I sit and do nothing I am. They seek to eat us piece by piece. This Frankish peace is no peace at all. I will smile and feign belief in the word of the Emperor and his King but when Brittany is defeated then the Franks had best watch their borders."

He nodded, "And your lords arrive when?"

"Soon. I need maps of the borderlands. I will ask my lords for the numbers of men that they can send to me. How are our finances?"

"Thanks to your raids they are healthy. What you lack is a large army."

"I know. Had Guthrum not relinquished his power I might have sent to him. I have few allies."

He smiled, "I am sure you will find a way." Dómhildr returned with wine, bread and cheese. Padraig smiled, "Eat lord. You need to keep your strength. I will be at your side. On that, you can depend. God has willed it so." I wondered at his words. It sounded like there was a hidden message beneath them.

The next day my wife came to me and she was beaming. "In seven months from now, you will have a second son."

"I am pleased, my wife. Take care with this one and rest. I would have a healthy son like William."

"Fear not lord for my priest has interceded with God. He will be born healthy and he will be a leader to follow you."

For some reason, I liked not her words. They seemed to imply that William did not exist. However, at the time, I was too busy planning a war to take them in. Padraig, although a priest, understood war. He did not concern himself with the killing and the right or the wrong of it. He looked at it as an exercise in numbers. I had grown an idea for a way to send a message to my lords. Padraig and I sat with my moneyer, William of Rouen, and came up with a solution. When they showed me the result I was well pleased. "I want fifty of these minting. Then I will have the die. Padraig will keep it safe." I was becoming a very suspicious man. I found myself questioning everything. I had been betrayed too many times in my life already.

My lords arrived before the deadline I had set. I knew that they would. Each of them felt a bond with me. Some, like Bergil and Sven, had been oathsworn. Others, like Ubba Long Cheek and Saxbjǫrn, had chosen to follow my banner. Bjorn the Brave had done great service in the siege of Paris. Erik and his son Bagsecg were a link back to the days of my grandfather. Each was tied to me but by a different thread. When the Lady Poppa discovered that they were all arriving she hid herself away. I did not mind for that meant the Frankish spy would know nothing of what we said.

With my oathsworn watching my doors I told them all that I had learned. I told them of the conspiracy and the fate of Nefgeirr and Halfi Axe Tongue. They listened in silence. "We have been duped and we need to be as cunning as our foes. We go to war."

They cheered. Sven Blue Cheek said, "And about time too. It does not sit well to grow fat and lazy. A warrior should be lean and hungry."

I held up my hand for silence. "We need a system. I want each of you to commit every man in the lands you rule to thirty days of service a year."

Sámr shouted, "Make it sixty, lord! My men would be happy about that!"

I nodded, "And those who wish can make it sixty but by making it thirty then we can keep our walls watched and protected while we go to war."

Silence fell until Sven Blue Cheek said, "I have grey hairs on my head and in my beard but you, Lord Göngu-Hrólfr, are wiser. This is a clever plan."

We spoke of how we might use our men to the best effect. Bergil Fast Blade asked, "When do we attack? Soon?"

I shook my head, "First you need to ensure that you have neither spies nor traitors in your lands. Saxbjǫrn was betrayed from within. The enemy knew that they were coming. I will send a sign. I have had my moneyer cast a special coin. It will be larger than a penny and made of silver. On one side there will be a horse while on the other a lion." I smiled, "The horse carries us to battle but we go with the heart of a lion." I saw nods. They liked the symbolism of the lion. When you receive the first coin you prepare for war and the second tells you that we are to fight." I took out the coins and, walking around them I gave each one a single coin. I watched them examine the coins. William had done a good job. As there would be a limited number of them he had taken great care in the striking of each coin. The fact that there would never be a large number meant that the die would stay sharp. It would be hard to make a copy for they would not be in general circulation.

Sámr asked, "But where do we fight?"

"In the land of the Bretons. We need to make certain that the borderlands, the Haugr, Bayeux, Ciriceburh and Valognes can be defended when we are away. We cannot use our ships for they watch for them. Their heartlands are protected. Angia and Sarnia are like sentinels. At Ýlir I will make a progress around your strongholds. I will tell you all then of my plan."

Finnbjǫrn Stormbringer frowned, "But we are all here now, lord. Why not tell us now?"

"First, I do not know. I have much to discover about our enemy. We fought King Alan before. I would make this the last time. I have to unravel the threads of our enemies' plans. The King of the Franks and the King of Wessex are involved but I am not sure yet how. What I do know is that we are seen as an abomination that the three of them wish to see eradicated."

Sven Blue Cheek was the most experienced and loyal of my lieutenants. He nodded. "Then we ride to war and fight as Vikings."

"Aye. Bagsecg Eriksson will lead all the horsemen that you bring. I know it will not be as many as in days past but that must change. Each of you will lead your own men in battle. You will all fight under your own banners but the plan will be mine. I made a mistake in allowing Saxbjǫrn and the others to punish King Alan. I will not do so again. If you are attacked then send to me for help."

"How? The message might be intercepted." Ubba looked concerned.

I held up the coin. "You all have the horn to summon me. Send a rider with the coin and I will come. Trust in your walls and trust in me." I looked around at all of them. "The enemy warriors are cunning. I know that you are warriors all and that you have courage but we need to act as one. If there is any hint of danger then send word to me. I do not want any of you to suffer the fate of Haldi or Nefgeirr." Looking back, when hindsight gives a man perfect vision, I should have looked each man in the eye but I did not and I paid the price or perhaps the Norns had already decided our direction.

My lords stayed for two days. It gave me the opportunity to discuss with each of them their unique situation. We were thinly spread and clung, largely, close to the coast. Each stronghold was less than half a day from their nearest neighbour. That was a strength but the ones on the Cotentin, Valognes, the Haugr, Carentan and Ciriceburh were vulnerable for Angia and Sarnia lay close by and they would be on the front line of an attack. They lay the closest to Brittany. Even Sámr's stronghold at Bayeux was a little too close to the enemy to be considered safe. Caen was my rock. Sven would be the one who would hold my flank. It was Sven Blue Cheek who would know my heart.

When the others had departed Sven stayed on for another day. We rode abroad with Harold and Haaken as guards. They rode fifty paces behind us for I wished to speak openly with Sven. It had been some time since I had ridden my mighty horse, Gilles, and there was a temptation to allow him to open his legs and gallop. I refrained from doing so. Sven had to know my thoughts. There were others that I could trust, Bergil, Sámr and the others but Sven had a sharp mind and he would be able to see flaws in my thinking. We did gallop for a few miles and then I slowed. I told him all of my news and all of my suspicions.

"Kill the priest! It is simple enough."

"But I know not how deep the betrayal goes. How does he get his messages to our enemies?"

"He is a priest. A hot knife will loosen his tongue."

"But how will we know the truth? No, my friend, I have to discover this web of lies. I have an idea. I will find someone to spy upon the spy."

"But how will you find someone to trust?"

"That is another reason for the delay in the start of the offensive. I have someone in mind but they will need coaching."

He nodded. "And Lady Poppa?" I gave him a sharp look. "Come Hrólfr you have danced around her since you began to speak with me. You suspect that she and the priest are in this together. It would make sense. She is related to Alan of Vannes. There is a limit to how much he can discover. Lady Poppa? She is privy to all that you do." He gestured behind. "She is with you even when your guards are not."

My shoulders slumped, "She has changed. It began before the Paris raid. If I did not know better then I would say there was another man but that cannot be. Perhaps she regrets her marriage to me."

"It is more likely that she thought she could change you." He laughed, "You might have the title of the Lord of Rouen but in your heart, you are still a Viking. You will always be so. She might have thought she could tame your hair, shave your beard and make you civilised!"

He was right. That sudden thought made me sad for I would never change and that meant I had lost my wife. "You are right. I will have to take another woman when Poppa has given birth to my next child. One son is not enough."

"You are right there, lord. How is William? I have not seen him."

It was a sore point. Perhaps to punish me Poppa had kept my son with her. She and the priest were teaching him more of the words from their holy book.

"We will see him before you leave. When next I travel he will come with me. He should learn what his father does."

"Good and if I were you, lord, I would act sooner rather than later in the matter of the priest and Poppa. Delay hurts us more than our enemies."

He was right but I did not hear the Norns spinning. It almost cost me all.

Chapter 6

My excuse was that I had much to occupy my mind. I visited with Ágáta first. She had dealt with the slaves. "How did the new slaves settle in?"

"Well, my lord. All have been bought by good masters. I bought Popæg for the hall. You were right about her. She is good with children and helps Lady Sprota. I bought her children too. They can be trained to be house servants." She smiled, "Keeping a family together is helpful." I nodded. "She is learning our language and young William likes her. Lady Sprota teaches William that which he needs to be a lord but Popæg laughs and teaches him how to deal with knocks and falls."

I looked at Ágáta. She would always be honest with me. "And my wife?"

She hesitated and considered her words before she spoke, "She is a wise woman, lord and she leaves your son to those who understand what he needs. She seeks to save her soul for she is, oft times closeted with the priest."

I lowered my voice. "I neither like nor trust the priest. Does he have dealings with any who travel beyond our walls?"

She nodded, "Many priests visit with him. They seek his advice. Often they bring him gifts." She was innocent and could not see malice in a priest. I now saw the network. The question was how could I exploit it?

"You have women who are good with a needle?"

"Aye lord."

"I would have two new banners made. One for here and one to go to war. They should be made of red material and have a yellow horse upon each one."

"Red is expensive."

"No matter. See Padraig and he will provide the funds."

I sought out Egil Flame Bearer. He was outside the warrior hall at the small anvil my men used to shape metal. I saw that he had recovered the split byrnie from the Breton lord I had killed. He was trying to join it. He looked up and shrugged, "I thought better one which was damaged than none at all."

"Leave it if you would and walk my walls with me."

"Aye lord." He hurried after me. I shortened my stride so that he could keep up with me.

"You told me that you would be my oathsworn."

"Aye, lord, and I meant it."

We reached the fighting platform. I waved a hand at the sentries and they moved toward the towers to give us space. "You impressed me at Sant-Brieg. You were brave and fought well. Your sword skills need work but now that you have a better sword that should be easier."

"I will try!"

"Good. See Harold Strong Arm. Tell him I said that you need lessons." He looked pleased. "When we next go to battle I would have you carry my new banner." I saw his face brighten like a new dawn. "Before you become excited know that this is not something to be undertaken lightly. You will have to carry the banner in your left hand and that means that you cannot use a shield. Your job will not be to fight our enemies but defend the banner. There will be no shield wall for you and the only treasure you will take from the field will be from those you kill who try to take the banner or from those that I kill."

He beamed, "Then I will be a rich man."

"Good. And there is one more task. I will not go into the details yet but I would have you watch my gate when you can. I would know of any strangers who enter my halls and whom they see. This can be any you do not know. You just report them to me and no one else."

"I will be the best of sentinels."

"Good. And you need to eat more. You are too scrawny!"

He laughed, "That will be a pleasure!"

I was busy for the next few days. I did not get to leave my town. I made time to start William's training as a warrior. I chose my time well. I waited until he was due to go to the priest, who now kept out of my way, and then I asked him if he would like to learn to become a warrior. Of course, he said yes. We practised in the open area between my hall and the wall around my wall. It was where my men practised their skills. They always gave us enough space.

He was too young and too small to even begin to think of using a sword. A stick was all that he could manage. We had old ropes which I had coiled into circles. With a pair of sticks, we played a game. I used my stick to throw a coiled rope at William. He had to catch it with his own stick and then throw it back. I knew that my wife, watching from the terrace, would think it a silly game. Nothing could be further from the truth. It would help him to develop quick hands and give him good reflexes. At first, he dropped it more than he caught it but soon learned how to do it. I was able to go faster and he, in turn, was able to flick it back and catch me unawares. When he tired of that game we played with sharpened sticks and a hay bale. In the early days, I just had him throw the sharpened stick at the hay bale. When he mastered that I took to standing before the hay bale. He had to run at me and, somehow, hit the bale. At first, he failed but that failure gave him the drive to succeed. He learned to change his direction and throw it when I moved to block him. He learned to have quick feet and hands. Of course, it was easier with me than it would have been with someone smaller.

Egil had obeyed my commands and he would be found each day watching the gate. When I realised that William now had developed skills I had Egil help me. It enabled me to watch my son and coach him. He needed good hand skills. The two of them took to throwing a rolled ball of yarn at each other. Egil was remarkably thoughtful. He saw what I wanted and he stretched William without making him look foolish. Then he took to using two balls of yarn. It taught my son to use both hands at the same time. He learned to look not at the yarn but at Egil's eyes. Over the next month or so William became quite skilled and he and Egil became friends.

Poppa was not happy. "These foolish games are at the expense of his lessons with Father Æðelwald."

I had decided to be more honest with my wife. "And that is because the less time he spends with that oily priest the better. Besides, the priest seems preoccupied with you and our unborn child. That, my wife, is the only reason that he is tolerated and it would not take much for me to banish him from Rouen."

I saw her mouth open and close as she thought to make some barbed comment. One look at my face convinced her to remain silent.

It was at Sólmánuður that we had visitors and our troubles began in earnest.

"Lord there are three drekar in the river."

I looked up at the sentry. He was one of the town watch. "Do they have shields hung at the side?"

"No lord."

"Then I will come. Snorri, fetch some of our men. Let us go and greet these visitors."

I was wary of any drekar I did not know. Since Guthrum's conversion, we had lost touch and contact with the Danes. The Clan of the Wolf had withdrawn within itself and so few longships came up the river. These three were the first in a long time.

By the time I got to the wharf, they had tied up. I saw from their ships and their dress that they were Danes. The leader was a youngish warrior of perhaps twenty-five summers. He had a good byrnie, His sword had a decorated scabbard. His hair and moustache were adorned with bones. I knew of warriors who did this. More often than not the bones were animal bones but the warriors made out that they were human. It was an affectation.

I held out my arm, "I am Lord Göngu-Hrólfr Rognvaldson, Lord of Rouen!"

"And I am Godfrid Godfridsson. My father was the Duke of Frisia."

I had heard of the Dane's father. He had ruled from Dorestad for a while until he was murdered by some of his own men although there was a rumour that the King of the Franks had tired of him and been behind the murder. "I was sorry to hear of your father's murder."

"Thank you, lord. The ones who did the deed are dead and now I seek to punish the master who ordered it."

"The master?"

"King Charles of the Franks!"

I shook my head, "That would be foolish with three ships. When the last raid took place there were more than three hundred and fifty ships."

"Nevertheless, I will try."

"You misunderstand. I have an arrangement with the Franks. I protect the river from those who would raid the Franks. At the moment I guard it. That may change but…" he gave me no chance to finish for he was angry.

"You would dare to stop me from avenging my father?"

I felt my oathsworn behind me. No one spoke to their lord like that. My voice was quiet but filled with authority. "Tread carefully young man. You are in my land now. I say again you cannot go upriver and that is for your own good."

I wondered if he would use violence. I did not want a bloodbath and so I raised my arm and, without looking, knew that ten archers lined the walls with arrows nocked.

"I ask you again to return downstream. There are many other places and people you can raid and you will not suffer as much as you would here."

I saw him glance over my shoulder. He was red-faced and angry. He jabbed a finger in my direction. As I stood a good head above him he looked vaguely ridiculous. "This is not over. The King of the Franks is my foe and now you have joined him."

I said, quietly, "If you wish to live a long life do not make an enemy of me, my young friend."

He stormed off. He and his men boarded their drekar. We watched them turn, slowly, and head back to the sea. Æbbi Bonecrusher and my hearth weru joined me. They were mailed and armed. "You are not needed, yet. I fear, however, that our young Dane will return this night. Have our men rest. Let the town watch keep a look out until dark. Call up every man who owes me service. I need them on the walls. We will try out our new system."

"Aye lord."

Padraig arrived, "Trouble lord?"

"A young Dane wished to raid the Franks. He would not listen. Have the ships moved upstream and then have a chain and logs run out across the river."

"He will return?"

"He thinks his manhood has been impugned. He will return."

I went and told Ágáta that there might be trouble and then my wife. I almost smiled. I had given her a dilemma. I had done that which she would have wanted. I had stopped the Danes from raiding the Franks but I had put her in danger. She was bereft of words and that rarely happened. William asked me when we were alone, "There will be a battle?"

My son was young but it was never too early to help make a young boy into a warrior. "The Danes will attack us and they will die."

"How can you be so sure, father?"

"Because they will try to scale walls which are high and we are expecting them. Attacking a walled town is never easy and needs preparation. We will be safe."

"Can I watch?"

"No, and before you ask why I will tell you. If you watch I will need a warrior to watch over you. He will have to be a good warrior and he would be better placed fighting our foes, would he not?"

He nodded, "You are right but I will be a warrior soon enough and I will not need a protector."

I made certain that my men all ate. The town watch were old men and they would be of no use in a night battle. I had well over a hundred warriors to defend my walls. Two-thirds had been on my recent voyage. The Danes had more than a hundred and twenty but they had walls to climb. We would make them a killing ground. On my walls, I had stone-throwers. We would send stones and flaming kindling at their ships. Nothing diminishes a warrior's ability to fight like his ship sinking.

I spoke with Padraig. I knew that I could rely on him to have the needs of my people at heart. I could fight my enemy knowing that he had all else in hand.

I was mailed and ready before dark. There was no sign of the Danes but I knew that they would be waiting for true dark. They would row silently up the river and climb my walls. I had braziers over the gatehouse and at the corner river towers. The walls were completely manned but only two or three men could be seen. To the Danes, it would appear as though we were unprepared.

Egil joined me. I had not asked him to but I had made him my standard-bearer and he was diligent. Æbbi Bonecrusher smiled at his enthusiasm. I turned to my lieutenant, "Have we darts, stones, javelins and bows?"

"Every ten paces there is a pile of each. The crews of the stone-throwers know to wait for my command. We have water ready by the gate in case they try to burn it." He shook his head. "You might take a small Saxon burgh with three drekar crews but not Rouen. This will be a waste of good men."

"He is thinking with his manhood and not his head. He is young and felt foolish. Had he thought about my words he would have seen the sense in them." I sat down with my back to the wall. I was recognisable. I did not want them to think that I was on my walls.

There was no moon. With no ships tied close to us any longer and the town awaiting the attack there appeared to be complete silence. Thus it was that I caught the slight noise of the wash from the leading drekar as it was rowed upriver. They had muffled their oars but you cannot muffle a keel. I nodded to Æbbi Bonecrusher and he peered over the wall. He held up three fingers. They had returned with all of their drekar. He hurried off to the west wall to warn the men. I nodded to Harold Strong Arm who did the same on the east wall. This was the time for patience.

Æbbi Bonecrusher returned and he donned his helmet. It was dark enough for me to stand knowing that I would not be seen. I picked up my helmet and held it. I could not see the enemy but I could smell them. They had the smell of unwashed warriors who had lived off pig and pickles. The air was filled with their pungent smell. I picked up one of the javelins which lay close by. It was just something to occupy my hands. I would not need it for a while. I caught a glimpse of something white moving. It would be a warrior who did not wear a helmet. They would be seeking a sight of our sentries. They would look up to look for a potential target. Their archers were not as good as mine but, unlike the Franks, they would have them. I wondered how they would scale my stone walls. I had not built them but they were formidable. They were the height of two tall men. Behind me lay a second, taller wall in which my family would be safe. I heard the ladder scrape on the wall. I wondered where they had found them. Perhaps they had had the wood and made them. Of course, if they had planned on taking Paris they would have needed them before they came upriver.

The silence could not last and when an arrow was sent at one of my men I heard a shout of alarm. "Stand to!" The Danes gave a roar and arrows slammed against the walls.

"Stone throwers!" The stone thrower crews did not need to know where the ships had landed. We were next to the river and they knew the range. The crack of the four machines sounded like thunder. I heard three splashes and a crash. I forced myself to ignore the sound of the machines and concentrate on the Danes. I glanced over the top and saw that they had ladders and they were also using shields and the mortared stones to climb. I pulled back my arm and sent my javelin at the ladder to my left. I hit the warrior but he was wearing a byrnie. He did not fall but he would be wounded. Others sent darts, stones and arrows as well as javelins toward the Danes. There were cries as some of my men proved luckier than I was or perhaps more skilled with darts, stones and javelins.

Æbbi Bonecrusher shouted, "Throwers! Use fire! Let us see these treacherous Danish bastards!"

Fire was dangerous but we had stone walls and we had water. We had placed braziers close by the stone-throwers. The missiles were made of old dried rope coiled into a ball and soaked in oil. They were placed in the throwers and hauled back. They would be ignited only at the very moment that they were released. Even if we did not hit their ships they would illuminate the sky. I heard the clash of steel as Danes made the top of the wall. They began hammering with their axes on our gate. It was a futile gesture for the gate was studded with huge iron bolts. Not only did they strengthen and brace the gate they also blunted axes.

The walls were suddenly lit as though the sun had risen when the four missiles were ignited. They soared and arced at different times. When men's faces were seen then arrows, stones and other missiles were sent at them. I saw that one drekar had already been holed by a couple of stones and was listing. Only one of our flaming missiles struck a drekar and the crew quickly extinguished it by throwing it into the river but the damage had been done. The crews of the war machines adjusted their aim.

"Lord, they have made the fighting platform." Petr pointed forty paces from us where I saw the Danes gaining a foothold.

It was inevitable some Danes would defeat the men of my town. "Æbbi, Harold, Egil, with me. Petr, Haaken, hold here!"

I swung my shield around and ran down the fighting platform. It was wide enough for three normal men but I filled it. Harold and Æbbi followed me with Egil as a reserve and to guard our backs. I saw Sven the Smith felled by an axe. He had slain two Danes and slowed their progress but he had paid the price. As his killer swung around I brought my sword from on high. The Dane's axe swung toward me but Long Sword outranged him and it struck his shoulder. I must have broken a bone for he dropped his shield and I punched him from my wall with my shield. Æbbi Bonecrusher ducked beneath a sword and rammed his own up into the skull of a second Dane.

"Lord, they are behind us!"

I whirled and saw that more Danes had climbed to the fighting platform and Egil was fighting two of them. Harold Strong Arm was my oldest warrior but he had lost none of his skills and he whirled around. His right arm was a blur as he brought his own sword down onto the head of the nearest Dane. Egil was holding his own. I saw that there were two men on the fighting platform and another climbing. "Æbbi, throw the bodies over the wall. Clear the ladder!"

"Aye lord." There was the sudden roar of flames climbing into the sky. It distracted one of the Danes on the fighting platform. A warrior could not afford to be distracted. My sword hacked him almost in two. His companion took a step back and I ran at him. I almost slipped in the blood from the man I had just slain but I kept my feet and, pulling my arm back, rammed it deep into the last Dane's chest. From the ladder came a crash and cries as Æbbi Bonecrusher dropped a mailed body over the side. It was the end of resistance. The last men who had made our walls were killed. I turned and looked at the river. One drekar, heavily overladen, was heading downstream. A second was on fire and one had but its mast showing above the river for it had been sunk. We had won!

I turned to Egil, "You did well there."

He shook his head, "But Harold killed them. I did not."

Harold put his arm around the youth. "You faced two fierce Danes and did not falter. I have been killing men since before you were born as has Æbbi. You will do, Egil Flame Bearer. Our lord has made a good choice for the one who will carry his standard."

By the time dawn came, we had cleared all of the enemy dead. There was no sign of Godfrid. He had fled. Padraig and Egil stayed with me as we wandered the river bank. We found none alive until we reached a small clump of reeds and overgrown shrubs. I spied something moving in the reeds. It was Egil who spotted the wounded Dane. He was trying to crawl to the river. Egil drew his sword. I said, "Hold!"

He stopped. "He is a Dane, lord! He tried to kill us!"

I shook my head, "No, Egil, he followed his lord and obeyed him. There is a difference. See he has barely begun to shave." The Dane had turned his head at the sound of our voices. I saw that his face had been badly burned. He wore no mail and he was young. I put his age at less than fourteen summers. He flailed his arm around.

Padraig said, quietly, "He cannot see. The flames have burned his eyes."

Padraig spoke in Norse and the boy keened, "Then kill me now! Give me the warrior's death I beg of you!"

He held up a hand for a sword. I drew my dagger and my short sword. Padraig shouted, "Lord, I pray you, hold."

"The boy is blind. Better he dies quickly than…"

"Than what, lord? Is life so worthless that you would throw it away?"

"He will have a warrior's death!"

"How about a warrior's life?"

"Egil is correct, he fought us and he lost. There is no dishonour in a death with a sword in your hand."

Padraig's eyes pleaded with me, "Lord, I ask for little. I do not condemn and I do not preach. Give me this soul for I would save both his eyes and his life."

I knelt next to the youth. "What is your name?" He said nothing. "I am Lord Göngu-Hrólfr Rognvaldson, Lord of Rouen. Hear my voice." He nodded. "I hold your life in the palm of my hand but life is precious. I would not extinguish a life without good cause. What is your name?"

"Godwin Godwinson. Kill me, lord."

"I have a priest here. He is a good man. He would save your life and give you back your sight."

"Is he a galdramenn?"

I smiled even though the youth could not see the smile, "He has skills and he keeps his word. If he cannot give you back your sight and you still wish it then I swear that I will give you a warrior's death myself. What say you? Are there still things you wish to do?"

He nodded, "This was my first raid. I was given life by Godfrid's father. I felt honour bound to serve his son."

"And you have done that. Your lord is gone. He left with little honour. You have honour. Have a life."

After a short time, he nodded, "If your wizard priest cannot save my sight then I choose death."

I stood, "Good." I turned to Padraig, "You have made a bargain here, Padraig. I hope that you can deliver."

He made the sign of the cross, "Aye lord, as do I but I see hope in this young man and I see the future. The Good Lord has sent him to me and I promise that I will do all that I can to save his sight." I nodded. "Egil, help me raise him to his feet."

I watched the two of them as they helped the maimed warrior and took him inside my walls. I could hear the webs being woven. This was truly *wyrd*. Godfrid had not finished with me but I did not worry about him. He lacked subtlety. He might still be a nuisance as Beorn Straight Hair was but I could deal with nuisances. King Alan of the Bretons and Æðelwald of Remisgat were a different matter. If I was to defeat them then I would need to be as cunning as they were. Was I up to the challenge?

Chapter 7

Egil seemed to feel a sort of responsibility toward Godwin. My standard-bearer was but a little older than he was. His concern meant that he spent a little more time inside my hall than outside as he helped Padraig to minister to the Dane. I was still trying to come up with a plan which would defeat the Bretons when he came to me. I was in my quiet chamber looking west. I had my charts and my lists. I also had some of Dómhildr's latest brew and I was enjoying it. He tapped on the door and I frowned. I enjoyed my solitude. I sighed, "Come!"

He shuffled in, "I am sorry lord but …"

"How is Godwin?"

"Padraig can truly make magic. Godwin can see light. He no longer lives in a dark world. He is now trying to raise the Dane's spirits. He is alone in the world. Each day his world gets brighter and there is a little more hope."

"Then I am pleased." I looked at him. He had come to me with another purpose. "And…?"

"Yes lord. I have not forgotten the task with which I was charged. I have seen strangers entering the town. They are all priests and they all visit with Æðelwald of Remisgat. They come every three days. Sometimes they are alone and sometimes they are in company. He sees them alone and then they leave. They rarely stay more than an hour."

I began to feel excited. I had proof. Padraig had been tasked with watching the priest. He had not reported visitors. That was because he had not seen them as a threat. They were priests! "Egil, the next time one comes I would have you follow them. I just need to know which road they take. Do not risk your life. You still have much to do. Godwin was sent as a lesson to us all. Heed it."

"I will lord."

After he had gone I looked west along the river. I had sent Gandálfr with *'Wolf's Snout'* to ensure that they had gone without causing too much mischief. Godfrid and his last ship had long gone. They had raided the land at the mouth of the river but they had not hurt my people. The animals they had lost could be replaced and the houses which had been destroyed could be rebuilt. Godfrid would remain a problem so long as he was alive but the world was wide and there were many seas. He could cause trouble but it was equally likely that he could come to harm. He struck me as a reckless youth. A more serious problem lay to the south of me. The Bretons had not responded to my taunt. That was worrying. My lords were still building up their forces. The losses at Carentan had been heavy. Had Godfrid come as an ally then we might have had sufficient men to make war sooner. Since Guthrum had converted, the Vikings who lived in the Danelaw seemed less belligerent. It was as though becoming Christian had sucked the fight from them.

I took a decision. "Harold Strong Arm!"

My oathsworn joined me as soon as the sentry summoned him. "Aye, lord?"

"Tomorrow we ride abroad. Have ten men prepared and a horse for William. It is time that my son saw some of the land he will one day rule."

It was not a long ride I planned. Erik Gillesson's horse farm was within riding distance of the river. Egil had told me that the priests who saw Æðelwald of Remisgat did not come across the river. That meant the land south of the Seine was free of spies. There might be danger and there might be enemies. By riding south, I would make Æðelwald of Remisgat curious. He would want to report it to his master. I was spreading bait and I hoped the priest would take it.

William had a copy of the blue cloak my oathsworn wore. The first men to wear it had been Alan of Auxerre and his horsemen. The long sword on the breast was also my sign, Long Sword. I had contemplated making it red and using the yellow horse but decided against it. The dark blue cloaks helped to hide us for they were dark. William was pleased to be wearing the same as my oathsworn. He also wanted one of the helmets we wore. He was too young and too small to need one but he looked enviously at my men as they donned theirs. I hung mine from my saddle. We crossed the river on the ferry. I think my wife had given up on William for she did not come to say goodbye. Sprota and Popæg did. Popæg shouted, "Heed your father, Master William." I saw her glance at me. "And do not fall from your horse. I do not want to have to mend a broken coxcomb!" The last words were aimed at me.

Snorri shook his head, "For a slave that one has a mouth on her, lord. She needs a good beating!"

William frowned, "Popæg is a kind lady. I will not allow her to be hit."

Snorri laughed, "She has a defender then eh, Master William? Good! You are on the way to becoming a man."

William stroked his pony. This would be the first time he had ridden his animal away from the confines of Rouen. "My father is training me in the ways of war." He looked at me, "When will I have a sword, father?"

"When you can lift my short sword with two hands then you can have a seax made."

I saw his eyes light up. My short sword would still be too heavy for him for some time.

On the other side of the river, we mounted and Æbbi Bonecrusher rode on one side of William while I rode on the other. It meant William could only see ahead but he did not appear to mind and I watched his face as he took in every word of our conversation. I was taking in the farmers in their fields. These were the ones who would follow Erik and Bagsecg into battle. They had fields filled with animals and with crops. They waved. Those on the road spoke to us and thanked me for the peace they enjoyed. These were the warriors who had given up the sword. They could and would fight for me but these would not go a-Viking. They had given up the drekar and taken up the plough.

Æbbi shook his head, "I do not think I could be a farmer, lord."

"Me neither but they are necessary. Their taxes allow me to keep many men under arms. I think that is why the Bretons have yet to react to our attack. Every farm we have seen has had all the farmers and their families working. It will be the same in the land of the Bretons. This is not like Norway or the land of Danelaw. Here a warrior can make war in winter. They will attack but it will be after Haustmánuður. That is why we ride. I would be ready by Tvímánuður. I intend to ask Bagsecg to have his men ride abroad. At the end of the week, we will ride to Carentan and I will speak with Saxbjǫrn. He is in the most parlous position."

My lieutenant nodded, "When Halfi Axe Tongue lost Benni's Ville it put the Bretons close to Saxbjǫrn. I wondered why you did not try to retake it, lord." There was no criticism in his words merely curiosity.

"When the town and port fell all of our people were killed. So many men were lost that we would not have had enough people to populate it. I know we lost our only port on the west coast of the Cotentin but had we tried to regain it then we would have bled our men away for no good purpose."

We rode in silence. I know that the land my grandfather had taken with the Clan of the Horse was now the most vulnerable. That had been the result of my brother. We now had four strongholds and each was vulnerable to an attack from the Bretons. We needed a battle where we could use our skills to defeat the Bretons and force peace upon them. I needed Alan of Vannes to cede the Cotentin to us. To do that I had to hurt him.

Erik had a good home. Montfort was well named. He had built a wall and had a strong hall which could be defended. The Risle river gave him protection on three sides too. The bottom of his hall was a stable. He could keep fifty horses there. Erik and his family were horsemen. The crops they raised were to feed their animals as well as them. Their whole purpose was to breed horses. Uniquely amongst the men who followed me, Bagsecg and his warriors did not wear mail. The blood of the Franks coursed through their veins and they were horsemen. The lack of mail meant they could cover greater distances without damaging their horses.

"Erik, we need to know what is happening along our borders. I need you to send your men, in secret, to look for signs of the Bretons."

He nodded, "There has been little sign of movement, lord. Here we are further away from the Bretons than any."

"Aye, I know. I will ride to Évreux and see if they have news."

Erik frowned, "But they are further away from the Bretons than us."

I nodded, "Yet they are closer to the Franks. We are at peace and I have kept the peace but news from Wessex and Cent makes me think that this is an illusion and that they are trying to trick us. If your riders see signs of any armed men then I need to know. By Tvímánuður we will be ready to attack and your men will be the screen of horsemen who finds our enemies."

Nefgeirr had been lord of Évreux but only for a short time. Now, Bjorn, the Brave was lord there. He and Leif Shield Bearer had asked for the honour of defending our most vulnerable of settlements. It was just over fifty miles to Paris. The Seine was less than eighteen miles north. If trouble came then it would take some time to bring aid to them. They were brave men. My best archer, Petr Jorgensen, lived here too along with Arne Three Toes. All of them had proven to be rocks in battle. I did not expect trouble at Évreux but I felt honour bound to visit with them.

They had built a wooden wall and dug a ditch since the last time I had visited. A gatehouse had two men upon it watching. We must have been spied from some distance for Bjorn and Leif greeted me. Both were bare-chested.

"We were hewing trees and clearing a wood, lord. This is good land. Come, we hunted yesterday and there is a haunch of venison. You might like the ale here although it is not as good as Dómhildr's."

We dismounted and left our horses drinking from the water trough. Bjorn and his men rode abroad. My son looked around him for this was unlike the world of Rouen. Here the houses had turf for their roof. There was no stone to be seen anywhere. Most of the activities, such as weaving, bread making, pot making and the like took place in the open. The children of the settlement had no time to play. They helped their parents in whatever trade they plied. He was a clever boy and I saw him take it all in. We entered the warrior hall which was a large communal hall. Thralls brought over the platters of cold meats and the horns of ale. Bjorn's wife, Ada, watered some down for William.

"Have you seen any warriors in this land?"

The two men looked at each other, "Strange that you should ask that, lord. Three days ago we found the tracks of horses heading north and east, toward Paris. Petr backtracked them. They had come from the southwest. Yesterday he and Arne took four men to follow the trail."

"You thought them to be Bretons?"

"Possibly. If they were not Bretons then they had passed very close to Breton land. King Charles' men tend to keep north of the Seine or east of Dreux. Count Odo controls Paris." We had fought Frank and Breton at Dreux. They both knew that we would contest any land which lay to the north and west of that line.

"Then we will wait until he returns. This is an itch I cannot scratch. I am unable to see what the horses mean."

We ate, drank and then spoke of the war which was imminent. When we went outside I saw that the sun had passed its zenith. "I like this not, Bjorn. Petr should have returned. Ada, watch William for me. We will ride and see if we can find Petr."

William looked as though he was going to argue. Ada had three children of her own and knew how to handle them. "Master William all of us obey your father and you are not an exception. Come you shall help me make a new batch of ale. You can help my children."

Bjorn said, "I will come with you for I know the rough direction Petr would have taken."

We rode along a greenway which was obviously well used for in places it was bare earth. We all rode with helmets hung from our saddles for we wished to be able to hear as well as see. The clash of steel and the cry appeared to come from some way ahead of us but we knew it spelt danger. Drawing Long Sword, I dug my heels into Gilles and my horse opened his legs. The sounds of battle became more obvious as we neared the conflict. Gilles leapt over the body of a dead warrior. The man wore no mail but he had a helmet and a shield. A bent sword lay close by.

I announced our arrival to alert Petr, "Clan of the Horse!" A warrior lunged at me with a spear. I jerked Gilles' head around as I slashed down with my sword. I caught his spear and then his arm. Blood spurted and he ran back into the shelter of the trees. There were horses milling around. Some had riders and some did not. I recognised Petr and Arne. They were to my left but the ones to my right, who were fighting each other, I did not. I did not know who to fight.

Petr shouted, "Lord, the enemy warriors have blue shields or red shields!"

I wheeled Gilles and headed into the fray. I saw that there were devices painted on the shields. Two men with red shields were attacking a bearded warrior who had lost his helmet. Gilles ploughed toward them. One began to turn which allowed the bearded warrior to gain the upper hand. I swung my sword from behind me. I hit the red shield and knocked the warrior from his saddle. He was not using stiraps. As the bearded warrior smashed his sword through the helmet of the man he was fighting the remaining red and blue shields decided to flee. The arrows from Petr and his men took out another three before they headed into the woods. Bjorn led my hearth weru after them.

The bearded warrior looked around for more enemies. When he saw none he smiled, "I thank you, mighty warrior. Had you not come to my aid then I might have followed my companions." He waved an arm at four bodies lying close by him. "I am Fulk le Roux son of Ingelger, Count of Anjou."

"And I am Lord Göngu-Hrólfr Rognvaldson, Lord of Rouen."

His eyes widened, "You are a Viking! Yet you ride a horse like a Frank!" I smiled. Petr and the others led their horses from the woods.

Fulk looked at them, "I thank you for your arrows. I would have perished with my men."

Petr nodded. "It was when we heard them speaking Breton that we knew we had to aid you. We fight Bretons. We did not know you."

My men returned. I gestured at the bodies of his comrades. "Fulk, do you wish to bury your men here or at Bjorn's settlement down the road?"

"Not here, lord, for I fear that animals would disturb them."

"Put the bodies on the horses and take anything of value from the enemy dead. I would know who they are."

"I can tell you that, lord. They are Bretons sent by King Alan. My father died last year and the Breton king tried to take over Anjou. We fought him and lost. I was sent by my mother to seek help from King Charles. They caught up with us yesterday. I fear I have lost the warriors with whom I grew up."

"Fear not. We can get you to Paris safely but it will be by river."

As we rode the few miles to Évreux I learned that it was Fulk's mother who was well connected. She was related to the King of the Franks. We buried the Count's dead and headed back to Rouen. I was anxious to be within my own walls by nightfall. I discovered that Fulk's father was not a great warrior but Fulk, although only twenty, was. However, he needed the guidance of an older man. I told him of the battles we had had. He was a sensible young man and I knew he was absorbing all that I told him. We reached the ferry just after dusk. I knew now that the Norns had been spinning. Anjou fought the Bretons. I had an ally. The fact that he had been defeated by the Bretons did not matter. So long as he was a thorn in the side of King Alan he would make the Breton leader look over his shoulder.

My wife was unwell and did not join us when we ate. Although Fulk was disappointed it allowed us to get to know each other a little better. William was so tired that he lasted but half an hour before he fell asleep and was whisked off to bed. Fulk, Padraig and my oathsworn were able to enjoy both the wine and the conversation.

"I thought all Vikings were barbarians." Fulk held up the wine, "But I can see that you are not."

Æbbi Bonecrusher laughed, "My lord, we can be barbarians but we have learned to appreciate some of the finer things in life."

"And can you defeat the Bretons?"

I would not confide in the young man for I did not know him well enough but I gave him hope. "We have beaten them before and we will do so again but, for the moment we farm and we prepare for war." He nodded. "Tomorrow we will secure you a berth on a ship heading upriver. When you see the King, you might tell him that I have forestalled an attempt by the son of the Duke of Frisia to attack Paris. Tell him that I still honour our side of the treaty." He took my words at face value but there was a hidden message for the Frankish king. If I chose to break the treaty because of his duplicity then he would be the one to suffer.

There were ships heading upstream and they were tied up at the wharf. Many captains liked to break their journey at Rouen. We were safe and we had good ale. It was easy to arrange a berth for Fulk. "If you return by the river then stay with me again. I would have a further conference with you."

He shook his head. "I will have an escort from King Charles and we can head further east, toward Burgundy. I had thought we had left in secret. Obviously, we were followed. King Alan has spies."

After he had gone I asked Padraig. "How is Godwin?"

"He is healing. The salve I use works but it is a slow process."

"And is he still belligerent?"

"No, less each day. I think speaking with Egil helps. They get on."

"Is Egil with him now?"

"No lord. I thought he was with you. He disappeared not long after you left yesterday."

A chill ran up my spine. "And Æðelwald of Remisgat?"

Padraig smiled, "He left to visit a brother in a monastery to the north. He had word that the man was sick."

That did not fill me with joy. Egil had followed the priest. Was my standard-bearer in danger? I told Padraig what I had asked Egil to do. "Lord, if you suspected Æðelwald of Remisgat was conspiring with priests then why not confide in me?"

I stared at him, "Padraig I trust you in all things save one. You are both priests. Over the last years did you notice the visits from priests?"

He shook his head, "I just thought... you are right lord. Perhaps your trust in me is misplaced."

"There is nothing wrong with the trust I have in you. It is just that you are blinded by the church in certain matters. I will take men and look for Egil."

I summoned ten men and we prepared our horses. We were just a mile north of my walls when we discovered Egil. I would not have recognised him for he wore an old cloak with a hood and an archer's cap. I reined in. "Out for a ride, my lord?"

I put my arm down to haul him up. As I did so I said, "No, we were looking for a young fool! Why did you follow Æðelwald of Remisgat?"

"Because you asked me to."

"I said to follow the men. This priest is dangerous. However, I thank you. What did you discover?"

"He went to a church at Bois-Guilbert. He stayed the night. There were horsemen there. They spoke Frankish. Two left a short time after they met with Æðelwald of Remisgat and they headed east. When I woke this morning, the other horsemen had gone. I left when the priest did but I ran ahead so that he would not know I followed him."

"You have done well."

"What does this mean, lord?"

"It means, Harold Strong Arm, that the King of the Franks is playing a dangerous game. When we go to war with the Bretons we cannot take our full force. I will have to leave most of the men to guard my walls. Æðelwald of Remisgat obviously thought my ride yesterday heralded the beginning of the offensive. He has made a grave error. Let us hope that we can exploit it."

Fulk would be in Paris within a day. My message would get to the King. The Bretons were a different matter. Were they getting their information from the same source? I had been too keen to live in peace. The siege of Paris had made me complacent.

William was waiting for me when we returned, "We have not practised for days! I am keen to see if I can beat Egil with the hoop game."

I knew that Egil would be tired but he grinned and threw off his cloak, "Come then, Master William, let us see."

My men took Gilles to the stable and I sat to watch. I saw Æðelwald of Remisgat as he entered my gate. He saw me and I saw the surprise on his face. He had thought to betray me but, by accident, I had tricked him.

That evening my wife surprised me by dining with me. She was friendly and almost affectionate. "I am sorry I have kept apart, my love, but I was worried that I might lose another child. I am keen for this one to be born healthy."

"As am I. And you have been alone for I hear that Æðelwald of Remisgat was also absent from Rouen?"

"Was he? I did not notice." I heard and saw the lie. "And where were you, my lord? William said you visited Vikings."

I laughed, "As all of my men are Vikings that is not a surprise. We visited with Erik and Bjorn. I wanted to ensure that we had enough horses and we do. Évreux is also well defended."

The meal was almost pleasant except that I knew she was gathering information to use against me. I had to make certain that I fed her that which would not hurt us. When she retired she said, "Lord, if you do not mind I would sleep alone again tonight." As I had not lain with her for a month that was hardly a surprise. "I have to rise frequently to make water."

"I am keen for this child to be born, my love, so that we can return to a normal life."

She pecked at my cheek. "All will be normal soon enough."

Perhaps I was overthinking things but her words seemed to have a veiled threat about them.

The next day Egil reported that another priest had come to Æðelwald of Remisgat but he had come from south of the river. I decided that I would confront the priest when he left. Baldir was the captain of the guard at the river gate. "When the priest who arrived this morning tries to leave, hold him here. I would like to question him."

"Did we do wrong to allow him in, my lord?"

I shook my head, "No. But I need to know whence he came. He may have knowledge which is of use to us."

It was not until late in the afternoon that a sentry summoned me. Æbbi Bonecrusher came with me. I saw that the priest was not a barefoot friar. He had good leather boots. And although he was cloaked it was a good cloak he wore. The large cross around his neck was ostentatious. It was there for effect. As soon as he spoke I became suspicious.

"Have I committed a crime, lord, that you bar me from leaving?"

"No Brother…?"

"Brother Jean."

"I am Lord of Rouen and I would know who comes and goes in my town."

"I have travelled here before and I have not been stopped."

"Then I am eager to know what draws such a well-dressed priest to my home." I saw in his face that he had not wished to give me so much information. "Perhaps our church is of interest to you. Or is it our defences? I detect a Breton twang to your words. Are you a spy?"

He now began to panic. "Of course not, lord. Æðelwald of Remisgat is a wise and learned man. He has many books and I often come to confer with him."

"And where do you go when you leave here?"

The hesitation in his words told me that he was preparing a falsehood. When he answered me, "Dreux," then I knew that he lied.

I feigned belief, "That is a long way from here. You have a difficult journey ahead of you. I wish you well, brother."

When he had boarded the ferry Æbbi Bonecrusher said, "Why let him go, lord? He is the spy. We have the proof."

"And what can he have learned? That I rode to Montfort and Évreux? That we prepare for war? He knows not when we strike. What he has learned is that I am suspicious. We will not see this spy again. The next priest who comes to see Æðelwald will be detained and he will be questioned."

Once again, the Norns were spinning. The next day a rider came from Ubba Long Cheek, Valognes was under attack! He needed my help.

Chapter 8

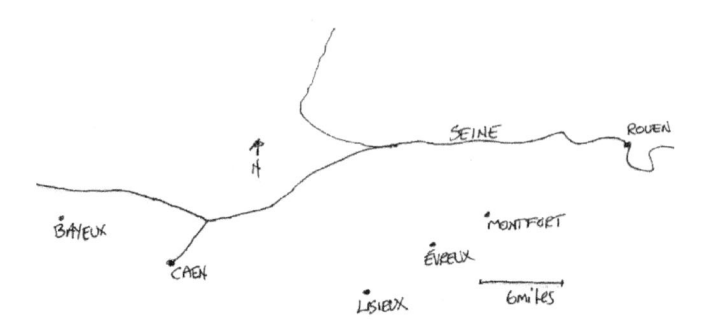

I could not take my whole army. King Charles the Fat was planning something. The aged king was trying to save his crown and I thought that we might be the prize he sought. I took my hearth weru. We were mounted and we could pick up more men at Montfort. If we changed horses at Lisieux and rode hard then we could spend the night at Caen. That would enable me to bring men from Bergil and Sven Blue Cheek. Sámr Oakheart at Bayeux would provide the rest. I assumed that Finnbjǫrn and Ragnar the Resolute would have gone to Ubba's aid.

"Padraig, I leave you in command here. You have good men."

"But I am no warrior!"

"Baldir can command the warriors but it is the day to day decisions which you will make." I handed him my seal. "And I would have you watch my son too."

He nodded, "I will do my best, lord."

We had good horses and we reached Montfort in a bare couple of hours. The horses managed a rest while Bagsecg summoned the forty riders who lived nearby. It was not enough but it would have to do. We reached Lisieux in the early afternoon. Our horses were tired. Gilles had no choice. No other beast could carry me but the others all exchanged horses. Bergil had more men. He brought twenty horsemen and his lieutenant, Einar Shield Brother, would bring a hundred warriors by foot. We rode for Caen and reached it after dark. I walked the last mile for Gilles was weary. It meant Egil and I were the last ones inside Caen's walls. Sven Blue Cheek was the most organised of my lords and by the time I reached him the horses had been stabled and food prepared.

"We have been caught unawares then, lord," he said it calmly. It took much to panic Sven.

I nodded, "My plans assumed that we would have more time. Ubba has made a mistake. He should have sent to one of you first."

"There might have been a reason."

Just then one of the sentries hurried in. "Sorry lord, but there is a rider from Lord Sámr. There has been a battle."

"Send him in."

I knew it was a disaster before he spoke. It was not his dishevelled and dirty look nor even the hangdog expression on his face, it was the hairs on the back of my neck. The spirits were talking to me. My grandfather was in the room and he was giving me warning of impending doom.

He dropped to one knee, "Lord Göngu-Hrólfr Rognvaldson, Lord Sámr sent me. He gave me this." He handed me the coin. I nodded. "The Bretons came and attacked Lord Ubba's stronghold. He sent a message to you and to the other lords in the Cotentin. The men of the Haugr and Ciriceburh marched to his aid."

"Not Lord Sámr?"

"He did not send to Lord Sámr. We heard of the battle and the attack from the survivors who fled to Bayeux. My lord's town is under siege. I barely made it out. The enemy surrounds it."

Sven could hear that the man's voice was about to break, "Fetch this warrior ale." He looked at me, "If they fled to Bayeux then it may mean that Carentan has fallen too."

I shook my head, "Saxbjǫrn had prepared for a siege. He knew he did not have enough men to fight an enemy but he had enough men to defend. He has Franks inside his walls who can defend. They may be hungry but they will be there when we arrive." The man had drunk and looked a little better. "Go on."

"This is what we were told lord by the first men who fled inside our walls." I nodded. What he meant was that the ones who arrived first had fled the field first. They would not know the outcome. "When the two lords came to the aid of Ubba Long Cheek the Bretons fell back and the three lords followed. The Bretons avoided Carentan and the lords thought that they had the enemy on the run for they outnumbered them. When they reached Saint-Lô, they found it was a trap. King Alan brought large numbers of men from the west and they broke the three lords' shield walls. They fled to our town."

I shook my head, "My lords do not lack courage."

Sven said, "Just common sense."

"It is my fault. We have let the use of horses diminish in the west. Only Erik and Bagsecg here have horses in any numbers. Horsemen could have kept closer to the enemy as they fell back. They could have scouted and discovered where the enemy warriors were. This changes our plans. Sven, I want you to wait here for Bergil's men. I will go ahead with the horsemen that we have. We cannot fight a battle but we can give hope to Sámr and show that we have not forgotten him. We will have sixty men who can fight on foot and Bagsecg's forty can keep watch on the enemy horse."

Sven said, "My walls are solid. I have men who can defend the walls. We will empty Caen of warriors. You will find more warriors in the farms twixt here and Bayeux."

"Then we will warn them that they will need to join you." I shook my head. "I should have sent for Bjorn the Brave and his men. They have the best of archers."

Æbbi Bonecrusher shook his head, "Looking back is easy lord and besides, we need Bjorn to watch for the Franks. He guards the back door to Rouen."

Æbbi was right but it did not help me. I had been outwitted again and I had let down my grandfather.

Gilles was better for a good night's rest and grain. We would have another hard ride. Egil and Æbbi Bonecrusher flanked Bagsecg and Bergil. "Egil, you will need to stay as close to me as Gilles' tail. I had thought to have trained you more before our first battle but I fear that you will have to learn while we fight. Men will watch our new standard."

"I know, lord. Last night I spoke at length to Sven Blue Cheek. I know that which is expected of me."

"Æbbi, I know it goes against the grain but the hearth weru will be needed to fight and not just to protect me. Egil and Long Sword will have to be my hearth weru."

"It will be hard, lord but we obey you in all things."

"Bagsecg, you will need to keep horsemen from us without losing your own. Be as the horsefly and annoy them. There is no dishonour in fleeing. We need to hold them until Sven and the bulk of men arrive."

We had learned that Sámr had more than a hundred men to defend his walls. We knew not how many had survived the disaster. The messenger, Ardhal, had guessed at between fifty and a hundred but that was a pure guess. I estimated that if we had four or five hundred men we would be lucky. No one knew the size of the Breton army. Our army was growing, albeit slowly. As we passed farms we called men to arms. None of these would have mail but they would know how to use weapons and they would happily fight to protect the land from the Bretons. They knew that if the Bretons won they would lose their farms. We were clinging to a narrow strip of land by our fingertips.

Sámr had built his hall on a high piece of ground above the river. Although the river could be forded we would be able to cross by the bridge. What we had to do was to draw any enemies away from the bridge to allow us to attack the men defending it. We stopped at the deserted farm which lay in the woods next to the road. We could see the town of Bayeux. It was surrounded by Bretons but there did not appear to be an attack going on. I had fought in sieges, most notably Paris. Fighting was intermittent. Men tried to take one part of a wall and then they retired to evaluate their success. I stood in the eaves of the trees. There was cover for us. If we did not use the road then the sixty of us could move through the trees, shrubs, bumps and hollows. Once we were four hundred paces from the enemy camp then there would be no cover. Although the Bretons would have surrounded the town the bridge was their only way of using a ram to break down the gate. The ones who waited without their walls would be there to stop aid from reaching Sámr and to stop men from fleeing.

"Bagsecg, I want you to ride to the southwest and approach the Breton camp from that direction. We will move down to close with their camp. My intention is to take and hold the bridge. You and your men can withdraw here and use your horses to threaten the Bretons. I need as many drawing away from the bridge as you can manage. When Sven arrives on the morrow then you can join with him and fight your way through them to reach us."

"It is a risky plan, lord."

"The alternative is to wait and we know not how long Sámr Oakheart can do that."

"Then we will do our best." He turned his horse and our forty horsemen headed south. We hobbled our horses and I led my sixty men toward the Bretons.

As we moved Bergil Fast Blade said, "You know it will be almost dark when we reach them."

I nodded, "This plan only works if that is true. In the dark, our small numbers will be disguised by our ferocious warriors. They will think we have more men than we actually do."

He nodded, "If it works then it will be worthy of a saga!"

"I care not for such things. My shield brothers and lords are more important."

As we moved west I wondered about the Breton attack. This had nothing to do with Poppa's priest. The spy had only left my town when Ubba was already fighting. They had known of the date of my intended attack and Æðelwald of Remisgat had discovered it. How had he been able to hear what was said in private? If I survived then I would question him. I had tried to be too clever. It might have cost me men. I was not as clever as my grandfather; I just thought I was.

We were able to move quite quickly for most of the time. We moved in small groups and moved from cover to cover. The problem came in the open sections. I thought we had been spotted when we heard the horn and then I realised it was Bagsecg. He had shown himself to the enemy. At the very least it would halt any attack on the walls and it might draw a large number of men away. The sun was becoming lower in the sky ahead of us. That would also help us for it would mean we were charging from the darker east. More horns sounded. We had reached a small line of bushes and shrubs. I peered through. We were half a mile from the Breton lines. I saw men mounting their horses. We would have fewer men to face. We had another two hundred paces to move. We would be in dead ground with the road to our left. I swung my shield around and drew Long Sword. Óðalríkr Odhensson and Egil Flame Bearer were behind me. Óðalríkr Odhensson had come of age during the Paris raid. He had shown himself to be courageous and capable of thinking on his feet. He was not hearth weru and I was glad that he had joined me at the fore. Harold Strong Arm and the rest of my men would be the battering ram which would gain us the bridge.

I knew that as soon as I rose I would be seen. That could not be helped. I just hoped that someone inside would see us too. Sámr had archers and even a few arrows might see us take the bridge. I began running toward the Bretons. I had my sword raised. We did not shout. Miraculously we had covered twenty paces before we were seen. Two men turned and when they saw us they shouted the alarm. Others turned. I saw a handful of arrows fly from the walls of Bayeux and two men fell. The sun was now setting more quickly and the stronghold and town were silhouetted. I brought my sword across my front as Bretons charged at us. They had no idea of numbers for the sky was dark behind us.

My sword struck one Breton diagonally across the chest. Óðalríkr hacked with his sword across the middle of a second. Óðalríkr had mail but Egil did not. A spear was thrust at Egil but my standard-bearer had quick reactions. He spun away from the spear and stabbed the spearman in the neck. My hearth weru made a wedge and charged at a body of Bretons who tried to bar our route to the bridge. Bergil led the rest of our men in a shield wall. My long legs had taken me almost to the bridge. It was now a race for horns sounded to recall the men who had chased after Bagsecg and his horsemen. It was too dark for arrows to be used from the walls of Bayeux. We had to kill as many of the Bretons at the bridge as possible so that we could turn and face the onslaught which I knew would come.

Harold Strong Arm had led the wedge and it had struck hard and sent the Bretons sprawling into the ditch. I heard Æbbi Bonecrusher shout, "Double line!" My warriors formed a line to block an attack from that side. Bergil and the others were hewing and hacking at the men on the other. That left the bridge for the three of us to clear. There were still six Bretons on the bridge although one had an arrow in his leg.

"Guard my flanks!" It was not a reckless and foolhardy attack. I was measured and knew what I was doing. The Bretons had swords and Long Sword outranged them. I was more than a head taller than the tallest of them. I had a bigger shield. I stepped forward and swung hard. I did not need to aim. There were six of them. I broke one Breton shoulder and sliced deep into the arm of a second as swords struck at my shield. I punched with my shield for I was still stepping forward, behind me Óðalríkr despatched, first one and then a second wounded Breton. Egil swung the standard at the side of the head of the Breton on their extreme left. I brought my sword from on high to split a Breton head. Egil's sword flashed and the Breton he had wounded died. There were two who were left. They held their hands up for mercy but it was too late and both died for my men had their blood up.

I said to Egil and Óðalríkr. "Quickly turn and face." As they did so I shouted, "The bridge is ours! Fall back!" The bridge was wide enough for five men. However, I occupied the space of two.

I saw that I had lost men. Some of my hearth weru had given their lives for their lord. They would be in Valhalla but it still saddened me. Bergil led his men back. They had cleared a large number from his side. Bergil stood next to me and Egil and Óðalríkr stepped behind us. There were wounded men and they were dragged closer to the far end of the bridge. Æbbi Bonecrusher was the last of my hearth weru and he joined me and Harold Strong Arm on the front of the bridge. The first Bretons who raced to catch my hearth weru paid a price for their eager haste. Four swords met them and cut them down. They could not get around us and the approach was a direct one. The four of us wore mail and were the best of my warriors. Each of us could have fought like a champion and the men who ran at us first were Bretons with little mail and not as much skill as we had. When we had slain ten of them I heard a Breton voice order them to halt. The hiatus gave me the opportunity to organize.

"Egil, unfurl the banner! Óðalríkr, stand behind Egil. I want spears over our shoulders. Lock shields." I did not know what Alan, King of the Bretons would do next but I knew what we had to do. We had less than fifty men and we would form a block on the bridge. The Bretons would have to push us all the way back to the walls of Bayeux. That would take time and time was our ally. Sven Blue Cheek was hurrying to our aid. The longer we fought the greater chance he had of deciding the day.

As the enemy formed my hearth weru behind me began a chant. As they chanted they banged their shields. It seemed to echo from the walls and then I realised that Sámr and his men had joined in. The sound rolled and grew like an approaching thunderstorm. It joined those within and without Bayeux. It put steel into my men's hearts for they were no longer alone and it put fear into the enemy.

The men of Rouen go to war,
A song of death to all its foes
The power of the horse grows and grows.
The power of the horse grows and grows.
The power of the horse grows and grows.
A song of death to all its foes
The power of the horse grows and grows.

The power of the horse grows and grows.
The power of the horse grows and grows.
A song of death to all its foes
The power of the horse grows and grows.
The power of the horse grows and grows.
The power of the horse grows and grows.

A Breton horn sounded and from the dark came a roar. It would have sounded terrible if it were not competing with the sound of my men and the men of Bayeux singing. I saw the shapes in the dark. There was the glint from spearheads. Whoever had ordered them to charge had sent a solid line of spears. It should have had a greater effect than it did but the Bretons had to negotiate their own dead. The last ten men we had slain lay littered like fallen leaves before us. The first spearman stepped onto a body and then tripped. Bergil Fast Blade lived up to his name. His hand darted out and skewered the hapless spearman. There was another body to be scaled. I had Long Sword and I swung it. I heard it crack and splinter spears. Stumps were rammed at our shields. Æbbi and Harold were fearless. I heard a spear slide along Æbbi's helmet and then the soft sigh of death as the Breton was killed by a vengeful sword.

Long Sword was of no use once the enemy closed with us and I rammed it into the wooden bridge beside me. I drew a seax. In the close confines of the bridge, it was a better and deadlier weapon. I was face to face with a Breton. He had drawn his sword. Our shields were pressed together. Behind me Haaken the Bold's spear jabbed forward. It caught the eye of the man next to the Breton who faced me. As Haaken twisted the man was unable to move. The Breton who faced me heard the scream and his eyes widened in fear. I lowered my right arm and insinuated it between the two shields before me. I began to push up. The Breton who faced me could not move his sword arm. My seax came up and I felt it touch something hard. The man had scale mail. I pushed harder. The seax was sharp enough to shave me. It tore through the leather bindings of the scales and moved up through the padded shirt. I pushed harder and the tip touched flesh. I knew that for blood dripped down my hand. The man's eyes widened and his mouth opened. A seax is a ripping weapon. I tore from side to side eviscerating the warrior. Blood and entrails fell and covered my hand. I withdrew my seax. The two dead men were pinned before us by the press of dead bodies. Their shields were held in place by leather straps fastened to lifeless hands. I saw that there was another

Breton to my right. My hands were sticky with blood. I raised my hand to the right and punched sideways. The seax struck the Breton fighting Æbbi. Then it entered his side and he roared. As he turned to look at me Æbbi headbutted him and I drove the seax deeper into his flesh. I must have struck something vital for he went limp.

It was a bizarre situation. The four of us held five dead bodies before us. The Bretons could not get at us for there were too many dead on the ground for them to push at us. They had many more men than we did but we were a solid mass of men and metal. The sides of the bridge protected us and they could not move us. A Breton voice shouted, "Push!"

I laughed for it had no effect whatsoever. I slipped my seax into my left hand and as a spear was jabbed over the dead men toward me I grabbed it behind the spearhead. I pulled backwards and the man lost his grip. I quickly reversed it and punched over the dead men. I towered over the Bretons and I was stabbing downwards. I hit something. Pulling back my arm I jabbed again and again. I had no idea what I struck. All that I saw was a sea of helmeted faces.

A horn sounded and I heard an order, "Pull back and reform!"

As the pressure went the five dead bodies slid to the ground. They formed a barrier. I would leave it there for the next attack would not be able to get close to us. My men began to bang their shields and cheer. I joined in. Egil's voice was in my ear, "Lord, a message has been passed forward. Pái Skutalsson brought it. Our wounded are within Bayeux. Lord Sámr Oakheart says we can withdraw within the walls if we wish."

"No. We hold the bridge and we can make them bleed here! We will stay but ask him for ale! The men will be thirsty!"

Just then I heard the thunder of hooves and to the east, horns sounded. Bergil laughed, "That will be Bagsecg. It is so dark that the Bretons will have no idea how many men attack."

The attack by our horsemen bought us enough time to dress our lines and to be handed fresh spears from inside Bayeux. We drank ale and we waited. The sounds of battle in the distance receded. If Bagsecg had done as I had asked then he would have hit and run. Then there was silence. It was not complete silence. The Bretons were moving but they were not forming for an attack. There were moans from wounded men who had not managed to fall back. I could hear them trying to crawl through the corpses of their comrades. Some would join them all too soon. There was no further attack that night. We were all weary but as dawn broke a slight breeze came from the west and the red standard held by Egil fluttered above my head. As it did so there was a cheer from the walls behind us. We had survived the night and we still held the bridge. Now we had a long day to wait for Sven Blue Cheek.

I reached into my pouch and took some dried venison. I began to chew. I would fool my stomach into thinking it had had a full meal. As the sun's rays became stronger I saw that the Bretons were arrayed some three hundred paces from us. Either King Alan had an enormous army or he had gathered it from around the walls to face me. A horn sounded and I saw the King and one of his lords dismount, take off their helmets and walk toward us. They wanted to speak!

Chapter 9

Handing my shield to Egil I said, "Bergil, come with me. We must have hurt him that he wishes to speak with me."

Harold grumbled, "Watch for treachery, lord."

I sheathed Long Sword and handed my helmet to Harold, "Fear not I know a snake when I see one."

We walked forward. My long stride quickly brought us a hundred paces from our men. We arrived there at the same time as the Bretons. I had met Alan of Vannes before. I did not like him. He had been unheard of when Salomon had been Count and after a vicious civil war, he had merged as the new count. The Emperor had granted him the title of King and I was certain that he had not won the crown and the title fairly.

He smiled the hollow smile which is on the lips and not in the eyes. "I see you have not lost your touch Lord Göngu-Hrólfr Rognvaldson. You are well named, Long Sword."

"And you have not lost your touch either, Alan of Vannes, you manage to avoid drawing your sword and putting yourself in danger."

I said it loud enough for my words to carry to his men. He coloured. "I would have you gone from my land!"

"Your land? We took this from the Franks. When my brother gave it to you it was not his to give. It is ours."

"I will tell you what I will offer, Lord Göngu-Hrólfr Rognvaldson. Have your people leave the strongholds they occupy and I will allow them to leave unharmed. Keep Bayeux. I do not desire it."

I laughed, "I care not what you desire. If you wish those strongholds then take them. When you wrest our swords from our dead hands then you may crow. Until then either draw your blades or leave."

"This handful of men and the tiny band of horsemen you brought will not save you. We slaughtered many of your warriors."

Duke of Normandy

"And paid a high price amongst your own men." I was guessing but I saw that my words had hit home. "And you have enemies! The problem with carrion is that they cannot be trusted. Even now the King of Frankia and the Emperor are plotting with the Count of Anjou in Paris. What will you do when Anjou attacks in the south and we still remain in the north? Will you be squeezed like a piece of ripe fruit?"

My barbed arrow had struck home and he became angry. "You are neither Frank nor Breton! This is not your land! When your folk lived on Raven Wing Island you should have been squashed as insects."

"Perhaps but we were not and now we grow in strength. Even your Emperor and the King of the Franks deal with us. It was Charles who gave me the title of Lord of Rouen. He gives out titles like minor favours. They keep him in power and they are meaningless."

"I am King!"

"You are King so long as the Emperor says so. Now, Alan of Vannes, the sun is rising do you and I fight to settle this? Shall we save unnecessary bloodshed and fight man to man?" He actually recoiled. "I thought not. Then either leave or bring on your men. I have seen them in the dark. I would like to slaughter them in the daylight. Make sure they empty their breeks before they fight. I like not the smell of human dung when I fight!"

"This will not end well for you, Lord Göngu-Hrólfr Rognvaldson!"

"We will see."

I turned my back on him and walked back to my men. They banged their shields and they cheered. I noted how awkward it was for me to negotiate the bodies. The Bretons would struggle to hold their formation when they attacked. When I reached my lines, I saw that Sámr had sent out fresh bread and twenty archers. Harold Strong Arm said, "Lord Sámr thought that the archers would come as a shock to the Bretons. I hid them behind our last rank." He handed me my helmet and some bread. It was still warm and tasted better than any bread I had ever eaten. That showed my hunger. I washed it down with the ale from my skin and then took my shield and turned.

This time the Bretons had gathered only mailed warriors. They had shields which were a little smaller than ours and they held long spears. This would not be as easy. Bergil seemed to read my thoughts. "They have the bodies to cross, lord. They will come at us piecemeal."

The Bretons must have thought the same. Their warriors marched in a solid block until they reached the first of the bodies. They were a hundred and fifty paces from us. Our archers would be able to send arrows at them when they were fifty paces closer. We allowed them to remove the first bodies unhindered. The greatest number of dead lay at the edge of the bridge. They were three and four deep. They spread around the sides. It would take a brave man to remove those bodies. Emboldened by our lack of response the metal snake edged closer preceded by men without mail who scurried like ants to drag the bodies to the side. I turned, "Egil, pass the word. When I drop my sword then the archers can release!"

"Aye lord."

When I raised my sword, the Bretons stopped and looked. They anticipated an attack but I just stood with Long Sword towering over the bridge. One of their leaders, in the front rank, shouted, "On!"

The Bretons came forward. They were at the part where the bodies lay in great numbers. There were twenty men removing the bodies. The Bretons must have realised that we would have to negotiate the wall of bodies if we were to get to them and they were confident. When my sword dropped, the body carriers stopped. It was a mistake for twenty arrows plunged down. Ten bodies were immediately added to the barrier. Another flight added three more bodies and then the survivors fled.

I shouted, "Cease arrows!"

The advance slowed. The Bretons had to keep their shields up. That protected them from arrows and enabled them to see their feet. I said quietly, as they approached, "On my command, the four of us race forward and use our spears. We fall back immediately."

"Aye lord."

I would not use a spear for Long Sword would do the job as effectively as a six-foot spear. I shouted, when the Bretons were thirty paces from us, "Arrows!"

My shout helped them to prepare and only one arrow found flesh. The warrior broke off the shaft. They came forward more confidently.

I shouted, "Cease arrows!" The second flight had just hit shields and helmets.

When they were ten paces from us and approaching the ground covered with bodies I shouted, "Now!" The Bretons heard the command and expected arrows. They stopped and joined their shields. In three strides I had picked my way through the bodies. I rammed Long Sword into the neck of the leader with the red plume in his helmet and tore it out sideways to bite into the neck of a second Breton. Bergil, Harold and

Æbbi rammed their spears into the bodies of another three men. Spears were poked at our mail. "Back!" Even as we stepped back Bergil had managed to spear another Breton. The centre of their attack now lay dead. We made the safety of our line and the restraint of the Bretons was discarded. Even as I shouted, "Arrows!" they charged us. Some tripped and fell over the bodies. We speared and stabbed them. As arrows fell I sheathed Long Sword and took out Hrolf's Vengeance. It would be better in the close confines of the battle to come.

The Bretons were angry. These had been chosen as the best that the King had to offer and we had hurt them. So far they had had to lose men without the opportunity to strike back. Now they struck. A spear came at my face. I flicked up my wrist and my shield blocked the strike. I pulled back Hrolf's Vengeance and rammed it blindly forward. I was rewarded with a cry as the razor-sharp blade found flesh. Bergil and the others jabbed their spears forward and men fell. Then a shower of javelins descended upon us. I heard a shout from behind me as one found flesh. One clanked off my helmet and a second stuck in my shield. I am a strong man and I used it as a weapon. I swung my shield from left to right. The javelin fell from the willow boards when it hit a Breton on the side of the head.

In a battle of shield walls, it is the spears which become shattered. The heartbeat between a spear shattering and drawing a sword is the most dangerous time for a warrior. Harold Strong Arm took a spear to the side of his leg. Æbbi Bonecrusher shouted, "Get Harold to the rear. Haaken, take his place!"

Egil used his free hand to drag back Harold. Haaken still had a spear and when he stepped forward his spear killed the exultant Breton who had speared Harold. We were now so close to the Bretons that we were face to face. The wall of dead meant that they were higher than the rest of my men. That was both a blessing and a curse. Their footing was less than steady. The bodies on the bottom had been there for half a day. Some had filled with body gases and they shifted as though alive. Hrolf's Vengeance was a good sword and was true. My grandfather had kept a tip on the blade and that found gaps in mail. I punched and I slashed. I had to endure blows to my own helmet, mail and shield, but mine were well made. I was bespattered and besmeared with blood and the guts of those I had slain.

A horn sounded and the Bretons withdrew. The battle was not over but Alan of Vannes understood that tired men make mistakes. Perhaps he hoped that those with me would tire too. We were Viking warriors. I was tired it was true but I could fight all day if I had to. Behind me, I heard the gates open as Sámr sent men with food and ale for us. We had wounded and they were taken inside too. The spear aimed at my helmet had given me another scar but it had already stopped bleeding. I did not need food but I needed the ale. My mouth was dry.

"Was Harold badly wounded?"

Æbbi shook his head. "He will be inside now and complaining to the healers. It was a gash to his thigh. It needed tending but within a month the limp will have gone." My men were experts at assessing wounds. In the night attack, I had lost four oathsworn. That was four too many. Harold was the best swordsman I had. He trained others. He would make William more skilled than I was.

The Bretons had withdrawn well beyond bow range. I saw a huddle of lords around their King. We were too few to leave. If King Alan departed without inflicting serious damage to us then he would lose face with his men. He had stolen power but there were others who could shift the allegiance to another rival for the throne. He needed a victory. He needed my death. As I sat on the parapet of the bridge I saw the whole conspiracy so clearly. The three kings, Alfred, Charles and Alan were working together to rid the world of Vikings. Charles and Alan wanted to know how King Alfred had defeated the Danes. For Alfred, he wanted power and influence. He wanted to rule the island of Britannia and be a major influence in Frankia. I smiled as I supped the last of the ale. That he would never do. The Land of the Wolf might not be the power it once was but Ylva Aidensdotter still lived there and her magic would help defeat the men of Wessex. My grandfather had made the choice which set the clan on this path. A man could never go back and weave again the web that made him. I envied the Clan of the Wolf. They had an ancient land which protected them and the power of a powerful witch. We did not.

Egil pointed, "Lord, they are up to something."

I looked where he pointed. Half the men had departed and I heard the sound of axes and then hammering. Bergil looked at me, "It cannot be a ram. If it is then by the time it is built we will have more men here."

"I hope it is a ram. That way we could attack them at night." I looked again. The work was taking place further downstream. I knew what they were doing. It made perfect sense. "They are building a bridge. They will outflank us." It was so obvious that I wondered why they had not thought of it earlier and then I answered myself. They had managed to take the bridge in their first attack. They had not needed to build a second one. Our unexpected arrival had done the damage. We had been right to force march with so few men. I turned to Bergil, "Take charge here. I will go within the walls and speak with Sámr. He can see further than we can and I need to know the whole story of this disaster."

"Aye Lord, and Sven Blue Cheek?"

"Sven is coming on foot and he needs as many men as he can get. Bagsecg will have kept him informed of our position. We have not yet begun to hurt. He will come and when he does he will wreak havoc amongst the enemy."

As I approached the gate it swung open and Sámr greeted me. "I knew that you would come, Lord." He pointed to his stone tower as we walked into the centre of his settlement. "The men in the tower tell me that the enemy warriors are building a bridge."

"Aye, I know. That means we have some time to prepare."

"Do you wish to exchange warriors? Yours have marched and fought for a long time."

I stopped and said quietly, "The men in your walls have seen the Bretons win. Even your warriors, Sámr Oakheart, have not tasted victory since Paris. Mine have. Let us leave them on the bridge. What happened?"

"Ubba is badly wounded. He has lost his left leg. Finnbjǫrn is dead. He and his oathsworn held up the enemy to allow the rest to escape. Ragnar the Resolute lost many men. The messenger they sent did not come to me. Ubba did not send to Saxbjǫrn for he knew how few men he had. Lord, when you speak to him be gentle. He blames himself for the loss of so many men."

I turned, "Sámr, this is not a game. We do not move pieces around a board and if we lose we restart. We hold men's lives in our hands. All that Ubba needed to do was to send me a message and stay behind his walls. They served Rurik One Ear well and they would have laughed a siege away. We have given the Bretons heart and they have seen that they can defeat Vikings. When we now go to war we must be totally ruthless. We must make their land a charnel house just to keep you and the other lords safe." I saw that he was crestfallen. "I do not blame you but when I met with you all I thought I made it quite clear that when war came we would all act together."

"You did."

We headed to the tower. I would speak with Ubba and Ragnar before I returned to the bridge but their feelings were secondary. The battle hung in the balance. When I reached the top, I recognised Thiok the Rus. We had rescued him and two others years earlier. He was a good man and I trusted his judgement.

He pointed, "They went to the wood where your horses were kept. I thought at first, they had spied them but they had not. They went to hew down the trees. Bagsecg sent half of his men to save the horses and the other half harassed the axemen. They rescued the horses and took them east."

I nodded, "Toward Sven Blue Cheek. Is there any sign of them?"

He shook his head. "The axemen hew the trees and they are brought down out of range of our archers."

Sámr said, "I pulled all of the archers to guard the place we think they will cross. It is where the river narrows. The archers have the range."

I had enough information and I scanned the enemy lines. The tower gave a complete view of the land and I saw that to the north the siege lines were barely manned. Sámr could have led his men and destroyed the ones who were there. The bulk of the army was before us. I saw that they had horse lines well away from the siege lines. They were well guarded. Bagsecg's attack would have forced their hand. I could now see that there were not only Bretons there were other allies. I recognised some of the standards of Aquitaine. There were other standards I did not recognise but from the mail and the helmets, they were Frank or from Anjou. Fulk had told me that King Alan was trying to steal his county from under his nose. I estimated that we faced more than six hundred men. I knew not how many guarded the horses or were cutting down trees.

"How many fighting men are within these walls?"

He hesitated and then the old Sámr came to the fore. "Men we can rely on, less than two hundred and fifty. Men to man the walls perhaps three hundred and thirty."

"Then we need to hold them until Sven arrives."

"We will still be outnumbered."

I smiled, "He will not know that." I could see that they had more logs ready. "Soon they will begin to build their bridge. I will leave you." I pointed to the bell which hung from the tower. It was not large. "Thiok, when you spy Sven ring the bell three times."

"Aye lord. But they will be more than a mile away."

"I will know he is coming. The Bretons will not."

I sniffed the air. The wind was from the north. It smelled of the sea. I licked my finger to check the direction. It was from the north and east. It was perfect. I made my way down the ladder. "Will you speak with Ubba and Ragnar?"

Shaking my head, I said, "Now is not the time. I need to defeat the Bretons first."

As I stepped toward the gate, men began chanting my name. I waved and spoke to those I recognised. I knew that the defenders had been wavering. My arrival and our actions since then had helped to stabilise them and give them hope. All hung on the edge of a knife. At the gate, I picked up the kindling which would be used to keep the brazier burning and the jug of oil used to start it. As I left the gates and walked to my men I had worked out our strategy. I glanced to the south as I crossed the bridge.

Bergil and my lieutenants awaited me, "They have almost built the bridge but it is not yet in place. When it is they will attack here to divert us. We will have no archers to aid us. We will have to work quickly. I want the enemy bodies taking and piling over there to the southwest of us. We will light this kindling and burn the bodies. The smoke will blow toward them and, I hope, add to the confusion."

"Confusion, lord?"

"Our archers know where they will build the bridge. It will be at the narrow part of the river. Even with smoke, they know where to send their arrows. The Bretons will think we are insulting them and they will be angry. They will try to take advantage of the fact that we have removed a barrier of bodies for them. I have but it is to allow us to attack. The smoke will help us. As soon as they advance we make a wedge and we charge their flank."

Bergil shook his head, "It is a risk, lord."

"A slight one. We have endured their attacks for long enough. More than half of the men on the bridge have yet to fight. Today they can bear the brunt of the fighting. Now hurry, daylight is burning."

My men worked quickly and the Bretons, three hundred paces from us, did not realise what we were doing until it was too late. My men took weapons and mail from the dead. It would allow the bodies to burn faster. It was only when Haaken the Bold used the flint to light the kindling that they realised what we were about. Broken spears and spent arrows were also used so that by the time Haaken the Bold had rejoined us the fire had caught. Flames licked and the fire crackled but it had yet to really take off. A Breton lord began to organise his men and they made a solid block to come toward us. As the wind fanned the fire so the flames took hold. Soon fat would burn and there would be smoke. From the river, I heard the sound of arrows hitting wood and the screams of men who had been hit. The attack had begun. King Alan had been forced to divide his forces. That was not in his plan.

"Wedge!"

With Long Sword at the fore, I began to march from the bridge. It would take us fifty paces to truly form up. When the Bretons saw what we intended they sounded their horn and the Breton lord ordered his men to make a shield wall and advance. I raised my sword and began a chant so that we could run at them. It was not a fast run but sixty mailed men were a considerable weight.

> *The men of Rouen go to war,*
> *A song of death to all its foes*
> *The power of the horse grows and grows.*
> *The power of the horse grows and grows.*
> *The power of the horse grows and grows.*
> *A song of death to all its foes*
> *The power of the horse grows and grows.*
> *The power of the horse grows and grows.*
> *The power of the horse grows and grows.*
> *A song of death to all its foes*
> *The power of the horse grows and grows.*
> *The power of the horse grows and grows.*
> *The power of the horse grows and grows.*

The Bretons were late and they were disorganised. The smoke from the burning bodies was confusing them. I held my shield in front of me. The Breton spear which came from the smoke smashed into it and I continued on. I brought my sword over from on high and hit the warrior in the third rank. A Breton spear from the second rank rammed into my right shoulder. It was a glancing blow but it broke a link and my skin. I punched with my sword as Bergil's spear hit the Breton in the middle. Breton horns sounded as King Alan redeployed men to face us. He could not see how many men followed me. As far as he was concerned it might be the whole of the garrison. We still had our integrity but the Breton line was in tatters. Haaken the Bold had slain the Breton lord who led them.

There was a temptation to hold but a voice in my head told me that Sven Blue Cheek would not let me down. It was worth pushing on.

We were no longer running and we had stopped chanting but we had the rhythm of war: block with the shield swing the sword, step forward. The men all around me were oathsworn and to be trusted. I did not have to worry about being attacked from the side. A warrior fighting with confidence has an edge over an enemy who does not. This time the Bretons had even ground over which to run. They did not trip but faster men reached us first and threw themselves at the handful, or so it seemed, of foolish Vikings. The training I did with William I had enjoyed when I was young. I moved my two hands as though they were both my strongest. My shield blocked and punched. Long Sword swept in long arcs. I tore through limbs. I bent swords. I knocked one Breton to the ground as he raced toward me. I stamped my foot on his chest as I passed him.

I heard a horn to my left. It was Sven. Our cow horns sounded different from the Breton ones. Sven was coming. A second horn from ahead told me that Bagsecg and his men had made an attack. When I had been at the tower I had seen how vulnerable the horse herd was. The Bretons before us slowed. Some halted and looked around for the two new enemies. We neither slowed nor stopped. Men ploughed on. Our wedge still remained formed and bristled with weapons. The men who had fallen had been replaced. I saw King Alan. He was just fifty paces from me. He had a good view of the battlefield and he knew that he had lost. He had more men than we did but we had broken him and with fresh troops coming to my aid he would lose. I saw him turn and his standard-bearer sounded the horn four times and then waved the standard. They were falling back. It was not a rout. It was a retreat. They marched backwards, their weapons still facing us. We had travelled four hundred paces when Sven and his men appeared on our left. I saw his raised sword and he led his men to charge into the flank of the Bretons.

King Alan's allies deserted him first. His lords then ran for the horses which remained. Even as I looked I saw Bagsecg and his men driving horses east.

Æbbi Bonecrusher said, "Lord, the men need rest. I do not think we can continue to pursue them."

He was right, of course. I did not think that Sven would be either but I knew that Sven Blue Cheek would see the Bretons we had slain and wish to do something about it. He would continue until his men could go no further. I nodded, "Egil, plant the banner here! We have fought our battle!"

I sheathed Long Sword. If any needed despatching then I would use Hrolf's Vengeance. I slid my shield over my back and I hung my helmet from my seax. We were not far from the Breton camp. King Alan had had tents. Egil and Óðalríkr Odhensson were still with me. My hearth weru were slumped on the ground. They were exhausted. Bergil went to the men he had brought. Some had died and he was a good leader. He saw to his men. Most of my men were with Sven. I would see them when they returned.

As we neared the tents I saw movement. I drew Hrolf's Vengeance and hurried toward the tent. There was a priest and a warrior. They were stuffing papers and maps into a small chest. The warrior turned and swung his sword at me. I just reacted. I grabbed his sword hand with my left and then rammed my sword into his middle. The priest dropped to his knees and began to beg his White Christ to save him.

"Shut your whining priest! Who was the warrior I slew?"

He said nothing and I put my sword to his throat. "Tell me and I will not only let you live, but I will also let you go!"

"He is Lord William of Orleans."

A Frank! "Go before I change my mind." He scurried away. "Egil, he has mail and a good sword. They are yours. Óðalríkr Odhensson, you may have the rings on his fingers and his gold. Guard those papers. They are valuable to me. Then search the tent. Who knows what else the Bretons may have left."

If these papers proved as valuable as the ones I had taken in Cent then the losses we had suffered might not be as disastrous as I had first thought. When we had found everything of value we left the tent and headed back to Bayeux. Our men and the men of Bayeux were working their way across the battlefield. The wounded were given a warrior's death and whatever they had of value was taken. Óðalríkr Odhensson had fought many battles and that was why he had good mail, a fine sword and a helmet which could take a great deal of punishment. I saw that Sámr had begun to pile up the enemy dead. The fire I had begun with the bodies still burned and his men were slinging the Breton dead upon it. Disease and carrion followed the dead.

Our own dead were laid reverently out by the bridge. They would be buried in their mail and with their swords. There would be no marker save for a mound. So long as Bayeux remained Viking then their bodies would be safe. Without even speaking to them I knew that Ubba and Ragnar would want to go to the battlefield where they lost their men and bury them with honour. The difference would be that their bodies would have been mutilated by the Bretons and there would be neither mail nor sword.

As I entered the gates the defenders and the townsfolk clamoured around me. Others had fought in the battle but I was the symbol of the clan. To the ordinary people, I was the reason for the victory and they tried to touch me. They thought I was lucky and they hoped the luck would rub off. The men and boys tried to touch the scabbard of my sword. Swords were powerful. Swords had the spirit of their maker within them and were seen as almost magical. I stopped no one. I knew how close we had come to losing. Indeed, we might still have lost. Until I could discover the fate of the towns in the Cotentin we had lost. Sámr's wife, Elise, came and reaching up on tiptoes, kissed me. I had to incline my head to allow her to do so.

"Lord Hrólfr you look tired. I have had a room prepared for you." She gestured and a servant appeared. "Petr will show you."

"First, I must see my lords." I turned to Egil and handed him the chest. "Take this to the room and then come and find me. I will be with the healers and Ubba."

Lady Elise said, "They are in the chapel."

There were many Christians in our land and I allowed them to worship. Their priests made good healers. They were not as good as a volva or a galdramenn but they were conscientious. I knew where the chapel lay. It was outside the hall.

Ragnar the Resolute was just coming out. He dropped to one knee. "Lord I have let you down badly. So did the others but a man must answer for his own mistakes. We thought we could defeat the Bretons and we were tricked. It has been an expensive lesson. I lost my brother, two nephews and a son!"

"The cabbage is out of the ground, Ragnar the Resolute. You can do nothing about the past. It was the Norns."

He shook his head, "No, lord, the Norns spun and we had a choice. We each went for glory. As we chased the Bretons south we boasted of how we would tell you of our victory and how we had saved you from an unnecessary journey."

I put my hands on his shoulders, "You put this behind you. Finnbjǫrn is dead and Ubba has lost a leg. You can learn from this. Your port is now the strongest on the Cotentin. You command the Cotentin."

He looked shocked, "I almost lose you your land and you reward me?"

"You have not changed. We named you the Resolute for that is what you are. You have inner strength. Draw on it now. You made a mistake. You will make others. I have made mistakes and that makes us human. Learn from it and become stronger."

"I will and I will not let you down." He lowered his voice, "Ubba is not a well man."

"The wound?"

He shook his head, "His mind!"

It was dark inside the chapel and there was the smell of blood and ointments. Tallow candles sputtered and spat. I saw bandaged warriors. Some, like Ubba, had lost limbs. All would live. If they were not likely to survive then a shield brother would have ended their lives. A priest came to me, "Lord Göngu-Hrólfr Rognvaldson, I pray you to speak with Ubba Long Cheek. His spirits are low."

"Will he live?"

"Live? Yes. It was a clean wound and I took the leg off above the knee. He might even walk one day. That is not the problem. He does not wish to live."

"I will speak with him." I wandered over to the cot upon which he was laid. I could smell singed hair. They had used fire to seal the wound. Ubba's eyes were closed. I pulled a chest over and sat on it. He opened his eyes. They widened. "Now then, Ubba One Leg! Were you so tired of your own name that you sought a new one?"

"Lord, how can you bear to look at me. You should take Long Sword and end my life and I would be grateful."

"But if I did that I would lose a warrior who is one of the best I have led."

"Did they not tell you? I was the reason Finnbjǫrn and Ragnar did not follow your instructions. Loki must have put the thought in my mind that I could defeat the Bretons and give you more land to rule. Instead, my warriors lie unburied."

"We won!"

"What?"

"King Alan has fled back to his own lands. He has failed to take a single town. He has hurt us but we have his horses and we slew many of his men. We will go to war but when I say! That will now have to be in Þorri. Can you learn to walk by then? Perhaps ride a horse? Had you had more horses then you would have caught the Bretons or seen their trap. There is a reason we use horses Ubba One Leg!"

"I do not like horses."

"I think that now is the time to become familiar with them. Build an army for me. Teach your men your skills. When I am ready I will summon you and we will march or ride together."

He took my hand and placed it on his brow, "I swear I will not let you down a second time."

"I know you will not."

I returned to the hall. I waved Egil over. "Before we go to the chamber we will drink. I could manage a whole barrel!"

"I will fetch what I can."

Sámr's hall had a long table and I sat in the middle. This was not my hall and I would not take the head of the table. My hearth weru came in. They slumped next to me. "We must be getting old, lord, for I am weary beyond words. My sword is as blunt as a lump of iron and my helmet is covered in dents and dints!"

I laughed, "Æbbi Bonecrusher, then take the coin you collected and buy a new one! Buy two!"

Harold Strong Arm limped over, "He is too tight, lord! I believe he still has the first farthing he ever stole!"

I looked at my wounded warrior, "I did not see you in the chapel!"

He shook his head, "I do not like the smell of churches. I went to the gatehouse for fresh air."

Sámr came in, "More likely to see if you could continue to fight!"

"It was a scratch."

Sámr shook his head, "I have just spoken to Bergil. One of Bagsecg's riders told him that Sven Blue Cheek is returning with the rest of the army."

"Good. Can you cope with all these men, Sámr Oakheart?"

"The Bretons brought cattle to feed their army. We can manage and if not then we would do without for if you had not come then all would have been lost."

I nodded and emptied the horn of ale which Egil had offered me. "Aye, I made plans but they did not turn out the way I expected."

Ragnar had been seated quietly at the end of the table. He looked up and said, "But your plans did work. We each left more than enough men to guard our walls. Your new system is a good one. You were just lacking in your choice of lords."

I waved his comments away and held up my horn for Egil to refill, "I told you before we use this as a lesson. We know where we are vulnerable. Bagsecg has captured horses. Each lord will take an equal share. My grandfather had a dream of Viking horsemen. Thanks to a treacherous brother that dream was shattered. Let us make Hrolf the Horseman's dream a reality."

The mood changed in an instant and they all shouted, "Hrolf the Horseman!"

I began to sing the song of my grandfather and all joined in. I was touched that all knew every word of the saga.

The horseman came through darkest night
He rode toward the dawning light
With fiery steed and thrusting spear
Hrolf the Horseman brought great fear

Slaughtering all he breached their line
Of warriors slain there were nine
Hrolf the Horseman with gleaming blade
Hrolf the Horseman all enemies slayed

With mighty axe Black Teeth stood
Angry and filled with hot blood
Hrolf the Horseman with gleaming blade
Hrolf the Horseman all enemies slayed
Ice cold Hrolf with Heart of Ice
Swung his arm and made it slice
Hrolf the Horseman with gleaming blade
Hrolf the Horseman all enemies slayed

In two strokes the Jarl was felled
Hrolf's sword nobly held
Hrolf the Horseman with gleaming blade
Hrolf the Horseman all enemies slayed

Chapter 10

I waited up for Sven Blue Cheek to arrive. Most of my men just collapsed having drunk all that there was and eaten well. Two hard days had taken their toll but I had to speak with Sven and Bagsecg for they were the ones with the true picture of the land and how it lay. They arrived together. Bagsecg was walking. They led captured horses laden with the detritus of battle.

Sven Blue Cheek looked genuinely pleased to see that I lived. We said nothing until we went into the hall. The floor was littered with sleeping men. We could have had a battle in the hall and none would have woken. Egil lay asleep but he was in my chamber with his body wrapped around the chest. As Sven drank I told him of the papers I had taken.

"That is what makes you who you are, lord. I would have left them."

I shrugged, "They may help but I did not use the last ones well enough. I will now."

Sven nodded, "We kept our swords in their backs until we had passed where they defeated Ubba's men. I had my men bury our dead in one mound. Their bodies had been despoiled. It would have done their lords no good to see them. Ragnar's son and his brother were almost unrecognisable."

"I have made him lord of the Cotentin."

"That is good. He will be stronger for this and it will not happen again."

I turned to Bagsecg, "I told the lords that we would share out the captured horses."

"Aye lord if I can keep the breeding stallions and mares."

"Of course."

"And we need horsemen riding horses like Gilles. I lost twenty men because we were not wearing mail. We need both kinds of horsemen."

That night we began to formulate a plan. We had to change how we fought for we had enemies all around us. Just before I went to my chamber I said, "One thing has me puzzled. Beorn Straight Hair; where was he?"

"Why worry about his absence?"

"He betrayed Saxbjǫrn and fled to the Bretons. I do not like the fact that he was not here. It reeks to me of mischief."

Sven looked puzzled, "He has received his gold and he has gone. He is not worth worrying about. He is a nithing!"

"When I know where he is then I will cease to worry but we have been undone a little too often lately. I will view everything with suspicion."

Egil slept at the foot of the bed. He had fully taken on the role of standard-bearer. I was so tired that I almost collapsed on the bed. Perhaps it was the ale, the tiredness or perhaps the disaster but whatever the reason for the first time in a long time I dreamed.

I was a bird and I was high above the land. I saw my grandfather. He was riding Gilles. He stopped at the top of a hill. I saw that he spied the land of the Seine. Ships plied the river. Farmers toiled in the field. I saw what he could not. Danes were crawling toward him. I saw Godfrid and I saw Beorn Straight Hair. I swooped to warn him of his danger. He smiled at me. I kept swooping but all that it did was to distract him. The Danes rushed up and began to hack at him and Gilles with swords and axes. I was thrown high into the air and when I looked down he was gone. I heard keening and I dived down once more. It was coming from my hall. There sat Gefn and she was weeping. She was shaking her head. In her hand, she held a girl child. Even as I alighted I could hear the bell sounding the alarm. I flew high above the river and I saw an army marching toward Rouen. There were many standards and banners. They followed a cross. They were heading for Rouen. Drums sounded and grew louder and louder.

I awoke. Someone was banging on the door. I wondered why Egil had not opened it and, as I jumped from my bed, I realised he was not there. I shouted, "Come!"

One of Sámr's servants was there. "You are summoned, lord. A rider has come to us from the Haugr."

Duke of Normandy

I wondered what this disaster was. I poured some water into the basin and sluiced down my face. I headed for the hall and Egil appeared, "I am sorry lord, I went to fetch food."

"It is no matter." We entered the hall. I saw Bertrand, one of Bagsecg's riders. Sven, Bergil, Ragnar and Sámr were speaking with him. When I entered they all stopped.

Bergil said, "Lord Bertrand has grave news. Tell Lord Göngu-Hrólfr Rognvaldson what you learned."

"Yester morning Lord Bagsecg chose four of us to ride to the Cotentin to seek news of the Bretons. He was worried that not all of the Bretons might have left the land and he feared they would do mischief."

My captain of horses had done that which I should have done. "Where is the messenger now?"

"He has headed for the Haugr."

Sven said, "I would listen first, lord, and ask questions later."

I nodded and took the ale which Egil proffered. "Go on."

"We all broke our journey at Carentan. There we found that they had been attacked but the attacks had been repulsed. I was sent to the Haugr. Lord, it has been completely destroyed. I found a child of ten years who had hidden when the attack came. It was Danes. They came without shields on their drekar. The men Finnbjǫrn had left thought that they were friends and admitted them. They were put to the sword and the buildings fired. The Danes left."

I shook my head. The curse which had hurt my clan had destroyed my grandfather's home. The meddling priest had much to answer for. "The boy, what did he tell you and how did he survive?" I knew that I sounded suspicious but I had to ask the questions.

"His name is Thorkell Svensson. His father was left in command of the walls." I remembered Sven, Thorkell's father. He had been one of my father's most trusted warriors. He must have been almost fifty years of age. "He sent his son away to hide. He told him someone had to tell you what had happened. The boy is small and quick. He evaded the Danes. He hid in the wrecked tower by crawling into a tiny space. He was able to watch and hear. The men were butchered as were the boys. The old, both men and women were slain. Sven White Hair was given the blood eagle. The few women who were left and the children were taken aboard the drekar. Thorkell waited until he saw them leave and then emerged. When I found him, he was burying the dead."

"Where is he now?"

"I left him with Saxbjǫrn the Silent. I knew I needed to return as quickly as I could."

Sven Blue Cheek said, "Lord, the boy heard them speak. You were right to worry about Beorn Straight Hair. He led the Danes and there is more." I looked up. What more could there be? "The Danes were the ones who tried to take Rouen. It was Godfrid. They serve Alan of Brittany."

Now part of my dream made sense. The attack on my grandfather in my dream was an illusion. It was symbolic. If that part was real then the other two elements were also true. I held my hand out for Egil to refill my horn. I was thinking. "And the other settlements? Valognes and Ċiriċeburh?"

"They are held. The Danes tried the same trick at Ċiriċeburh but the captain of the guard did not trust them. He dislikes Danes and he refused to open the gates. The riders who went to them caught up with Bertrand. Benni's Ville is destroyed and there are none who live at Bárekr's Haven but we knew that the Bretons had done harm when they raided Valognes." Sven spoke calmly but I knew that he understood, as I did, the magnitude of the problem. I emptied the horn and I began to formulate my response. I knew I had been silent for some time when Sven Blue Cheek said, "Lord?"

"We are hurt and we bleed. I had a dream which disturbed me and Bertrand's news did not come as a surprise." I looked at Ragnar, "The lords of the Cotentin are under siege. You need to spend the next months growing your forces. You need to be vigilant and use what men you have left to watch for treachery. Unless you know the drekar which sails into your harbour regard them as foes. Ubba will need help but Saxbjǫrn has shown us that we can be strong even though we have been hurt."

Ragnar nodded, "Aye lord."

"Sámr, Sven, Bergil; you will hold this line and this road. Visit each other regularly. Use your new horses well. Bagsecg, you will be the most important for you must breed more horses. I see into the future. I see great danger. We learn from this disaster and we become, like Saxbjǫrn, stronger!"

"And you, lord, what do you do for I know that you will not sit idly by?"

"I will take *'Fafnir'* and a crew. We will sail into the heart of King Alan's land and we will kill these Danes. We will leave a message for King Alan."

They nodded. Sven said, "And your dream? Where was the danger? Who was the danger?"

I said simply, "Rouen and the Franks!"

The day was spent preparing for Ragnar and Ubba to return home. Those of Finnbjǫrn's men who had survived were given a choice. They could either join one of the Cotentin lords or serve me. Ten chose to follow me. They were the ones who had lost families. I was going to punish those who had taken their families and they would have a greater chance of vengeance if they followed me. I walked Sámr's walls with Sven and Bergil. We offered suggestions to improve its defences. Bayeux was the front line. Like Lisieux, it was further from the sea than we might have liked and aid would be slow to reach it.

"Sámr Oakheart, I would have a ditch dug around your town and let the river fill it. Build a stronger gatehouse."

"Thank you, lord, that is good advice. If we had coin then we would build in stone."

"Come, the new grass we will go to war and there will be coin for you. You are luckier than the lords of the Cotentin. You lost fewer men. You have boys you can train as warriors. Ubba and Ragnar had boys taken as slaves or killed. Your warriors will need to father more." Part of me was thinking about my wife and the child that she was expecting. The dream had said it was a girl. Was that true?

We rode east. We were not in a celebratory mood. Despite the fact that King Alan had not achieved his objectives it did not feel like a victory. There were too many dead. Carentan and Saint-Lô had both shown me that my opponent knew me too well. I was predictable and that was not a good thing. I spoke with Sven and Bergil. To be truthful it was more Sven for he was wise in the ways of war. Bergil was not. Even Sven Blue Cheek struggled to think of a way to defeat the Bretons. "We have an army which is better than the Bretons but to defeat King Alan we would have to strip every town of its warriors."

"Ragnar showed us that we can do that. We make our strongholds stronger. We need more drekar. I will not seek any from beyond our lands. I do not trust them. We have the winter to build more ships. If we are to succeed then we need to fight Alan of Brittany in his land and not ours." I turned to look at Sven. "When I sail to punish these Danes, I will also examine the coast. I will seek somewhere we can land and hurt them. Bagsecg is quite right. Our horsemen are good to scout but not to fight. We have to fight as old-fashioned Vikings until we have more horses and men to ride them. My grandfather had the right idea but Alain of Auxerre and his men will not come again. Next time we will make our own horsemen. That will take time. I hope the Allfather grants me that time."

By the time we reached Rouen, we had been away for almost fourteen days. I am ashamed to say that the first thing I did was to give the box of papers to Padraig and the second was to order my drekar readied for sea. It was only then that I sought my wife. Of course, I should have wondered why she was not there to greet me but I was preoccupied and it was I who felt guilty. She smiled when she saw me. She did not hug me. I knew she would not. She disliked the smell of horses and sweat. She was now heavily pregnant.

"Did all go well, lord?" I shook my head and told her all. She patted my hand, "You do yourself a disservice, lord. You have driven the Bretons hence and our land is safe." She smiled, "While you were away the Bishop of Paris came to visit us. He is a friend of Æðelwald of Remisgat." I immediately began to feel anger rise. She must have sensed it and continued, "He came from King Charles to thank you for rescuing the Count of Anjou. He sent a necklace for me and a medal for you." She handed it to me. There was writing around it.

"What does it say?"

"Hrólfr, defender of the Seine!" It is a great honour. Your star is rising, husband."

I might have been excited if it had not been for the worry that as Æðelwald of Remisgat was involved it was all part of the conspiracy. My wife was too innocent or perhaps she was too desperate to be one of the Frankish nobility again.

"When you have bathed and changed we will eat. We have much to speak on."

I bathed quickly but I did not return directly to the hall. I went to see Padraig. He needed to know my plans and I needed to know what he had discovered.

"The maps are useful lord. They tell us more about the waters you will sail and it identifies their strongholds. The parchments," he held them up, "are even more informative. King Alan the Great and King Charles the Fat are allies. The Bretons will be given the Cotentin if you are driven from this land."

"You are sure?"

"There are letters and documents which make it quite clear. The land between will be given to King Alan's son, Pascweten, and he will be Count of Caen. Bowing the knee to King Charles he will be a buffer between them."

"Clever. Is there any date for when they will attack?"

"I am guessing, lord, that the attacks on Carentan and Valognes were the start of the offensive. They might have hoped that you would be defeated and even killed. You are the glue which holds this land together lord."

"Perhaps. Tell me, was any mention made of Danes or Vikings in the documents?"

"No lord."

I told him all. I explained how we had won and what we would do next.

"This revenge raid against the Danes is not necessary, lord."

"I believe it is. There are more out there like Godfrid and I do not want them to join together and make war against us." I jabbed a finger at the maps. "Find somewhere you think the Danes would be hiding." I had a sudden thought, "Godwin, is he healed?"

"Almost."

"He knows Godfrid. I will speak with him. Make sure that Egil is there too."

He smiled, "Your son and the Dane get on well. If you are trying to subvert him then the two of them will have more effect than you or I."

I nodded. As I went to the hall I saw the complexity of the Norns' threads. It was unlikely that Godwin would know where Godfrid and his ship were to be found but he could tell me things about the crew and the ship. I had taken Egil on and he had proved to be more useful than I could possibly have imagined.

Æbbi Bonecrusher was waiting outside my hall, "Lord, what are your plans?"

"We need a full crew to take *'Fafnir'* to the land of the Bretons. We seek the Danes."

He nodded. "There are but ten oathsworn left lord."

"You know yourself, old friend, that oathsworn are not chosen. They choose themselves. Ten will be enough."

"I do not think that one drekar will be enough, lord. We need two."

"Can we afford to leave my home so ill defended?"

"It will be well defended and Gandálfr is keen to sail his ship. *'Wolf's Snout'* is a fine ship."

"We need the best of crews!"

"I will ask Gandálfr and Magnús Magnússon to help me choose them. There is much talk in the alehouses about the treachery of the Bretons. Finnbjǫrn was popular. Ubba led many of the men who now live here. There are plenty who wish to wreak vengeance on the Danes."

"Then tell the two of them that I will see them tomorrow. I would sail sooner rather than later. I have a child to see into the world and I would be here for the birth."

My wife had organised a feast for me. Dressed in clean and colourful clothes I felt like a new man. William was keen to speak with me about Godwin and then to discover what had happened in the battle. My wife seemed a little quiet and reflective. At the time I put that down to my garrulous son and her pregnancy. When I asked her, she said that the baby was healthy, so far as the women who knew such things could discern, and all would be well.

"I confess, husband, that the slave you brought, Popæg, has proved to be a gift from God. She is a little rough and uncouth and she cannot speak our language well yet but she knows babies and children. Sprota is teaching her our words for she will be able to take much of the work from her shoulders."

"I am pleased." The Norns had spun well. I had not known when I had sought slaves that I would find one to satisfy my wife. I promised myself that when I returned from this raid I would speak at length with this mighty matriarch.

Before I went to see Padraig and Godwin I needed to see my shipwrights and captains. Erik Leifsson and Gandálfr were already at their ships. Neither had been needed for a couple of months and both captains had ensured that their ships were well maintained. My lieutenant had given them the barest details of our raid. "Padraig has new maps. I will have him make you copies. We will not be at sea for long. We destroy the Danes and then sail along the Breton coast so that the two of you know where we could land."

"We invade?"

I was wary. I trusted my two captains but there were others in the shipyard who might be spies. "We raid. King Alan thinks that he has hurt us. We will raid his ships and his ports. He will become weaker and we will be richer! There may be spies in the port. If any ask questions then tell them we return to Wessex to make more profit." There had been much speculation about the papers I had brought back. "Tell any who ask that the papers told us where there was a great treasure to be found." I counted on the fact that the Franks, Bretons and Saxons would believe that gold held the greatest sway over our hearts.

They were satisfied with that. I left them and went to speak with Padraig. Egil had already taken William there. Padraig had his own room. It was close to the chapel. He used it for quiet reflection. When I saw Godwin, I could not believe the changes which had been wrought. Although his face was still scarred he was able to open his eyes. Padraig had given him a straw hat with a brim as his eyes were still sensitive to light. As I entered I heard the three youngsters all laughing. Padraig winked. The priest had the ability to conjure and it always impressed the young. When he saw me, Godwin started a little and stopped laughing. To him, I was still the enemy. I was the one person in the room he had little contact with. I had a battle to win. I began by smiling.

William said, "Padraig is a wizard! He can make coins appear from my ears! We will be rich for he can produce many such coins!"

I saw now why they were all laughing. "An excellent idea but we would not wish to use all of Padraig's power, would we?"

My son nodded seriously. He opened his hand to look at the coins.

"Godwin, I am pleased that you are healed."

"Thank you, lord. You gave me a life and Brother Padraig gave me a life which was worth living."

I looked at him. I was not able to have true eye contact with him as he could lower his brim and hide his eyes. I wanted him to see my eyes and the truth within them. "And now you have a choice to make. We have healed you. Would you leave us and make your own way in the world or would you join the Clan of the Horse?"

To William, it was an easy question to answer. He would stay with us but Egil knew the dilemma in Godwin's mind. Could he desert his oar brothers?

I would not be foresworn in this matter even though it might cost me. "Know you that I intend to hunt down Godfrid. He used treachery to enter one of my towns and took many women and children as slaves. If you joined my clan you might have to fight Godfrid."

He raised his head so that I could see into his red eyes. Padraig had told me that the scarring around the eyes was permanent. "Lord, I was not in Godfrid's crew. I have a complicated story."

"I have time and I would hear it."

"I am neither Frisian nor Dane. I am a Saxon. My village was raided when I was a babe in arms, or so my mother told me. My father and brothers were killed. I was raised in Frisia. My mother worked in the hall of a Frisian chief. I lived there until I had seen five summers. There was a dispute with the Count of that land. The chief was executed for the Count wished for his land. We were sold with others. A Dane who lived in Beodericsworth bought us. The Christians now call it St. Edmund's Bury. The Dane liked my mother and took her as one of his wives. It meant I was treated well and taught how to use a sword. I was not freed you understand. My mother was also retained as a thrall but she was not beaten and she had fine clothes. Two years since his brother was seeking a crew. Ragnar, the hersir who owned me, gave me to his brother. Einar was a good warrior. I liked him. He gave me my freedom a month after we set sail. We raided Wessex. It was after one such raid that we met Godfrid. We were in Dorestad and we were selling our treasures when he asked us if we would raid with him. It made sense for his father ruled Frisia and Einar saw it as a way to become richer. We were a poor crew. None of us had mail."

"Then how did you manage to raid successfully?"

He shrugged, "We were lucky. We never raided burghs but kept to the small villages, hamlets and large farms." He shook his head, "It all changed when Godfrid's father died. Godfrid commanded ten ships then and he tried to avenge his father at Dorestad. He lost four ships there. Two more deserted him. He decided to seek support from the King of the Bretons for he thought that he would fight the Franks. On the voyage south, a storm blew up and we lost another ship. I thought that we had ill luck and ought to turn around. Einar did too but he said he had given his word."

"Alan of Brittany, did he offer support?"

"That was the strange thing. Einar told his crew all. He was in the meeting. He said that Alan of Brittany was not at war with the Franks. It was a ruse but if Godfrid thought to make war then he should sail to Rouen where he would find an ally. Einar was not convinced for he had heard that you were an ally of the Franks. Godfrid gave him a byrnie. It worked. Einar followed him."

I sat back in my seat. Now it all made sense. I wondered at the sudden rage from Godfrid. He had expected me not only to allow him upriver but also to join him.

"Have I said something wrong, lord?"

"No Godwin. I see the Norns at work. Their threads are cleverly bound."

"Godfrid had a plan. He said that Einar and Folki would lead their crews against the gates of your town. He said that we were best suited for we had no mail and we could move quieter and quicker. It made sense. We thought that you kept a poor guard. Einar fell when he led men up the ladder. He landed at the bottom of the ladder. His back was broken. He told his oathsworn that we should save ourselves. We could not win. Then he died. When we tried to get back to our ship it had been taken by Godfrid. He was sailing away. Your men's spears, stones, arrows and darts took a fearful toll. We had no option but to try to sail Godfrid's ship, **'Ghost Dragon'**. She was stuck. Even so, we boarded her and then we were hit by one of your fiery missiles. It bounced before me and scorched my face. I fell overboard. The river was cooling but I must have passed out. When I awoke I was in the shallows and I could not see. I crawled to where you found me. I had lost my sword and my seax. If I had not then I would have taken my own life."

"That would have been a waste, Godwin. You would not have gone to Valhalla."

He waved a hand across his face. "Odin would not have me and besides, Padraig has been telling me about the White Christ. Perhaps his heaven might be a better place for me."

I glared at Padraig who spread his hands, "Lord, you said I could not try to convert your people. All I did with Godwin was give him counsel."

"Words, priest! I thought I could trust you!" I saw William and Egil look anxiously from Padraig to me and back. They were unused to us having heated words.

"And you can. My words have saved a young warrior. Calm down and ask him the question that is in your mind! Then you can dismiss me. Then I will return to my rock in the wild seas west of here." He paused. "Before he was taken he was baptised. The White Christ is beneath his skin and all that is on the surface is a veneer. He was a slave what else could he do?"

I knew that I was being unreasonable and I blamed Æðelwald of Remisgat. I had given orders that no priests could visit him and they had sent a Bishop. I was being laughed at in my own hall and I could do nothing about it. "You are right, priest. Godwin, would you join my crew?"

"Aye lord for I was abandoned. My jarl was used by Godfrid and all of the crew I served alongside are dead. I owe Godfrid nothing. He is a corrupt and evil man. I would have vengeance on him."

"And after?"

He shook his head. "I have too much running through my mind to make such decisions, lord. I was blind and Padraig has saved my sight. Perhaps there is salvation in the White Christ but I will serve you until Godfrid no longer breathes. I will not swear an oath to you but I give you my word that I will do all that I can to fetch you within a sword's length of Godfrid."

I clasped his arm. "And that is all that I can ask. Tell me do you know where Godfrid met the King?"

"Aye. It is a port. It was not Vannes. The King came from Vannes. It was called Nantes. The Romans had been there and there were many waterways around the port. It is a busy port, lord."

"Good. Then you shall join my crew. Go with Egil and chose a helmet, shield and weapons from the armoury." I saw that William wished to be with them and I smiled, "Go with them but you are too young for a sword."

When they had gone Padraig said, "I know you are angry with me lord but the boy was going to take his own life. Jesus' heaven was a hope for him and he grasped it like a straw. If I had not done what I did then he would be dead and you would be no closer to finding this Godfrid. He has told you where to find Godfrid and I have no doubt that you can do great mischief there."

Padraig was not afraid of me. Most men would have quailed and crumbled beneath my gaze but he was willing to take whatever punishment I offered. I smiled, "You are right! Do not try this with any of my warriors."

"Judge me when you have seen how Godwin performs. I think you will be surprised."

Chapter 11

It took two days for us to be ready for sea. I spread the word that Wessex was our target. Many did not believe the story for all had heard of King Alan's attack but there was no proof and as I prevented any man or ship from leaving my port then the news would stay in Rouen. There might still be spies lurking in my town. The three kings were all resourceful men. Ships came and went but they would not sail until after I had left and no one could outsail me! We left at the start of Gormánuður.

My son, William, had wanted to come but that had been out of the question. Over the two days of preparation, I saw how close he was to both Egil and Godwin. Godwin was a surprise. He could speak Saxon, Danish, Frisian and Frank. He also had skills with weapons. He would never be the biggest warrior on the crew and he would struggle to row for as long as some but he was wily and cunning. He had quick hands and knew how to fight. He also had an instinct for survival. His wounds might have killed many men but he had clung tenaciously to life.

Padraig had copied all of the maps for my captains but we knew where we were sailing. We knew as much about the coast as any sailor. When we returned we would know more! My plan was to sail west until we were beyond Angia and Sarnia. Then we would sail due south. We would approach Nantes and Vannes from the south and west. That way I hoped we would achieve complete surprise. Vannes lay to the north of Nantes and the river on which it lay, the Liger. Vannes lay in a small bay with an incredibly narrow entrance. Godwin had told me, although I already knew, that the Bretons had two watchtowers on the headlands. A ship might sneak in unseen but it was impossible to get out without a fight. Godwin had been able to describe what we would see very accurately. Padraig said that was because he had been blind for a time and forced to make pictures in his head. He had spent hours of darkness remembering and the things he remembered the last were the freshest. That served us for we knew what we would find when we entered the dragon's lair. *Wyrd*.

I told Poppa and Padraig that we would easily be back before Ýlir. It was a month away but the Norns had spun and one never knew. In many ways, my dream had prepared me for the fact that the unborn child in my wife's womb might well be a girl. I did not mind so long as she was born healthy. As Rouen receded in the east I found myself regretting not doing something about Æðelwald of Remisgat. I knew he was a spy and that he was working against me. Perhaps he always had. We had blamed the curse for our bad luck but thinking back it all began when Æðelwald of Remisgat came to my grandfather. We had all made the mistake of thinking him ineffectual because he was a priest. We had been wrong to do so. I comforted myself with the thought that I might only be away for fourteen nights or so.

I immersed myself in my drekar. I had fewer oathsworn this time and more men who were not known to me. But warriors such as Pai Skutalsson, Habor Nokkesson, Thiok Clawusson, Magnús Magnússon and Óðalríkr Odhensson had chosen to follow me and all were warriors who could be oathsworn. We did not row down the river. There had been rains upstream and the river was in full spate. We had a fast voyage to the river mouth. *'Wolf's Snout'* followed us. Gandálfr had even more men he did not know. Despite my secrecy and purported target older, wiser warriors knew our true target. The attack on my walls and the disasters we had suffered against the Bretons meant that many men were drawn to sail with us because they feared that if they did not then their world might come to an end. There were warriors who had thought they had given up the sea but now knew we had to fight for our land. I knew not if spies watched from the two headlands at the river's mouth but it made little difference. We sailed due west. We had little choice. The wind was from the south and east. Perhaps Odin was sending us a wind to fool our foes. It was getting on to dark and so I went to the steering board and curled up. All of my problems were now on the land. At sea, I had other problems. I trusted Erik and I trusted his ship's boys. I slept.

When I woke it was to a wet and grey world. It was raining. During the night someone had covered me with an old piece of sail. Even so, my hair and beard were wet. I stood and saw that there were two other, larger pieces of old sail. One was forward of the mast fish and the other aft. Men were huddled together underneath them. The weather was an ally.

Visibility would be limited. We could even risk sailing closer to Angia and Sarnia. I would not, of course. My plan was a good one and I would not change it. We would sail west until nightfall and then turn due south. We would slow at that point but there would be no danger of hitting any land. The lack of sun and stars would make finding our exact position more difficult but even Erik was familiar with the waters around the Cotentin and Brittany. We just had to recognise one piece of coast and we would know our exact position.

The rain and the wind made the sea rougher than we had had of late. I glanced astern and saw that Gandálfr had closed up with us. He did not want to lose us in the murk. I took the piece of bread Godwin offered me and the horn of ale from Egil. The two had formed a bond and attached themselves to me. Godwin was a little fearful of some of my men. He was uncertain if his attack on Rouen might have coloured their judgement. He need not have worried. Once a man joined my crew he became as one with them.

Godwin pointed east, "Godfrid was not a confident captain. He did not like to sail out of sight of land. He would not have sailed in these conditions."

I nodded, "If you have any more information about your former leader then let me know."

"He was never my leader. I followed Einar and he followed Godfrid."

Over the years I had seen many crews like Einar's. Often, they sailed the smallest of drekar. Sometimes that might only have six oars on each side. If they were to raid successfully then they needed to sail in the company of larger warships and that meant taking orders. Sometimes that worked out but at others, it could spell disaster.

"When you are in port how many of the crew sleep aboard?"

He grinned. I knew that when he did so it hurt his face for his skin was still red and cracked and smiling still made him wince. Padraig had given him a salve. The saltwater would aggravate the pain. If he grinned then it meant he was genuinely happy about something. "The ones who upset the captain. There were some, like his oathsworn, who would never have to do a duty. I knew some of the ones he did not like. They rarely saw a port. Karl the Wanderer was one of those. He said he did not mind for it meant he never spent coin. He confided in me once that when he had enough coin he would leave Godfrid and find a fairer captain."

I was getting a good picture of this captain. He was the antithesis of the best captains I had known. If anything, he seemed quite similar to the snake of a brother who had usurped my land and helped to destroy our clan. A small watch meant I would not have to use many men to take his ship. In addition, they would likely be men with no real attachment to either the ship or the captain. What I planned was risky. We would be going ashore to kill Godfrid and Beorn Straight Hair in Nantes itself. The fact that King Alan would not be there gave us an advantage. Perhaps it was deliberate. He might use the Danes but he would not want them close where they could slit his throat.

"And how many crewmen did he have?"

"That is harder for me to answer lord. He stole our ship. His, the **'Ghost Dragon'**, had twenty-four oars on each side and ours, **'Wave Skimmer'**, just sixteen. I do not know how many of his warriors survived. At the most, it would be a hundred men for I saw some die but there might have been others who survived the attack and were taken aboard." He shrugged, "Perhaps even some of our crew, the watch we left on board."

After speaking at length with Godwin I had a much better idea of the layout of the port of Nantes and my decision to use Nantes would be vindicated. Vannes was both older and better defended. Vannes had a narrow entrance and could be better guarded. A couple of islands added to the defence. Nantes lay on the river and all of the wharves and quays lay on the northern bank. The land was lower-lying and there was a network of smaller streams and rivers feeding into it. There was, as yet, no wall around the town. The warehouses, halls and houses melded into one. It was a jumble. That presented certain problems. Our aim was to get to Godfrid and, if he was there, Beorn Straight Hair. Godwin had told us that there were men in Nantes who were the warriors of the lord who ruled Nantes for Alan of Vannes. He was honest with me and told me that he could not give an exact number. We had to get into the port unseen. I needed to disable **'Wave Skimmer'** and then find Godfrid. I would have to use Godwin like a hound.

As we ploughed west Magnús Magnússon came to see me. He had been a mighty warrior who loved war until he met a young Frank from a village north of Rouen. Now he seemed content to farm. Or so I had thought until he had volunteered to come with me. I believed he was one who had chosen to sail one more voyage to save the life he had built. He now had two children. He was rich. He had been one of the most successful warriors who had followed me and even before he was wed he had not spent all his coin on warrior frivolity. He had bought well. His thralls were the best and he paid overseers to run the farm. When his last child, a son had been born, he realised that he would not have many more opportunities to go to war. He was ageing. Unlike many warriors, he did not have a death wish. He wanted to live to mould his son into a warrior.

"Lord, I know that you have a plan in your head for that is your way. I am unsure how many more raids I have left in me. I would know how we fight."

My men were used to speaking to me thus and I nodded, "Getting in should be easy enough. We step the mast and we row up the river at night. From what Godwin says the Bretons regard Nantes as a safe port. They have neither tower nor wall. Godwin does not remember a night watch."

"But there may be one."

"Aye, Magnús Magnússon, I will assume there is one. Gandálfr and his crew will take and hold the wharf. We will enter the town. We have a big crew. There are sixty of us and half are mailed. Godfrid will be in the best hall in the town. We find it."

"That is the plan, lord?"

"We may have to fight the local watch and the lord but I do not think they will be expecting this." I lowered my voice. "We have spies in Rouen. The enemy leaders have planted spies in the towns of my lords. I have left quickly so that word cannot get out to King Alan or Godfrid or any of the other enemies who seek to destroy us."

"Then this raid is the beginning?"

"It is. I hope that we will be successful. I hear the Norns spinning and I am not foolish enough to say that we will win but if we survive then when we sail home we sail close to their coast. We look for landing sites for come the new grass we will return and hurt the Bretons so much that they do not even consider going to war with the Vikings again."

He smiled, "Then I have returned at the right time. I still have hair which has not seen the frost. My eyes are sharp and my arm is strong. This mail and helmet are the best that I have ever owned. My boy is too young to learn of war yet. I will have one last, long bloodletting and then, when our enemies are defeated I can hang up my sword and become a fat farmer. I will tell my son of all that we did and I will make him a warrior to follow William Long Sword."

"When we have defeated the Bretons, we war against the Franks."

He laughed, "I knew that before I set foot on this drekar." I cocked my head to one side. "I live not far from Franks. I have spoken with them.

They resent our presence on their land. The defeat of Saxbjǫrn was greeted as though it was a Frankish victory. They thought it heralded the beginning of the end of Viking rule. I knew differently. I have fought alongside you, lord, and I know that you do not give up easily. When your brother tried to kill you and you were reborn it was as though the gods themselves had changed you. We will prevail." He smiled, "But that did not stop me from digging a ditch around my hall and placing my hall on a mound with a wall around it. I came to serve you but I have six bondi at my hall to guard it. When this is all over I will hire another six. What I have I hold and keep!"

Over the next two days, as we headed first west and then north, others confided in me. Many had thought, as I had, that the end of the siege of Paris meant we had secured our foothold on this land. Like me, they now saw that was an illusion. They wanted to keep the land and knew that it would entail the spilling of blood. They knew that warriors would die. The difference was that these were the warriors who had followed me as young men and now had families. They were ensuring the future for those families.

Even when we turned north we did not have to row. The weather was still foul but the wind, from the south and east, still powered us. We travelled more slowly but soon we would have to turn and that would mean rowing. Each mile north meant less rowing for the men. On the third day out of Rouen Lars woke me, "Lord, the captain said it is time to turn. We have passed Ushant and the tide race speeds us along. We can now turn and sail into the wind."

I nodded. I made water and then, cupping my hands shouted, "It is time for us to begin to earn our passage. Make water, eat and drink; today we row."

The men were quite happy to row and there was none of the grumbling you found in a weak crew. From what Godwin had told me Godfrid rarely had his men row. Many complained. That showed him to be a weak leader. My men knew that I would take an oar too.

Despite his recent wound, Harold Strong Arm had insisted upon sailing with us. He would not land at Nantes. He was a true warrior and knew that he might not be able to keep up with us and a shield wall could have no weak links. He would guard the drekar. He could, however, row. "Well, lord, we will see if '*Wolf's Snout's*' crew is as good as we are."

There was a healthy rivalry between the crews and the captains. If my men sailed in Gandálfr's ship they would swear it was the best of ships. They were loyal to each other and the vessel in which they sailed.

"Aye Harold but it will be a hard row. We will be at the oars all day."

"Good! It will strengthen my sword arm!"

All the crew would begin to row while we stepped the mast and turned into the wind. We had an hourglass which my grandfather had bought, at great expense, when he had sailed the seas seeking me. After an hour half of the crew would rest. An hour later and they would replace the other half of the crew. There would then be two-hour stints at the oars. If Erik had calculated correctly then we would be off the mouth of the Liger when darkness fell. We would sail through the small islands at dusk. With luck, we would not be seen. Drekar with stepped masts were almost invisible. It would take three hours to row up the river to Nantes and we would arrive, with luck, two hours before dawn. Saxons I had spoken to did not know how Vikings could row so far and then fight a battle. That was because we were Vikings. The hard row would merely prepare us.

Egil and Godwin would both row but they would be close to the bow where their lack of experience would not hurt us. They were both paired with more experienced rowers. We took our oars. Erik waited until we were all in position and then shouted, "Run out the oars!"

I shared an oar with Haaken the Bold and we ran the oar out until it was parallel with the sea. The ship's boys began to furl the sail.

"Row!"

I began the chant. We would only sing until we had way upon her.

The night was black no moon was there
Death and danger hung in the air
As Raven Wing closed with the shore
The scouts crept closer as before
Dressed like death with sharpened blades
They moved like spirits through the glades
The power of the raven grows and grows
The power of the raven grows and grows
With sentries slain they sought new foes
A cry in the night fetched them woes
The alarm was given the warriors ready
Four scouts therewith hearts so steady
Ulf and Arne thought their end was nigh
When Hrolf the wild leapt from the sky

Flying like the raven through the air
He felled the Cymri, a raven slayer
The power of the raven grows and grows
The power of the raven grows and grows
His courage clear he still fought on
Until the clan had battled and won
The power of the raven grows and grows
The power of the raven grows and grows
Raven Wing Goes to war
Hear our voices hear them roar
A song of death to all its foes
The power of the raven grows and grows.
The power of the raven grows and grows.
The power of the raven grows and grows.

The crew liked the song of my grandfather and soon we had a healthy sweat. Erik turned us into the wind but we just kept the same pace with the oars. After an hour Erik shouted, "Step the mast!"

Haaken the Bold and half of the crew rose and left the other half of us to row. They went to the mast and unshipped it then stored it on the mast fish. They had an hour to rest and drink before they relieved us. As we rowed I saw that the sky was no longer totally grey. There were patches of blue. The weather was changing.

We had stopped singing and I was enjoying the simple rhythm of rowing. I watched my men working as a team to bring down the mast and secure it. We would now be invisible until we reached Nantes. We would raise the mast before we left but until then we would be low to the water. I had heard of sailors who had spoken of seeing sea monsters. I am not saying there are no sea monsters for the seas are wide and I have not yet crossed the great ocean but the ones they saw were drekar. Our dragon prow rose on crests and fell in troughs. To a simple sailor, it would be a sea monster. Their work finished Haaken and the others made water and ate. The ship's boys had little to do and so they ran out lines for fish. With luck when we were relieved there would be freshly caught fish. The silver magpies of the sea, with their almost purple flesh, were delicious eaten within an hour of catching. The rest would be salted and air-dried. We would not starve on such a short voyage.

When I saw Lars turn the hourglass I knew that my shift was almost up. I had rowed for two hours and I felt it. Egil and Godwin would be in an even worse state. Haaken came down the centreboard and stood behind me. He slid on the bench next to me and put his hands on the oar. "Ready, lord." I slipped out and stood up. The changeover was seamless but then we were very experienced. Some of those by the prow were not as smooth and I heard the clatter of oars. We would be slowed, albeit briefly until the men had the rhythm again. There was a bucket of seawater by the mast fish and I dipped and held my hands in the salty water. There would be a salve for those like Egil and Godwin but for older hands like mine seawater was effective. It cooled and it helped to cleanse any cracks in the skin. I would apply some seal oil after I had eaten. Before I began to row again I would wipe my hands on my cloak. It would help to make the cloak resistant to water and prevent my hands from slipping on the oars. The new men would need to learn such routines. I ate quickly. Harold Strong Arm and I were the first at the water and we were applying the seal oil when Egil and Godwin appeared. Their hands were bloody.

Harold shook his head, "Foolish warriors. Here wash them in the saltwater." I saw them both wince when the saltwater hit the raw flesh. Harold was like a mother as he gently dried the hands.

I fetched the precious salve we used. "Hold out your hands." I smeared the salve on them and then took some of the cloth we kept for new rowers. I wrapped their hands in the cloth. "You should have wrapped cloth around your palms before you rowed."

Egil said, "I thought my hands were hard enough, lord."

"You will need many more voyages before they become the leather that is our hands. After you have eaten then wrap more cloth around them and lie down." Egil cocked his head to one side. "Until you are used to it your back will ache. Lying on the wooden deck helps."

They nodded and Godwin said, "We do this all day?"

"All day."

"Godfrid's crew rarely rowed."

That was more information which would help. The endurance of a long row prepared a warrior for a long fight in a shield wall. The repetition of the oar was replicated in the rhythm of sword and shield. Blade to blade my men would win even against Vikings.

"The wind is shifting, lord. I do not think we need to rig the mast again for by the time it has turned we will be close to the coast and I know you would have us hidden." I nodded. "The wind will make the rowing easier and give us a swifter passage."

"Good."

The break from rowing seemed to fly by. I saw the sand almost ready to run out and so I went back to relieve Haaken. He gave me a rueful smile, "Is it my imagination, lord, or was this not easier when we were younger?"

"I do not think that this was ever easy, Haaken. If it is any consolation then Erik thinks it will be easier toward the end."

"I hope so but however long it lasts these Danes will suffer for the pain they have caused me!"

For the next few hours, I endured the monotony of the row east. I used it to plan how I would defeat King Charles. I had been duped. I now knew that. He had given us peace so that he could build a conspiracy and defeat me. That gave me hope. If he was a warrior he would have crushed me. He did not think that he could crush me. We had honoured his borders and protected his rivers. When we had defeated King Alan, in the spring, we would then begin to build up our numbers to defeat King Charles. I would send emissaries to those lords I knew I could trust. The Clan of the Wolf sprang to mind. I would invite them to send ships to Rouen. I would not give them the reason but until I could look them in the eye I would not be able to trust them.

When I finished my last session at the oars the coast was in view. It was a smudge. This time those who had mail donned it. When we were in the river we would relieve the others so that they could prepare for battle and then we would be the ones who would land first. Unlike the others, I would not take my shield. I would use Long Sword two handed. Hrolf's Vengeance would be ready at my waist in case it was needed. With two seaxes, one in my belt and one in my boot, I was ready. Some men either darkened or reddened their eyes. Some bantered with Godwin that with his red eyes he already had terror etched by the Norns. It was then that he began to be called Godwin Red Eyes. I was not sure how he would take the name but when I saw Egil speaking quietly to him I knew that it would be alright. It was not an insult it was a statement of fact. It was also a badge of honour. That he had survived such an injury impressed those older warriors like Harold Strong Arm. Harold had been a warrior who had served with my father. One of the few to have survived the Danish treachery and the time of my brother he was the most experienced man left from the time of the Haugr. When he died he would not be replaced easily. He was made of rock. His wound had slowed him and as he was no longer a young man I wondered if it might end his time as hearth weru.

I ate and I drank and then I spoke with Erik, "From what Godwin tells me we do not need to turn the drekar around until we leave. It will take you and Harold, along with the ship's boys, time to step the mast."

"I know, lord. The boys know what they are doing but it will help that we have a strong warrior like Harold Strong Arm to aid us."

"Perhaps that is the work of the Norns. Had he not lost the leg or not been wounded then it would have been the ship's boys alone who performed the task."

We were sailing into the dark of dusk and so we needed two pairs of eyes in the prow. Once the mouth of the river had been without people but since we had begun to raid and with the arrival of so many people there were now farms on the hillsides and boats drawn up on the beaches. One day they would build a tower. Sven Blue Cheek had already done so at the mouth of the Orne. It would light a signal fire to alert him of danger. As we sailed through the sea like estuary it made no difference if we were seen. We would travel faster than any messenger sent to warn Nantes that the Vikings were coming.

I relieved Haaken who quickly donned his mail, ate drank and made water. He relieved me before any of the others. He was oathsworn and he knew that I had to be the first ashore. I would have hearth weru around me when I landed. Haaken and the others would join them as soon as the ship was secure.

I went to the prow where Lars was watching for sandbanks, shoals and rocks. Egil and Godwin were there. "Egil Flame Bearer, today you have no standard but you will need to guard Godwin."

The Saxon shook his head, "I need no protection. I am a warrior."

I hardened my voice, "And you know Godfrid. Until he is ours you and Egil stay just behind me. I do not want to have to shout for you. I want you close enough to hear me whisper."

"Aye lord."

Godwin had told us that there was an island in the middle of the river. They had not fortified it. It would be a good marker. It would warn us that we were close. Egil had sharp eyes. Perhaps Lars was looking down at the water. "Lord I see the island."

"Well done Egil. Go and tell the captain and warn the crew."

There was an excited buzz of conversation as Egil passed the word. I heard the sealskin boots of my men as they tramped up the drekar. I had arranged it so that the men who landed with me were the more experienced half of the crew. Haaken the Bold would lead the other half for me. Æbbi Bonecrusher was the first to arrive, along with six of the hearth weru. Haaken had just one with him and Harold would be staying aboard. Pai Skutalsson, Habor Nokkesson, Thiok Clawusson, Magnús Magnússon and Óðalríkr Odhensson were close behind. They had retrieved their shields from the side of the drekar. I saw the less experienced men watch them hang the shields from their backs. They emulated them. The mail they wore and the scars they bore were testimony to their experience. The younger ones would learn from that.

I could now smell the land. It was the smell of animal and human waste. It was the smell of wood burning. It was the smell of cows and animals. There was also the noise of the town. We had just the creak of the oars and the swish of the bow wave but the land had the sounds of dogs barking. Cows lowing. There were still men drinking or whoring for an occasional cry came from ahead. It was reassuring that none reacted. Godwin had told us that the Dane was the pampered son of a Count. I had hoped that Beorn Straight Hair had not given him discipline and it appeared that he had not. There were no men watching his drekar. We saw the Danish drekar, *'Wave Skimmer'*. She was in the centre of a line of smaller ships.

"Egil, tell the captain to lay us alongside the drekar. We will board over her." If Godwin was correct then the men left on watch aboard the drekar would not be doing their job diligently. A prisoner might tell us where Godfrid was.

The sleeping crew would be alerted when we neared as we would have to order the larboard oars to be run in. There was no way of avoiding that. I pulled myself up onto the larboard side of the ship. I did not have a weapon in my hand. I held on to the forward stay and balanced. On a river, this was easier than when we boarded at sea. There was less motion. I heard an order which seemed to ripple down the drekar, "In larboard oars." That half of the rowers would stack their oars and be ready to follow us quickly. On the second drekar, Gandálfr would choose where he landed. I saw two large knarr tied up close to *'Wave Skimmer'*. With a lower freeboard, they would be boarded easier than the drekar.

Even as we closed with the drekar I saw a face appear from the deck. We were close enough for my long legs to take me and I leapt across the gap. My left foot landed on the gunwale and my right connected with the sentry's face. He fell backwards. The bump of our hull and the sound of a giant landing on the deck woke the other five men but it was too late for them. Æbbi and my hearth weru closely followed by Thiok Clawusson, Magnús Magnússon and Óðalríkr Odhensson ended their lives.

The man I had hit was coming to. I reached down and picked him up, "Do you want to live?" He nodded. "Then where is Godfrid?"

Godwin had been right. Godwin's crew had little loyalty for their lord. The sentry pointed, "He is in the large hall just up the hill. There is a square close by."

Harold Strong Arm appeared on the larboard side of my drekar. I thrust the Dane toward him, "Here, he can help you raise the mast. Then let him go."

The man looked terrified, "Where lord?"

"I said I would give you your life. I did not say I would give you a life! Run, find a hole in which to hide! I care not!"

Already my men were pouring down the gangplank. Although there had been noise it appeared not to have disturbed any others in the port. I raced down the gangplank and said to Æbbi, "Head to the square. He is in the hall there." In my eagerness to discover the whereabouts of Godfrid I had forgotten to ask about Beorn Straight Hair. I hoped he was here too. Once again, my long legs meant that men struggled to keep up with me.

"Aye lord."

I turned to Godwin, "Where is the square?" He pointed to a wider road between an alehouse and a warehouse. I drew Long Sword and turned up the cobbled street.

The town's folk had now heard the noise and doors opened as people looked out. The cry, "Vikings!" rang out. It was obvious that we were not Godfrid's Danes. Some of the cries turned to screams and shouts as my men killed the men.

The door to the hall opened as we entered the square. Men began to pour out. Some wore mail others were just in the clothes the Danes had slept in. I did not falter. I held my sword above and behind me. I began to swing it as I approached the five Danes who ran at me. The two on my right had no helmets and when my sword sliced down it hacked through one skull and into the neck of the second. A spear rammed into my mail. Egil and Godwin were, as I had asked, behind me and Æbbi was next to me. The three Danes all died for their weapons had been aimed at me and my men slew them quickly. Egil and Godwin might be inexperienced but even they could kill an experienced warrior who did not defend himself. The men who poured forth had just heard the noise and rushed out. They came at us one by one. My oathsworn and most experienced warriors had joined me. We had not made a shield wall but we were in a solid line and we hacked, hewed, stabbed and slashed at the Danes who ran at us. When the remainder began to form a shield wall I raised my bloody sword and shouted, "Godfrid of Frisia, I am Göngu-Hrólfr Rognvaldson come to end your worthless life! You are a treacherous coward and you will now pay for your crimes!"

The Danish leader burst out of the hall. He wore a byrnie and an open face helmet. He had a Frankish axe in his hand. "I am not afraid of you Göngu-Hrólfr Rognvaldson! You are a lumbering troll whom I will hew down to size!"

He and his oathsworn ran at me. This would be a test of his men and mine. I could not fight all of them alone. My oathsworn were to my right and Pai Skutalsson, Habor Nokkesson, Thiok Clawusson, Magnús Magnússon and Óðalríkr Odhensson on my left. Egil and Godwin had heeded my words and were behind me. I heard a horse and a rider gallop from the side of the hall. I had no time to speculate. He could be someone fleeing or someone seeking help. We had to kill the Danes first and then worry about reinforcements.

The Danes advanced. They had the slope with them and we had both rowed and fought. In theory, they should have been fresher. I could smell the ale on them. Some were still drunk. That did not mean that the warrior would be easier to defeat for a drunk could be like a berserker. He could fight on with the most terrible of wounds. However, a drunk had slower reflexes.

Godfrid saw that I was not using my shield. I watched him pull back his arm. He had either forgotten or did not know that I had a longer sword than any other warrior. The axe never reached me for Long Sword smashed into his shield and made him reel. One of his oathsworn saw that my right side was unprotected. He lunged at me. Magnús' sword stabbed him under the ribs and his sword came out through the Dane's neck. With such men around me, I could fight without fear knowing that both sides of me were protected. Instead of bringing my sword back over my right shoulder, I allowed it to continue the swing and then used a backhand blow. Godfrid could not have fought someone with a long sword before for he came at me again, swinging his axe. My backhanded blow hit his axe handle and sheared it in two. The head flew in the air and clattered off a Danish helmet.

Godfrid's open helmet meant that I could see his face and I saw fear spread across it. He drew his sword. I swung at his shield again and this time he was ready. He did not reel but I saw him wince at the power of the blow. There was a crack as my blade hit the willow. He should have struck at me with his sword but the blow had hurt him and he stepped back. I used a backhand blow to strike at his sword. He blocked it and sparks flew as the blades rang together. He stepped back again. I saw him ready for a blow to his shield but, instead, I swung at his sword. He was not ready for it and he stumbled to his left. I have long legs and, as he fell backwards, I stamped hard with the heel of my boot on his knee. He gave a scream, like a vixen in the night and he completed his fall backwards. His sword fell from his hand.

I brought my sword over and hit, first his head and then his prostrate body. It was a quicker death than he deserved. "This is for the people of the Haugr. You will wander the seas crying to be free!"

"Killer!"

I whirled as one of Godfrid's oathsworn launched himself at me. Had he not shouted then his sword might have connected. As it was I whipped my sword around and almost cut his body in two. My own warriors redoubled their efforts as they butchered the last of the Danes.

By the time dawn came up all of the Bretons in the port had finally fled. With the wharf and all of the ships there in our possession, as well as the houses, we began to strip the town of all that it contained. There was so much that we would need another ship. We loaded *'Wave Skimmer'*. Harold Strong Arm told us, as we sailed home, that Godfrid had renamed her *'Ghost Dragon'*. All Vikings knew that you did not rename ships. It made them cursed. Godfrid and his men had paid the price for their foolishness. As the houses and churches were emptied they were fired. The flames soon spread and, by the time we were ready to sail they had reached the wharf. We had no need to wreck the ships there; the fire would destroy them and the wharf! The Haugr was avenged but as Beorn Straight Hair had escaped us Carentan, Saint-Lô, Nefgeirr and Halfi Axe Tongue remained unavenged.

The wind had come around to blow from a more southerly direction. With sails billowing, we would be able to sail home without rowing. Harold Strong Arm captained *'Wave Skimmer'*. We had lost warriors in the battle of Nantes and it meant we had fewer crewmen on each drekar but as we would not need to row it did not matter. I told Harold and Gandálfr that we would be sailing as close to the coast as we dared. We had had our vengeance and now we needed to scout out our enemy. We would be returning when the new grass came and we would bring a veritable fleet to punish the Bretons. Most of the men rested as we headed down the river. There were wounds to heal and stories to be told. Our people did not write things down. We told them. The voyage home would be the time to speak of the valour of warriors and their deaths. Men would begin to refine their stories into sagas and songs. I stood at the prow listening to the songs and stories while watching the coast slip by.

We had charts and maps which identified the ports and settlements but I needed to find places which were close by where we could land and then attack them. Vannes would be too strongly defended. I saw that as we passed the narrow bay. It was ten miles wide by eight miles deep but the entrance was a bare eight hundred paces across. Once inside the tower guarded entrance any attacking drekar would have to negotiate a myriad of islands and rocks. By the time a fleet arrived, then the walls would be manned and chains pulled across to trap drekar within.

There were inlets close to Vannes but I dismissed them for we needed to be deep inland with a land we could ravage. That would be the only way we could draw out King Alan. We passed the entrance to the River Blavet. I knew that upstream was a town which also served as a port. The port was some seven miles upstream. We could attack there and do so knowing that we could escape. I stored that information.

As we turned west to sail around Finisterre I saw that the land there was not suitable for an attack. Rocks like savage teeth guarded it. We spied fishing boats fleeing upstream at the westernmost part of the Breton land. There had to be a port there and that, too, could be raided. Finally, as we turned north to sail toward the Seine I saw the familiar coastline between Saint-Brieg and Mont St. Michel. When the sun began to dip in the west I knew that I had seen enough. I headed back to the steering board. My men were, largely, asleep.

Egil and Godwin were by the mast fish speaking. They looked up guiltily as I passed. Egil said, a little too eagerly, "Have you decided, Lord Göngu-Hrólfr? Do you know where we will attack?"

"I think so. I need to look again at the parchments we found in the Breton camp. The River Blavet looks like a good place to land and we can entice King Alan away from his fortress walls. I shall speak with

Duke of Normandy

Padraig." They exchanged a guilty look, "Come, Egil, I will have no secrets from you. You did take an oath. Godwin has yet to do so. Speak!"

I must have spoken loudly for a couple of men sleeping nearby shifted. "Come to the prow and I will know that which is in your hearts."

At the prow, Godwin looked at Egil who nodded. "Lord, you have been good to me. I came to hurt you and you saved my life and Padraig saved my eyes. I owe you but I have a secret in my heart that I am fearful to mention. I would incur neither your wrath nor your displeasure."

I spoke quietly, "A warrior who speaks the truth, from his heart, has nothing to fear. If I do not like the words you speak that will have nothing to do with you if you speak the truth."

He nodded, "It is the truth, lord, that I swear. I wish it were not but it is. Now that Godfrid is gone and the crew I sailed with are dead then I am your man and I would swear an oath but I cannot swear an oath while I have kept a secret from you."

I smiled. He had an honesty about him which was refreshing. "Speak Godwin. Nothing you can say will make me think worse of you."

He took a deep breath. "When I was recovering and could not see I stayed in your hall at Brother Padraig's cell. He is a good man and ministered to me well but he had other calls upon his time. Often, I was left alone. I did not sleep at normal times. Sometimes the potion he gave me to sleep would wear off and I woke. When I began to be able to make out shapes I decided to avoid waking him. I discovered where I could make water or find a jug of ale." He smiled. "It helped me to recover for I was not helpless. I did not tell Padraig. I saw things for people assumed I was still blind. I saw Popæg when she went to William. He had woken crying and she sang him to sleep. I saw the guards who did not walk the walls and sometimes slept in the corner of the tower."

"If that is the news you have to tell me then I already know those who do such things. Although I confess I did not know of Popæg's care for my son."

Egil nodded, "She cares for him more than Sprota lord. Sprota has a young merchant from the town who pays her much attention."

I was learning about my own home. Perhaps it took a half-blind man to see that which I could not. "Godwin, do not dance around your news. Tell me!"

He seemed to hold his breath and then he burst out, "I saw Æðelwald of Remisgat enter your wife's chamber and they embraced." He paused. "I saw him come from her chamber in the morning." I was stunned. "It was when you were raiding, lord." I saw his red, scarred and now scared eyes staring at me. There was no lie there but he was terrified that the truth might result in his death.

"Perhaps your eyes deceived you."

"This was when my eyes were almost healed and I know what the priest looks like." He shook his head. "After the first time I watched and each night he went and each morning he left. I would have told Padraig but he is a priest and I thought that they might be friends."

I knew that what he spoke was true. He was not lying. It was not in his eyes and many events now took on a new meaning. No wonder I had been shunned from her bed. She had stopped worrying about William. Sprota had allowed another to care for my son. Then a thought struck me like a fist in the stomach. Was the child my wife was carrying mine? If it was born in Ýlir then there was a chance that it could have been mine but Gormánuður meant that it was the priest's. I turned to Godwin, "I believe you. The two of you must keep this news to yourselves. Godwin, you can swear an oath to me and I would have you do so now on Long Sword. If you are oathsworn then you cannot tell another." I took out the sword and held it by the blade.

He grasped the hilt, "I swear to Lord Göngu-Hrólfr Rognvaldson that I will be your man. I will give my life for you."

I nodded. "Now rest, I have much to think about."

Chapter 12

The night helped my black mood. I now wondered if Poppa had ever truly cared for me. Had I been a way for her to be lady until something else came along? Æðelwald of Remisgat had made it quite clear that he wished my land to be Christian. Poppa also wished the same. That I understood but to couple! In my hall! I realised that I was losing my temper and so I walked the deck. I had the power of life and death over both of them. King Charles the Fat might object but I now had evidence that he was conspiring against me too. I owed him nothing. The problem was William. How would he view my actions? I did not sleep but walked my deck until dawn came. I saw the estuary in the distance. I needed proof. I believed Godwin but there were Christians in my land who might disapprove of any action I took without proof. It took until we reached the estuary at noon for me to formulate my plan. I knew that we would have to row up the river. It was ever thus. There were too many loops for us to carry the wind.

I spoke with Erik. "I would have us reach Rouen at midnight."

He frowned. "The men are rowing well and we can make it sooner."

"The men have rowed hard enough. But I wish you to land me and some men at Bardouville. I will ride home and warn the families of our late arrival." I knew there was a hersir at Bardouville. He would have horses and the journey over land would take an hour or so at the most. I would be there long before the arrival of my drekar.

He shrugged, "It does not bother me and it is good that you think of your men."

I hated being so deceitful but until I had proof I had no choice. I sought out Æbbi Bonecrusher. "I intend to leave the ship at Bardouville. Choose two of my hearth weru and yourself. We will ride with Egil and Godwin."

He frowned. "Is anything amiss, lord?"

"Perhaps but I will say nothing until we reach Rouen. I need good men who can be relied upon."

"Then that is any of your hearth weru!"

"You choose."

I went to the prow and stared east. Was this the curse which Æðelwald of Remisgat had brought upon my family? My grandfather and I had thought that a spell would end it. Now I saw that it needed blood and blood it would have.

Heading up the Seine could be tortuous. We had the sail rigged but the ship's boys were up and down so frequently that they risked rope burns. The men had to row. It was not hard rowing but there were fewer in each ship now. I took a turn at the oar. It helped me to expunge some of my anger. When I reached my hall then I needed to be cold. What I intended was not to be undertaken lightly.

We reached Bardouville two hours after dark. The oarsmen were happy to stop. "Take all the rest you need. I will tell your families that you will be home soon."

My men cheered and I felt guilty for the deception. There was a wharf at the settlement and although it was dark Audun Fair Hair, the hersir, came to see me.

"Audun I need eight horses."

"Of course, lord."

"I will return them soon."

"Do not worry, lord. Keep them as long as you like. We have plenty."

The road to Rouen ran along the river and we rode hard. The horse was a normal-sized one and my feet almost touched the ground but I cared not. If Godwin was wrong then my wife would still be pregnant and Æðelwald of Remisgat would be in his own cell and far from my wife. I did not believe that for one moment but the thought made my anger less hot. I hoped for an explanation which would allow me to continue to be the husband of Poppa. We rode hard. The roads were dark and they were empty. We reached the west gate of my stronghold.

"Who goes there!"

Æbbi Bonecrusher had been silent all the way from Bardouville. His voice was well known, "It is the lord of Rouen! Open the gate."

While we waited for the gate to open he turned to me, "Lord I am hearth weru and I follow you anywhere but I know not what is happening."

"Æbbi Bonecrusher, you have to trust me. We are going to my chamber for I fear treachery. I cannot fill your head with my thoughts. You have to witness with your own eyes that which I hope is not true. The Norns have been spinning and there is malice in their webs."

He clutched his horse amulet and nodded. "I will be there, lord, to watch you and protect you; even against Skuld!"

We hurried to my hall. When we reached it, I sent for the captain of the guard, Bjorn. "Three drekar will be arriving soon. Watch for them and admit them. None else either leaves or enters Rouen."

"Aye lord. There is news lord. Great news!"

"And I will hear it later." I turned to Æbbi. "I need just you, Egil and Godwin. Have the others wait in the Great Hall until we send for them."

He nodded and spoke to the others. They would stable the horses before they went to the hall. We had ridden without mail and I had left Long Sword on my drekar. For what I needed then Hrolf's Vengeance would have to do. It seemed appropriate as the priest had also betrayed my father and grandfather.

I led my men to Padraig's cell. The priest was not yet asleep. He was reading. He looked up in surprise. "Lord, are you prescient? Have you heard the news?"

My heart sank. It felt like the last nail in Poppa's coffin. "No, I have not." My voice was flat and I saw the surprise on the priest's face.

"Your wife has given birth to a healthy daughter, Gerloc. God is to be praised."

I nodded for I felt numb. "Where is Æðelwald of Remisgat?"

I could see that my words had surprised him, "I am guessing that he will be in his cell, lord."

"And that is close by?"

"Next door. It is silent. He must be asleep."

"Then let us go wake him." I left Padraig's cell and went to the next one. I opened it. We held a burning candle and we saw that the bed had not been slept in. "Let us seek him, eh Padraig? Let us find this priest from Rome!" I nodded to Æbbi who made sure he was behind Padraig. Until I had proof then I could trust no one. As we passed a sconce I said, "Egil, fetch a torch!"

He grabbed one and we ascended to my chamber. As we neared it Padraig murmured, "Lord, is this well done?"

"We shall see, priest. It is good that you healed Godwin and his eyes for he saw that which was under your nose! Do not run or Æbbi will end your life!"

Padraig stood erect, "Whatever you think I have done I had ever been true to you."

"We shall see."

We reached my chamber and I hesitated. Only Godwin and Egil knew what I intended. I turned the handle of the door as though I was raiding a church and wished to enter silently. The room was in darkness but as soon as Egil, with the burning brand, entered it was bathed in light. My daughter was in a crib but in the bed and naked lay Æðelwald of Remisgat and Lady Poppa. They were in each other's arms and they were naked. There was a moment when they slept. Padraig, Godwin and Æbbi Bonecrusher entered and saw them. Padraig made the sign of the cross and Æbbi Bonecrusher's hand went to his sword. I put my hand on his and restrained him. The light woke them and when their eyes opened and they saw us I saw terror in them.

"My lord I was comforting your wife!"

Even now when all was clear he was still dissembling. "Æbbi Bonecrusher, take him hence. Do not allow him to dress. Godwin and Egil go with him. Hold him in the Great Hall. Have one of the hearth weru guard this door."

"Aye, my lord!"

Æbbi Bonecrusher picked up the priest and threw him from the bed. Gerloc woke and cried. The priest stood and came toward me. I backhanded him so hard that he flew across the chamber and his head smacked on the door. Godwin and Egil grabbed him. My wife was weeping. "See to the child. See to the child of a faithless priest!"

I watched Padraig reel as my wife held Gerloc to her breast. He looked at me. I nodded, "You understand numbers. Where was I nine moons since?"

I saw realisation dawn and he made the sign of the cross. "I did not know, lord."

I nodded. "I can see that now but Godwin, the half-blind Saxon, could see and he has opened my eyes to this deception."

My wife gave me that imperious look she had when first we met. "You are a barbarian! I thought I could change you and bring you to God's grace but I can see that was impossible. King Charles the Fat has promised that Æðelwald and I can have sanctuary with him in Paris."

I smiled, "And that will not happen. This is what will happen. Tomorrow my men will escort you and Sprota to the house of nuns by the river. It is right that you go there for you had me build it. As for Æðelwald of Remisgat, he will not live. He will die. He will die if for no other reason that he broke his vows as a priest. I do not believe in the White Christ but I believe in vows!"

She paled, "But my child!"

My voice hardened, "The child is not mine but she will be brought up as though she is. I will find her a wet nurse and she will never know of her mother's sin. The world will never know unless you choose to tell it."

"But Æðelwald?"

"Will be executed by the Lord of Rouen for being a spy and conspiring against me! Or would you have me make your infidelity public knowledge?"

She shook her head and I knew that I had won. She would not wish her infidelity to be common knowledge. I had wanted to kill her but that punishment was not enough. She would suffer as she saw her daughter brought up as a lady. As for Æðelwald of Remisgat, he would suffer and he would tell me all about the conspiracy before I ended his pain. "Say your farewells to your daughter. Padraig, find Popæg. She will know of a wet nurse and, priest, I have not yet done with you. I will have the truth and all of the truth. I hope you are ready for that inquisition."

Padraig nodded, "My heart is true but I am sorry, lord, I should have seen this. That Godwin, a half-blind man, could see what was before my very eyes saddens me and I am disappointed in myself!"

When Popæg came for the child her eyes told me that she had suspected something. Unlike Padraig, Popæg was a woman, a woman of the world, and would have sensed that all was not well. She gently picked up Gerloc. Poppa put her hand out to stop her but Popæg said, gently, "I swear my lady that she will be cared for. She will come to no harm and she will be loved." My wife's face was riven with tears as she nodded. Popæg looked at me, "Lord, your son is also with me. He is asleep."

"Thank you. Say nothing and I will speak with him when he wakes."

"Aye, lord." She left.

Sprota appeared and looked from me to Poppa. "Is this true, my lady, does he know?"

"He knows, Sprota. We are being sent to the House of St. Hilda."

Sprota shook her head, "No, my lady! I have a man! I would be wed!"

My harsh voice made Sprota start. "Then you should have thought of that when you covered up my wife's infidelity. Do you think that I would have you living in my town after what has happened? You will be confined here until I have made arrangements."

I left and closed the door. "Petr, no one enters or leaves."

"Aye lord." His face showed that he knew what had gone on. He was hearth weru and he would remain silent.

When I reached my hall, I saw that the priest now wore a cloak to cover his naked body. Æðelwald of Remisgat looked up as I entered. His face was already swollen from my blow. He looked defiant, "You cannot kill a priest!"

I laughed, "You forget that I am a barbarian! Will I be excommunicated by your Pope? Perhaps King Charles the Fat will punish me?" I jabbed a finger at his face. "I know of your treachery. I spoke with the men you met. You thought I was not aware that you were a spy?" His face fell. "You think me a crude barbarian and you feel superior. You abused your position and you abused your church. You will die. Resign yourself to that. There are two choices for the death which awaits you. You will choose your manner of death. I can make it swift or I can hand you over to Æbbi Bonecrusher and my men. They will make you die piece by piece. It will take days and you will beg for death yet it will not come."

"King Charles will punish you! He will take your title from you! He will drive you hence!"

"Fool! I know that the Franks, Bretons and Saxons conspire against me. What I need from you before I give you a swift death is all that you know of their plans."

He gave me a sly look. "I could tell you lies and you would not know!"

I turned to Æbbi Bonecrusher, "What do you think?"

He took out a seax and put the tip under the priest's right eye. He put his face close to Æðelwald of Remisgat and said, quietly, "Oh I would know, priest. Know this, I would rather you told us nothing for I would punish you for what you have done to my lord. When I take you away you are mine until you die!"

The priest saw then that he was doomed. "I would confess to Padraig! I will not go to my God unshriven!"

"I am not certain that your God would have you after your crimes but I will allow this. Godwin, fetch the priest." He scurried off. In the distance,

I heard the noise from my walls. My drekar had come. "Æbbi, when he has confessed take him to the armoury in the cellar. It is quiet there and none can hear screams."

"I will tell all! Let me stay here!"

"Look on this light for the last time. For soon you will have a world of darkness." Padraig appeared. "The priest would confess. My men will stand apart but you will not be out of their sight. When you are done he will be taken away."

Padraig nodded. I left the hall. I never saw the priest again. I had wanted to end his life myself but I needed his knowledge more. I put the faithless couple from my mind. I had the problem of William yet to solve. I could not tell him the truth for he would not understand. He would have to be told a story which made sense. He was a clever boy and he was all that I had left now. I headed for the main gate. Egil and Godwin flanked me. "You two have done well. Go to your chambers. Rest."

Godwin said, "Lord, I had my cot in Brother Padraig's chamber. Do I return there?"

Egil said, "I think, Godwin, that we will both move to the warrior hall. Is that not right, my lord?"

"It is. You will both receive a good share from this raid on the Bretons. When we go to war you will have war gear which all will envy."

Egil said, "I once thought that was all that I wanted now I see that there are other treasures which can be won and lost which are more important."

In contrast to those of us who had ridden through the night the rest of my men were in high spirits. We had done that which we intended and one enemy was dead. Our losses had been light and our gains great. The Haugr was avenged and the winter would be a better one for all my warriors. We had another drekar and all of the weapons we had taken from the Danes. When we fought King Alan we would have steel and we would have a fleet.

I sought out Harold Strong Arm and Haaken the Bold. "How is the leg, Harold?"

"A little better lord why?"

The sun was rising. "I need to ride down the river. I would have you come with me."

"Aye, of course, lord."

"Haaken fetch horses."

By the time Haaken returned with the horses the sun was warming the air and we headed toward the convent. Harold and Haaken were two of my oldest hearth weru and I needed to tell them of my wife. They would ensure that any rumours were quashed. When I had told them Harold said, "I am not married, lord, but I would have strangled her with my own hands. Why are you being so generous?"

"She is the mother of William. Would you have me drive a wedge between us?" He shook his head. "This is the Norns. All those years ago they began to weave their threads. The priest came to my grandfather and inveigled himself into his graces. He was blind to the danger. Now I see that the curse was not just that the priest saw my brother's birth but the priest himself."

"Should we rid ourselves of all Christians then, lord?"

I shook my head, "No Haaken for we are bound up with them. Most of our men have married Christians. Many have Christian children. We have to live in a world of the White Christ, I hope that when the priest dies his thread is cut and the curse will end."

The Mother Superior listened as I told her that my wife and her lady would be entering the nunnery. I did not give the reason. If Poppa wished to make up a story then that was her choice. "But I want to make one thing clear. If you wish me to allow your nunnery to continue to exist and to prosper, if you want me to continue to protect you from all enemies then you make certain that Lady Poppa and Sprota never leave your walls."

"You would have us as their gaolers?"

"It is for you to decide that. You have nuns here who come as young girls and never leave. Is this a prison for them?"

"It is their own choice."

"Then perhaps the Lady Poppa will see this as her choice." She nodded. She had no choice.

The town was thronged when I returned. I was greeted like a conquering hero but although I smiled my spirits were low. "Have horses readied for my wife and her lady. Tell them they have the day to pack. You two will escort them to the nunnery."

"Aye lord. We will do as you bid."

Popæg was in the Great Hall. I saw that there was a wet nurse, a young Saxon, feeding Gerloc. William was there with Padraig and both Egil and Godwin were with him. All looked at me expectantly. Only William smiled and he ran to my arms, "Father! Egil has told me of the raid! We have punished the Danes!"

I nodded, "Aye we have. Come with me, my son. Let us walk my walls. I have words I need to say with you."

He took my hand and I led him from the hall. I was aware that we were followed by the eyes of the others. When we reached the fighting platform I waved the sentries away. "Son, your mother and Lady Sprota are going away." William nodded. "They are entering a nunnery. Your mother will become a nun."

"Does she wish to do so?"

I sidestepped the question, "She will serve God, her God, and she will find peace."

"And will Æðelwald of Remisgat go there with her?" My son had an innocent look on his face. "He is her special friend. She often told me that. Will he go so that he can comfort her at night? She often needs comfort at night when you are away."

I shook my head. "No, Æðelwald of Remisgat is also leaving but he is leaving my land. You will never see him again." I became angry again. My son had seen but his innocence had protected him. I began to regret my clemency toward the priest. My son's fingers squeezed my finger. I had to forget the faithless pair and concentrate on him. "Popæg will care for you now. Does that make you happy?"

He grinned, "She is soft and comfortable, father. I like her and she has wonderful stories!"

"Good."

When we entered my hall the faces of those within turned to us. "Popæg, I would give you your freedom. You are no longer a slave."

She nodded, "And I can leave your hall if I wish?"

Her words felt like a blow. Had I miscalculated? Was it impossible for me to read women? "Of course. I am a man of my word and I have given you full freedom. You may leave. You can take a ship and return to Cent if you have a mind."

She nodded, "Then I choose to stay but if I am to care for your children then I need payment." She plucked at her clothes. "These are not the raiments of a lady and you will need a lady to care for your children."

I smiled. I had not miscalculated. "Of course. Padraig, see to it."

He smiled, "Aye lord!"

My world began to attain some sort of normality.

Chapter 13

Æðelwald of Remisgat told us all that he knew. Æbbi Bonecrusher was convinced of his words. He was given a quick death and his body was weighted with stones and thrown into the river at night so that none saw his passing. His masters might suspect his fate but they would not know it. I gave orders that all priests who arrived in my town were to be detained and questioned. After the first two came asking for the priest no more came. King Charles and King Alan now knew that their spies would no longer report to them.

We confirmed much that we suspected. The priest had been the conduit between the two kings. He did not tell us directly but we knew that King Alan had been promised the Cotentin in return for weakening us. The most disappointing news was that my wife would have been made Countess of Rouen after I had been defeated and publicly executed. Æðelwald of Remisgat would become Bishop of Rouen as a reward. King Charles the Fat, it seemed, would be turning a blind eye to a bishop and a countess' relationship. Any remorse I might have felt about putting her in a nunnery disappeared when I heard how she would have callously cast me aside. After his death, I rode, with William, to my lords. They needed to know both the infidelity and the plot. I told them all privately. Each time I told them the pain grew less. They were as angry as I had been when I had discovered them together. We were away until Mörsugur.

Normally my wife would have been preparing for Christmas. The warriors celebrated the winter solstice and I wondered what we would do this first year without my wife. Padraig and Popæg came to me when I returned. Padraig spoke but I knew that the two of them had conspired together.

"Lord, we would have a Christmas celebration. You and your warriors will celebrate the solstice but more than half of those who live in your home are Christian."

I nodded, "I do not object."

They looked at each other, "And there is one thing more, lord."

"Yes, Padraig?"

"We would baptise Gerloc." I said nothing. "Lord, her parents are Christian. The wet nurse and Popæg are Christian. Even if you do not like it she will be brought up a Christian."

Popæg said quietly, "You said she would be cared for. This is important lord."

I nodded, "Very well but do not expect me to witness this."

"We will do it discreetly, lord."

Popæg kissed my hand, "Thank you, lord. You have a hard shell but I know that there is a Christian heart beating within."

"You are wrong. My heart belongs to the old ways and will for all time." I should have known that the Norns were spinning.

I knew that Gerloc was not mine but she was innocent of any misdeed and I found myself becoming fond of her. That was partly the fault of Popæg who made certain that I saw the child each day. I can see now that she was a clever woman. I did not mind. I had my son and he was healthy. A daughter, even one fathered by another, was something to enjoy.

Now that I knew for certain that King Charles the Fat intended to break the treaty I had my men watching the ships which used our river. When I launched my attack then King Charles the Fat would suddenly find that he had no river to use. My men hewed trees and my smiths attached chains to them. When I chose I would block my river in two different places. We would become a fortress. Bagsecg and his horsemen made sure that the land between Montfort and the river was both safe and secure. My lords, mindful of the two disasters, also kept scouts looking for any threat. Our drekar were repaired. Those lords, like Sven Blue Cheek who had not used their vessels for some time, had them drawn from the water and given a thorough overhaul. Each lord knew my deadline. It would remain a secret until seven days before we set sail. The Bretons and the Franks would know that we were coming but only I knew the exact landing place.

One early morning at the start of Gói my sentries reported two drekar were heading upstream. After Godfrid we were wary and I had my walls manned. As the drekar came up the river I recognised the leading one. It was *'Dellingr'*. Her captain had been Harold Haroldsson. He had been my father's shipwright and had helped me to defeat my brother. When I became Lord of Rouen he said that he had done what he had promised and secured me a home. He asked to be released from his oath so that he could sail the seas with his son. I gave him *'Dellingr'*. The men who sailed with him were the others who had not had enough of raiding. That had been more than fifteen years ago. I saw that *'Dellingr'* looked old and tired. From the few oars which both ships used they were under crewed. The years had not been kind to her or perhaps she had been badly used. The one which followed her was smaller but newer.

I went down to the gate to greet my old friend. Only Harold Strong Arm of my hearth weru would remember him and I summoned him too. The man who stepped from the ship was not Harold Haroldsson. He was too young for that.

"I am Lord Göngu-Hrólfr Rognvaldson. I recognise the ship. I often sailed in her."

"I am Leif Haroldsson. My father served you. I have brought the ship home to die. She leaks and her wood is rotten. The next storm will see her die and my father would not have wished her to take men with her."

I nodded, "I can see that there is a tale here. We have room in the warrior hall for your crew although it may be a little crowded."

He shook his head, "For tonight my men will stay aboard and I will speak with you." He sounded serious and so I nodded and led him into my stronghold.

"I knew that your father had sired a son but I knew not where your family lived."

"We lived west of Ċiriċeburh. My mother was a Frank who had been born there and she wished to die there. My father came for us when he was given the drekar. It was too late for my mother. She had died. There were few Norse left by then and my father took all of the men and we went A-Viking."

We had reached my hall and I waved over a slave to fetch ale.

After quenching his thirst Leif continued. "We raided first the Bretons and then the Saxons of Wessex. We were successful. The other drekar you see in the river joined us. Lars Bjornson is a young warrior. Then we heard of treasure in the Blue Sea off Africa. We were told that the savages there were half-naked and did not have metal weapons."

I nodded, "The stories were exaggerated?"

"Aye lord. The treasure was poor and they fought hard to keep it. We lost many men and my father decided to sail for home. He dreamed that he had died. He said he saw Hrolf the Horseman in his dreams and that the jarl was in Valhalla."

I refilled his horn for I could tell that the memory was a painful one. "My grandfather died in Wessex but he had a good death."

He shook his head, "Would that my father had had such a death. Our drekar sprang a leak and we landed on the coast where the Moors reign. He remembered that Erik One Arm had been a slave there and he did not want to land but we had little choice. We had to find a beach and coat the hull with pine tar. The Moors came in the night when we waited for the tar to dry. My father suffered a wound to the leg. We lost warriors but we escaped. We set sail but the wound in his leg worsened. By the time we reached the Liger, he was close to death. We landed on the southern bank, away from the Bretons, so that we could light a fire to burn out the poison. We were too late. His last thoughts were of this land. We had heard that you were Lord of Rouen and he said that I had to bring the drekar back to die with dignity here in Rouen."

I rose for I thought the tale had come to an end. "No, lord, the story does not end there. While we were burying my father, a ship came downstream and some Franks landed close by us. We thought that they came to fight and although we were outnumbered we were prepared to sell our lives dearly. They did not wish to fight us. They wished to talk. The leader was a strong warrior. He said he was on his way to Rouen to speak with you. *Wyrd* eh? I told him our tale and that we were headed there. He asked me to give you a message."

"Who was this Frank?" I was suspicious. Was this another Frankish plot to deceive me?

"He said his name was Fulk le Roux and that you had saved his life." My face showed my relief for Leif smiled. "You know him then?"

"Aye, and I am relieved. Go on."

"He said he had heard of your raid on Nantes. He said that he would make war on King Alan from his lands and asked if you would do the same from the north. He said that if you did you both had a better chance of victory."

I filled my horn and drank deeply, "You bring both good and bad news. I am sorry about your father, Harold, but the news from Fulk is the best that I could hear." I looked at the young warrior. "So what is it that you wish?"

"We would follow you. Both Lars and myself have had enough of sailing the seas. We have little treasure to show for ten years of raiding. I am almost thirty summers old. I would take a wife and have a family. My father never saw grandchildren."

"Then you are welcome." The Norns were spinning their thread. I looked out to the east. "I have an idea, come with me."

We went to the eastern wall of my town. Beyond it lay open fields and the river. There were no farms there yet for it had been disputed until the raid on Paris. My men had spread south of the river. I waved my arm. "We can give **'Dellingr'** a home and it can be your home too. It would be fitting for your father was a shipwright. The land to the east is for you and your men. We turn the drekar upside down and make her your hall. With turf walls and a roof, it would be a fine hall."

I saw his face light up, "Lord that would seem to me to be the perfect solution. My father's spirit is in the drekar. He would be with us. We could make a wharf next to the hall for the drekar."

"Before you agree to follow my banner I need to warn you that we are surrounded by enemies. We go to war with the Bretons soon and then we will fight the Franks. Your lands may become a battleground."

"You have given us the land. The least we can do is to fight for it!"

"Then let us go and tell your men. If you are anything like your father you will wish to consult with them first."

"Aye lord."

His men were all of the same mind. I saw that all of them were of an age with Leif or perhaps younger. We took down the mast, spar and sail. We left them on the wharf. The holds had been emptied of half of the ballast. We would not need it on the short journey and all that remained were the men and their chests. As we prepared to sail upstream I asked him about that.

"We had older men. Many were the men who had helped my father build ships. That is how the drekar lasted so long. She was repaired frequently. Gradually the older ones died. We picked up younger men when we landed at ports like Dyflin, Dorestad, Bruggas and Lundenwic. My father learned from the horseman and he chose wisely."

He saw that his crew were ready to cast off and he looked at me, "It is your ship and it is an honour to sail on her last voyage."

"Cast off!"

As they rowed I saw some of my men on the walls watching her. They all knew what we were doing for I had told them. Harold Strong Arm had been particularly interested. For them, this was a poignant moment. It was the death of a ship and yet the birth of a hall. Many wished to see the moment.

As we headed upstream he asked, "Lord, are there many women in Rouen?"

I nodded, "In Rouen and in the land hereabouts but we do not take them. We want no blood feuds. You will find that they are willing to choose a Viking for my men are all rich."

He nodded, "I saw their mail. Few of my men have mail."

"Do not worry, the Bretons do and I intend to enrich you and impoverish them."

We did not have far to row. There was no wharf and the ship's boys simply held the ropes while we disembarked. The men carried their chests ashore and put them at the spot that we had chosen for the hall. It was on a naturally higher piece of land. The decking was taken up and laid like a road. Then we attached two mighty ropes to the dragon prow and we began to haul her out of the water. We had taken half of the ballast out to make this part easier. I joined them for this was something I had never seen before. I had heard of warriors who had done this as a statement. It meant they had left the sea. For Leif and his crew, it was not the same. This was a new beginning. We hauled. The crew had spread seal oil in the wood and the ship moved easier than I had thought. I saw the weed hanging from the keel and saw what Leif had meant. The ship was dying.

We stopped shy of the place we would use and the men began to cut the turf. It was stacked soil to soil, grass to grass. It took most of the day to remove the turf and then we had to pull the drekar around and begin the hardest part. We took the last of the ballast from the keel. The stone would make the hall stronger. We would have to pull her over. Before we could do that, we had to remove the dragon prow. It would be reattached to the keel. We had to saw off the sternpost. That done we pulled. Half of the crew held ropes to act as a brake. Once the ship was vertical then its weight would pull it over. Even though every man on both crews toiled it still landed heavier than we had hoped. Luckily, she was undamaged. We had almost done all that we could but we still had to embed her beneath the soil. The sun was setting as we trudged back through my gates. We would feast with my warriors and the two new crews. In truth, they barely made one crew but until we had built their halls they would continue to be two crews.

The feast was a success. Harold Strong Arm told some of the tales of Haroldsson and we heard of the places they had visited. I saw him looking wistfully at Leif. His friend had had a son and Harold Strong Arm had no family at all. He looked over and saw my son, William, with Popæg smiling at the child. I think it made him yearn for something he had never had. William was allowed to stay up despite Popæg's critical eye and he took it all in. "Father, can I come tomorrow when you finish the hall?"

Padraig laughed, "I do not think it will be ready tomorrow, William."

I said, "You are wrong, priest. Leif, Lars and their men will sleep inside the drekar hall tomorrow night."

"But how?"

Leif explained, "First we cut two doors in the hull. We use the wood from the deck to make a floor. We know it will fit perfectly. We cut a hole in the keel for the fire and we will be ready. After that, we use the turf to make the walls and the roof. By the end of a few days, we will build our wharf and tie up *'Dragon's Eye'*."

Padraig shook his head, "Quite remarkable."

I turned to the two captains. "You will not have long to lay out your farms for we sail in twenty days. We have the longest journey of all of my ships and we gather at Ciriceburh."

Lars said, "Do not worry about us, lord. My drekar is a young one and there is neither worm nor weed in her keel. We will be ready. What our men lack in mail they make up in heart."

I smiled, "I never doubted it for an instant."

I did not get to spend much time with the two men for I had much to do. I was taking just two crews from Rouen. The rest would stay under the command of Harold Strong Arm. His leg had healed but I needed someone to command Rouen and he was a perfect choice. He would ensure that we were not attacked. Perhaps it was his reflective mood but he seemed quite content to stay in Rouen. Bagsecg and Bjorn the Brave would also stay at home and watch the border with Frankia. Petr Jorgenson and his archers would sail with me. With Leif and Lars, we would have ten drekar. Olaf Two Toes had died and the men from Djupr would be led by his son, Siggi Olafsson. There would be two drekar from there and two from Caen.

The night before we left I spent with William, Padraig, Harold Strong Arm, and Popæg. I spoke to William but my words were aimed at the others. "William, tomorrow I go to raid the Bretons. I may be away for a moon but I will come back. If I do not it is because I am dead."

Popæg rolled her eyes and William gripped my fingers. Padraig said, "But your father will return."

"My son is a Viking. He knows that when you step out of your door then you are in a dangerous world. Do not tempt the Norns, priest and Popæg, do not roll your eyes at me. I hope to return. I want to return but if it is not meant to be then I will die with a sword in my hand and Harold Strong Arm will ensure that William Longsword becomes Lord of Rouen and leads the clan!"

Popæg tutted, "And I pray that you return home too. The boy has lost his mother and it would not do to lose his father too."

Harold Strong Arm gently squeezed Popæg's arm, "Our Lord is the greatest warrior in the land, any land. He leads the finest warriors. Odin will watch over him. He is just being careful." She nodded and smiled at Harold. He looked at me. "You know that I will do as you ask, lord, for I have no children of my own. I will look after William as though he was my own son."

That pleased me and I changed the conversation to more pleasant matters.

Erik Leifsson was now much more confident about sailing my drekar. We led and *'Wolf's Snout'* and *'Dragon's Eye'* followed. All three ships were in perfect condition. We had supplies for a month and plenty of weapons. This time we were not raiding. We were going to war. We were going to end the threat of King Alan. Thanks to Leif's news and his meeting with Fulk le Roux I was more hopeful about our chances of defeating him. King Alan would have to divide his army and that gave us the chance we needed.

We had benign winds and we reached Ciriceburh in a day and a half. Half of our fleet was already there. While the crews would sleep aboard the lords landed. We would stay in Ragnar the Resolute's hall until Ubba's ship and Saxbjorn's joined us.

Ragnar had regained some of his confidence. "We have many young men who wish to sail with us." He looked at me. "It is like the old days with your grandfather."

"If I was half the man my grandfather was then I would be happy."

Bergil laughed, "If we are talking of size then you are twice the man your grandfather was!"

The banter was a good sign. Leif and Lars found themselves in a brotherhood. They said little but I saw their confidence grow. Sven Blue Cheek leaned over to me, "Lady Poppa and this priest, it is not your fault, lord." I nodded. "Since you told me I have gone over all that you did. This was the work of the Norns. All those babies who died were a sign. You were meant to have one child and William Longsword, when we raise him, will be the leader to assume your mantle."

I smiled, "You said 'we raise him'. You have sons of your own."

He smiled, "Lord I am but a warrior. I saw in you when first I met you someone who is greater than any other warrior I have ever met. The Norns put me here to guide you and to mould you. If I am spared then I will do the same for your son."

I nodded and told him what I had said to Harold and my son before I left. Sven smiled, "I do not risk the Norns but your thread is still strong. It will not be a Breton blade which cuts it."

When the last ship arrived, it was Saxbjǫrn's, we held a council of war. I spoke and they listened. "We will land at the Blavet river. There is a small village there and we can make a longphort in the river. We will advance across the Breton heartland. Each warband will raid alone but we will be close enough to each other to combine when the Bretons come."

Saxbjǫrn asked, "Can you be certain they will come, lord? Perhaps they know of our plans and will be raiding our homes."

I knew that the battle where he had lost so many men had had an effect on Saxbjǫrn. He had brought just forty men. He had to have left twice that number in Carentan. I saw Sven, Bergil and Sámr, scowl at Saxbjǫrn the Silent.

"Saxbjǫrn did you know where I intended to raid before we met here?" He shook his head. "The guards who watch our doors are Ragnar's oathsworn and they sail with us."

Ragnar growled, "And if any man suggests that my men are foresworn they will answer to me."

"None does that, Ragnar. Saxbjǫrn had a traitor in his camp. That traitor is still alive. I believe he is with King Alan." I saw Saxbjǫrn's eyes narrow. "We are threatening King Alan's home. It is well defended from the sea. We will hurt the people who are closest to him and he will come. As soon as he does then we combine to make one warband. We bring him to battle and end this in the Breton heartland. The more you take from those in the Blavet valley the sooner the Bretons will come and we will fight them on ground of our choosing. We will be neither tricked nor trapped this time. They will not know where we strike. We will have the advantage and we will retain it!"

Sven, whom all respected, nodded, "It is a good plan. If there is a flaw then it is in the resolve and discipline of each of us." He glared at each lord. "We keep in touch with each other and when we are summoned then we make haste to join Lord Göngu-Hrólfr Rognvaldson."

We spent some time speaking of the signals we would use. When all was settled then I stood, "We leave after dawn. We sail up the river at night. I know that we do not know the river but I want surprise to be on our side. Lars Bjornson has the smallest drekar. When we reach the river, I will transfer to his ship and we will lead the way upstream." I saw the pride on Lars' face which was quickly replaced by worry. Moving from drekar to drekar at sea was never easy. I smiled. I had no fear of the sea.

I sought out Saxbjǫrn. "Saxbjǫrn I know that you are worried about this raid. If you do not come then there is no dishonour."

He shook his head, "If I do not go then I might as well hang up my sword and become a farmer. I am fearful and that is not the way a Viking should go to war. Besides if Beorn Straight Hair is there then I can avenge my shield brothers." He lowered his voice, "Lord, I have been troubled by dreams. Halfi Axe Tongue and Nefgeirr were as close as brothers. All the men who died were close to me and each night I am haunted by their faces."

"It was not just down to you, Saxbjǫrn, you were betrayed."

"And that is why I must come for when I have slain Beorn Straight Hair then the dead might let me sleep."

I led a mighty fleet west from Ċiriċeburh. There were two rivers closer to Vannes and I could have used either of them but I wanted to ravage the Breton lands as much as I could before the battle was joined. We would be twenty-five miles from Vannes. I counted on at least one and perhaps two days of grace before King Alan knew where we were. In that time, we could lay waste to that most valuable of assets the Bretons had; their land. Now was the time they would be ploughing and seeding. Now was the time when their animals would have young. I would be hurting King Alan's people's ability to make war. I would also be encouraging his rivals to topple the King from his throne.

The wind was gentle and we did not move as fast as I would have liked and so we had to row for part of the voyage. It was not arduous and helped to prepare our crews. The wind brought their chants to us in drifts.

Each crew had songs which helped them. As the coast drew near and the sun began to set we pulled next to **'Dragon's Eye'**. The two ships were secured by ropes and then a bridge of oars was made so that I could walk over. The oars sagged alarmingly when I reached the middle but they held and I saw Lars sigh with relief when I jumped down to his deck. I waved farewell to my crew. I knew that my oathsworn were unhappy that I was to sail with another crew but it had to be. We headed for the river. The Norns had spun and I had cast the bones.

Chapter 14

At its mouth, the river was over half a mile wide but it gradually narrowed. From the Breton maps, we had taken we estimated it to be an eight-mile row. We had not stepped the mast but we had furled the sail. I stood at the prow with Arne, one of the ship's boys. The river was far straighter than we might have expected. We were forced to slow where it narrowed and there were three turns in quick succession. The crew were keen to impress their new lord and the oars slid silently through the river. They seemed to sigh and did not splash. Arne and I used hand signals. He suddenly tapped his nose and pointed to the steerboard bank. I sniffed. It was wood smoke. We were nearing a settlement. I had been estimating the time and this would seem to be eight miles up the river. It was hard to see in the dark but I thought that the river was about seventy paces wide. It would be perfect for a longphort. I waved to Lars to put the steering board over. Leaving Arne to continue to watch I went down to the steering board. *'Fafnir'* was very close to our stern and I signalled to Egil at the prow. We were landing. I donned my helmet and slung my shield over my back. As the steerboard oars were slid in I peered over the side. The riverbank looked to be mud with overhanging trees. We would be able to tie the ship to them.

When the ship's boys jumped so did I. I landed ankle deep in soft, sucking mud. I dragged my boots from the slippery bed and used the overhanging branches to haul myself up the bank. Once I was on solid ground I listened. I could hear cattle and I could smell smoke from further upstream. Leif joined me with his oathsworn. I pointed upstream and, nodding, he loped off. I would join him soon. I turned to watch Erik bring my drekar next to Lars'. She was a little bigger but it would not be a problem. She began to tie up. *'Wolf's Snout'* was next. The longphort was being built. This would be a temporary one to help us land our men quickly. More men landed and I drew Long Sword and ran off up the trail toward the smell of smoke.

Hennebont proved to be bigger than I had expected. Leif and his men waited two hundred paces from the first building. He had done the right thing. Had he gone charging in then many of the Bretons might have escaped. I leaned in and spoke to the two leaders quietly, "Leif, take your men and cut them off from the north. Lars take your men and do the same from the east. I will wait here for our warriors." The two chiefs led their men east and I was left alone.

Gandálfr and Æbbi Bonecrusher brought the two crews to join me and I was not alone for long. Lars and Leif's men were not mailed. The ones who joined me were and I had more than eighty men. Eighty Vikings were a force to be feared. I pointed with my sword. "We have the town surrounded. We hit them and hit them hard!"

I turned and began to run. Inevitably we were heard for mail made a noise. Boots pounded and the alarm raised. This was a small settlement and most people had cows which needed milking. Bread would have to be baked. We were on the outskirts when we were seen by a farmer. His cry of "Vikings!" rang out and woke the village.

I swung Long Sword at the farmer who shouted. My sword bit into his arm and then his side. He fell writhing to the ground. "Egil, Godwin! Search the farm!" It was important to get into the homes before the treasure each family had hidden could be moved.

There were more cries as my men spread out. In the distance, I heard shouts as some people tried to escape and give warning to the farms, churches, villages and towns which lay close by. The centre of the settlement had a tower. Einar Arneson fell clutching his shoulder. He had been hit by an arrow.

"Petr!"

Petr Jorgenson and his archers hurried forward. The archer and his companion tumbled from the tower to crash onto the cobbles. There was also a hall, and half a dozen warriors led by a lord rushed out. "Æbbi Bonecrusher, shields!" With my oathsworn around me, we advanced on the lord. More men poured from the hall. They had taken the time to don mail and helmets. These would need us to fight them. I did not bother with my shield. The Breton lord had a spear which he lunged at me. I flicked the head aside with my sword and my long legs took me closer. The Breton's head only came to my chest. I could not head butt him. Instead, I rammed my knee up between his legs. He grunted and doubled up. I brought the pommel of my sword down upon the back of his neck, just below his helmet. He dropped to his knees and I reversed my sword and stabbed him in the back of the neck. His warriors fought even harder when their lord died but Haaken the Bold and Æbbi Bonecrusher were more than a match for them. I swung my sword across the backs of two men. My sword bit through leather, flesh and bone. I swung it the other way and my sword went through the back of a warrior's neck.

"They are dead, lord. All have fallen!" Petr the Slow's voice was fearful. He had thought I had gone berserk. I had not but the joy of battle had been in me. It sometimes happened that way.

I nodded, "Secure the town. Send for the drekar. We will use this as a longphort now." I sheathed my sword. The Breton warriors and their lord lay dead. Elsewhere the men who had fought us were now corpses too. The women, old, children and the men who had surrendered were gathered in what must have been the village square. I headed down to the river. Æbbi Bonecrusher followed me. There was a wooden wharf. It would make loading the drekar easier. I saw that there were five ships tied up already. "Have those boats moved upstream and emptied."

"Aye lord. If the rest goes as well as this we will have an easy victory."

"I expect a day or so as easy as this and then the Bretons will know we are here. Then they will come for us and we will see who is stronger; Bretons or Vikings!"

By the time dawn broke, we had the drekar tied up to the wharf and my men had been fed. Only three crews had had any work to do and so the other crews were sent out to raid the land. Our three crews began to load the drekar and gather the animals from the settlement. The mail and weapons from the men we had killed were spread amongst the three crews. Lars and Leif's men were given a disproportionally larger share. My warriors knew it made sense. When we faced the Bretons in battle we needed as many well-armed and mailed men as we could get. Lars and Leif were keen to get more treasure and so they crossed the longphort to raid the northern shore. Gandálfr took his crew there too.

I had Egil and Godwin search the small church and the hall. They knew how to search for papers. I spoke with the priest. He had not offered resistance and so he was allowed to live. He was a brave man for he showed no fear when I questioned him. Padraig had told me that most priests were not afraid of dying. They believed they would go to their heaven. "Who was the lord I slew?"

"Judicael of Nantes. You will pay for his death. He was a cousin of the King. The King had marked him down for a large piece of land in the Cotentin!"

That confirmed what we already knew. The Bretons thought that we were a spent force. So far, we had raided them with one or two boats. This raid was different although they did not know it yet. We had almost five hundred men.

"And who is the lord who rules this land?"

"That would be the King's son, Pascweten. He is Lord of Vannes." I nodded. The priest asked, "And what will happen to us?"

"To you?"

"The people of Hennebont. The ones you have not slaughtered."

"Do not try my patience priest. When your King Alan sent men to raid the Haugr they slew all. I have been restrained."

He looked contrite, "And that is why I ask about our fate, lord."

"When we have had enough of this land we will ask the Lord of Vannes if he wishes to buy you. If he does not then we will sell you in Dorestad or Bruggas." I saw the priest wrestling with his thoughts. "The outcome is in the hands of Pascweten. I care not who pays for you so long as someone does." I had no doubt that they would be bought by Pascweten, son of the King. This was the land which was closest to his heartland. If he lost this then he risked losing all. He would pay.

Egil and Godwin found small chests of coins as well as many jewels. The wife of the lord had expensive tastes. She also thought that she was better than her people. She objected to being in such close proximity to her people. My men just herded them even closer just to annoy her. There were maps and papers as well as a finely decorated holy book. With the candlesticks and altar linen from the church, we had already made a rich haul. My men began to slaughter the animals. We had an army to feed and although we would take some animals back it made sense to take the younger ones. The older and larger animals were butchered. Some of the meat would be salted. There were wine and ale barrels which we would empty and then fill with salted meat. Most of the meat was put on to cook. We had many mouths to feed. We had large fires and took the huge cauldrons from the hall. Along with the vegetables we had taken and the bread our warbands would eat well when they returned.

Petr Jorgensen came to me as the animals began to be slaughtered. "Lord, we have found six horses. I would take my men and scout ahead of the warbands."

"Good. If you can get to Vannes then so much the better."

"We will try."

I went to the drekar. Erik Leifsson was in command. He was my captain and so would command all the other drekar. The drekars were not yet secured. "Lord I would be happier if we faced downstream. We have time to do it now while there is daylight and we are empty. The river is high and it will be easier than if we try to move them in a rush. The two warbands that are headed north will not need to cross until later. We have time."

"You are in command, Erik. It is your decision."

He looked relieved, "Thank you, lord."

I pointed to the Breton boats, "Before we leave we will destroy these ships. Take whatever gear you need from them."

"They are good ships."

"And we will not have enough crew for them. We need to hurt the Bretons. Losing their boats, their wharf and their animals will do that."

All that remained was to await the return of my warbands. Æbbi Bonecrusher and my men had organised food for us. They had roasted some meat on the fire. We sat in the lord's hall and ate from his metal platters. They would be taken home with us. We drank from goblets and not horns. The meat was cooked to perfection. Charred on the outside, bloody juices ran down our chins. We used bread to mop up the gravy that remained on the platters.

Haaken the Bold said, "I could get used to this, lord."

I nodded, "One day when you tire of being hearth weru and take a woman then you can have a hall and do this every day."

He shook his head, "There are just nine of us left now, lord. I doubt that any of us will enjoy old age." He laughed, "And that is why we became your oathsworn. It will be a short life but a glorious one!"

My other men all cheered and banged the table. It seemed to be a common view. Egil and Godwin ate with us and I saw, from their faces, that they had a different future picked out for themselves. That was also good.

The first of the warbands arrived back in the middle of the afternoon. It was Ragnar the Resolute. They were driving cattle and they had captives with them. As four men sported wounds they had not had it all their own way. Over the next few hours, the rest returned and all had been successful. Two men had died and twenty wounded but it was a small price to pay for the success we had enjoyed. Every church and farm east of the river for twenty miles had been ransacked. Gandálfr, Lars and Leif had also had great success in the west.

Sámr had managed to go the furthest east. Petr had passed him on his way to Vannes. "Men did escape, lord. Two men on horses fled as we approached. I am sorry."

"It was to be expected. All it means is that we move east tomorrow and choose our own battleground." I waved a hand at the captives, the animals and the treasure. "It is hard to see how we could take back any more. Erik can begin to load the ships tomorrow. The men of Valognes have done well today. They can guard the longphort and the captives. There were just forty men who came from Ubba's home and they have suffered the greatest losses in the raid so far." I put my arm around Sámr, "Now eat! The food is good and before we go I would like to drink all the wine, ale and cider!"

Petr and his men rode in after dark. They had four spare horses. "Lord there are men heading for Vannes. The countryside is filled with Breton riders. We slew four of them. It means I can mount another four men tomorrow and we can find them."

"Do not take risks!"

He laughed, "Lord the riders are Bretons and they are good but they carry spears. They could have ten times our number and I would not fear them."

I spoke with all of my lords and discovered that the best site for a battle would be a few miles east of our position. There was a fjord-like feature which meant one side of our battle line would be protected by the sea while on the other side there was low lying ground. The small piece of high ground meant the Bretons would find it difficult to outflank us. More importantly the Bretons would have further to march from Vannes to reach us. They would be tired. We would all be well fed and rested.

We left before dawn. Petr and his archers sped ahead of us. We would not be surprised. We marched in warbands. I led with Sven. Lars and Leif's men guarded one flank while Saxbjǫrn and Ragnar the other. Gandalf brought up the rear. Although most of the farms and houses had been raided my men still found treasure, animals, pots and linens in the empty buildings we passed. We fired them when they had been ransacked.

We were just a mile from the battlefield when Ulf rode in, "Lord there are twenty Breton riders heading this way."

"Shield wall! Archers!"

My crew had twenty men armed with bows and they formed up behind our three ranks of spears. We were so quick that despite the Bretons being mounted we were ready for them. The Bretons liked to line their fields with shrubs and trees. We were unseen until the last moment. When they rode over the small rise they had a shock when they were confronted by a solid wall of Vikings.

"Loose!" The twenty archers sent their missiles over our heads. Some found flesh and others found horses. The effect was dramatic. Leaving one dead warrior they fled. King Alan and his son would know where we were. The question remained what would they do about it?

We reached the ground that Bergil Fast Blade had discovered. It was perfect. It allowed us to have a line of warriors one hundred men across. With well over forty archers behind us, the rest of our men would be a reserve, led by Ragnar. They would fill any gaps. Saxbjǫrn and his small band of hardened and mailed warriors would be our anchor on the left. Sven was on the right. Sámr and Bergil were on either side of me. The men had time to empty their breeks and make water on the low boggy area to the north of Saxbjǫrn the Silent. Saxbjǫrn used some rocks to make a small wall as added protection. We waited.

Not long after noon, our archers rode in. "Lord they come. The Bretons have two hundred horsemen. The rest of their army is a mixture of men with spears and farmers. They number more than five hundred." He paused, "There are Vikings with them."

"Beorn Straight Hair?"

He shrugged, "I would be guessing if I said so. There is a small warband of them. I would say no more than forty. Some have the Danish axe."

I knew then that we had not accounted for all of Godfrid's band or perhaps the Bretons had hired Danes. It mattered not. "You have done well. Join the archers and take command of them."

The Breton scouts appeared first. These were the ones we had bloodied and they had learned their lesson. They halted some distance from us. Two turned and rode back, no doubt to report to whoever led the Bretons. My men had had time to eat and to drink. Our weapons were sharp and the wait had allowed us to examine the ground over which we would fight. A good warrior knew that stepping upon a rock at the wrong time could be disastrous. Battles were often decided by such things. A warrior who slipped and fell could cause a shield wall to be breached and a battle lost.

Egil had my standard behind me so that they would know who came to punish them. I held a spear. If they used horses then a solid wall of spears was the most effective deterrent. Their army began to filter before us. They spread out. I almost laughed for if they came at us with the full length of line that they arrayed then they would become severely disordered when they came to the pinch point. It was then that I realised the King was not with them. Had Fulk le Roux drawn off the King? The leader had polished armour and I took it to be Pascweten. He and his oathsworn rode horses. I saw that he had fifty mailed men and they looked, from a distance, to be using stiraps. I also saw the Vikings. They were led by Beorn Straight Hair for I recognised his shield.

Someone must have advised Pascweten for he drew in the men on the flanks. I saw then that he intended to break us in the centre. The Vikings and the farmers lined up on the enemy right. There were well over two hundred or more of them. The presence of Bjorn would please Saxbjorn. He would have vengeance. On the enemy left they had the rest of the foot. The centre was made up of their horsemen. Pascweten looked to have divided them into two. I knew that the Bretons liked to use throwing spears and darts. The first group of horsemen were so armed. The ones with stiraps formed the second group and they had lances. It was a good plan. The throwing spears could be sent without fear of our spears. What they did not know was the number of archers we had brought. They would hurt the light horses and their riders!

I saw that the Bretons had brought their priests and their crosses. We had a weapon to counter their cross. We began banging our shields and chanting.

Clan of the Horseman
Warriors strong
Clan of the Horseman
Our reach is long
Clan of the Horseman
Fight as one
Clan of the Horseman
Death will come

The chant seemed to roll along the line and down to the water. It felt almost hypnotic. I knew that it made me feel as though I was no longer alone. I was part of a greater being and entity. I was part of the clan and we were unstoppable.

Above the chants and the banging, I heard the strident notes of a horn. The Bretons began to advance. "Lock shields." Our shields came around as one and clicked as they touched. The spears of the front rank were braced against our right feet while those of the second and third ranks appeared above our shoulders. I saw the Breton line move. The horsemen moved quicker and they would be the ones who would hit us first. Pascweten was counting on his men's ability to weaken us so that when he charged with his lances they would strike at the same time and he would break our line in two. His father would not have tried such a move. He would have known that we would not be shifted. The son was trying to show that he was a greater leader than his father! The horses thundered on the uneven ground as they headed toward us. These men would stop thirty paces from us and throw their javelins. If they were skilled then they would wheel and do so. As they neared us I saw that they held three such weapons in their hands. That meant three such attacks to be endured. Petr needed no orders. My archers were on a slightly higher piece of ground. They could not see over me but they could over the rest of my men. Petr would judge when to launch his arrows. All the time the men on foot were drawing ever closer. My captain of archers did it to perfection. As the horsemen began to wheel and draw back their arms the arrows fell. They found flesh both human and equine. Equally important they disrupted the men who were throwing. It is hard to concentrate when arrows are falling. Even so, many of the javelins hit us but we all had large shields and we saw the spears coming for us. Some were slow to react and javelins found their bodies. The duel of archers and horsemen continued until the Bretons had used up their supply. Less than half rode back toward their main line.

I took out the throwing spear which had stuck in my shield and I rammed it haft first into the soft soil. Others did the same. Some took the javelins to return them to the Bretons. The wounded were taken to the healers in the rear and they were replaced so that we had a solid line of unwounded warriors.

The two bodies of foot were even closer now and Pascweten led his horsemen. They tried to keep a straight line so that their attack could be more effective. It was neutralized by the uneven terrain. This time the hooves thundered for they were bigger horses and the riders mailed. There were, however, fewer of them. Horns sounded and the men on foot raced toward my men. There were no archers to keep them at bay for I had all of the archers. Petr launched his arrows a little earlier. I saw one horse struck by three arrows. Its head fell and it pitched the rider to hit the ground. Before he could recover he was trampled by his comrades. The horse and rider made a gap for riders who had to ride around the obstacle. I had used a spear on a horse myself and I knew when they would strike. They had stiraps and they would stand in them and ram their spears toward us. We were ready for such a move. The men who had picked up throwing spears hurled them at the horsemen. Throwing from the ground gave them a greater range and I saw some horses and riders struck.

"Brace!" I leaned behind my shield and angled my spear a little more.

Many of the horses baulked and would not complete the charge. Others did as they were ordered but struck a spear. Our spears had long metal heads and could do terrible damage to an animal. I heard a crack like thunder as the men on foot hit my other shield walls. The battle was now engaged all the way along the line. We were outnumbered but the Bretons had already taken the greater number of casualties. Pascweten was not in the front rank. He was in the third line of horsemen. Wearing open face helmets, I saw greybeards. These were veterans. These were the men who had fought alongside my brother. These had fought alongside and against Vikings. They knew how to fight us. This Pascweten knew his business.

The rider who rode at me did as I expected and stood in his stirups. He lunged down with his spear. It was almost eight feet long. I moved my spear to the left. He had a good horse. He had a brave horse. His spear hit my shield and I slightly angled it. I heard the metal of the head as it scratched and scraped along the metal-studded shield. My spear hit the horse in the shoulder and its speed drove the spearhead deep within its body. I let go of the spear and put my weight behind the shield. The horse was mortally wounded. Its heart told it to continue but it did not have the strength. Its head dropped and I saw the rider, still standing in his stirups trying to save himself. The dying horse hit my shield and I would have been bowled over if I had not had warriors pushing their shields into my back. The rider flew from the saddle. Egil was so busy pushing that he forgot about the standard. The pointed tip struck the

Breton in the throat. The standard was torn from Egil's grip as the dying warrior sailed to land behind the third rank of warriors.

In one move I had drawn Long Sword and moved forward half a step. "Hold them!"

I saw that half of the men who had ridden at us had either been wounded or unhorsed. Haaken the Bold stepped from the line to despatch one luckless Breton. I watched as men from the second rank took the places of those wounded or killed in the front line. I was tall enough to see that our right had held but Beorn Straight Hair and his renegade Vikings were pushing back Saxbjǫrn and his men. Ragnar the Resolute reacted quickly and I saw men racing to bolster our left. The last of the Bretons in the first rank came at us again. I swung Long Sword. It smashed into a spear and then tore across the muzzle of a horse which reared. The rider fought to stay in the saddle. I lunged at his middle. A spear scraped along my mail but I felt my sword's tip tear through scale mail and into flesh. As the Breton fell backwards he pulled his horse and he was crushed beneath his steed.

Pascweten must have thought that he could end the battle. His right had almost won and we had suffered wounds in our front rank. He raised his spear and led his best warriors to charge us. Many of our spears were shattered. I saw fresh weapons passed forward. Egil shouted, in my ear, "I have the standard again, lord!"

"It has been blooded. It is good! Wave it so that all know I live."

As the horsemen thundered toward us they had obstacles before them. Their own dead and dying warriors and horses lay like a barrier before us. I swung my shield around to my back so that I could use Long Sword two handed. Pascweten was coming for me. With two mailed men on either side of me, they ploughed through the dead and dying. I had no spear and he could see that. This would be a test of my skills and those of the son of King Alan. I saw his arm pull back. He was not going to risk standing in his stirraps. There was no shield to stop his spear and my chest would be a huge target. I knew where he would strike. The games I played with William taught you how to coordinate the hand and the eye. They gave you the skill to hit a moving target. The target was the spearhead. I swung as Pascweten rammed it at my chest. I saw the head of the spear come toward me. I watched Long Sword as it hacked through the wood of the shaft. The spear had almost reached my mail when I did so. The tip of the sword continued and scored a long line down the left flank of Pascweten's horse. It was well trained and did not flinch. The horse drove over Petr the Slow. Its hooves crushed his skull but my brave hearthweru did not move. He was swinging his sword even as he was falling. It tore open the horse's throat. This time the horse fell sideways and crushed some of the men in the front rank.

Our shield wall broken, I turned and ran to Pascweten. He had kicked his feet from his stiraps and he held his shield in two hands as I hacked down at him. My blow split his shield in two and he rolled away. He grabbed his sword but I had blood in my head. Petr was not the only oathsworn I had lost and I wanted vengeance. My first blow buckled his sword and he fell backwards. My second blow took his head. The riders closest to him looked in shock at their leader's decapitated body. Haaken the Bold and Æbbi Bonecrusher, two of the last of my oathsworn still standing, leapt at the men and hacked them from their horses. I took the helmet from the dead Breton's head and held the bloody skull by the hair. As I glanced to my left I saw Saxbjǫrn as he ended the life of the traitor, Beorn Straight Hair. The cheer from behind me told me that we had won. The Bretons were fleeing. Those on my right followed them but we were too exhausted. I stood amidst a charnel house but Pascweten, heir to Alan the Great, lay dead and we had won the battle. Now could I win the peace?

Chapter 15

We had dying warriors and horses to despatch but as I looked around I saw that we had lost many warriors. Two of my hearth weru were still with me. Harold Strong Arm guarded my home and my son and I had lost all but two of those who had sworn to give their lives for me. They had kept their word. Egil lived yet. He grinned. "I thought when the horse and rider died that my service to the Lord of Rouen was over."

"You gained honour for you did not flinch. Godwin?"

"He lives. He did not have to face the horsemen." He waved an arm, "It was bloody!"

"And they will pay. It will not be in blood but they will bleed gold." I turned, "Ragnar, have those who did not fight clear the field. Burn the enemy and bury ours. Start to take the mail and weapons back to the longphort."

"Aye lord. Our men have been avenged."

"Perhaps. We have killed the King's son but King Alan still eludes my blade"

Saxbjǫrn limped over. He had been wounded, "And I can sleep at night." He held the head of Beorn Straight Hair. "Not a Dane remains alive."

"You have done well." I turned to my captain of archers. "Petr, take your horsemen and follow the Bretons. I would know what they intend."

"Aye lord." He ran to his horse and waved over his men.

"A great victory, lord!"

"Thank you, Sven Blue Cheek, but King Alan was not here and it feels hollow."

He waved a hand across the field. "His army is defeated. We killed more than a hundred horsemen and horses. The King has lost a son. Had I offered you this when we left Ċiriċeburh you would have bitten off my hand."

I nodded, "You are right but look at our dead."

Æbbi Bonecrusher and Haaken the Bold approached. "You are right lord, we have lost warriors but even now they are in Valhalla and are being hailed as heroes. They were not foresworn and all died with a sword in their hands. They took many Bretons with them. Our line did not break and we won. Celebrate and do not mourn. We will honour our dead and tonight when we drink, we will remember them!"

We made camp just east of the battlefield. The wind was from the sea and took the smell of death toward Vannes. If we buried our dead then they would be despoiled by the Bretons. Instead, we made a pyre where they had fallen. Their swords were killed and placed in their hands and they were burned. This was not a Christian burial. There was no chanting. This was not something we wrote down. Each warrior who wished to say goodbye to their shield brothers or just remembered them silently. As the flames licked higher around the bodies it was easy to see their forms in the smoke as they rose to Valhalla. We had all heard the story of Dragonheart who had gone to Miklagård and died. He had gone to Valhalla but then returned for his work was unfinished. He had lived long after he saw Valhalla. The stories he told were now the stuff of legend. When we looked up and saw the smoke rising we knew what Valhalla would be like. I could see Petr the Slow as he was offered a horn of ale by my grandfather. When the fire died down we returned to our camp.

We butchered and cooked the dead horses. Men cleared the field of all that was valuable. I had Pascweten's body and head covered with a cloak. We would need them. My riders returned well before dark. "They are fled to Vannes, lord."

I nodded and waved my lords around me. "We will stay this night. Saxbjǫrn, take the rest of the treasure and the wounded to the ships. You can use the horses we captured. Lars, take your men to help them."

Saxbjǫrn had been wounded but like the rest of those who would be returning to the ships, the wounds would just be honourable battle scars. The ones whose wounds had been more serious were given a warrior's death. Saxbjǫrn nodded, "Aye lord. Now that I have avenged my shield brothers I will hang up my own shield. This wound will slow me in battle. I will be your lord of Carentan. I will make my warriors ready to fight for you but I will ride to war no more."

I had known this was coming. I had seen a change in him. The deaths of so many of his men had made him doubt himself. A warrior who doubts himself gives his enemy an edge in battle. They ate and then left. All of the wounded were mounted and the other horses carried the spare treasure from the fight back to the drekar. Leif was the most inexperienced of the lords who sat around my fire. Egil and Godwin acted as servants fetching ale and food. With just two oathsworn left to me I needed their presence and I trusted them both. "Lord is this over? Will they fight again?"

Sven Blue Cheek chuckled, "I hope so. If they do then Brittany will be ours." The young warrior looked confused and Sven explained. "We broke them today. They lost five for every one of ours. They made the mistake of bringing farmers for they thought to drive us hence easily. More than half of their army was made up of men who are not warriors. They will not fight again."

"But suppose King Alan comes?"

"If he was close by then he would have led his men. Thanks to Lord Göngu-Hrólfr Rognvaldson we have an ally in Fulk le Roux."

I shook my head, "More like the Norns, Sven."

"You do yourself a disservice, lord. The Norns put the warrior from Anjou before you but you chose the right path." He turned back to Leif. "It is more likely that they will sue for peace."

"And then we prepare for a bigger war. We prepare to take on the Franks." I smiled at Leif, "There your new home, Leif Haroldsson, may well become a battleground."

"We now have more mail and better weapons lord and we can make our new home stronger."

Bergil's wife was with child again and I saw the concern on his face as he asked, "Will it be soon, Lord Göngu-Hrólfr Rognvaldson?"

"If King Alan had been here then I would have said yes for he and the Emperor are working together. I can see now that the title of king, which Charles bestowed upon the Breton, was the price he paid for an alliance. If King Alan had been here then it would have told me he was trying to draw me away from my home. This defeat for the Frank's ally helps us and delays the war. They will try to find other allies to fight us. They may even hire Vikings." I pointed to the pile of Viking bodies which still lay where they had fallen. "Since Guthrum was converted there are many of his men who are swords for hire. The Franks pay well. Bergil Fast Blade, you will see your child born and begin to walk before we have to fight." I waved a hand at them all. "You have that time to build up your forces so that your walls are strong and you have enough to leave on your walls and to bring more men than you brought this day. When we fight the Franks, I want the victory to be so complete that they never fight us again. Then we can return our attention to these treacherous Bretons."

It was noon when the Bretons appeared. Although they brought many men they did not come for war. We arrayed our lines to show them that we were ready to fight but when the priests came toward us I knew that these would be peace talks. The fine robes told me that it was a bishop who had been sent. "Lord Göngu-Hrólfr Rognvaldson I am the Bishop of Vannes, Rudalt, Count of Vannes, wishes to talk peace with you."

"Who is this Rudalt?"

"He is the youngest son of King Alan."

I nodded and pointed to a spot close to where Pascweten had fallen. His body lay nearby covered by a cloak. The meeting place was close enough for Petr and my archers to kill any who attempted treachery. "I will bring four lords. This Count of Vannes can bring the same number."

Sven Blue Cheek, Sámr Oakheart, Bergil Fast Blade and Ragnar the Resolute came with me. I left Leif in command. Æbbi Bonecrusher and Haaken the Bold would be there to advise him if that was needed.

Rudalt was young and he rode as did the three lords who came with him. He looked down, "We would have peace, Viking."

I nodded and said, "Then get down from your horse pup lest I take its legs and force you to the ground."

He coloured and I saw him glance at one of the older lords with him. He had been advised already to be respectful. The Bishop said as the young Count dismounted, "Let us remember the dead who lie about this field, lords. They are yet unburied."

I smiled, "Our dead have gone to Valhalla already. If you wish to honour your own dead then let us speak quickly before the rats and foxes return to feast upon the dead."

Rudalt glanced at a pile of bodies which appeared to move. It was rats. He said, quickly, "We would have peace. What do you want?"

"Firstly, I need to know if you have the authority to negotiate. I do not want your father to come back to me and say that he does not agree with that which his son has spoken."

The Bishop spoke, "I am here so that all will be done well. Whatever we agree is agreed by the King."

"We will leave this land." I saw the relief on all of their faces although the older warrior still looked sceptical. "However, there is a price.

Firstly, King Alan will agree that my settlements on the Cotentin are Viking and will remain untouched. They are not Frank and they are not Breton. If you cannot agree to that then now is the time to end these talks and to draw swords."

They looked at each other and the young Count nodded and said, "That is agreed."

Secondly, we have many Bretons we took. They are unharmed. We have them gathered at the river close to our drekar. If you would have them back then you must buy them."

"Buy them?" Rudalt frowned.

"We have to pay for this war. We either sell them to you or to the slave markets in Dorestad!"

The Bishop said, "We will buy them!"

"I also have your brother's body and his head. Would you wish them for burial?"

"Of course!"

"Then there is a price for him too." He nodded. "The price for the body and the captives is ten thousand silver pieces or the equivalent in gold."

The Count looked at the Bishop who nodded, "Agreed." The church would be providing the coin.

"You will bring it to the place you call Hennebont. Do not be tardy for we need to eat. A hungry Viking raids. As a measure of our goodwill you can take your brother's body this day." I pointed to the cloaked form. "How long will you need, Bishop?" I knew that Rudalt was a figurehead. The Bishop held the power.

I saw the older warrior hide his smile. The Bishop said. "It will be with you by noon tomorrow. The captives are unharmed?"

"The only ones who died were the men who fought us. They have been fed and are unmolested."

The Bishop said, "I would send one of my priests with you so that the captives can be given hope."

I nodded, "They have that already but I do not mind." They rose. "Before you leave know this. We can be a good neighbour so long as we are left alone but we are the deadliest of enemies for unless you take our head we will fight you. If your King wishes more land there will be easier enemies from whom he can take it." I saw the Bishop nodding. He understood my words. If this was not the end of the war then we would unleash a beast upon the Bretons that they would not be able to contain.

The priest brought a cross with him which he carried before him. Perhaps he thought it gave him protection. Before we left my men brought me three horses they had found wandering on the battlefield. They were bigger horses and I was able to ride. We headed back to Hennebont. The Bishop had been right to send the priest for the relief amongst the captives made our last day easier. The decks on the drekar were lifted to enable us to load the treasure. I had decided that each man would be given an equal share of the treasure we took. I know that some men would have thought that it was overgenerous. It had been Poppa who needed coin and I was rich enough. I had chests of coin already in Rouen. I would reward my men and that would draw more men to my standard. I needed a larger army.

The chests arrived as had been promised. I let the captives go. They fled, with the priests and the men who had escorted the chests. We were left in an empty town. It took until dark to load the ships and replace the decks. Then we loaded the animals. I took back the three large horses. One by one my drekar headed down the river until there were just two left. Mine and Gandálfr's. Our men fired the town, the wharf and the ships Then we hoisted the sail and headed down the river. The red sky seemed to reflect my standard. The burning town would be a reminder of the folly of attacking Vikings.

As we sailed downstream, letting the current and the sail do the work, I thought about the campaign. I had left twice as many men at home than I had brought with me. Admittedly most of them did not have mail but they were all warriors. They were not the Breton farmers we had faced. Bjorn the Brave and Bagsecg had more than a hundred and twenty warriors between them They had not been used. If war came early it would be unwelcome but we would cope. To win I wanted time to strengthen our forces. The silver we had been given would make us all better armed. I would use my own coin hoard to equip my oathsworn.

My two hearth weru sat at the prow. They were talking about Harold Strong Arm. "He will be angry that he was not there with them when they died."

I heard their words. Harold Strong Arm had told me that his days of fighting in a shield wall were gone. I knew what they did not. He would command Rouen. I let them finish their talk. The two would be reliving the battle and the deaths of their friends. They had been engrossed and not seen me listening. They turned when they saw me. Haaken said, "You have but two hearth weru lord. It is not enough."

I nodded, "And that is why I come to speak with you. When we return I would have you spread the word that I need oathsworn. You three will ensure that the ones I have are the best. Mail and good weapons are not a prerequisite. I need men who are strong in heart. I need men who do not wish for a family. I have gold and silver. I will buy what they need. They will be equipped as Alan of Auxerre and his men were. When we fight they will stand out upon the battlefield."

Æbbi Bonecrusher gave me a curious look. "Did you not see, lord, that the Breton whose head you took also had a red standard? On his standard, however, was a curious creature."

Haaken said, "It was a lion. I have seen them before. They live in hot places. They are like a wolf but they have shorter fur and do not hunt in packs. I have heard men call them the King of the Beasts!"

I smiled, "I used one on the coins I gave to my men. It is a powerful creature."

Æbbi Bonecrusher laughed, "Then this Pascweten had a high opinion of himself."

"He was a fair warrior. He knew how to fight." I thought back to the battle and I remembered the red standard. By closing my eyes, I saw the lion. "It was a battle of the red and the horse won."

Haken frowned, "Save that you do not ride to war on a horse."

Æbbi Bonecrusher said, "But we are the Clan of the Horse."

"Led by a lion! Think how many times our lord fights alone and for us. I think it would be a better sign for you, lord."

"I am loath to change my standard again."

"No matter what the standard we will always be the Clan of the Horse. You should consider it, lord."

"I will, Haaken the Bold, but we have, I hope, a year at least before we need to go to war again."

The three horses were tethered in the centre of the drekar close to the mast. We had lost men in the battle. We only had forty men left aboard and we were not as crowded as we might have been. We were heavily laden. Erik had had to remove some of the ballast. It was fortunate that we did not have far to go for a storm would swamp us. I made plans to land at Ciriċeburh, Carentan and Caen if there were problems. We would not risk either the ships, the crew or the animals. The Allfather had sent the horses for a purpose. There was a stallion and two mares. Erik Gillesson and his son would be able to breed horses capable of carrying mailed warriors. Nor was there any rush to reach home. I had no wife waiting for me. William would have missed me but soon he would join me when I sailed or rode to war. I did not have his mother to prevent him from becoming a Viking. With that in mind, I sought out Godwin. He and Egil were examining the treasures they had taken from the battlefield. They had both taken fine scabbards from dead Bretons as well as daggers. Egil also had a good sword.

They looked up as I approached. "I would have the two of you watch over the horses on the voyage back. If they look to become anxious then calm them."

"Aye lord."

Godwin nodded astern. We had just left the estuary but there was the faintest of glows from the burning town and wharf. "I recognised some of those who fought with Beorn Straight Hair. They were Godfrid's men."

"Then I hope that is the end of them. The last thing we need is a blood feud with Vikings." He nodded, "You still wish to serve me?"

"I do lord. I have not disappointed you have I?"

"No Godwin. I am well pleased with you. I would have you be as a bodyguard for my son, William. I will not leave him at home but I am Lord of Rouen and I command men. When he comes with us I would have you watch him and ensure he comes to no harm." I smiled, "Either from another or from himself."

He laughed, "William is a lively boy. I will be honoured, lord."

"That makes you oathsworn to the two of us."

"I do not mind, lord."

"There may come a time when you do. If you wish to wed or to leave me then just ask and I will release you from your oath." He nodded. "This means that you must sleep in his chamber. I will speak with Popæg when we reach Rouen."

We left the protection of the land and our motion became livelier. I joined Godwin and Egil and we quietened them. Godwin began to sing to them and that helped. He sang a Saxon song. It had the desired effect and despite the movement of the drekar, they seemed happier. I went to Erik, "We will put in at Ciriceburh. It will do the animals good and I think this storm may become violent."

The other captains, except for Saxbjǫrn, must have had the same idea. Luckily for us, Ciriceburh was one of our larger ports. Two stone arms made a breakwater and a safer anchorage. Ragnar had improved the defences since the Breton attack. Our caution was justified when the lively weather turned into a full storm. The animals we had brought back, horses, cows, pigs and sheep were all housed within the walls of Ciriceburh. Had they not been then we might have lost them. Ragnar sent riders to Valognes and the other settlements to announce the news of our victory. He, Ubba and Saxbjǫrn could now begin to reclaim the land lost to the Bretons. They had sworn to allow us to hold the Cotentin. This time Bárekr's haven and Benni's Ville would be built more strongly. When war with the Franks came Ragnar would bring just one large warband. We would not let go of what we had gained so easily.

We sat out the storm and then headed home with a fresh but benign wind from the southwest. Gradually the other drekar slipped away to return to their homes and Gandálfr, Lars, Leif and myself continued to Rouen. We had to take to the oars once we reached the river. It added half a day to our journey for we had the fewer crew and we were heavily laden. We did not reach Rouen until dusk. I was relieved to see that my standard still flew. I had thought about the words of Haaken the Bold. Perhaps there was something in what he said. A golden lion appealed to me.

Harold Strong Arm had had men watching the river and by the time we tied up the wharf was crowded with families waiting to see their menfolk. The tears marked those whose men had died. Fortunately, there were not many. None of my dead oathsworn had families. William and Popæg, along with Harold Strong Arm, were there. We did not need to tell Harold of the loss of hearth weru. He saw just Æbbi Bonecrusher and Haaken the Bold. As William ran to me I saw Popæg squeeze his arm. Had the Norns been at work?

I swung William up into my arms. He shouted, "You have giant horses! Did you win?"

"Aye, I won!"

"I missed you!"

"I shall not leave without you again. You shall come with me."

"Truly?"

"Aye, but there are conditions!" He nodded, somewhat fearfully, "You must be able to ride a pony."

"I can nearly do that now!"

"And Godwin Red Eyes will guard you. You obey him as though I had spoken."

He seemed relieved, "That will be easy! I like Godwin."

I turned to my son's nurse, "Popæg, Godwin will need to sleep close by my son. Is that a problem?"

She smiled and said, "Not a problem my lord. I will have another cot placed within and I will find another chamber." She seemed quite happy at the thought.

"Harold, we have lost oathsworn. Haaken and Æbbi will speak with you. How goes the river and my land?"

He nodded to the river. "We have counted the ships which ply our waters. More sail upstream than stop here."

"So if we halted trade then the Franks would suffer more than we?"

"They would."

"Good. I will see to the unloading of the horses and stable them. Have the rest of the treasure we took taken within. Tomorrow we hold a feast. We have to celebrate the victory and sing of the dead!"

That evening William was so exhausted that he fell asleep in my arms. Popæg brought Godwin who picked him up and carried him to bed. Padraig had been nervous all night and as soon as we were alone I asked him why.

"Lord, while you were away I had a letter from the Lady Poppa."

I sat up. "It was addressed to you and not to me?" He nodded. "What did it say?"

"She begged me to intercede on her behalf. She said that she missed her son and daughter. She knew that she had made a mistake and wished for forgiveness. She asked for a second chance. She said everyone is allowed one mistake and you must forgive her."

His voice and his eyes pleaded with me. I nodded. "Interesting. Not once does she speak of me. It is her son and daughter she misses. I daresay that she misses the lifestyle she enjoyed but I am not in her thoughts. If she came back how could I trust her?"

"Lord, Jesus tells us to turn the other cheek and to forgive our enemies. She was never your enemy. Surely you can forgive her."

"If I was a Christian then perhaps I might forgive her but I am not. She conspired against not only me but all the people who follow me. I cannot forgive her even if I want to and I do not want to. She made her bed when she coupled with that priest. Now she reaps the reward. Go to the nunnery and tell her my decision. I want no more missives from her. Is that clear?"

"Yes lord. You are a hard man."

"I am a Viking and this is the way we are."

"And you will now live alone?"

"I am not alone. I have my son. Gerloc is a pleasant child, you, when you are not preaching, are also good company. I have my warriors what else is there?"

"What about women, lord?"

I laughed, "If I wanted a woman I could have a dozen with the click of my fingers. You manage without a woman. Why should not I?"

"Lord, I am a priest. I serve God and the church."

"And I am Lord of Rouen. I serve my people."

Chapter 16

William rode with me when I went to see Erik and Bagsecg. I still had just two oathsworn and I took Egil and Godwin. William had shown that he was a good rider. With Egil and Godwin flanking him then he was safe. We took with us the three horses I had captured. They had been cosseted in my stables. The grooms thought them better than any horse they had seen save Gilles.

Erik ran his eye over them. He was impressed. "We now have stock to breed a powerful horse herd but it will still take three years or more before we see results."

"We may have that and more. What have you learned about the Franks? Are they preparing for war?"

He smiled, "There are three King Charles. Or at least there were. The Emperor Charles the Bald has now declared that Young Charles, they call him Charles the Simple, is to be the new King of the West Franks. He has appointed the Duke of Aquitaine to guide him. Charles the Fat is either dead or so close to death as to be of no use as a king. There are two kings of the West Franks at the moment. Charles the Simple is young and so is Ranulf Duke of Aquitaine. Ranulf is seen as the military mind who can teach Charles how to defeat you. Odo, whom we know from the siege of Paris, is not happy and so until the political situation is calmed then the Franks can do nothing."

"What if we attacked?"

"Then that might be the one event which unites the Franks. Count Odo hates you and would put aside his own ambition to defeat you." I could see that Erik was right. He was half Frank and knew their ways better than I did. Poppa had also understood them but that bridge had been burned. "The Franks look in and not out. They are wary, even afraid of us. Only Odo, who has called himself King for a year, is ready to war with you."

I smiled, "Then I like his honesty. It is these dissemblers I dislike. This new King, he is young?"

"Barely twenty."

"Do you have spies still?"

"You mean William?" I nodded. "Aye, I do."

"Then have him visit Paris and discover all that he can. These Frankish politics are complicated. I need to know more about this new King."

"The rumour has it that he is not yet crowned for Odo clings on to the crown."

"Rumours are no good to me. I need facts. Where is this Charles the Simple! What of this Ranulf of Aquitaine? And where do the Bretons fit into all of this." Even as I spoke I wondered about Fulk le Roux. Charles the Fat had been a supporter and ally. If Fulk was defeated then Alan of Brittany might choose to ignore the promises made by his son. "I will ride to Bjorn the Brave and stay this night in his hall. As soon as William the One Arm discovers any news send it to me."

"Aye lord and I will let you know when your new stallion has covered the mares!"

The road to Bjorn's hall was much easier knowing that there was anarchy in Frankia. The Empire was not the powerful force it had been during the reign of Charlemagne. The Franks seemed to think that simply by naming a man Charles he would inherit the qualities of that fearsome Emperor. It was obviously not true.

The farms which lay between Montfort and Bjorn's lands were all prosperous. I saw crops in the fields and there were many animals. Bjorn was a Viking without a drekar. The river lay well to the north but he and his men were a new breed. They were shipless Vikings. Unlike most of my warriors, they were happy to use horses. Being so close to Erik and Bagsecg gave them an ample supply of hardy horses and they used them. They still fought on foot but, if they had to, then they could use stiraps and fight from the back of a horse.

He swept an arm east as he explained, "I have my men ride the borders of their land at least once every seven days. They look for that which has changed and they look for signs of change. Apart from the attack on the noble from Anjou it has been quiet hereabouts."

"Then perhaps we can delay war for a little longer. You have young men who are being trained to fight?"

"We have and all of us have sons who will fight one day."

"You know of this Charles the Simple?"

He shook his head, "Not as much as we should. He is the son of Louis the Stammerer. His title does not suggest that he is a great man and we know he has yet to be given the crown. He is King but not yet anointed and crowned."

"And could you defend your hall?"

"We have a palisade and we have a ditch. The ditch is filled with water and there are stakes within it. We have a well and thanks to Petr Jorgensen we have good archers. If they attack us they will have to fight tooth and nail to reduce our walls."

William enjoyed being with the young families of my warriors. In Rouen, he had few children with whom to play. Those who had families lived beyond my walls and had farms. I was tempted to stay longer but I still had much to do in Rouen. Lars and Leif had a home but it was not yet defensible. When the Franks made war, their halls would be the focal point of any attack. I wondered if that thought had been planted in my head by the spirits when I suggested that they build there. It was the sort of thing my grandfather would have done. I owed it to Harold Haroldsson's son to keep him as safe as I could.

On the way back to Rouen, William was chatty. The loss of his mother did not seem to have bothered him, in fact, he was far more outgoing than he had been. "Now that I ride with you, father, will I be given a sword and mail?"

I laughed, "Mail would be a waste. By the time it was made you would have outgrown it. If you wish to feel like a warrior we can have the tanners make you a leather jerkin and cap."

He looked disappointed, "A sword then."

"You could not lift a sword. Let us say a seax."

"They will be a start. And do we go to war soon?"

"We have no need to for our enemies are not yet ready to threaten us. We will make war on them before they can take our land from us."

"Mother said that this land was not ours. She said we had stolen it and that the rightful owners wanted it back. What did she mean the rightful owners?"

"This land has been fought over by many people. It is the strong who hold on to it. We hold it and that makes us the rightful owners."

He seemed satisfied by my answer. "I like this land."

"Good, for one day you will rule it."

"After you are dead?"

"Probably."

We rode in silence for a while. Then, out of nowhere, he said, "Will Harold Strong Arm marry Popæg?"

We all turned in surprise, "What makes you say that?"

"They kiss a lot and hold hands. She laughs when he is in the room." He shrugged. "I would not mind."

I looked at Egil and Godwin. Egil said, "I knew nothing, lord."

Godwin said, "I know nothing either lord save that they do seem to cast affectionate glances at each other. Is it forbidden?"

"It is not forbidden it is just that I am surprised." I knew I would have to ask Harold when we reached Rouen but I was uncomfortable bringing up the subject.

It is strange but as soon as I entered my hall and saw the two of them in the same room I knew that William had not misunderstood. This was something I had not expected and so I sent for Padraig. I met him in my private chamber where I could study maps and plan. I spoke first about the Frankish King. "What is it that you know, Padraig? I have rumours and inferences but you are a learned man. Other priests pass through my town and I know that you will have spoken to them."

He nodded, "King Charles, also called the Simple, is the Emperor's choice of King. Odo Count of Paris has declared himself King. At the moment Odo has the support of Paris and that is all. I have heard," he smiled, "from merchants and not priests, that a group of nobles is gathered at Rheims to have him crowned and anointed."

"And what do we know of this Frankish King?"

"That he is young and has little experience. He is not a warrior. I think that is why the people of Paris preferred Odo. He is the warrior who saved Paris from the Vikings."

"Then I have time before he can mobilise against me." Padraig hesitated. "Oh, come now Padraig. You have read the letters and you have spoken to the priests."

"With respect, lord, that was Charles the Fat and we know not what this new King will do. Either he is nothing like Charles the Fat and will not break the treaty or he is in which case he will have to secure his own country first."

The priest was right. There would be no attack this year and probably not the next year either. I had time. "Good. Now, what do you know about Popæg and Harold Strong Arm?"

I saw that I had taken him by surprise for he flushed and then smiled, "He is an older warrior and despite her manner, Popæg is still capable of bearing children. They are comfortable together and I believe that they would wed but…"

"But for Göngu-Hrólfr Rognvaldson whose feet are so large that he tramples on people's feelings!"

"I did not say that lord but…"

"Send him to me and I will speak with him."

"My lord…"

"He was my oathsworn. We have seen friends die and we have stood side by side. Words cannot hurt either of us. Send him to me."

When he entered he was nervous. Had Popæg been with him I would not have known what to say but this was Harold Strong Arm. I spoke to him the way I always had, bluntly. "I understand you wish to marry Popæg?"

His mouth opened and closed and then he smiled, "Aye lord."

"Then what is the problem?"

"I am oathsworn and…"

"And we have agreed that you will not fight in a shield wall. You will be the keeper of my hall. Marry her!"

"Thank you, lord…I…"

I waved an arm to silence his protests, "I am just disappointed that you felt you had to hide it."

"It was not that lord. I was attracted to her but spending as much time together as we did, looking after William, well it sort of accelerated things and then you were back and… I am sorry."

I grinned and clasped his arm, "And Padraig is right! I am a little frightening to be around." A sudden thought struck me. "Do you think William is afraid of me?"

"Afraid? No. In awe? Certainly!"

When we rejoined the others Popæg looked a little worried. When Harold Strong Arm went to her and almost picked her off the ground then she knew that all was well. Although Æbbi Bonecrusher and Haaken the Bold were pleased for their friend and the impending wedding their priority was oathsworn and over the next months while the wedding was being arranged they were bringing men to me. They insisted that I have the final choice over those who would defend me. I initially chose eight to join Æbbi Bonecrusher. We would not be going to war for a year or so. Committing to me was a lifetime's work. I still had time and who knew what the Norns might throw my way.

Their first choice both surprised and pleased me. It was Egil Flame Bearer. "He is young, lord, but we watched him when he held your banner. He is as resolute as Ragnar and he has skills. He handled himself well when he followed the priest. That is the sort of thing those who followed the Dragonheart could do so well. His friendship with Godwin bodes well for your son and it is time that one of the hearth weru carried your banner."

Egil joined me. Arne and Audun Petrsson were brothers. Their father had died fighting alongside Ubba. They travelled all the way from Valognes to join me. Haaken knew of their skills. Their two older brothers had families and Arne and Audun were happy to commit to my cause. Haraldr Blue Eyes was known to me. He was the only warrior whose size came close to mine. He had lived and farmed to the north of Rouen. The gods had sent a disease and, when he was away fighting with me, his family had all been taken. He took it as a sign that he was not meant to have a family. He buried them and joined me. Olaf of Djupr was the second son of Olaf Two Toes. When his father died he sought to emulate the old warrior who had fought for so long at my side. He was an easy choice. Stig of the Haugr was, like Egil, young. Like the Petrsson brothers, he had lost much. He had been sailing on his uncle's knarr when the Haugr was taken. His family were either slaughtered or enslaved and he blamed himself for being away at sea. He wanted vengeance and serving with me guaranteed him the opportunity to do so. The last two who were chosen were from Montfort. Erik Gillesson sent them. They were half Norse and half Frank. Both were excellent riders and Erik told us that they were the best warriors he had. One was chosen by the Norns for he was called Hrólfr the Horseman. That had been my grandfather's name and was an obvious choice. The other was the grandson of Bagsecg, my grandfather's blacksmith. When his father had been killed in battle and his mother died, Erik had brought him up. Sven Mighty Fist had inherited his grandfather's physique and was the strongest warrior I had ever met.

They all swore an oath and moved into the new warrior hall we had built attached to my hall. All were given a blue cloak with a silver sword and a helmet with a nasal. They were Vikings and chose their own swords. The ones who had no mail were given some. Finally, each was given a horse. Gilles had been used by Erik to breed horses and we had enough large ones for those like Haraldr Blue Eyes and Sven Mighty Fist who were too big for ordinary horses.

They swore their oath to me after Popæg and Harold were married. She was a Christian and Padraig performed the ceremony. It was more formal than the simple one used by my Vikings but Harold did not mind. He understood his new wife and her need for the cross around her neck. As he said to me, while we waited in the chapel, "I will die a Viking. And as for children? I had given up any thought of having them and if the price to become a father is for them to be brought up Christian then it is *wyrd*."

A day after the wedding, as I headed east with my hearth weru I thought about Harold's words. Few of my men had married pure Norse or Danish women. Most had the blood of the Franks in their veins and almost all of them were Christians. There was no conflict in their homes. Audun and Arne had had a Christian mother and had attended a church for their mother had had them baptised. They seemed able to reconcile that with a desire to kill enemies. They would not turn the other cheek. My people and my warriors were changing. Should I?

I turned to look at my new men as we left Rouen. The red standard fluttering above the blue cloaked horsemen made for a striking sight. When we fought people would know where to find me and that was good. I still wondered about making the horse into a lion. I resolved to do nothing until I had a sign from the Allfather.

I left my hall to speak with Lars and Leif. I had walked my walls and seen their home grow. Now I wished to inspect it closer. They had done a good job. The wooden palisade was well protected by a ditch which was filled with river water and had to be crossed by a removable bridge. There were two small towers above the gate and each held a couple of archers. The inside was well organised and neat. The hull of their drekar was now a mound of turf with a spiral of smoke rising from it. There were other buildings too. The bread oven lay far from any building save the smithy where a smith's hammer rang out. There was a second hall made of wood and turf. A granary stood on stilts and I saw that there were women working at a brewhouse.

Leif greeted me as I dismounted. "It is good to see you, lord." He waved an arm around the interior of his home. "What think you of our hall?"

"I think you have done well and there are women too."

He nodded, "The women of Rouen are friendly and there were many unattached women who sought a husband. Some had lost men in the wars and there were also orphans. Half of our crew are married and many of the women bear Vikings within them."

While we walked around and he showed me the features he had built, we talked. "Lord, my men and I would raid."

"The Franks?"

He shook his head, "I know that you are not ready for war and we are not foolish enough to begin a war which might put our new families in harm's way. We have heard that Alfred of Wessex grows old. His son Edward and his nephew, Æthelwold, both vie for the crown." He smiled, "One advantage of spending so many years as wanderers is that we know how to gather information. The ships which trade with you tell us these things."

"Alfred has always suffered from ill health what makes you so sure that he is close to death?"

"His family are gathered at Wintan-Caestre. They look within and not without. We would strike soon and take advantage of the situation."

"Then you have my permission but I ask one thing. If you find any maps, parchments or papers then do not destroy them. Bring them to me. I have a priest who can interpret them and the information they contain is valuable."

"I will do so."

After we left him we rode as far as the last farm to the east. Bárekr was as much a Frank as a Viking. He had a farm which he could defend but he preferred farming to sailing the seas. Like Bjorn the Brave he seemed untroubled by his Frankish neighbours and I returned home happier.

Four days later a one-armed man rode into my town. It was William, Erik's spy. He had been a warrior but he had chosen to follow Erik and the fact that he was a Frank helped him to blend in with the people of Paris.

As we sat with Padraig and Æbbi Bonecrusher he gave us his news. "Odo, Count of Paris is dead and Charles the Simple has been crowned."

I asked the obvious question, "How did Odo die?"

William shrugged, "His death is shrouded in mystery and the people of Paris are not happy. Odo was the one who saved them from the Danes."

I smiled, "And me."

He shook his head, "Had they followed your advice then Paris would have fallen. The new King has not gone to Paris. He is busy securing support in the rest of West Frankia. My lord told me what you wished to know. There will be no war this year. If there was then you would win for they are ill-prepared. If you chose then you could claim vast areas of Frankia."

"But I am not yet ready. The attacks by the Bretons took from us the warriors who would have won the war for us. We are thinly stretched. The gods, it seems, are not yet ready for a war. We will wait."

I handed him some coins and Padraig asked him, "And the Church? Who do they support?"

"Like the people they are divided. Those in Paris favour any but one of the family of Louis the Stammerer. The rest back the King for he has the support of the Emperor and the Pope."

"Why is the Church important?" I was curious.

"Because they are wealthy and they will support the king who will ensure that they can survive." He sighed, "It is no surprise that the men who met with Æðelwald of Remisgat were priests and from the Roman Church. It is in their interest to weaken you."

I smiled, "And your church does not engage in such practices."

He shook his head, "We are simple priests who deliver God's word to people."

I knew he was speaking the truth. "William, I would have you keep me informed about any change in the political situation. We need advance warning of an attack by the Franks."

"Do not worry, lord, you shall have it."

A month or so later, as I was preparing to ride abroad, a drekar came into my river. After Godfrid we were wary but there were no shields on the gunwales and like Leif's ship it looked as though it had suffered damage at sea. I went to greet them. The captain was Haraldr Greybeard. I had never met him. He was Norse. He clasped my arm when I landed. "I wondered if the giant who is too big to ride horses still lived. I am Haraldr Greybeard and I was a distant cousin of Rognvald Eysteinsson."

"My adopted father."

"Aye, he was a good man. I would have left the fjords when he did but I sought my fortune in Miklagård." He laughed. "Many of us tried but few made many coins from it. When I returned Harold Finehair was King and I did not get on with him. We fell out and he declared me an outlaw."

"In my view that is a mark of honour."

"My crew and I raided for a while and then we heard of a land beyond the western sea." I found myself clutching my horse amulet. He smiled, "I know you thought we would fall off the edge of the world." I nodded. We did not. There is something out there for we found strange birds and sea creatures but we saw no land. We saw a sea of weed but after many months we turned to come home. Some of my men began to die for the air was as hot as in Miklagård. I thought to come here for I do not like the Danes and we have heard, from others, that you need good swords and warriors to wield them."

"We do. You are more than welcome."

"We will need to repair our ship and, I am afraid, that for a while we will be beggars for we have no coin. We are men and we need to eat."

"Fear not we have raided well and you will have all the food you need. I will have my steward see to it. Upstream is a settlement of others like yourself. You can build your own home there. When you have settled in then come and speak with me. I will tell you of my plans."

This was *wyrd*. The Norns were truly spinning. First, a thread from the Haugr was spun and now one from Norway. My grandfather's dream of a secure land in Frankia looked like coming to fruition. Padraig sent food to the new warriors and stones so that they could build a bread oven. It would take them time to repair their drekar but we had time. I now had a purpose. I would seek the weaknesses in the Frankish defences.

And so we prepared for war but this would not be a sudden war. This would be planned and coordinated. I intended to know the land we would use to attack the Franks. I had a year to become as familiar with the ground as it was possible. Now that I had my own bodyguard I was more confident about riding close to enemy lines. We rode first to Djupr. The Franks were barely to be seen. In the twelve days we rode we saw not a single Frankish stronghold. We then headed east. We saw nowhere with fortifications until we came to Beauvais. It had an old Roman fort whose stone had been reused to make a stronghold. I knew that by threatening Beauvais I could draw the Franks from Paris. Then, a month later, we crossed the river and headed south toward Chartres. This land was even more secure for we held all up to Évreux. Bagsecg and Bjorn kept a tight hold on the land. Paris was more formidable than Chartres but if we could take that then it would send a message to the Franks that we were serious. After speaking with many merchants who passed through our town it became obvious that the Franks thought we would tire of farming and go back to wandering. That might have been true of many other Vikings but not my clan. We were here to stay.

As I rode back I realised it was almost a year since I had put Poppa in a nunnery. It was time to prepare for war.

Chapter 17

Lars and Leif had a successful raid to the land of Wessex. There they gathered information as well as treasure, mail and female slaves. King Alfred was dead. Guthrum had died years before and so those who ruled in the land the Romans had called Britannia were unknown to me. On their way back, they had called at Bruggas. They had spread the word that I was making war and needed ships. Such a call to arms would bring us many ships. This time I would select the best and not just take any drekar and its crew.

I summoned my lords four months after we had ridden to Chartres. My new men and I had had months to get to know one another and we were now a tightly bonded band. I felt sorry for Godwin for he had been left at home with William and I know that he envied Egil. One problem I did not have was Poppa. When my lords had visited she had always made them feel unwelcome. She looked down upon them. They did not have the fine manners of Frankish lords. My lords were warriors. We had eaten raw wild sea birds with our fingers when we were hungry. We had drunk water which was so full of wildlife that it almost constituted a meal. None were dainty when they ate.

As Popæg and Harold were now married she was the only woman at my table. My lords did not bring their wives. Popæg was also with child. This amused Haaken the Bold and delighted Harold. None said anything untoward to Harold. He was held in great affection by all of my lords. The result was a convivial feast which was not only a council of war it was also a celebration. As such it was the finest of feasts. William was now able to drink small beer. He had grown. Popæg thought it was because he now ate what she called proper food. He ate what my men did. There was lots of meat and plenty of bread and cheese. He would be as big as his father. Gerloc had also grown in the many months since her mother had left and she now had a personality. She was not my child but she felt like it for I saw her each day and she called for me by name, I was Gong-Gon! It was her way of saying my name.

Haraldr Greybeard, Lars and Leif attended. Since their arrival, they had all become part of our clan. As Padraig pointed out we were less of a clan and more of a people. The Franks and Bretons called us Norsemen. That would do for a while but we were more than that we had Danish, Frankish, Breton, Saxon and even Hibernian blood in our veins. One day the Allfather would tell me what we were but for the present, I basked in the comradeship of my hall.

We feasted and drank well. Popæg kissed her husband goodnight and took a reluctant William, who had been falling asleep for some time, to his bed. Godwin made to rise but Popæg shook her head, "Stay with the men and enjoy the feast. I will watch the bairn." She smiled, "Besides Harold Strong Arm will be of little use to me this night!"

My lords all roared as Harold shrugged. He was the most experienced warrior save for Sven Blue Cheek and he could cope with banter. Marriage had made him a happy man. Haaken the Bold had ensured that my hearth weru guarded the doors to my hall and we could speak openly. I saw Haraldr Greybeard look askance at Padraig as I stood and began to speak. He was wary of the followers of the White Christ.

I waved a hand at the priest. "Like you Haraldr Greybeard I am sceptical of all priests but this one is different. He does not follow Rome's dictates and he can be trusted. You have my word on that!" I saw him nod and Padraig raised a horn of ale to him.

Saxbjorn, who had drunk more than I could remember belied his name by shouting, "Tell us how we defeat these Franks then, lord. We have punished the Bretons. Let us do the same with the Franks."

"First, the Franks are more numerous than the Bretons. You would have to ride for a month or more to cross the lands they rule. Our aim is not to conquer more land. We have enough in the Cotentin and between Djupr and Bayeux. I want us to raid and hurt the Franks along the border. I wish us to make the land a wasteland. Charles the Simple is not a warrior. The last warrior they had was Count Odo of Paris and he is dead. This Frankish King will not relish a war and we do what we did with the Bretons. We get them to ask for peace and to swear to allow us to keep what we have."

"And do we trust them?" Ragnar the Resolute was still suspicious of all things Frankish.

"The Franks relied on spies. As you know I harboured two in my own hall and it cost us dear. That tells me that they fear us. Our own spies tell me that there is still division in the lands of the Frank. Here is my plan. It is simple. There are two targets, Paris and Chartres. Sven will lead the warriors from the lands between Caen and Ciriceburh and I will lead the warriors from Montfort to Djupr. Sven will raid the lands between our border and Chartres. And I will do the same north of the river. My first target will be Beauvais. This is not a quick war. We will grind them down. I do not expect either Sven or I to finally begin to besiege our targets for two years. Our farmers have crops to plant and harvest. They have animals to rear. Only when we are ready to besiege Paris and Chartres will we use every warrior that we have. By then the Franks will be too weak to launch a counter-attack. King Alfred of Wessex is now dead. He was an ally of the Franks and the Bretons. His son, Edward, has to fight the Danes. Merchants have told us that Fulk le Roux has made great inroads into Brittany. If King Alan was foolish enough to attack us then Fulk would easily take Breton heartland. Do not expend all of your men in one attack. I will take just Bjorn and Bagsecg with me, along with Haraldr and the men of Leif and Lars. With just those four hundred men we will cause such mischief that the Franks will think that I have brought three hundred ships again." I waved a hand at Haraldr and Leif. "The Allfather has sent us these new allies. When we begin to make our own lands secure then there will be Frankish land for those who are new to this land. More ships will flock to our banner. I promise you that there will come a day when the King of the Franks accepts that I rule this part of his land!"

There was a huge roar as my lords shouted and began banging the table. The feast then became a normal Viking one; we sang songs and spoke of dead warriors. The next morning, I spoke with each of my lords before they left. I wanted them to understand my mind. I did not think that any were reckless. Our two Breton disasters had shown that but I did not want warriors like Saxbjorn and Ragnar to try to make amends. It was unnecessary. The last to leave was Sven.

"I am inexperienced in sieges, lord. The one at Paris was a failure. "

"We did not lead that siege. They wasted too many warriors on the walls of Paris. We do not need to make war machines or attack the walls. That is wasteful. Surround the town and stop them from receiving help. This will not be for a year, probably two. We must coordinate our attacks so that Paris and Chartres are attacked at the same time. That way we split their forces. They may even keep a reserve in case we attack with a third army."

He shook his head, "We had over three hundred drekar the last time we attacked Paris. You will have much fewer men."

"But we will not need drekar. When we begin the war, I intend to stop all trade up the Seine. We might spend up to half a year ransacking all that the land between our land and the Franks has to offer. They will have no food up the Seine nor from the Seine valley. The siege begins when I advance to Beauvais. I learned from our failure. We may have fewer men but they are better men for we lead them and not the sons of Ragnar Lodbrok!"

We hauled our logs and chains across the river to stop any Frank from using it. Then I led the men of Rouen toward Beauvais. My first attack was on two fronts. I sent Bagsecg and Bjorn across the river at Elbeuf. They raided all of the settlements along the river. Their aim was plunder. With Bagsecg's horsemen as a protective shield Bjorn the Brave led his men to capture animals, grain, weapons and slaves. A day later I led my men, all two hundred of them, in a wide sweep east from Rouen. Bárekr's farm marked our starting point. It would also mark our camp. My intention was to devastate the land for a month at the very least. Bagsecg and Bjorn would return across the river when the settlements on the river were destroyed.

The first four days were easy. We encountered no opposition at all. By the third day, families were fleeing and we found empty farms, which we burned, and animals too old to take and those we slaughtered. We could have moved faster had we used horses but I did not have enough for all of my men. As we closed with Beauvais then I would use horses. What I wanted was the pandemonium of families who fled. There would be more mouths to feed in each town further east. The Franks would be eating that which they needed for the winter.

I sent back the animals to Rouen. The slaves went with them. The treasure and weapons we kept at Bárekr's farm. On the fifth day, the enemy found us. Or rather, thanks to Leif and his men who had found horses, we discovered the enemy. There were two hundred men. Half of them were mailed and the other half were not. They were spotted when they were twenty miles away. Haraldr wondered why we went to meet them rather than waiting at the farm.

"I would do all of our fighting on the soil of the Franks. This will now be our last night at Bárekr's until we return to Rouen. We fight this battle and then find a Frankish farm. We are more than halfway to Beauvais. I am hoping that these men come from Beauvais."

We marched confidently east. Leif's men had kept in touch with the Franks. They had horsemen but they did not use them as scouts. They were lords and they wore mail. It would prove to be a mistake. We waited for them at the Epte River. It was not a wide river. It was less than forty feet wide and could be forded but there were trees on the west bank and we took shelter there. We had parity of numbers but I wanted the Franks to think that they outnumbered us and that we were afraid to fight. I placed Leif's ten horsemen to the north of the woods where they would be seen. Our twenty archers sheltered in the eaves of the wood and the bulk of my army hid themselves in the woods. When I gave the order, they would burst forth.

William and his bodyguard, Godwin, were with us. He had been in no danger up to now and I did not think that he would be in any danger now but Godwin had been given clear instructions. If he thought that William was in danger he was to take him back to Bárekr's farm. I knew the young warrior would heed my command. Egil had the standard furled. We would not use it yet. It meant he could fight as hearth weru.

We watched as the plumes and standards of the nobles appeared over the skyline. An arm pointed at my horsemen and the Franks began to gallop toward them. Those on foot followed. They were eager. Siggi commanded our twenty archers. "Make each one count Siggi."

"Aye lord."

As ordered Leif and his mounted men fled when the Franks neared the river. There was a huge splash as they hit the water. The splash and the spray disguised my archers' arrows. Four men fell and two horses were hit before they realised that they had been ambushed. The leader made the fatal mistake of halting. My archers did not stop nor did the men of Frankia who fought on foot. They poured down the slope.

I drew Long Sword. I would not need my spear, "Ready warriors! When they are in the middle of the river we burst forth. Archers you had better move quickly."

"Aye lord."

The Frank who led the horsemen now compounded his error. He sent twenty of his horsemen after Leif while the rest turned to join the men on foot and attack the archers. Siggi ignored the men on foot. The horsemen were more valuable. They had mail, good swords, helmets and horses. No doubt they would have coins in their purses. With just twenty archers sending arrows we could not cause huge numbers of casualties but we hurt them and we hurt their horses.

I saw the first of the Franks who fought on foot reach the middle. They too splashed and sent showers of river water in the air. Once they had passed the centre then they would be able to see us. "Charge!"

Our archers dropped their bows and ran toward the horsemen. I led my men into the river. I leapt from the bank to land within my sword's length of a warrior with a short mail byrnie, spear, shield and helmet. The wave I created struck him in the face as I brought my sword down to split his helmet and head in two. As he fell into the river it began to turn red. I stepped forward for my long legs made it easier for me than my other men and swept my sword in an arc. It tore into the side of the neck of one man. A second lunged at me with his spear but I flicked Long Sword around and the head missed my arm by a handspan. I was too close to use my sword and so I punched him in the side of the head with my fist. As he slipped below the water I stabbed down and skewered him in the middle.

Egil shouted, "Lord, the horsemen!"

I saw that while the men on foot were being slaughtered the horsemen were making inroads on our left and three of my archers had been killed. "Oathsworn!" I waved my sword and they skilfully disengaged to follow me. We ran at the horsemen. Even as we approached them another archer was speared. I swung my sword at the nearest rider and it hacked through the horse's skull. The horse fell to the side and took the rider with it. I lunged at the next rider and my sword went into his thigh. The first fallen rider was trapped beneath his horse as its hooves flailed around. He drowned. My oathsworn were all good swordsmen and they were not afraid of horses. We were mailed and could take hits. When another five riders had fallen I saw the leader raise his sword and shout, "Fall back!"

"After them! Kill as many as you can!"

When men rout they are the easiest of targets. Men killed this day could not fight us again. By the time we reached the other bank the horsemen had escaped but Gandálfr, Haraldr and Lars led their men to hunt down the men on foot.

I heard the hooves of horses, "Turn!" There were just eleven of us and five archers but we were enough. Fifteen of the horsemen who had pursued Leif now returned. They saw their path barred. Siggi and two archers had reached the west bank and picked up their bows. Their three arrows decided the Franks. With Leif and his men coming behind them they had two choices, fight us or surrender. They chose to fight. Their horses were tired and they laboured across the river. Our three archers hit both men and horses although none were fatally wounded. As they reached the top of the bank we stepped forward and swung our swords. We were not afraid of horses but the horses were terrified of the wall of steel which confronted them. My sword ripped open the throat of one horse and as it fell backwards it crushed its rider against the river bottom. Egil avoided the spear which came at him and sank his sword into the unprotected groin of a second. The river was soon filled with fatally wounded Franks. We captured eight horses. We had won. I watched Godwin lead my son from the safety of the wood. My son had a seax and he raised it, "My father, Lord Göngu-Hrólfr Rognvaldson!" It was an accolade of which I was truly proud.

We had passed a farm just half a mile from the river and we camped there. We buried our dead by the river, on the west bank, and then stripped the enemy dead. After gathering the enemy dead, we burned them. The flames leapt up into the late afternoon sky. When it became dark the survivors of the battle would see the flames and know that their fellows were being burned. It would further demoralize them.

We had not brought priests with us but we did have warriors who knew how to heal. Luckily the wounds were relatively minor. Some men needed wounds to be stitched. There were three broken limbs. They would be sent back on two of the captured horses with some of the treasure we had taken. Bárekr's farm would be the collection point.

Haraldr and his men had not fought in such a battle for a long time. They had lost more men than the rest of us. I could see that it bothered the warrior. "Do not fret, Haraldr. Your men acquitted themselves well."

He pointed at Egil, "Yet young warriors like that looked far more accomplished than my men and he looks so young."

"Egil Flame Bearer is a special warrior. He has dedicated himself to becoming the best that he can be. Save for the time he spends with my son William he just practises his skills."

"And your son is young. Do you not fear for him?" He shrugged, "I have no children or none that I know of. I am not sure that I would risk my future in battle."

"The Norns spin, Haraldr, and there is little point in fighting them. If the Norns wish William dead then that would happen if he was within Rouen's walls and protected by an army. Godwin is a good warrior and he will see no harm comes to him. This way my son sees from an early age how to lead and how to defeat the Franks."

"I can see that I have much to learn from you."

We spent that day at the river. Horses needed rest as did we. Our scouts still ensured that we were not in any danger.

The next day saw us advance another fifteen miles. We stopped when we saw the walls of Beauvais. They were made of wood and they were defended. It was getting on to dark. "Haraldr, Leif and Lars, you will make your camp here. Light one fire for every five men. I will take my men around the other side. When dawn comes have your men advance to bow range and wait."

"Wait?"

"They will be more worried than we are. I will send a rider with instructions."

"You do not know yet what you will do?"

I laughed, "Let me see their defences and how they react when they see that Lord Göngu-Hrólfr Rognvaldson has come!"

I turned as William said, "And what of me?"

"You will stay here with Godwin. We have a night ride through ground we do not know. When you are more skilled in such things then you may come with us. Until then you stay here with Godwin and Haraldr."

"Aye lord." He was learning to obey commands, even those he did not like. He was learning to be a warrior.

As we headed through the dark Egil asked, "Do you know what you will do, lord?"

Haaken the Bold laughed, "Of course he does. We will march up to their gates and demand that they surrender."

I could see that Egil could not see how this would work. "Lars and his men will light one fire for every five men. Normally we light a fire for ten or twelve men. They will think we have more men than we do. Tonight, they will send riders for help. They will have counted our fires. We take and kill their messengers. I will ride to their walls with the heads of their messengers and demand their surrender. They will refuse. I will wait for a messenger will have ridden to Haraldr and the others. They will advance and those in Beauvais will think we have doubled the numbers. The walls have a little Roman stone with a palisade on the top. The men we slew were from Beauvais. They will have little heart for a fight."

"And if they do none of that lord?"

I smiled, "Then we will scale their wooden palisade and slaughter them."

I was confident that they would surrender without much of a fight. I would, eventually, leave Beauvais for my intention had been to show what we could do. We would continue to raid as we headed back to Rouen. The land around Beauvais was flat but we had to cross fields rather than roads. It took longer to reach the far side than I had anticipated. I sent two of my oathsworn, Hrolfr the Horseman and Sven Mighty Arm, to ride ahead once it became clear that our circumnavigation of the town would take longer than expected. We passed two farms and we occupied them. The farmers and their families were forced to flee south. Word would spread of our presence but it was to the east and Paris where the danger lay.

We reached the road which passed through the wood to the east of the town and found my two oathsworn. They had a dead messenger and were holding his horse. "I am sorry lord, there were two of them. The other fled back inside the town when we appeared. This one thought he could outrun us."

"Good, just so long as none escaped to Paris." I turned to Gandálfr, "Make camp in the woods. We light no fires."

My men were happy to have cold rations for they anticipated the fall of a town. Confidence breeds confidence. We put out a screen of sentries and we slept. I walked with Æbbi Bonecrusher to view the town. He pointed to the walls. They were manned and it was more than a night guard, "The death of their messenger has alerted them to our presence, lord."

"It is not how I planned it but this helps us. The messenger saw two warriors on horseback. They have not heard the thunder of horses and may think it is a scouting party. They will worry. In any event, it does not change what we do. We march forward at dawn and plant ourselves before their walls. Egil will get to hold my standard so that they know who we are."

There was no sudden movement on the walls and I knew that we remained unseen in the dark. Our blue cloaks were most effective at night. It made us invisible. We returned to the camp and slept.

Rising before dawn, after eating we headed to the edge of the wood. We left the horses, save one, at the camp. The one we brought we tethered at the edge of the wood. I was trying to make them think we had more men than we actually did have. I had my men spread out in a long line. When we were all in position, I raised my sword and we stepped forward, almost as one man. The effect was dramatic. Horns sounded and I saw movement on the walls. We came from the dark and, as the sun rose above us, we saw the defenders of Beauvais. My men began banging their shields as we moved closer to the walls. We marched steadily using the rhythm of the shields to keep us in line. My men knew when we would stop for I had told them before we left our cold camp and, as I raised my shield, thirty paces beyond bow range they stopped and held their shields before them. It would have come as a surprise to the defenders who expected us to charge like barbarians. My men were not like that. We knew how to fight a controlled battle.

When we stopped we ceased banging shields and the last bang seemed to echo across the ground toward the walls. It was replaced by silence. I allowed the silence to linger. I saw, on the fighting platform of the town wall, men's faces turn to look at their neighbours. What were we doing? I turned to Beorn Long Legs, "Go back to the camp. Mount the horse and ride back to the others on the other side of the town. Tell them to sound horns and advance to the walls. Then fetch the men we placed in the farms and bring them to the south walls."

"Aye lord."

He ran back to the woods and we stood in silence. A short while later the hooves of his horse could be heard thundering. Like our banging they echoed as he galloped south, hidden beyond view. Still, we stood in silence. Eventually, I saw more faces appear on the walls. My plan was working.

"Egil, show them the standard. Wave as though you are signalling." In my head, I had been counting time. The hooves of Beorn's horse had receded and I was timing this to have the greatest effect.

"Aye lord." He untied the cord which held the banner tightly to the staff and, raising it, began to wave it.

Just at that moment, I heard Haraldr sound the cow horn. Within a few moments, some of the men facing us had left the walls. Still, we did not move. When the twenty or so men we had left in the farm appeared to the south, led by Beorn on a horse, I deemed it time to speak.

"Come Egil, it is time to speak." I had a good eye for distance and I stopped at what I thought was beyond bow range. I was twenty paces from my men. I took off my helmet and handed it to Egil. An arrow flew from the walls and landed six paces short of me. I stepped forward and walked to the arrow. I picked it up and snapping it in two spat on it and threw it back toward the walls. Without turning I said, "You can come closer now, Egil."

When he was next to me I took out Long Sword and rammed it into the ground. It looked like a cross. I cupped my hands and shouted, "I am Lord Göngu-Hrólfr Rognvaldson. I have you surrounded. Surrender to me and I will let you live. Fight me and you all die. You know I keep my word."

I saw a heated debate on the gatehouse. Now that the sun was fully up I saw that the gate would not offer much resistance when we attacked. There were two small wooden towers and there was no ditch before it. If they chose to fight then I knew we could take it.

I watched as a warrior took his helmet from his head. He shouted, "I am Lord Robert of Beauvais. You killed my younger brother and I would have vengeance." He let his words echo. "They say you are a warrior and a man of his word. Let us settle this blood feud like men. I am the champion of my people and I would fight you to let God decide this. If you win then my people will surrender. When I win your men will disperse and return to Rouen."

This was an easy decision to make. "Agreed. And we fight here between our men?"

"Aye, and I will ride my horse for I am a noble and do not fight on the ground like a peasant. What say you?"

Egil started, "That is not fair, my lord. He will ride you down!"

I turned to Egil, "He will think that he will. Fear not. I am happy with this." I took my helmet from him and shouted, "Agreed!"

I turned to Gandálfr, "Make a wall of shields. Egil, return to the others and fear not. My grandfather was a horseman. I have ridden to war. This arrogant Frank thinks that he will win but he has yet to fight a Viking with Long Sword." I took off my cloak and handed it to him. My shield was on my back and I was content. I had a plan.

I walked forward so that the distance between myself and the walls was halved. When he emerged, he would have a short distance to reach me. His horse would not be travelling as quickly. I held Long Sword in two hands and kissed the blade, "Allfather, help me this day. Show the Franks that you are stronger than their White Christ."

The gates creaked open and Robert of Beauvais emerged. He was wearing a full-length byrnie. He had a shield but it was smaller than mine. He held, in his right hand, a spear. It looked to be eight feet long and had a pennant on the end. He had a sword and it was hanging from a scabbard on his saddle. He had stiraps. The horse was magnificent. It was as big as Gilles. Robert of Beauvais must be a big man for he did not look small upon its back. He wore a helmet and, at first, I did not know why. Even with my Long Sword, I could not reach his head. Then it came to me. He was less confident fighting on foot. This was a horseman. There was a difference between us. I was more than a horseman for I was a warrior who could ride!

He did not wait but dug his heels into the flanks of his horse and charged directly for me. I had a balanced stance with Long Sword held above me. It was a big horse and it struggled to get up to speed quickly. Had this been an open battlefield he would have been able to increase his speed gradually. The horse was labouring. I ignored the spear. The first enemy was the horse. His spear was on his right and he rode at my left side. That was his first mistake. I had a sword held in two hands and I could strike from either side. The ground vibrated as the horse came closer. I saw the Frank pull back his arm for he thought me transfixed. I spun around to my right when the horse and rider were five paces from me. He could not shift his spear in time. It was on the wrong side of his horse's head. I brought Long Sword around in an arc. The spin increased the speed and power of the blow. My blade hacked through the left hind leg of the horse. It stumbled for three more strides and then fell, its lifeblood pumping away. My men cheered and I heard a wail from the walls. I ran toward the warrior.

Robert of Beauvais pulled his legs from the stiraps and rolled away as my sword swept down to where his body would have been a moment earlier. He was quick and drawing his sword he was on his feet in an instant. I saw that he favoured his left leg. His right had been hurt. I swung at his shield. He held it before him but my blow was so hard that I saw him wince and heard a crack. The shield was damaged. I switched my attack and swung at his right side. He tried to step back on his right leg as he countered with his sword but his leg was weak and he stumbled. His sword did not stop my strike it merely slowed it and the end of Long Sword bit into his leg. I was now using my speed to defeat him and his wounds, the fall and the speed all confused him and slowed his reactions. He should have been trying to attack me but, instead, he was merely defending. I was in command.

I changed my strike and used both hands to lunge at his chest. He brought both sword and shield up to protect himself. The tip of my sword hit his shield and he took a step back. He had the wit to step back on his left leg. He held his sword before him. I lifted my sword high above my head. He pulled his shield up. I spun to my right and brought my sword around in a long sweep. He tried to bring up his sword but it was not enough. Long Sword swept aside his weapon and ripped through the mail links on his coif. Had his sword not slowed down my blade then he would have lost his head. As it was my blade tore into his neck. I struck an artery and blood fountained from the wound. He remained upright for a moment and then the life left his eyes. He sank to his knees and then fell backwards. He was dead. I took off my helmet and raised it.

"Göngu-Hrólfr! Göngu-Hrólfr! Göngu-Hrólfr!"

I waved Egil forward. "Come let us see if they will honour their Lord's word!"

We marched close to the gate. It was a risk for an arrow could have ended my life but I think they were in shock at the speed with which I had defeated their lord and champion.

My voice was filled with steel. I still held my bloody sword. "Lord Robert is dead! Open your gates and admit us!" There was hesitation. I roared, "If the gates are not opened immediately I will put every man, woman and child to the sword! I will raze Beauvais to the ground!"

There was a shout from the walls. It was a woman's voice, "Open the gates! The barbarians have won and God has forsaken us!"

Chapter 18

The town was emptied of treasure, food, mail and animals. We harmed not a single person. The whole attack had cost them but two men and yet the Franks were hurt. We stayed for three days. My men raided the land to the east of Beauvais and we took more animals and food. With laden wagons, we headed home. We had done all that I had intended. We picked up that which we had left at Bárekr's farm and, after a week of slow riding reached Rouen. Our homecoming was announced before we reached my town. People lined the road. There were no captives but the wagons and carts were testaments to our success. Padraig had to order more warehouses to be built to store our surplus.

Over the next months, the lords from south of the river sent news of their successes. Although not as spectacular they had defeated all that the Franks had sent against us. We held the land west of the Epte and Risle rivers. Already I had warriors seeking to build strongholds closer to the border for the land was rich and fertile. I refused. I told each one the same. "Until I say so the land west of the Epte and Risle rivers will be as a wasteland. I want it empty. We have not yet won. That day will come but we need patience."

One result was an influx of drekar filled with warriors. Leif's visit to Bruggas had begun the trickle and it soon became a flood. They were eager to benefit from our success. None could go upstream for our barrier remained in place. We spoke to all of the captains and their men. Those we thought would help us we allowed to stay and build a hall. The rest we sent downstream. We had learned our lesson from Godfrid and those we sent hence were escorted by two of our drekar to the river mouth.

Six months after Beauvais we received a delegation from Paris. They had travelled by boat until they reached our logs and then walked to Rouen. It was humiliating for them. Count Richard of Paris and the Bishop of Paris were there along with Lord Robert's wife, Matilda.

When we had occupied her town, she had shown herself to be a strong woman and had not been afraid of me when she faced me. Her men quailed but she did not.

I greeted them in my Great Hall. I had had a large chair made. It fitted me but it dwarfed all else. I sat in it flanked by Padraig, Gandálfr, Haraldr, Leif, Lars and Æbbi Bonecrusher. The two men bowed but Lady Matilda glared at me.

"What brings you to my home? Was the barrier across the river not warning enough that you are not welcome?"

The Bishop smiled, "Lord, that is one of the reasons we are come here. King Charles of the West Franks wishes peace. He wants the river re-opened so that we may trade downriver again. He knows not why you broke the peace."

I pointed a finger at the Bishop, "You know the reason better than any! You conspired with your spy in Rouen to bring about my downfall. Your King wrote letters to Alfred of Wessex and Alan of Brittany to form an alliance against me. I am not a fool! You think because we are pagans we are barbarians. That is a foolish mistake to make. Lady Matilda will tell you that we have behaved with more constraint than barbarians normally show!"

"You killed my husband!"

"He challenged me!" I shook my head, "If this is all that you are here for then you waste my time, leave!"

Count Richard spoke, "No, Lord, we have an offer. King Charles will pay ten thousand gold pieces if you cease making war on him."

"A generous offer but as Guthrum of the East Angles discovered taking gold can result in defeat. I will have the gold but I will also have the title Duke. Not only that, your King will give me the title and deed of the land between the Cotentin and the Epte River as my domain."

I saw the Count shake his head, "That is too much."

"That is my offer. Take it or leave it."

The two men looked at each other, "We will have to take the offer back to our King."

"Then do so."

"And you will stop your war until then?"

"Of course not. We have yet to taste defeat and we like the gold we take from you. Until I am Duke and have a secure land for my people there will be war."

After they had gone I sent riders to Siggi Olafsson. It was time for the men of Djupr to make an attack. A second rider went to Bagsecg and a third to Sven. Padraig said, "You do not give them time to speak with their king."

"Exactly. I wish them to see how serious we are."

"And the title, Duke? You have not been bothered by such titles before."

"Nor am I now but the Franks are. Godfrid's father was made Duke of Frisia. He was given a land the same size as that which I wish. I am giving the Franks an offer that they understand." I was learning to play this game like the Franks. They valued crowns and I would use that.

Over the next months my three warbands raided the Franks and then withdrew. They and we became richer with the Franks weakened. They were haemorrhaging their men and their gold. When I wondered why the Franks had not responded Padraig gave me an answer. "Some of my brothers had been on a visit to Rome to speak with the Pope. They passed through Rouen on their way home. We had hoped for a reconciliation of our churches. They failed but while they were there they saw emissaries from King Charles. He is trying to enlist the aid of the Pope to rally all the Christians and drive you from this land."

"If he succeeded then that could hurt us."

Padraig nodded, "Luckily the Pope has his own problems and there is a lack of support for King Charles. You should know that it is your beliefs which might bring your downfall."

"What do you mean?"

"When the Moors came to Spain they represented a threat to the Frankish way of life. All petty disputes were put aside to fight them. You have confused the Franks for you look much like they do but there is talk of Christians joining together to drive the pagans into the sea. They want you Christian or dead!"

I tapped my chest. "How can you change that which is in here?"

"It has happened, lord, men who had stronger beliefs than you became Christian."

"Then we will have to defeat the Franks sooner. I want to be ready to attack Paris and Chartres by next year. Make certain we have enough grain and weapons."

His words had worried me. I rode with Egil, Godwin and my son along the river. We now had settlements east of us. These were the recently arrived warriors. We would be going to war and I now had enough men and, if I needed them, ships. How would I hold it? From what Padraig had said I was the problem. I was a pagan and the Christian leaders who were my neighbours could not accept that. Britannia was now Christian. Only the lands of the Norse and Danes were not. That did not make us wrong and the followers of the White Christ right. How could a man change? I still did not understand Guthrum's conversion. Had his defeat by Alfred torn the belief from his body?

William had grown. Boys his age now came to war with our armies. They slung stones at our enemies and fetched and carried for the warriors. He had a good leather byrnie. It was studded with metal and would prepare him for the time, in a year or so, when he would wear mail. He had a metal helmet and a short sword. He rode easily as though born to the saddle and I knew that next time we went to war he would not have to hide in the woods with Godwin. He also took more interest in war and the way we went to war.

"Father, how will we use these new men?"

"The last time we attacked Paris we had too many leaders. There were too many voices making decisions. This time I command and I will direct each warband."

Egil said, "I was a boy when you raided Paris. I have grown up hearing warriors speak of the raid. There were many hundreds of drekar were there not?"

"There were but some were small. Every warrior who had a sword and a leaky ship flocked for the treasure. It was doomed to failure. We will not fail for I do not wish to capture Paris."

William asked, "Why not?"

I laughed, "How would I hold it? Taking Paris would surely bring every Christian leader to try to retake it. It is the threat which will secure that which I want."

"And what is that, lord?"

"Simple, Egil, a homeland which is ours. We will defend it but I would have the world acknowledge that it is ours." I looked at William. "The rest is up to you and those who follow you."

"I do not understand."

"Your grandfather visited a witch in a cave far to the west, Syllingar. There the witch, Skuld, told him that one day his descendants would rule half of this world in the west. She said that their influence would ripple through the ages. Your grandfather did his part. He gained us a toe hold on this land. Thanks to the curse my brother almost lost it until I was sent to the bottom of the ocean to be reborn. My part is to secure the land you will inherit. When I am gone then your oathsworn and your lords will help you to make your land greater than it is. I will watch from Valhalla with my grandfather and all will be well."

I am not sure if my words intimidated or inspired him but whatever effect they had they resulted in silence and deep thought. We visited each of the new warbands and I spoke at length with their lords. Without divulging too much of my plan I told them what I expected. I gave each of them permission to raid upstream as often as they wished. I told them that whatever they took would be theirs but they were to give me all the intelligence and information which they could gather. One of them, Ragnvald of Dorestad, asked, "Why lord?"

"Why what?"

"You let us raid and offer a home yet you do not ask for anything in return."

"But I do. I expect loyalty and obedience. Your raiding will bring you profit and will serve my purpose. When I call upon you then your service will be the price you pay." He nodded. "All that I will say is that if I were you then I would speak with the other captains so that you do not step on one another's toes. The land close to the river has been raided often. If you were to ask my advice then it would be to sail upriver and then head inland. Beauvais has nothing left to give. Seek other places."

Over the next months the new warriors along with my lords continued their raids. The thirty days service was proving effective although I had not needed to use my coins again. I knew we were eating into the resolve of the Franks. I knew we were having an effect when, four months after the Bishop and Count had visited, Bagsecg sent a rider telling me that the Franks were sending an army south of the Seine. They were moving slowly. I knew what they meant. They were avoiding being ambushed.

Our men had rested well. I sent a rider to Sven Blue Cheek and Bergil Fast Blade. I asked them to bring their best men as quickly as they could to Évreux. I then took my six drekar and headed upstream to Elbeuf. We would march south and meet with my horsemen and Bjorn the Brave. We returned with the rider who had brought the message. I interrogated him as we rode.

"Where do you think the Frankish army began?"

"That is easy, lord, Paris."

"How do you know?"

"The standard of the Count of Paris and the presence of the Bishop of Paris. We saw many standards and banners of the French lords we fought last time we attacked Paris."

"But not the banner of the King."

"No lord."

Now I understood this game. The King was still reluctant to fight me but Richard of Paris was trying to emulate the exploits of Odo. If so he was making a grave mistake for he was bringing his army to meet mine and that gave us the advantage. The road west went through Évreux. There were minor roads he could use; we often did but a large army had to use the main road and we could block it. By coming through Évreux, the Franks could swing north and attack the men guarding the logs across the river. They could cut my lines of communication with Caen and the Cotentin. While the Pope dithered, they had discerned a pattern. They thought I had split my army in two. I had but not to my detriment.

As we had had to cross the river by ferry my army was spread out along the road. My oathsworn and forty other warriors rode horses and we would reach Évreux first. Sven Blue Cheek would take a whole day to reach us. Bjorn and his men were already at Évreux when we arrived. This showed that he was a warrior who could think for he had hewn timber and placed logs across the road. He had dug a ditch and embedded stakes.

"Where is Bagsecg?"

"He and his men are ahead of the Franks. So far the men of Paris have not tried to do anything about the horsemen."

"That is because they are waiting for me. I am the prize! They go slowly to draw me to them." I had left men raiding north of the river. Perhaps they thought I was with them and that was why they were moving so slowly. Unwittingly I had tricked them. The Norns had spun a complicated web. As my men came we allocated them a position. Our horses were tethered. We would just use Bagsecg's horses as a screen. By the time evening had fallen all but thirty of my men had arrived. With Bjorn's men we had one hundred and eighty to face the enemy. Bagsecg's sixty horsemen and Sven and Bergil's one hundred and twenty meant we had enough to face the Franks. Petr and his archers had been further south. They would not reach us until after Sven and his men but the fifty archers would be crucial to our defence.

The next morning, I mounted Gilles and rode with Egil and some of Bagsecg's horsemen. They had reported that the Franks were camped ten miles away. It would take time for them to break camp. Bagsecg and I gathered his men across the road five miles from Évreux. We chose a place where the enemy could see us from a long way off and where they could array for battle. There was an inviting wood just a mile behind us and I wanted them to think that we had planned an ambush. Egil unfurled my banner and let it flutter over my head. The Count's scouts spied us. Turning tail, they raced back to the main column. The Franks did not move as quickly as we did. When the ponderous steel snake arrived, they arrayed for battle. They faced our lightly armoured men with mailed horsemen. There were one hundred of them. Behind them I saw another hundred armed like Bagsecg's men; lightly armoured with javelins. It seemed to take an age for them all to deploy. Then the men on foot arrived and were marshalled into lines. The first were mailed. The second had helmets and the rest were the burghers of Paris. They waited. Eventually, after the Bishop had blessed them, a horn sounded and the whole line moved toward us. I waited until they were less than two hundred paces from us and about to charge and then shouted, "Fall back!" Our men were all waiting for the command and we wheeled and rode away as one.

 The Franks dug their heels in and they galloped after us. We kept a steady pace. They would close the gap with us but that did not matter. They would not catch us. As we neared the woods I turned and saw them slowing. They expected an ambush. When we entered the woods, they stopped. We slowed too and rode back to Évreux at a steady pace. Bjorn had cleared a killing ground before the town. Trees had been cut down and barricades built. The stumps had been left to slow down the enemy horse. The log barricades would afford protection from both men on horse and those on foot. By late afternoon Sven and Bergil had brought their men and we were almost complete.

 "How many are there, lord?"

 "Enough for us to eat well on horsemeat and to reap a rich reward in mail and weapons. They outnumber us but this Count is no Count Odo. They have helped my plan for this will be a second army we have hurt."

 William had waited with Godwin at Évreux. We had not risked him. He showed he was becoming a warrior by asking pertinent questions, "How can you be certain that you will hurt them? Ragnar and Ubba were both defeated."

 "They allowed themselves to be tricked by the enemy just as we have tricked the Franks. I did to them what they did to my men. They feigned flight. The Franks are too clever for their own good. Bagsecg and his men know exactly where the enemy are gathered. We know their numbers and we know their composition. When they attack there are ditches and stumps to negotiate. There are traps. There are wooden barricades behind which we can shelter and we have archers to thin their ranks. Even if we did not have the best warriors gathered here we could hold them off."

The Franks camped just two miles from Évreux. Normally we would have disturbed their sleep and kept them off balance but I wanted them confident. That way they would commit to the attack. We kept a good watch and we lit plenty of fires but they did not come in the night. Few warriors take on a Viking at night. They might not attack us at night but they would try to rid the land of us at dawn. Most of our men had had a day to rest. Only Petr's archers had just had half a night's sleep and that would not impair their rate of arrows. We were in position even as we heard the Franks stirring and preparing their horses. We still had Évreux's bread ovens and our men had eaten well. I stood behind the barrier in the centre of the road. We had left the road open until Bagsecg and I had returned. The horsemen were to the north and south of the road. They were there to deter the enemy from outflanking us. We waited.

The sun had been up for an hour by the time they approached us. The tree stumps warned them that we had prepared our defence and the Count wisely decided to dismount his mailed men. The log barriers came up to the chest of a man. It would take a mighty horse to leap such a barrier. The Bishop and his priests blessed the host. I saw the Count of Paris kiss the cross the Bishop proffered. They held their shields before them and they began to march toward us. The second rank held their shields above them. They were wary of our archers.

I turned to Petr. He and the archers were behind our second rank of warriors. "Do not waste your arrows on the front ranks. Save them for the ones behind."

"Aye lord."

I smiled as I saw the approaching Franks prepare to be struck by arrows which never came. When they were just eight paces from us they lowered their spears. All that they could see of us was the top of our helmets. I, of course, was the exception. They saw my chest and my head. They saw my standard fluttering. They began to move faster and then they found the ditch filled with the traps. It was the signal for Petr to unleash his arrows for he knew that the ones without mail were now in range. As mailed men stepped on dung covered stakes they fell and disrupted the line. Men without mail fell to my archers but still the Franks came on. They were propelled by the mass of men behind them. Bjorn and his men had had time to split some of the logs and make a fighting step. None of us had stood upon it yet. As the ragged line approached to within three paces of the barrier I shouted, "Now!"

I drew my sword as I stepped on to the step. The first eager Franks had run toward the barrier. It was roughly made and could be scaled but it meant that they were unbalanced. My first sweep hit two and knocked a third from his feet. The spears of my oathsworn jabbed and stabbed at the faces. All the time the archers were taking their toll of those behind. Still the nobles and their retinues came on. They had had enough of the barbarian who made their lives less comfortable than they had been. As bodies fell so the Franks found that they had their own fighting platform. It was one made of their dead. Warriors traded blows. Spears were thrust at me. My mail took most of those that reached me but one scored a deep cut on my cheek. Even as the Frank triumphantly shouted I brought Long Sword down upon his head and smote his helmet in two. The Franks were paying a heavier price than we were but my men were still being killed and wounded. Until we could whittle down those with mail it would be an evenly fought battle.

I was aware that I had killed and wounded so many men that Long Sword was not as sharp as it had been. I battered it against the head of a Frank who fell to the ground and sheathed it. I swung my shield around and took out Hrólfr's Vengeance. It was sharp enough to shave with and had a tapered point. Although I did not have the length of Long Sword my long arms helped me. I lunged at a noble with a yellow plume in his helmet. The sword plunged into his neck. Tearing it out sideways showered those around him with his blood. I know not if he was a leader of some kind but when he fell the heart went from the Franks. They did not rout nor even retreat, it was just that they did not prosecute the attack as vigorously. When Gandálfr slew a second noble with a yellow plume the Franks began to withdraw. They did so in good order but they fell back.

Sometimes you plan a battle and it all works out as it did in your head. This one had gone well and we had achieved all that we needed but I decided to take more. I turned to Godwin, who had the cow horn, "Sound the attack!" The signal would not just be for those behind the barricade it would signal the horsemen on our flanks.

I sprang over the barricade and my fall was broken by the bloody bodies of the Franks. As I began to run the ordered retreat became a rout. None wished to face the giant who seem to run in boots which could leap chasms. In their haste to flee they knocked each other over and men fell to the ground. I sliced, stabbed and slashed at those who stumbled before me. Egil had planted the banner at the barricade and he ran with me. The rest of my oathsworn kept as close as they could. Haraldr, Leif and Gandálfr all led their own bands. Panic swept through the Frankish ranks. When I heard the thunder of hooves from Bagsecg and his men then I knew that the battle was over. Ahead of me I saw the Count of Paris, his bodyguards and the priests mount horses and flee east. Those who could reach their horses did so and the rest just hurtled through the woods as they headed toward Paris.

They had fled so quickly that they had left their chests. The religious artefacts which so inspired the Franks were now ours. Their capture was a victory in itself. Leaving the horsemen to pursue the survivors we plundered their camp. We had won. It had been a hard-fought battle but the sudden end surprised even me. My men began banging their shields as we headed back to Évreux.

"Göngu-Hrólfr! Göngu-Hrólfr! Göngu-Hrólfr!"

William, my son, sat on his horse. He wanted what I had. He would be a warrior and he would lead. He had seen his father do it and he would do the same. Wounds on both sides had been similar but they had lost more men. Even more important was the fact that they had yielded the ground to us. My campaign had succeeded. When we had recovered from the battle then we could begin to win the war.

Chapter 19

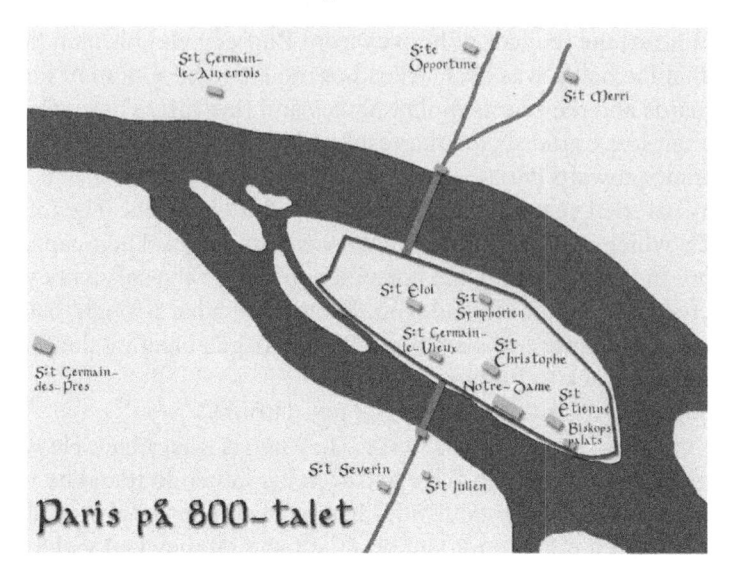

The victory bought us more than a year of peace and prosperity. It brought great riches and it brought more men to our banner. Those who had raided upstream had found little opposition. The Franks had been badly hurt. I wondered if they would come again. I wondered if they would sue for peace. Were they yet ready to pay my price and give me that which I wanted?

It became obvious as the weeks turned to months that they were not yet ready to meet my terms and so I sent more men to raid along the Seine. I met with my lords six months after the battle of Évreux. The measure of our success could be seen in their horses and mail. All had new mail byrnies. Polished helmets and finely decorated scabbards replaced the more functional ones we had previously used. Their cloaks were made of high quality material and dyed. When I looked in their eyes then I knew that they had not changed within. They had used their coin to buy the trappings of nobility. Inside they were still Viking warriors.

"At Harpa we take every man we can and we attack Chartres and Paris. We will have men raiding the lands around those two cities until they plead for peace. Last time they offered us coin. We want coin and a land. We want a land given to us to keep."

Ubba now had a wooden leg. He would not be fighting but it was right that he came to the meeting, "What about the Bretons?"

"Have they begun to cause us trouble again?" I looked at Ragnar for he was Lord of the Cotentin.

"Not yet, lord, but they have begun to fortify their border towns."

"Then leave half of your men there. Ubba you command in Ragnar's absence."

"Do you trust me not to repeat my mistake?"

"Of course." I pointed to his wooden leg. "Each time you see that leg you know of your mistake. You will not do so again." He nodded. "Sven does that leave you enough men to take Chartres?"

"Chartres is not as strong as Paris. We can cause trouble and make them hurt. I am not sure that we could prosecute a siege to a successful conclusion."

"All that you need to do is to hold your nerve longer than the Franks. For the last eight years and before that, since the other siege, we have bested them at every turn. We have won all of the battles. It is they who doubt that they can win and not us." I saw Ubba look at Ragnar, "Forget the Bretons. It is the Franks we fight. Does any in this hall doubt that we can defeat them?" They shook their heads. "Then on the first day of Harpa we being our attack. Tell no one our ultimate objective. As far as our men are concerned we do as we did when we first raided. We are heading east for plunder. I will have Bagsecg and his horsemen for we can make the land east of Paris ours too."

We did not feast or drink as much this time for everyone in my hall knew that this would either succeed or, like the last time, we would be paid off and return home with the threat of Christian backlash hanging in the air.

William had now broadened out. He had always been tall but the last few years had seen him fill out. He was ready for a byrnie. Godwin had convinced me that he was ready to fight. He even had two servants who would act as bodyguards too. Although still young Harold Strong arm's boys, Haaken and Hrolfr, could use a sling and ride. William would not fight but he was preparing to be a warrior and a leader.

Godwin came to me just before we left, "Lord, I have protected William and I have helped him to become a warrior."

"Aye you have."

"When we return from this war I would be released from my vow." I nodded. Thanks to my talks with Padraig I had been expecting this. "I have met a girl and she is not terrified of my red eyes. We would be wed and I would become a father. Watching William and Gerloc grow has made me yearn to have a family of my own."

"I release you and you may marry her as soon as you like."

"I will do so when we return from this war. I would have a clean break."

I knew that Egil would also be seeking such a release. Like Godwin he had met a girl. This battle would change my world even if we lost.

I had spent an increasing amount of time with Padraig. He was growing old and he was not a well man. We spoke of our heavens and of our different worlds. It was his condition which made him tell me of Godwin and Egil. "They deserve a life, lord. I have had little life save the one I chose. I have served you. I hoped that I would see you become a Christian. I failed."

"Of all men you were the one who could have done that. Your version of the White Christ is more palatable than the priest who shall not be named! I can see some virtues in your religion. I just cannot cope with turning the other cheek."

"We believe in one supreme being as you do, lord. We both agree that they are probably the same god. We have just given him different names."

"It is just that you forgive too readily."

He laughed, "The King of the West Franks is Christian as is the Bishop of Paris. I see no forgiveness in them."

"Are they not Christians then?"

"Let us say that they are pragmatic. A good Christian is one who has a heart which is good. It is one who cares for his people and his land. You have all of that."

"Yet I am not a Christian."

"No, lord, you would need to be baptised for that!"

Padraig had asked to come with us on this raid. It was not to see bloodshed but because he knew his time on this earth was drawing to an end. He had spent much of his life with me and he wished to see how it would end. I agreed for I was fond of him. We had had our differences but he had never let me down and my land was stronger because of him.

The fleet which sailed up the Seine was a fraction of the fleet we had taken all those many years earlier. We took barely forty ships and we had fewer men. But I was confident that we had more chance of success. Bagsecg and Bjorn the Brave were marching across country to meet us at the bridge across the Seine to the island. We would be there first but they would secure the southern bank for us. This time there was no barricade of ships to slow us down and the whole fleet arrived at the western end of the islands. Our approach had not been secretive and the two bridges to the island were still crowded with folk fleeing even as we approached.

Haraldr Greybeard had proved himself a good leader and he led half of the fleet to moor on the north bank close by Saint Germain le Auxerrois while the rest of us anchored off Saint Germain des Pres. Both churches were empty when we arrived and we used those as warrior halls. We would make ourselves comfortable. I had the easier task for two hundred men were marching to join us. Haraldr would have to fight enemies from the north. Siggi Olafsson was with Haraldr and between them I knew they would be able to defend the ships.

I think we surprised the Parisians. We saw, on their walls, the Count of Paris and the Bishop. The Bishop was mailed and ready for war. He was obviously not in a forgiving mood. We quickly captured the southern end of the bridge. The battle we fought was with those who remained in their homes. Some, especially the rich merchants, had men who fought for their valuables. They were either killed or fled. After we had taken everything of value we set fire to the buildings. We were safe from the flames for the wind was from the west. When the bridge caught fire, I had my men douse it. I was pleased that the southern end was charred for it told those in Paris that we could burn it any time we chose. Haraldr and Siggi did the same to the north. Like us they left the bridge intact.

Instead of building siege engines I sent out more than half of my men to raid the lands around Paris. The horsemen ranged as far east as they could go. The men on foot spread out for ten miles south of the river. Everything that could be eaten or was valuable was brought to the church. The people were chased away. The men were killed. This time they could not supply the island by boat for my horsemen controlled the river. I think that the occasional boat got through but none could bring enough food to feed the starving populace. A month passed and still we had not attacked. Sven Blue Cheek had Chartres surrounded and they were starving too. I refused all requests to speak with the Count or the Bishop. It would be King Charles or no one. We sent our drekar back to Rouen regularly with the treasure we had taken. Four months after we had begun the siege Bagsecg brought us the news I had been expecting.

"King Charles himself is coming with an army. There are East and West Franks. There are Lombards and Swabians. He has hired Burgundians too. Lord, it is a mighty army. It is to be counted in the thousands." He sounded worried.

I nodded, "And they are coming along the southern side of the river?"
"Aye lord although I saw horsemen to the north."
"And when will they be here?"
"Late tomorrow then they will be just five miles to the east of us."
"Good. You are our eyes!"

I took my drekar and Erik sailed me to the north bank. Haraldr and Siggi had made themselves comfortable and they had a well-defended camp. "Haraldr, tonight, I want you and your men to burn this bridge. Then using just one ship ferry three quarters of your men across the river. Do it in the dark and land them well to the west of the church. The King of the Franks comes and I would have him kept in the dark about our numbers. You will remain hidden behind the church until I summon you." My men trusted me implicitly. I had yet to fail. No matter how ridiculous my ideas they seemed to work.

As I sailed back across the river with the first of Siggi's men I put the finishing touches to my plan. I had first come up with this plan after the first siege. It was so many years ago now that William had grown from a youth to a young man. Bergil Fast Blade had grey hairs and Harold Strong Arm had lost all of his!

Æbbi Bonecrusher had gathered my lords at the bridge. Before us lay the burned houses. They were charred stumps. The desolation spread for three quarters of a mile south. "Petr you know what you must do?"

"Aye lord, I fill *'Fafnir'* with all of my archers." Petr's archers were the best. We had another hundred who would fight with me but Petr and his fifty would be my secret weapon. He smiled and clasped my arm, "Fear not lord I will not let you down. When you need me, I will be there."

"Gandálfr, you have all of the captured weapons?"
"Aye lord. There are wagon loads of them."

"Then when it is dark you make a wall of the javelins and spears to the south of us. I want to make it impossible for men to charge through them. Leif and Lars. Your men will guard that flank. Your warbands must hold off what might be an army!"

"Do not worry lord, we will."

"The rest of us will wait in three lines. We will endure whatever the Franks throw at us. Gandálfr will distribute the darts and throwing spears. Our archers will thin out the enemy but I want to make a wall of dead before us. We do not need to defeat the Franks. We just avoid defeat. Godwin, you and my son, along with Harold Strong Arm's boys have one task. You guard the bridge. If the men of Paris try to sally forth then fire it. If our left flank is in danger then fire it. We have so few men to spare that tomorrow boys must do that which should be left for men."

Godwin nodded. Of all men he understood fire. "Aye lord but this fire will harden iron and make it steel! We will not let you down!"

As we went back to the church I saw the fire begun by Haraldr. The north bridge was on fire. The only way off the island now was by the bridge close to us.

That night I sat with Padraig. He was giving me advice. He was not a warrior but he was a man of science and knowledge. When I had learned all that I could he said, "Lord, I would stand by you. I would hold the cross of Christ."

"You ask much."

"Yet I have asked for so very little. It will not hurt you for it looks like the emblem on your cloak." He had a cloak about his shoulders. He had said he had the chills.

"I will agree if you wear a helmet and carry a sword."

"I will not use a sword."

"I know. You have a reason to carry a cross and I will use it for my purpose."

"Very well."

We had warriors who were Christians. There were more than there had been but not enough to make me fear for my army. Padraig heard their confessions. He told me it would do no harm and might make them fight harder. I would reserve judgement on that. When he had gone I went to William and Godwin. "Godwin, do not risk my son tomorrow."

"Fear not lord. He will be there to greet you at the end of the battle."

I looked at William. Since his mother had gone he had become my son. He was dearer to me than any and yet I would put a huge burden on his shoulders. "You have grown over these past years. Do you think you can lead these people called…"? I shrugged, "I no longer know what to call us save, the people?"

"I will be ready one day, father, but I still have much growing in me. Do not lose your life tomorrow."

"I will try not to."

I managed but a few hours of sleep. I woke before dark. The air was filled with the smell of charred wood. Æbbi Bonecrusher greeted me with a horn of ale. "Egil will plant our standard on the top of the church, lord. That way he can fight at your side. Your hearth weru will be with you tomorrow."

"I know. I have put you in harm's way…"

"That is because you will be in harm's way."

"It is the only way I know to draw their best warriors toward me. That way we win!"

"Perhaps. Sven Blue Cheek once told me that following you was like trying to ride a wild pony. He was right. What he did not say is that following you makes you a better man."

"A better man?"

"Look at Harold Strong Arm. He is now happy and has children. I have known him for many years. When he was younger he was a dangerous man to know. After your father was murdered he became even more violent. Since serving you? Look at him now. When this battle is over I will find two more hearth weru for you. Haaken the Bold and I will emulate Harold. We will see if we can become fathers too."

As we went to the river I knew that this battle would change all of our lives!

We had cleared some of the charred buildings to make it harder for the Franks to get at us and to give us a killing space. I turned and saw Godwin and my son, along with their two helpers laying kindling under the charred bridge. I turned back to look from the island to the east. The men on the walls were watching us and wondering what we were doing. They would know of the imminent arrival of the King of France. As yet there was no sign of them. I expected their scouts in the early afternoon. If Bagsecg was correct they would camp at sunset. The burned buildings meant that the only place they could camp would be a mile to the east of us, almost level with the end of the island. I turned back and saw William carrying the pot of hot coals. It was a thoughtful act for Godwin had been badly burned once already. The two helpers would feed the fire until it was needed. There was a chance it might not be required.

Æbbi Bonecrusher said, "Come lord, you had little sleep, have food. Egil has brought some lamb."

Our raids continued each day and although my men had to travel further afield each time they still managed to bring back treasure and food. The lamb smelled delicious and I tucked in. As I ate I viewed our lines. They looked to be perilously thin, there were barely two hundred and eighty men to repel the first attack but Haraldr had another three hundred hidden in the church and to the south of us. Bagsecg could bring his eighty horsemen to join us when the enemy closed. There were also another two hundred north of the river. I was satisfied.

I had been to the river to make water when Bagsecg's scout rode in. "They are close, lord. You will see their scouts shortly."

Without making a fuss my men formed up. It was unlikely we would fight at night but we had to look prepared. It was a huge army and they rolled in for what seemed like hours. I saw the royal standard and knew that Charles the Simple had stirred himself to lead his army. My oathsworn and I were well known for our distinctive cloaks and helmets. He came forward to see us. As the King himself rode a few paces ahead of his men I led my oathsworn with Padraig in tow to view them. I rode Gilles for I wanted the King to see me. The cross would confuse the Franks as it had confused my men until I had explained it to them. "We do not care about a cross but they do. If they think we are Christians then it might weaken their attack. It cannot harm us."

"We do not have to become Christian?"

"No Æbbi Bonecrusher."

"Then it is good."

I saw the King point a finger in my direction. I was about to turn when Æbbi Bonecrusher pulled up his cloak, turned around and dropped his breeks. Turning back, he made water in the direction of the King. My men laughed for they thought it to be funny. If Æbbi had done that to a Viking then one of the enemy would have raced over to challenge him for such an insult. The Franks seemed bemused.

We returned to our lines and some men began to sharpen weapons which were already sharp. The sound would carry and the enemy would know we were ready. We kept a good watch but I slept. I slept better than I had done for some time for I knew that the next day would be momentous… one way or another.

The Franks wasted no time and as soon as the sun had risen their horns sounded and their mounted men rode toward us. This was not like Beauvais where we had a log barricade. We had charred buildings which would allow their horsemen to close with us but not to keep a straight line. When I say they came for us it was really for me. Their finest nobles and horsemen rode toward me. I was not on Gilles but I was head and shoulders taller than almost everyone else. The archers behind me had measured the range. They had strategically placed charred wreckage so that they knew when to release. They sent a shower of arrows. The mailed men did not suffer much but their horses did and when a horse fell it often killed its rider or brought down other horses. The already ragged line became even more ragged. As they neared us we hurled first darts and then throwing spears. This time many of them found flesh or threw horsemen from their saddles. I drew Long Sword when they were ten paces from us. I stepped from the line to allow myself a good swing and I timed it to perfection. The spear from the noble with the blue plume struck the mail on my left arm but my sword struck and severed his leg and drove so deeply into his horse's side that it veered off to the side and crashed into a second horse. I stepped back, I heard a horn behind me. That was Haraldr summoning his men. Our two lines would become four. Our archers continued to rain death. Æbbi Bonecrusher was on one side of me and Haaken on the other. Egil still watched my back. When I had stepped forward I had felt his shield supporting me.

My hearth weru hacked, sliced and stabbed at horses and men. We became an island as the Franks further south pushed my men back. They would not push us back. I brought my sword from on high as a spear came toward me. It seemed it was destined to strike me but Egil's spear came from under my arm to flick up the spear and to stab the horse in the throat. My sword came down and split the Frank's head.

I heard a shout from the left. The Franks had sallied from the island. I watched as Godwin and my son began to fire the bridge. It was a mistake to turn. I had my own battle to fight. Even as I turned a Frankish spear came for me. My sword was down. Æbbi Bonecrusher stepped forward and flicked up the spear with his shield. The warrior's horse reared and smashed down on Æbbi's head. Enraged at both the Frank and myself, I swung my sword and half cut the Frank in two. Haaken the Bold had been Æbbi Bonecrusher's shield brother for what seemed like all time. He went berserk. I had not seen it for some time and it was terrifying. He hurled his shield at the nearest Frank and it almost knocked him from his saddle. He chopped at the man and then ran at the rest of the milling horses and riders. He took them by surprise. They were not expecting it and he managed to kill or wound five before they saw what they had to do. Five of them speared him at once. My archers took advantage and they launched arrow after arrow at them. My oathsworn died but his death resulted in twenty dead Franks.

I heard a horn from the Franks and saw that they had another one hundred horsemen ready to come at me. I turned and saw that my son and Godwin had set fire to the bridge. Men caught in the middle of the bridge by the racing flames screamed as they were burned. I saw the Bishop of Paris hurl himself into the Seine to douse the flames. He was mailed and he did not surface.

"Shield wall!"

Bjorn the Brave and his men joined my remaining oathsworn. Egil took Æbbi Bonecrusher's place. The horsemen thundered on and then my secret weapon was used. Erik brought my drekar west from behind the Franks. They had sailed upstream and turned around the island to approach unseen by the Franks. Now with the current taking them, they sailed down the Frankish line. They were less than eighty paces from the Franks and they sent arrow after arrow into them. Mail could not stop them and the Franks had so many men that every arrow found flesh. My archers were attacking the right-hand side of the warriors. Their shields were on their left! I saw the King himself take cover as some of his closest lords and advisers died. We prepared to face the horsemen but the full weight of the attack did not materialise. Petr and his archers simply slaughtered the horses and their riders. Bodies of animals and men piled up.

"Charge!" We raced into the mass of dying horseflesh to avenge Haaken the Bold. I took the head from a lord who was trying to pull himself from under a horse. As I swung Long Sword, I was aware that Godwin and William had joined us. Harold Strong Arm's sons were slinging stones. I looked up. I had hoped for a stalemate, a draw. I saw the standard of the Franks and it was retreating. We had won!

The rest of our men flooded forward but I was spent. With Egil and the last of my oathsworn, I walked over to the body of Harold the Bold. He was smiling. He and Æbbi Bonecrusher would never have a family but they would be in Valhalla and they had died happy. We laid the two of them together. We would bury them when time allowed.

It was dark when the last of my men returned. The battle was over and the battle was won but had I won the war?

The first thing I had done when I knew that we had won was to seek my son. His mail had soot upon it and Padraig was tending to one of Harold's sons. I wagged a finger at him. "You should have run. The Franks almost caught you."

Godwin said, "No lord, Father Padraig here ran and blocked the sword of the Frank which would have slain him. I slew the Frank and then William was able to fire the bridge. We had made it too well for the flames leapt up and scorched his mail."

I turned to Padraig, "Thank you."

He shrugged, "I did not kill anyone and my blow saved a life." He smiled. "It was the Christian thing to do." He coughed and looked unsteady on his feet.

"Sit you have earned a rest."

As I returned to my men I reflected that two Christians, Godwin and Padraig had saved my son's life when a Christian Bishop had lost his. *Wyrd.*

By the time dawn had come our drekar was moored where the bridge had been and we had cleared and buried our dead close to the church. Æbbi Bonecrusher and Haaken the Bold were laid together. Their bodies were in the centre of the rest of our dead for they were the most honourable of all those that had died. Padraig had the idea of marking their grave with the cross he had carried. "It may stop the Franks from digging up their bodies." We planted the cross with the body of the White Christ upon it and the Franks did not disturb our dead.

We stripped the enemy dead and sought the treasure they carried. We headed back to our lines and we ate. I had half of the army stand to all night. I feared a second attack. It did not come. Instead when dawn broke a bareheaded rider rode toward us. "King Charles would speak peace with you." He pointed to a place which was being cleared of the Frankish dead. It was two hundred paces from our lines and four hundred from the Franks. More importantly, it could be seen from the island. "The King will have six men with him. He will sound a horn when he is ready." He looked at me expectantly.

"I will come."

I chose Padraig, Haraldr, Gandálfr, Bagsecg, Bjorn, Leif and William to come with me. A horn sounded and we walked. I saw that King Charles liked his comfort. He was no warrior. I had not seen him at the battle. He had tables and chairs laid out. My men waited until I sat and then they sat.

The King looked old despite the fact that he was far younger than I. His leaders looked old. The Bishop who was with him was also old. Had we defeated an army of old men?

"Lord Göngu-Hrólfr Rognvaldson you have won and I am here to ensure that you no longer raid my people. I need peace. My land needs peace. There are more of your kind than we can deal with. I would have you fight our enemies for us both domestic and foreign."

"You want a sword for hire?"

"No, I wish you to be lord of the land of the Northmen, Normandy. I give to you the land on both sides of the Seine from the Epte to the Risle. That land will be called Normandy for your people have now made it their own. You will have the title of Duke. You will swear to protect all the people of that land, Frank and Norse."

He looked at me expectantly. "And the land from the Cotentin to the Seine."

He hesitated and the lord next to him whispered in his ear. He nodded. "And the land from the Cotentin to the Seine."

I had all that I wanted. We had made so much money from the Franks that I doubted that they could fulfil a request for more. But where was the price we would have to pay? I looked at my men. They thought it was a good offer. Padraig nodded. I said, "Then I will be Duke of Normandy." I looked at William. "As will my heirs."

The King nodded and looked relieved, "Of course as Duke of Normandy, part of the Empire and a vassal of West Frankia you will have to be baptised a Christian." I heard the gasp from my men. "And to tie us together you will be betrothed to my daughter."

To give me time to think I said, "Daughter?"

He smiled, "She is but five years old but when she is old enough a marriage to you will ensure that the western side of my realm is safe."

The marriage would not be a problem. She was younger than my son! It was at least seven years away and much could happen in seven years. Could I become a Christian? Then I thought of the King's words. He wanted me baptised as a Christian. I had seen the ceremony. A priest put water on your head and gave you a name. That appeared to be it. I already allowed churches in my land and Christians. In my heart, I would still be Göngu-Hrólfr. Inside me I would still be a Viking. I could hear the Norns spinning and hear my grandfather's telling of the tale of the cave. If I was to fulfil the prophecy then I had to do this or continue to fight. I looked at Padraig. Two Christians had saved my son. This was *wyrd*.

    I stood and held my arm out. The King looked confused and two of his lords helped him to his feet. He put a hand out. It was soft and perfumed. I clasped his arm. "I will be baptised, by Padraig, my priest. I will rule the land of Normandy for you and I will care for all the people and protect you from raids along the river. I will become the Duke of Normandy!"

Epilogue

When we returned to our camp I explained to my lords my decision. I did not have to but I wanted them to know exactly what I was doing and why. I told them that they did not have to be baptised. The King insisted upon seeing me baptised. Padraig performed it in the church we had used during the battle. I was given the Christian name of Robert. Padraig later told me that it was the closest name to Rollo or Hrolfr. I had had so many names in my life that the change of name did not worry me. The King also gave me a chest of gold. I think he thought it obligatory when dealing with Vikings.

As we sailed down the river in laden drekar I explained to William all the reasons for my decision. He accepted them. I feared that Sven and the others would not. I had sent a rider to Chartres to tell Sven to raise the siege and to invite my lords to Rouen.

When I reached Rouen there were great celebrations. Word had come down the river on drekar faster than mine. The ones who lived in Rouen were largely Christian anyway. Padraig did not live to see Sven and the others. On the journey downstream he had become increasingly ill. I had sent for healers but he had shaken his head, "Lord, I am dying. I have known it for months. I die and go to heaven with a clear conscience and know that I have done that which I was sent here to do. I have made the Norsemen, Christian. You will lead a great people and William will do so when he is old enough but it will be a Christian people and that I take much of the credit for."

He died within the hour and I confess that I shed a tear. I had spent more years with him than my wife Poppa. He was buried with honour. The King had given me coins to build a cathedral and Padraig's body was placed in the crypt. The building was but a skeleton but part of its bones would be Padraig.

When Sven and my men arrived from Chartres I was a little nervous. I had no need to be. Sven Blue Cheek greeted me with a warrior's clasp. "You defeated the Franks and you have secured this land!"

"And Chartres?"

"We could have taken it but it would have cost us many men. We lost few warriors and came away rich. It is *wyrd*."

"And I am now Robert, Duke of Normandy!"

He laughed, "When we first pulled the half-drowned fish from the sea you had another name. How many men can be reborn as many times as you? I am content. In your heart, you are still the same Viking that I will follow until the day I die but I will call you by your new name Robert Duke of Normandy or perhaps Rollo. It suits you better. The Norns still spin for the prophecy they gave to your grandfather is fulfilled and your people will become greater! All hail the Duke!"

And so, my part in the prophecy came to an end. William Longsword would have to take it on. Even as we drank I could hear the Norns spinning. I had been baptised but I was still a Viking.

The End

Norse Calendar

Gormánuður October 14th - November 13th
Ýlir November 14th - December 13th
Mörsugur December 14th - January 12th
Þorri - January 13th - February 11th
Gói - February 12th - March 13th
Einmánuður - March 14th - April 13th
Harpa April 14th - May 13th
Skerpla - May 14th - June 12th
Sólmánuður - June 13th - July 12th
Heyannir - July 13th - August 14th
Tvímánuður - August 15th - September 14th
Haustmánuður September 15th-October 13th

Glossary

Ækre -acre (Norse) The amount of land a pair of oxen could plough in one day
Addelam- Deal (Kent)
Afon Hafron- River Severn in Welsh
Aldarennaöy – Alderney (Channel Islands)
Alt Clut- Dumbarton Castle on the Clyde
Anmyen -Amiens
Andecavis- Angers in Anjou
Angia- Jersey (Channel Islands)
An Lysardh -The Lizard (Cornwall)
An Oriant- Lorient, Brittany
Æscesdūn – Ashdown (Berkshire)
Áth Truim- Trim, County Meath (Ireland)
Baille - a ward (an enclosed area inside a wall)
Balley Chashtal -Castleton (Isle of Man)
Bárekr's Haven – Barfleur, Normandy
Bebbanburgh- Bamburgh Castle, Northumbria. Also, known as Din Guardi in the ancient tongue
Beck- a stream
Bexelei – Bexhill on sea
Blót – a blood sacrifice made by a jarl

Blue Sea/Middle Sea- The Mediterranean
Bondi- Viking farmers who fight
Bourde- Bordeaux
Bjarnarøy –Great Bernera (Bear Island)
Byrnie- a mail or leather shirt reaching down to the knees
Brvggas -Bruges
Caerlleon- Welsh for Chester
Caestir - Chester (old English)
Cantwareburh- Canterbury
Casnewydd –Newport, Wales
Cent- Kent
Cephas- Greek for Simon Peter (St. Peter)
Cetham -Chatham Kent
Chape- the tip of a scabbard
Charlemagne- Holy Roman Emperor at the end of the 8th and beginning of the 9th centuries
Cherestanc- Garstang (Lancashire)
Cippanhamm -Chippenham
Ċiriċeburh- Cherbourg
Condado Portucalense- the County of Portugal
Constrasta-Valença (Northern Portugal)
Corn Walum or Om Walum- Cornwall
Cissa-caestre -Chichester
Cymri- Welsh
Cymru- Wales
Cyninges-tūn – Coniston. It means the estate of the king (Cumbria)
Dùn Èideann –Edinburgh (Gaelic)
Din Guardi- Bamburgh castle
Drekar- a Dragon ship (a Viking warship)
Duboglassio –Douglas, Isle of Man
Djupr -Dieppe
Dwfr- Dover
Dyrøy –Jura (Inner Hebrides)
Dyflin- Old Norse for Dublin
Ein-mánuðr- middle of March to the middle of April
Eopwinesfleot -Ebbsfleet
Eoforwic- Saxon for York
Fáfnir - a dwarf turned into a dragon (Norse mythology)
Faro Bregancio- Corunna (Spain)

Ferneberga -Farnborough (Hampshire)
Fey- having second sight
Firkin- a barrel containing eight gallons (usually beer)
Fret-a sea mist
Frankia- France and part of Germany
Fyrd-the Saxon levy
Gaill- Irish for foreigners
Galdramenn- wizard
Glaesum –amber
Gleawecastre- Gloucester
Gói- the end of February to the middle of March
Greenway- ancient roads- they used turf rather than stone
Grenewic- Greenwich
Gyllingas - Gillingham Kent
Haesta- Hastings
Haestingaceaster-Pevensey
Hastingas-Hastings
Hamwic -Southampton
Hantone- Littlehampton
Haughs/ Haugr - small hills in Norse (As in Tarn Hows) or a hump- normally a mound of earth
Hearth-weru- Jarl's bodyguard/oathsworn
Heels- when a ship leans to one side under the pressure of the wind
Hel- Queen of, the Norse underworld.
Herkumbl- a mark on the front of a helmet denoting the clan of a Viking warrior
Here Wic- Harwich
Hetaereiarch – Byzantine general
Hí- Iona (Gaelic)
Hjáp - Shap- Cumbria (Norse for stone circle)
Hoggs or Hogging- when the pressure of the wind causes the stern or the bow to droop
Hrams-a – Ramsey, Isle of Man
Hrīs Wearp – Ruswarp (North Yorkshire)
Hrofecester-Rochester Kent
Hywel ap Rhodri Molwynog- King of Gwynedd 814-825
Icaunis- British river god
Ishbiliyya- Seville
Issicauna- Gaulish for the lower Seine

Duke of Normandy

Itouna- River Eden Cumbria
Jarl- Norse earl or lord
Joro-goddess of the earth
Jǫtunn -Norse god or goddess
Kartreidh -Carteret in Normandy
Kjerringa - Old Woman- the solid block in which the mast rested
Knarr- a merchant ship or a coastal vessel
Kyrtle-woven top
Laugardagr-Saturday (Norse for washing day)
Leathes Water- Thirlmere
Ljoðhús- Lewis
Legacaestir- Anglo Saxon for Chester
Liger- Loire
Lochlannach – Irish for Northerners (Vikings)
Lothuwistoft- Lowestoft
Louis the Pious- King of the Franks and son of Charlemagne
Lundenwic - London
Lincylene -Lincoln
Maen hir – standing stone (menhir)
Maeresea- River Mersey
Mammceaster- Manchester
Manau/Mann – The Isle of Man(n) (Saxon)
Marcia Hispanic- Spanish Marches (the land around Barcelona)
Mast fish- two large racks on a ship for the mast
Melita- Malta
Midden - a place where they dumped human waste
Miklagård - Constantinople
Leudes- Imperial officer (a local leader in the Carolingian Empire. They became Counts a century after this.)
Njoror- God of the sea
Nithing- A man without honour (Saxon)
Odin- The "All Father" God of war, also associated with wisdom, poetry, and magic (The ruler of the gods).
Olissipo- Lisbon
Orkneyjar-Orkney
Portucale- Porto
Portesmūða -Portsmouth
Penrhudd – Penrith Cumbria
Pillars of Hercules- Straits of Gibraltar

Qādis- Cadiz
Ran- Goddess of the sea
Readingum -Reading Berks
Remisgat Ramsgate
Roof rock- slate
Rinaz –The Rhine
Sabrina- Latin and Celtic for the River Severn. Also, the name of a female Celtic deity
Saami- the people who live in what is now Northern Norway/Sweden
Saint Maclou- St Malo (France)
Sandwic- Sandwich (Kent)
Sarnia- Guernsey (Channel Islands)
St. Cybi- Holyhead
Sampiere -samphire (sea asparagus)
Scree- loose rocks in a glacial valley
Seax – short sword
Sheerstrake- the uppermost strake in the hull
Sheet- a rope fastened to the lower corner of a sail
Shroud- a rope from the masthead to the hull amidships
Skeggox – an axe with a shorter beard on one side of the blade
Sondwic-Sandwich
South Folk- Suffolk
Stad- Norse settlement
Stays- ropes running from the mast-head to the bow
Streanæshalc -Whitby
Stirap- stirrup
Strake- the wood on the side of a drekar
Suthriganaworc - Southwark (London)
Svearike -Sweden
Syllingar- Scilly Isles
Syllingar Insula- Scilly Isles
Tarn- small lake (Norse)
Temese- River Thames (also called the Tamese)
The Norns- The three sisters who weave webs of intrigue for men
Thing-Norse for a parliament or a debate (Tynwald)
Thor's day- Thursday
Threttanessa- a drekar with 13 oars on each side.
Thrall- slave
Tinea- Tyne

Tintaieol- Tintagel (Cornwall)
Trenail- a round wooden peg used to secure strakes
Tude- Tui in Northern Spain
Tynwald- the Parliament on the Isle of Man
Úlfarrberg- Helvellyn
Úlfarrland- Cumbria
Úlfarr- Wolf Warrior
Úlfarrston- Ulverston
Ullr-Norse God of Hunting
Ulfheonar-an elite Norse warrior who wore a wolf skin over his armour
Uuluuich- Dulwich
Valauna- Valognes (Normandy)
Vectis- The Isle of Wight
Veðrafjǫrðr -Waterford (Ireland)
Veisafjǫrðr- Wexford (Ireland)
Volva- a witch or healing woman in Norse culture
Waeclinga Straet- Watling Street (A5)
Windlesore-Windsor
Waite- a Viking word for farm
Werham -Wareham (Dorset)
Wintan-ceastre -Winchester
Wihtwara- Isle of White
Withy- the mechanism connecting the steering board to the ship
Woden's day- Wednesday
Wyddfa-Snowdon
Wyrd- Fate
Yard- a timber from which the sail is suspended on a drekar
Ynys Môn-Anglesey

Maps and Illustrations

The Norman dynasty

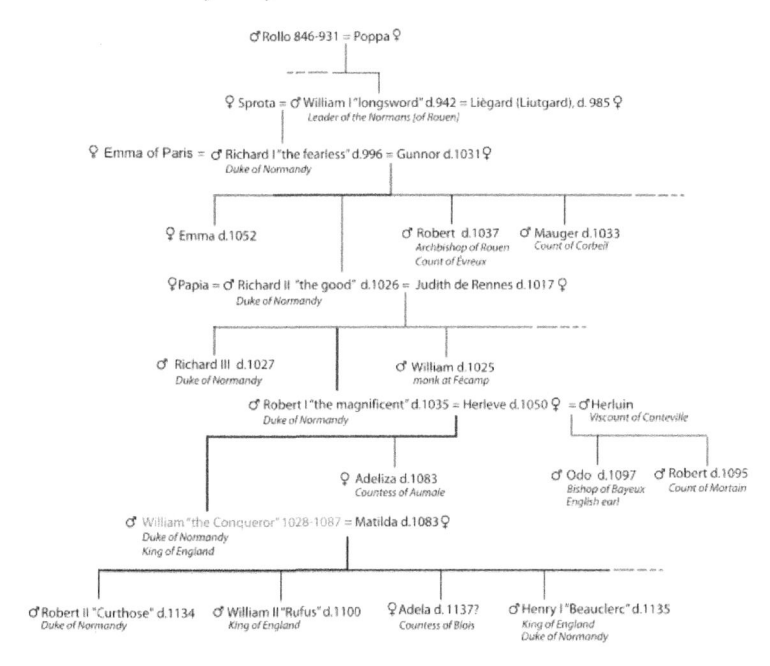

♂ Rollo 846-931 = Poppa ♀

♀ Sprota = ♂ William I "longsword" d.942 = Liègard (Liutgard), d. 985 ♀
Leader of the Normans (of Rouen)

♀ Emma of Paris = ♂ Richard I "the fearless" d.996 = Gunnor d.1031 ♀
Duke of Normandy

♀ Emma d.1052   ♂ Robert d.1037   ♂ Mauger d.1033
Archbishop of Rouen   Count of Corbeil
Count of Évreux

♀ Papia = ♂ Richard II "the good" d.1026 = Judith de Rennes d.1017 ♀
Duke of Normandy

♂ Richard III d.1027   ♂ William d.1025
Duke of Normandy   monk at Fécamp

♂ Robert I "the magnificent" d.1035 = Herleve d.1050 ♀ = ♂ Herluin
Duke of Normandy   *Viscount of Conteville*

♀ Adeliza d.1083   ♂ Odo d.1097   ♂ Robert d.1095
Countess of Aumale   Bishop of Bayeux   Count of Mortain
                      English earl

♂ William "the Conqueror" 1028-1087 = Matilda d.1083 ♀
Duke of Normandy
King of England

♂ Robert II "Curthose" d.1134   ♂ William II "Rufus" d.1100   ♀ Adela d. 1137?   ♂ Henry I "Beauclerc" d.1135
Duke of Normandy   *King of England*   *Countess of Blois* *King of England*
                                                                                     Duke of Normandy

Courtesy of Wikipedia.

Historical note

My research encompasses not only books and the Internet but also TV. Time Team was a great source of information. I wish they would bring it back! I saw the wooden compass which my sailors use on the Dan Snow programme about the Vikings. Apparently, it was used in modern times to sail from Denmark to Edinburgh and was only a couple of points out. Similarly, the construction of the temporary hall was copied from the settlement of Leif Eriksson in Newfoundland.

Stirrups began to be introduced in Europe during the 7th and 8th Centuries. By Charlemagne's time, they were widely used but only by nobles. It is said this was the true beginning of feudalism. It was the Vikings who introduced them to England. It was only in the time of Canute the Great that they became widespread. The use of stirrups enabled a rider to strike someone on the ground from the back of a horse and facilitated the use of spears and later, lances.

The Vikings may seem cruel to us now. They enslaved women and children. Many of the women became their wives. The DNA of the people of Iceland shows that it was made up of a mixture of Norse and Danish males and Celtic females. These were the people who settled Iceland, Greenland and Vinland. They did the same in England and, as we shall see, Normandy. Their influence was widespread. Genghis Khan and his Mongols did the same in the 13th century. It is said that a high proportion of European males have Mongol blood in them. The Romans did it with the Sabine tribe. They were different times and it would be wrong to judge them with our politically correct twenty-first-century eyes. This sort of behaviour still goes on in the world but with less justification.

At this time, there were no Viking kings. There were clans. Each clan had a hersir or Jarl. Clans were loyal to each other. A hersir was more of a landlocked Viking or a farmer while a Jarl usually had ship(s) at his command. A hersir would command bondi. They were the Norse equivalent of the fyrd although they were much better warriors. They would all have a helmet shield and a sword. Most would also have a spear. Hearth weru were the oathsworn or bodyguards for a jarl or, much later on, a king. Kings like Canute and Harald Hadrada were rare and they only emerged at the beginning of the tenth century.

Duke of Normandy

One reason for the Normans' success was that when they arrived in northern France they integrated quickly with the local populace. They married them and began to use some of their words. They adapted to the horse as a weapon of war. Before then the Vikings had been quite happy to ride to war but they dismounted to fight. The Normans took the best that the Franks had and made it better. This book sees the earliest beginnings of the rise of the Norman knight.

I have used the names by which places were known in the medieval period wherever possible. Sometimes I have had to use the modern name. The Cotentin is an example. The isle of sheep is now called the Isle of Sheppey and lies on the Medway close to the Thames. The land of Kent was known as Cent in the early medieval period. Thanet or, Tanet as it was known in the Viking period was an island at this time. The sea was on two sides and the other two sides had swamps, bogs, mud flats and tidal streams. It protected Canterbury. The coast was different too. Richborough had been a major Roman port. It is now some way inland. Sandwich was a port. Other ports now lie under the sea. Vikings were not afraid to sail up very narrow rivers and to risk being stranded on mud. They were tough men and were capable of carrying or porting their ships as their Rus brothers did when travelling to Miklagård.

The Norns or the Weird Sisters.

"The Norns (Old Norse: norn, plural: nornir) in Norse mythology are female beings who rule the destiny of gods and men. They roughly correspond to other controllers of humans' destiny, the Fates, elsewhere in European mythology.
In Snorri Sturluson's interpretation of the Völuspá, Urðr (Wyrd), Verðandi and Skuld, the three most important of the Norns, come out from a hall standing at the Well of Urðr or Well of Fate. They draw water from the well and take sand that lies around it, which they pour over Yggdrasill so that its branches will not rot. These three Norns are described as powerful maiden giantesses (Jotuns) whose arrival from Jötunheimr ended the golden age of the gods. They may be the same as the maidens of Mögþrasir who are described in Vafþrúðnismál"

Source: Norns - https://en.wikipedia.org

I have used the word town as this is the direct translation of the Danish ton- meaning settlement. A town could vary in size from a couple of houses to a walled city like Jorvik. If I had used ton it would have been confusing. There are already readers out there who think I have made mistakes because I use words like stiraps, wyrd and drekar!

The assimilation of the Norse and the Franks took place over a long period. Hrolf Ragnvaldson aka Rollo aka Robert of Normandy is not yet born but by the time he is 64 he will have attacked Paris and become Duke of Normandy. The journey has just begun.

Tower construction

Towers were made by constructing two walls with mortared dress stone and then infilling with rocks. When I visited Penrith castle in Cumbria in 2017 I saw a partly ruined tower which demonstrates this. It helps that the dressed stone was red sandstone! You can see the width of the tower. This one is 13th Century but the principle was the same in the 9th.

Author's collection

Rollo

I have used the name Rollo even though that is the Latinisation of Hrolf. I did so for two reasons. We all know the first Duke of Normandy as Rollo and I wanted to avoid confusion with his grandfather. I realise that I have also caused enough of a problem with Ragnvald and Ragnvald the Breton Slayer.

Rollo is generally identified with one Viking in particular – a man of high social status mentioned in Icelandic sagas, which refer to him by the Old Norse name Göngu-Hrólfr, meaning "Hrólfr the Walker". (Göngu-Hrólfr is also widely known by an Old Danish variant, Ganger-Hrolf.)

The byname "Walker" is usually understood to suggest that Rollo was so physically imposing that he could not be carried by a horse and was obliged to travel on foot. Norman and other French sources do not use the name Hrólfr, and the identification of Rollo with Göngu-Hrólfr is based upon similarities between circumstances and actions ascribed to both figures.

He had children by at least three women. He abducted Popa or Poppa the daughter of the Count of Rennes or possibly the Count of Bayeux. It is not known if she was legitimate or illegitimate. He married Gisla the daughter (probably illegitimate) of King Charles of France. He also had another child. According to the medieval Irish text, '***An Banshencha**s*' and Icelandic sources, another daughter, Cadlinar (Kaðlín; Kathleen) was born in Scotland (probably to a Scots mother) and married an Irish prince named Beollán mac Ciarmaic, later King of South Brega (Lagore). I have used the Norse name Kaðlín and made her a Scottish princess.

Poppa and Rollo

There is some dispute as the true identity of the woman called Poppa. Most agree that she was the daughter of a Breton count but the sources dispute which one. I cannot believe that a legitimate daughter of a Count would have been left with a Viking and so I have her as illegitimate. More danico was the term used by the Franks to speak of a Danish marriage. The heirs were considered legal, at least in the world of the Norse. William was famously William the Bastard.

I apologise for the number of Franks called Charles. All of them existed and they had the soubriquets I gave them. None were flattering. The family of the King of the Bretons are also accurate. Godfrid, Duke of Frisia was a Viking and he was murdered. As insane as it sounds the King of the Franks gave his 5-year-old as Rollo's bride. As Rollo was almost sixty it does not sound right but they were different times.

I created the Poppa storyline to explain how he had two wives and the priest as a spy served my purposes too.

The story is not yet done although I may not get to William the Conqueror.

Books used in the research
- British Museum - Vikings- Life and Legends
- Arthur and the Saxon Wars- David Nicolle (Osprey)
- Saxon, Norman and Viking Terence Wise (Osprey)
- The Vikings- Ian Heath (Osprey)
- Byzantine Armies 668-1118 - Ian Heath (Osprey)

Duke of Normandy

- Romano-Byzantine Armies 4th-9th Century - David Nicholle (Osprey)
- The Walls of Constantinople AD 324-1453 - Stephen Turnbull (Osprey)
- Viking Longship - Keith Durham (Osprey)
- The Vikings in England- Anglo-Danish Project
- The Varangian Guard- 988-1453 Raffael D'Amato
- Saxon Viking and Norman- Terence Wise
- The Walls of Constantinople AD 324-1453-Stephen Turnbull
- Byzantine Armies- 886-1118- Ian Heath
- The Age of Charlemagne-David Nicolle
- The Normans- David Nicolle
- Norman Knight AD 950-1204- Christopher Gravett
- The Norman Conquest of the North- William A Kappelle
- The Knight in History- Francis Gies
- The Norman Achievement- Richard F Cassady
- Knights- Constance Brittain Bouchard

Griff Hosker
August 2018

Duke of Normandy

Other books by Griff Hosker

If you enjoyed reading this book, then why not read another one by the author?

Ancient History

The Sword of Cartimandua Series
(Germania and Britannia 50 A.D. – 128 A.D.)
Ulpius Felix- Roman Warrior (prequel)
The Sword of Cartimandua
The Horse Warriors
Invasion Caledonia
Roman Retreat
Revolt of the Red Witch
Druid's Gold
Trajan's Hunters
The Last Frontier
Hero of Rome
Roman Hawk
Roman Treachery
Roman Wall
Roman Courage

The Wolf Warrior series
(Britain in the late 6th Century)
Saxon Dawn
Saxon Revenge
Saxon England
Saxon Blood
Saxon Slayer
Saxon Slaughter
Saxon Bane
Saxon Fall: Rise of the Warlord
Saxon Throne
Saxon Sword

Medieval History

The Dragon Heart Series
Viking Slave
Viking Warrior
Viking Jarl
Viking Kingdom
Viking Wolf
Viking War
Viking Sword
Viking Wrath
Viking Raid
Viking Legend
Viking Vengeance
Viking Dragon
Viking Treasure
Viking Enemy
Viking Witch
Viking Blood
Viking Weregeld
Viking Storm
Viking Warband
Viking Shadow
Viking Legacy
Viking Clan
Viking Bravery

The Norman Genesis Series
Hrolf the Viking
Horseman
The Battle for a Home
Revenge of the Franks
The Land of the Northmen
Ragnvald Hrolfsson
Brothers in Blood
Lord of Rouen
Drekar in the Seine
Duke of Normandy
The Duke and the King

Duke of Normandy

Danelaw
(England and Denmark in the 11th Century)
Dragon Sword
Oathsword
Bloodsword

New World Series
Blood on the Blade
Across the Seas
The Savage Wilderness
The Bear and the Wolf
Erik The Navigator
Erik's Clan

The Vengeance Trail

The Reconquista Chronicles
Castilian Knight
El Campeador
The Lord of Valencia

The Aelfraed Series
(Britain and Byzantium 1050 A.D. - 1085 A.D.)
Housecarl
Outlaw
Varangian

The Anarchy Series England 1120-1180
English Knight
Knight of the Empress
Northern Knight
Baron of the North
Earl
King Henry's Champion
The King is Dead
Warlord of the North
Enemy at the Gate

Duke of Normandy

The Fallen Crown
Warlord's War
Kingmaker
Henry II
Crusader
The Welsh Marches
Irish War
Poisonous Plots
The Princes' Revolt
Earl Marshal
The Perfect Knight

Border Knight
1182-1300
Sword for Hire
Return of the Knight
Baron's War
Magna Carta
Welsh Wars
Henry III
The Bloody Border
Baron's Crusade
Sentinel of the North
War in the West
Debt of Honour
The Blood of the Warlord

Sir John Hawkwood Series
France and Italy 1339- 1387
Crécy: The Age of the Archer
Man At Arms
The White Company
Leader of Men

Lord Edward's Archer
Lord Edward's Archer
King in Waiting
An Archer's Crusade
Targets of Treachery

Duke of Normandy

The Great Cause

**Struggle for a Crown
1360- 1485**
Blood on the Crown
To Murder a King
The Throne
King Henry IV
The Road to Agincourt
St Crispin's Day
The Battle for France
The Last Knight
Queen's Knight

Tales from the Sword I
(Short stories from the Medieval period)

**Tudor Warrior series
England and Scotland in the late 14th and early 15th century**
Tudor Warrior

**Conquistador
England and America in the 16th Century**
Conquistador

Modern History

The Napoleonic Horseman Series
Chasseur à Cheval
Napoleon's Guard
British Light Dragoon
Soldier Spy
1808: The Road to Coruña
Talavera
The Lines of Torres Vedras
Bloody Badajoz
The Road to France
Waterloo

Duke of Normandy

The Lucky Jack American Civil War series
Rebel Raiders
Confederate Rangers
The Road to Gettysburg

Soldier of the Queen series
Soldier of the Queen

The British Ace Series
1914
1915 Fokker Scourge
1916 Angels over the Somme
1917 Eagles Fall
1918 We will remember them
From Arctic Snow to Desert Sand
Wings over Persia

**Combined Operations series
1940-1945**
Commando
Raider
Behind Enemy Lines
Dieppe
Toehold in Europe
Sword Beach
Breakout
The Battle for Antwerp
King Tiger
Beyond the Rhine
Korea
Korean Winter

Tales from the Sword II
(Short stories from the Modern period)

Other Books
Great Granny's Ghost (Aimed at 9-14-year-old young people)

Duke of Normandy

For more information on all of the books then please visit the author's website at www.griffhosker.com where there is a link to contact him or visit his Facebook page: GriffHosker at Sword Books

Printed in Great Britain
by Amazon